PRAISE FOR MAGDALENE'S JOURNEY

"Independently and regardless of whether historical fact or imaginative fiction, this narrative calls up from the depth of our shared consciousness the ideas, the people, and the events that have shaped the adventure of humanity on this planet. Read with an open mind, it conveys the sense of awe and significance that envelops the ultimate meaning of our existence."

—Ervin László, Ph.D.,
Nobel Peace Prize nominee, Systems Scientist,
Integral Theorist and author of *The Intelligent Cosmos*
and *The Great UpShift*

"This book is a revelation of a new order of science and inspiration. The authors bring together state-of-the-art explorations by weaving together science, spirituality, imagination and transformative content. Present and future considerations of spiritual power are brought to a new perspective that illumines realms of consciousness and our relationship to personal and cosmic archetypes. Reading this remarkable book will open up the depth of your awareness and consciousness that the reader never knew she had."

—Jean Houston, Ph.D.,
world-renowned scholar, philosopher, futurist, and
award-winning author of *The Possible Human,*
A Mythic Life and *The Hero and the Goddess*

"The intimate courage and heart openness shared in *Magdalene's Journey* is a precious wayshower for these pivotal times of re-membering who we really are. The book guides us across the threshold of a limited perception of reality to a more expansive and richer exploration of its deeper nature. The essence of its fundamental message that we are microcosmic co-creators of a unitive and multidimensional Cosmos, invites us to awaken to our universal heritage and empowers our emergent potential to become co-evolutionary partners with our Gaian home and with the vast communities of a living Universe."

—Jude Currivan, Ph.D.,
Cosmologist, co-founder of WholeWorld-View and
author of *The Cosmic Hologram* and *The Story of Gaia*

"What do we know about the divine feminine and masculine, and how do we access the spiritual wisdom that lies within us? In this exhilarating, provocative book, the authors move beyond historical rhetoric, and through sacred storytelling invite us on an inward journey, so that we may discover how we can embody the divine masculine and feminine in our world and in our daily lives."

—Shamini Jain, Ph.D.,
Psychologist, scientist, social entrepreneur, founder of
CHI and best-selling author of *Healing Ourselves*

"There are few inspirational books around and even fewer that give inspirational messages using quantum physics. This is truly one of those rare exceptions. *Magdalene's Journey* is reader-friendly. Read and enjoy!"

—Amit Goswami, Ph.D.,
Quantum Physicist, author of
The Self Aware Universe and *Physics of the Soul*

"In a world where people are searching for meaning, this book comes at just the right time to help us make sense of the world we think we know, opening our minds to possibilities and realities so delicious that we feel transported and freed from the normal confines of everydayness."

—Natalie Petouhoff, Ph.D.,
Vice President, Fortune 500 company and
Wall Street Journal best-selling author
of *Empathy in Action*

"In Renée and Anthony's narrative, the two main characters of the book receive a series of amazing and loving visitations, which bring through powerful teachings about how unity consciousness, oneness, and love have the power to heal ourselves, others, and the planet. *Magdalene's Journey* helps us evolve out of outdated paradigms that no longer serve us. Their story weaves modern science into ancient esoteric wisdom so we can all expand and embrace new stories that have the power to heal humanity."

—Sandra Ingerman, MA,
world-renowned shamanic teacher and author
of *Shamanic Journeying* and *Soul Retrieval*

"*Magdalene's Journey* is an inspiring and important retelling of the life of Mary Magdalene. Long erroneously thought to be a woman lifted from a sordid life, we see Mary as a person of powerful spiritual realization who shared the mission of Jesus, who should be appreciated as an expression of the Divine feminine and a teacher in her own right. The authors skillfully weave history, narrative, science, and transcendent spiritual teachings into one uplifting experience."

—Joseph Selbie,
author of *The Physics of Miraculous Healing*
and *The Physics of God*

"Although the setting of this visionary tale stems from over two thousand years ago, the book goes beyond depicting a renowned woman's untold life. It shares both stories and teachings from yesteryear in a way that seeks to unify humanity regardless of belief system. At the crossroads of science and consciousness, we discover how little decisions can make a significant impact on those around us, healing ourselves and others in the process. This book may very well shift the way you perceive humanity's relationship to all living things and our role on the planet."

—MeiMei Fox,
New York Times best-selling co-author
of *Bend Not Break*

"This book challenges traditional thinking about Mary Magdalene's pivotal role during the time of Jesus. Have you ever wondered what really happened between them and her contribution to that chapter in history? You are invited to sense your own gut-level recognition of the truth about the surprising events being revealed as the gripping story of *Magdalene's Journey* unfolds. Not to be missed."

—Gabriele Hilberg, Ph.D., MFT,
Psychotherapist, co-author of *Einstein's Business*

"This very unique chronicle paints a more holistic view of history than the patriarchal one we've been wired to believe. Along the way, riveting characters from yesteryear bring forth spiritual wisdom that parallels what modern science is revealing today. Time and time again, we are brought into expanded states of awareness and consciousness, which give us pause to reflect and hear a deeper truth, one that at a soul level, we might already inherently know."

—Mark Anthony,
JD Psychic Lawyer, best-selling author of
The Afterlife Frequency, Evidence of Eternity
and *Never Letting Go*

"A fascinating, entertaining, and well-written story! But it's actually much more than that. The book explores deep concepts about the nature of reality and poses mind-boggling questions about the hidden mechanics of our world. Additionally, it introduces thought-provoking historical narratives that challenge traditional beliefs. Don't be surprised if your imagination runs wild while reading this book—and don't be surprised if those imaginative ideas continue to percolate long after you finish reading."

—Mark Gober,
International speaker, IONS (Institute of Noetic
Sciences) board member and author of
An End to Upside Down Thinking

"Across the world, one of the greatest religious mysteries involves the nature of the 'real' relationship between Mary Magdalene and Jesus. Dogma seldom equals truth, only a support for a specific hierarchy. *Magdalene's Journey* breaks us free from the shadows of patriarchy to present a delightful, intelligent, and deep storyline that tugs at the imagination and whispers, '*There is truth in this tale.*' Quantum science serves as the bridge to explain the couples' bond but also the way that yesterday's knowledge can impact today's culture. Perhaps—hopefully—it is time to restore the balance between the feminine and the masculine and transform this world into the realm of light it is meant to be."

—Cyndi Dale,
International teacher, speaker,
and author of *The Subtle Body* series

"The story of early Christianity was written by historical winners—largely male and authoritarian—too parsimonious to share the historical stage or point of view with the other half of humanity. An ephemeral guide and companion while narrating her story, Magdalene pierces the lives of an unsuspecting couple with deeply moving and wise dialogues that both clarify and animate ancient, lifeless dioramas into living communities with heart and pulse. Magdalene's descriptions of daily life, family entanglements, and political and social complexity root the reader in a memoir. You'll move from a comfortable perch into a fascinating and daring adventure."

—David Bolinsky,
Pioneering medical illustrator,
3D animator & TED speaker

"*Magdalene's Journey* is nothing short of astonishing. As I have evolved as a science writer, I have encountered brief glimmers of possibility around the edges of quantum science. This book weaves those possibilities into my personal spiritual journey in ways I'd never previously imagined. As an adolescent, I rebelled against a Christian Science upbringing by rejecting all organized religion. But as I began to study the sciences more deeply three decades ago, I found my mind and heart making connections and asking questions, leading me back toward Love. *Magdalene's Journey* lays out a blueprint for us to study on our way to a greater understanding of who we truly are."

—Janet Rae-Dupree,
Former writer at *New York Times*,
Forbes, *BusinessWeek & LA Times* and author
of *Anatomy & Physiology Workbook for Dummies*

"Imagine the combination of rich storytelling depicting Mary Magdalene's life and her vital role alongside Jesus with groundbreaking insights and parallels to modern science all in one book. A page-turner, you find yourself eager to dive into the next chapter of her life while rethinking your idea of truth along the way. A must-read!"

—Jill Lublin,
International speaker, publicist,
and author of *The Profit of Kindness*

MAGDALENE'S JOURNEY

MAGDALENE'S JOURNEY

The Untold Story of Mary Magdalene's Life & Teachings

RENÉE BLODGETT
ANTHONY COMPAGNONE

Magdalene's Journey

Published by Blue Soul Publishing.

Library of Congress Cataloging in-Publication Data
Names: Blodgett, Renée, author. Compagnone, Anthony, author
Title: Magdalene's Journey
Identifiers: LCCN: 2024908117

ISBN: 978-0-9842507-0-7 (Paperback)
ISBN: 978-0-9842507-3-8 (Hardcover)
ISBN: 978-0-9842507-1-4 (eBook)
ISBN: 978-0-9842507-2-1 (Audiobook)

Book cover illustration and section sketches by Dunja Kacic-Alesic.

Any variations from traditional and canonical versions of Mary Magdalene and Yeshua (Jesus) are the work of the authors and fall under the categories of visionary literature and historical fiction, both of which are discussed in the Afterword. To the best of their ability and without any guarantee of completeness or accuracy, the authors have also conveyed information about quantum science, religious, and creative works.

FREE RESOURCES

We have a website dedicated to *Magdalene's Journey,* where you can read through a Q&A and learn more about the inspiration behind the book.

On our Resources page, you'll receive a glossary of terms, book group discussion questions, and a recommended reading list, which includes some of our favorites in both science and spirituality.

On our Offerings page, you'll find our latest free gifts for readers.

VISIT:

https://magdalenesjourney.com
https://magdalenesjourney.com/resources
and
https://www.magdalenesjourney.com/offerings

DEDICATION

To Miriam of Magdala,
who was long silenced like
so many inspiring and pivotal women
in history. May your voice become
a beacon of light for years to come.

To Renée's mother
Irene Langford Blodgett.
Your spoken and unspoken
wisdom lives on.

To Gaia for teaching us
synchronicity and interconnectedness
through nature's beauty
and sacred geometry.

To the Divine Feminine in all of
us. To Her persistent love and
endurance across millennia.

And lastly, to our Blue Soul and
Magdalene's Sisters communities
who have supported our work
for many years. You truly have
become like family to us.

CONTENTS

PREFACE

Filled with deeply personal revelation and ancient, yet still timely wisdom, this passionate and raw narrative explores the life of Mary Magdalene, otherwise known as Miriam of Magdala. *Magdalene's Journey* shares Miriam's relationship with the apostles—both male and female—and her life with Yeshua, most renowned to the world as Jesus of Nazareth. After his death, her journey continues as she teaches everywhere she goes. This account hopes to serve as a significant upgrade to an outdated paradigm and distorted storyline in history.

Why Mary Magdalene?

Truth be told, we knew nothing about Mary Magdalene beyond name recognition. Despite our many spiritual experiences over the years, we ran from institutional dogma at an early age and because the references to Miriam of Magdala and Jesus of Nazareth often occurred in a religious context, they weren't on our radar.

You might say Miriam and Yeshua *found us*. Deeply rooted in simple but profound teachings, the combination of Yeshua's wisdom and Miriam's unspoken truth got under our skin. More importantly, it made its way into our hearts. It was as if we could tap into age-old knowledge even though we couldn't wholly comprehend how or why. As a renowned jazz musician friend once said to us, "We are all connected to the universe. We have access to all of it; most people just don't realize it." This work gave us the experience of that connection, and reading the book allows you to share that connection as well.

Miriam of Magdala's voice got stronger as her judicious words came to us night after night. Her journey took the shape of declarations about her life with Yeshua and the apostles, which challenge a much filtered and archaic narrative that has dictated to humanity how to understand history and the Abrahamic religions.

It didn't take long for us to discover a growing curiosity about this mysterious woman who was referred to by different names: Miriam of Magdala, Mariam,

Mary Magdalene, the Tower, Madeleine, or simply the Magdalene. Tossed aside like an inconvenient truth by the powers behind patriarchal Roman thrones and later the male-controlled Catholic hierarchy, she was mostly unknown. People who took the time to probe deeper still looked through that tainted lens, leading them to misunderstand and devalue her role as a healer and teacher. This role, one could argue, was equal to that of Yeshua's as the yin to his yang—complementary and interconnected forces that together deepened the power of their healing abilities.

The Catholic Church took positive steps to right omissions and distortions over the years, first declaring her a saint in 1969. This new, elevated title extended beyond the Catholic Church. Also on board were the Eastern Orthodox, Anglican, and Lutheran churches.[1] Second, Pope Francis created a major feast day in her honor 2016, decreeing she be referred to as the Apostle of Apostles.

Nonetheless, Mary Magdalene's centuries-old portrayal as a sinner and prostitute remained in the popular imagination. Her name has gained more recognition since the discovery of the Gnostic Gospels at Nag Hammadi in 1945 which talked about Mary Magdalene in new and unexpected ways. This discovery undoubtedly helped draw attention to the *Gospel of Mary*, an ancient text found in upper Egypt in the late nineteenth century. These profound writings were purchased in Cairo but never released to the public until 1955 when they were finally published. Cynthia Bourgeault notes, "It would be twenty years longer before an English version appeared and still another twenty years before popular editions became available."[2] Karen King reminds us that less than eight pages of the papyrus survive, which means that much of the *Gospel of Mary* is lost.[3] We're undoubtedly not the only ones interested in her life who wonder whether the missing pages will ever be found. It is still a mystery.

Many questions about Miriam of Magdala remain unanswered. Indeed, several gaps persist, pointing to a larger, unacknowledged question: How many powerful and pivotal women have been written out of history and holy books? Even for scholars and historians who have investigated this period, there's much they still don't know.

You won't find religious dogma in this story nor in Yeshua's teachings which are layered into Magdalene's narrative like an exquisite and treasured tapestry from yesteryear. When *Magdalene's Journey* talks about Biblical texts, it is merely to suggest that omitting or changing Yeshua's original teachings in these texts served Roman and later Catholic Church power structures.

When Yeshua walked the planet, rather than relying on external authorities, he emphasized an inward journey, a teaching that remains paramount today.

It is the essence of his message that the *kingdom lies within*. So too was his pointing to love as the glue that binds humanity and the cosmos itself.

Social Conditioning & History Meet New Paradigms

Magdalene's Journey presents a modern enhancement to reality as we have been conditioned and wired to accept it with our linear minds and constructs. The book attempts to capture a universal and revolutionary message about Miriam's and Yeshua's lives, now recreated in a period that can show us a new, fuller, and more tangible understanding of it.

Some sections may jar you. Regardless of whether we grew up in a specific denomination, or have simply absorbed ideas from culture, our upbringing has shaped so many of our belief systems. Cognitive dissonance may come into play here. Hearing information that challenges our belief systems can trigger a multitude of uncomfortable emotions. Often, we'll do anything in our power to bring a new way of looking at a situation, person, or thing back into accord with our understanding so we can feel at ease again.

In facing these possible dissonances, readers experience the book best when they let go of the conditioning and go within. Even more, when we surrender into our hearts, we begin to hear a different truth, one our Higher Self calls forward for us to remember innately within our own *inner kingdom*. Then, the uncomfortable inconsistencies of old beliefs can melt away, and a deeper awareness and broader insights have space to surface.

Although this is a work of historical fiction, it was inspired by parallel experiences in our own lives. Central to the wisdom in this book is knowing *no one truth exists*, only perspective layered upon perspective. These acumens are based on a combination of research, academic study, and personal experiences as authors.

This account of Miriam's life comes from unseen dimensions in the subtler realms to be heard now, perhaps because as a species we're more ready to receive her message and, more importantly, comprehend it. In response to the distorting power for far too many years, the book shares the need to rebalance the masculine and feminine energy in the world, starting within each one of us. Part of this task is understanding not just the important role of Miriam alongside Yeshua but also the vital, never-recorded roles women have played over the millennia. Miriam of Magdala's evocative and enthralling voice represents the divine feminine in all of us, emerging in a significant and life-shifting way at this time in human evolution. This rebalancing requires the inward journey Yeshua spoke about in order to intuitively know a different history.

In countering old storylines, Miriam's story weaves modern science into ancient esoteric wisdom when you least expect it. In this process, you may find that her journey expands your consciousness beyond what cultures and religions around the world have always adhered to as the *only* history, the *only* truth, and the *only* reality.

In *Magdalene's Journey*, readers are never asked to replace a truth they currently hold dear, whether backed by scientific evidence, experienced through faith, or acquired through social conditioning. Instead, we hope humanity can begin to look at concepts like magic and miracles in a fresh light. They truly are accessible to all of us. If we embrace the notion that we don't know what we don't know, we move forward with a curious and open mind. Then, who knows what is possible within this magnificent, more expansive consciousness?

This rich, bold, and at times emotional story may do more than provide a new perspective on an imposed and antiquated narrative about Miriam and Yeshua, two powerful, spiritual teachers from yesteryear; we hope that it also transforms the way you perceive and experience God/Godde, consciousness, and science as well as our role on this planet.

As a literary text that portrays new understandings, *Magdalene's Journey* stretches you beyond the expectations of traditional categories you might be prone to use as labels for this book such as science fiction, fantasy, or simply a novel. As you push beyond your comfort zone, maybe you might even reconsider your definitions of imaginary, visionary, reality, and truth. Miriam's story may prod you to re-examine history as well as answers to life's most pressing and paradoxical questions about humanity's very existence.

Are you ready to embark upon a wild journey back in time that heals us all in the present?

When you read, feel into the words with your heart, where our innate wisdom resides. All of us have this inner gift. We poured our souls into this book, and our desire is that you simply read it with an open mind, but most importantly, an open heart.

And with that, we'll see you on the other side.

• • • • • •

Part I:

Ancient Timelines

CHAPTER 1

A SEED IS PLANTED

Love inspires,
illuminates, designates,
and leads the way.
—Mary Baker Eddy

In the still of the night, a voice began to whisper until its timbre gained ground. It was a slow but steady thundering of tones that echoed into the luminous sky, the moon basking in the reverberation of its sound.

"As you would say in your modern colloquial language, I blew my own horn and danced to my own drum," Miriam began. "Deep down, I wasn't sure what path I would ultimately take, but I rebelled against the status quo as early as childhood. It first emerged as curiosity about life beyond my father's rules and then grew into an insatiable hunger for something authentic, larger, and deeper.

"Later, I protested against what was expected of me in a land that saw women solely as instruments to expand the tribe. I sought to act independently despite the fact women couldn't step into liberation during my time. It simply wasn't possible, for if the ancient Judaic rules of the day didn't stop you, your family would. At least they tried in my case.

"My father had ideas of whom I would marry, men who would complement and strengthen our family's position. You didn't stray far from your immediate community when it came to marriage. I was what you'd call today the black sheep and constantly looking for something more meaningful to do with my life. Simply put, I didn't want to be married off to someone I didn't love.

"My sister never understood me, and although my brother Lazarus was often puzzled by me, we shared a special bond. My mother didn't always agree with my decisions; however, she understood my mystifying ways far better than my father ever would. My father often feared I would do something to jeopardize our family's reputation. Ultimately, my mother became my main support after I left home—until much later that is—but I'll get to this chapter of my life in time.

"Yeshua and I knew each other when we were young. We had a connection through our families, religion, status, and money. We saw each other on sacred religious holidays and during private family gatherings for it was common to celebrate special occasions in our community. In our tradition, it was always a father's dream to marry his daughter off to a family of greater means which presented an issue for us. You see, although our families were acquainted, Yeshua's family was not as well-off and prestigious as ours.

My father often feared I would do something to jeopardize our family's reputation.

"We had a spark from the very beginning, but we could not act on it because of my father's wishes and plans for my future. Yet Yeshua and I both dissented from our own religion and the way things were traditionally done, something my father sensed. Even though I didn't understand this deeper connection in my human form, souls always communicate—my soul was communicating with his, and his was communicating with mine. A seed was planted very early on in our friendship.

"It was understood at some point Yeshua would travel to India for an extended stay to further his studies. Of course, this meant we didn't see each other for many years. During our time, girls grew to womanhood, and boys grew to manhood much faster, so although it should have been expected when he returned, many were surprised by how much Yeshua had changed, including me. It was clear he was no longer a boy but a man, and it was also apparent that his studies in the East made a remarkable impact on him.

"That unforgettable spark was still there when we saw each other again. When family members were not watching, we held hands, and both of us knew we shared something special, beyond what you refer to in your contemporary language as chemistry. We'd look deeply into each other's eyes, but there was no kiss since others were watching us, as was the way during our time. But we both experienced a deep-seated flicker of recognition and a sense of mission. While we didn't verbalize it as such, the seed of our lives and work together took root in a way we didn't comprehend during those early days. We would become the divine feminine and divine masculine merging with God.

"Around this time, Yeshua's cousin John the Baptist had a deep spiritual awakening, and Yeshua left to become part of John's spiritual work. Yeshua and I were not destined to be together during that period, not only because Yeshua went off to teach with John, but also because my father had arranged to marry me to a man of means, a man whom I didn't love. Of course, I refused, which my sister didn't understand as she was much more conventional than me. My rebuttal led to strain and difficulty at home, so I decided to leave. As you can imagine, my father was terribly angry and scorned my choice. The rest of my family was dismayed about my departure, but they didn't speak up since they too were raised in our tradition with all of its conservative rules.

"Some people will see I had no other choice but to leave, but others may not understand this insurgent behavior even in your modern times. Eventually, I ran away because my father wanted to marry me to someone I didn't love. I couldn't go through with it even if it meant leaving my family, and yes, even if it meant I would need to make my way in the world.

"I had very little money without my father's support; therefore, I didn't venture far from my hometown. Luckily, I was smart and strategic as a young woman, so I quickly learned how to make enough money to get by. As strange as this may sound to your modern ears, I initially earned money playing number games with bones, but the proceeds didn't last long. With few other options as a woman during patriarchal times, when a man propositioned me with money, I accepted. I supported myself in this way for around six months until I had saved enough money to give me the necessary security.

"To all those who have judged me for millennia and beyond, I ask you this: How many men and women did you sleep with before you married? Did you not have your own time experimenting with sex? You may have done it for pleasure, but I did it for money because I had to under my circumstances. What is worse? Don't judge me. And don't judge other women.

"You've read in your history that Yeshua was a woodworker, and he was indeed a gifted carpenter; however, Yeshua also spent time studying and teaching with his cousin John upon his return. Both were preparing the way for their new teachings by finding bridges between the old texts (the Torah and the Hebrew

Bible) and their roots in the lineage of Abraham, David, and Moses. Prophets and spiritual teachers always looked for these kinds of sacred connections.

"I had heard about John and Yeshua's meetings and decided to hear them speak. If I was still living at home, I wouldn't have been allowed to walk amongst their growing but controversial community. Although I was still quite young when I began to attend their gatherings, the teachings instantly resonated with me. The spark with Yeshua intensified, and since we were away from our families and traditional community, we had a chance to be with each other without judgment. As much as it would be easy to paint a dreamy picture of a courtship that flourished, it was not an easy time to live, and Yeshua was quite busy with his teachings. When we first kissed, it was fortuitously and certainly unexpected. You could say our heads came together by accident. Our cheeks came together by accident. Our lips came together by accident. Our passion was kindled by accident. Our love grew by accident. But over time, we consciously came together as one soul to do the work God had ordained us to do.

"Romance did not exist back then in the way you think of it today. We sought or rather took each other as companions in extremely challenging times. As companions who recognized a deeper mission between us, we grew to love each other. Through the teachings of John, the water healer or water dunker as they called him, our love for the work expanded along with our intimate love for each other.

"I can also explain it like this: When I first met Yeshua, a seed inside me ignited. Was it my soul recognizing his again, perhaps from past lives we shared? I couldn't have put it in those words from my time on this planet, but it was a spiritual connection of great significance and consequence. It was also magnetic, yet it went beyond a physical attraction to someone you see across a room. As much as some would like to idealize our relationship, it wasn't a traditional love affair. There was an inner knowing of something far greater even though I didn't fully understand it. I just knew I wanted to be next to him, discover more of who he was, and absorb his knowledge. I became a follower—one of his female apostles—and later, both a teacher by his side and his wife.

"But for a single woman in ancient Judea to run off and follow a Rabbi whom some began to refer to as the *Son of God* or even the Messiah, it was counter to my father's conventional ways. As a rebel, sometimes you need to make gallant choices necessary to move forward on your path. When we don't speak our truth and beat our own drum, a part of us dies inside. Our soul is crying out to be heard, and it is our intuition that answers the call.

"Looking into Yeshua's eyes for the first time truly planted a seed, and when we touched, the electricity running through my body left me breathless. It wasn't a longing to be with him; it was a knowing. A soul's knowing. We both knew. I also realized my life was with him and the community he and John had created to spread what became known as the *Good News*.

When we don't speak
our truth and beat our
own drum, a part
of us dies inside.

"If I hadn't left home and made the choices I did to live during a time when the idea of a liberated woman would never see the light of day, I wouldn't have done my life's work. I wouldn't have stepped into my purpose. With Yeshua, my life was forever changed, and I realized there would be no turning back.

"You understand humanity's multiple layers, don't you? You know when a seed of love gets planted and sprouts, it grows into love that transforms all things, don't you?

"My name is Miriam of Magdala, and over two thousand years ago, I fell in love with one of the greatest healers, shamans, sages, prophets, and teachers your world has ever known."

• • • • • •

CHAPTER 2

A REUNION OF SOULS

Wait for me where the skies meet
the sea, the Otherworld where our old
souls will meet again for the very first
time, where our imagination takes
flight and magic isn't a fairytale.
—Dahi Tamara Koch

Angelo was flipping through pages on his online media portal when he came across a controversial documentary on Jesus. Intrigued, he began to watch the trailer.

"You've got to listen to this guy," he called out to Rochelle, his wife of fifteen years. "They may have found new information about Jesus of Nazareth's death, including where he was buried."

She was watering plants on their New England deck, but the sliding doors were wide open so she could easily hear his voice. They were both interested in history, archeology, and ancient wisdom. She put down her watering can and stuck her head through the doors.

"Has it been validated? Or is it just speculation?" Rochelle asked him.

"I'm not sure," he responded, flipping through videos with overlapping content. "Here's another video that speaks about Jesus' personal life, apparently based on research. It suggests that Jesus went to India to study." His voice sped up, something that always happened when he got excited about updated accounts of history. "Hey, there's also something on the Essenes and the *Dead Sea Scrolls*."

"What are the *Dead Sea Scrolls*?" asked Rochelle.

"A bunch of ancient texts which have become known as the *Dead Sea Scrolls* were discovered in the 1940s—a few of them were almost intact manuscripts and others were fragments of manuscripts," Angelo replied. "Their discovery apparently led to a new interpretation and understanding of the scriptures. They were found in caves near the Qumrān Ruins, and a group called the Essenes are often linked to them."

"Hmmm, the Qumrān Ruins," Rochelle repeated. "The name rings a bell," thinking of her time living in Israel. "I didn't go there," she added, now wishing she had. She found the tombs and pyramids in Egypt far more interesting, but her experience may have been enhanced by the extra effort required to travel there at the time, especially on a low budget and as a woman moving around the country alone.

"Here's another video on sacred geometry," Angelo continued. "And one on Egypt around the time Jesus was alive."

Rochelle knew he was bookmarking them for later viewing. Sometimes they'd bring a big monitor outside in the warmer months and watch movies and documentaries under the stars.

Thinking of her time in Egypt, Rochelle said, "The ankh in Egyptian culture held significant symbolic meaning, and it was believed to represent eternal life. It is often depicted with Egyptian gods and goddesses in tomb paintings. Egyptians wore it as an amulet back then, but many people wear it today as jewelry. Some also connect it to the Goddess Isis, fertility, and the many other aspects she represented."

"It was alive in Judea as well, and variations of it existed in other cultures too, according to the description," Angelo said. "I love keys, for they represent the ability to unlock answers to life's most profound questions."

"That and access to the Holy Grail," Rochelle said with a laugh, knowing Angelo had made his way through *King Arthur, Harry Potter, Monty Python, Indiana Jones,* and other movies of their ilk countless times.

Angelo was lost in his scrolling, so Rochelle was about to return to their plants when she noticed he had stopped and his eyes widened.

"I found something else, which of course has shown up in many movies and books. Holy Grails are everywhere." He began to read, "'They have taken the form of chalices, spears, skulls, platters, stones, swords, cauldrons, and even books. What makes an object a Holy Grail is its possession of a special power that has been called the Holy Spirit by Christians, the Alchemical Force by Alchemists, and Kundalini by Hindu Yogis.'"[1]

"Yeah, I remember reading the Holy Grail is also connected to the chalice Jesus used during the Last Supper, seen as a symbol of power or to possess actual magical powers," Rochelle added. "But the real question is this: Was the Holy Grail merely myth or legend, or is there some truth to it?"

"There's always some truth to legend, isn't there?" Angelo said. "Meaning … later on, evidence has proved at least some of these legends true. How can we honestly know what is pure imagination and symbolism from hundreds or thousands of years ago and what is actual experience?"

"You mean, something like a chalice, skull, or stone can hold magical powers and unlock the mysteries of the universe or even do nonsensical things like extend our longevity or make us live forever?" Rochelle teased, giving him that coy look of hers that always made him smile.

But maybe Angelo had a point. Only yesterday, she had read something from Dr. Ervin László about science fiction drawing inspiration from myths and imagination: "Science fiction, as well as ancient wisdom, are often the precursors of legitimate science, and legitimate science often rediscovers creative fiction and ancient wisdom."[2]

Rochelle and Angelo loved to explore ancient and esoteric wisdom across all cultures. They both knew of portals, for example, but presumed they belonged to the worlds of science fiction and fantasy, not everyday life. They never imagined portals could exist, especially ones that could take them into other worlds and dimensions. If they did exist, it wasn't something they wanted to explore, or so they thought.

After returning from an extended stay in Asia five years ago, their interest in spiritual wisdom and practices—both ancient and modern—deepened. Sometimes Rochelle and Angelo hung out at a mindfulness studio housed in an original brick building with 1902 etched on the front. It was so fitting for Cambridge where architecture exhibited remnant styles of its early settlers. Tucked away in a narrow alley, it reminded them of the historical European towns and cities they had visited and lived in during their younger years. Sitting side-by-side in soft brown yoga back chairs, they'd listen to Sanskrit mantras and chants. Original bricks lined the walls and wide wooden beams throughout softened the studio's antiquity while the furnishings brimmed with muted Mediterranean colors conducive to stilling the mind. The studio was adjacent to Angelo's favorite café which also had an air of ancient spirituality to it. As you entered, statues of Buddha and Kuan Yin with a scenic water fountain cushioned between them greeted you. On the back wall, lush plants made themselves at home.

Even before their trip to the East, they shared a love of all things old. The tenants of New England's past found Rochelle and Angelo, and they found them. At home, rooms were filled with tables and dressers from Colonial and Edwardian times. Their shelves housed leather books from yesteryear teeming with the wisdom of Aristotle, Plato, Galileo, Dante, Newton, Kant, Descartes, Hegel, and countless others.

Soon, furniture, books, art, and statues from the past wouldn't be the only old things that would become an integral part of their lives. Little did they know they would meet two ancient souls who would turn their lives upside down. Neither one of them saw the encounter coming, so it felt more surreal than real even though both Angelo's and Rochelle's accounts of the experience were indistinguishable.

The encounter happened under the stars on a clear-skied spring evening. "Remember to look up at the stars and not down at your feet. Try to make sense of what you see and wonder about what makes the universe exist,"[3] Stephen Hawking once said, and they always resonated with the words. Rochelle loved the warmer seasons when they could lie on their deck or lawn, staring into the nothingness of space and the glistening stars.

After a prolonged meditation on their deck under a mystical sky, Angelo shifted into what could only be described as an altered state. Although he visibly still looked like the same Angelo Rochelle so dearly loved, his energy had changed.

"Are you okay, Angelo?" she asked him on that memorable night. There was no response, and his eyes remained closed.

Perhaps he is asleep, she thought.

However, she could hear heavy, slow breathing, unlike his typical sleeping state.

"You awake?" she called out, this time a little louder. He then began to speak in unusually slow utterances, one word at a time.

"I . . . am . . . heeere but . . . not . . . aloonne."

The voice sounded like Angelo's but not *completely*. What was different? She couldn't tell but thought perhaps he was merely dreaming. Then, his eyes sprang open.

"Were you dreaming?" Rochelle asked when she saw he was clearly not asleep. Then she noticed his eyes changed, the same color perhaps, but with a slight variance. They were deeper somehow, and he didn't blink. Not once.

"I was . . . not dreea-mming. I am . . . not dreea-mming," came the assured response. "I can . . . not moo-ove," he added in a whisper.

"Whaaat?" Rochelle cried out as if any other word following it was no longer possible. She grabbed his hand and asked him, "Can you feel me"?

"Yeesss," he replied and squeezed her fingers to accentuate his one-word response.

"Some-onne is heeere with us now," Angelo said, and unexpectedly his head tilted back, his eyes closed again, and his breathing became even slower. After a lengthy pause, which felt like hours to Rochelle, he began to speak.

"My name is Miriam of Magdala," Angelo finally said, but his voice had changed yet again. It certainly didn't feel or sound like Angelo, for Rochelle knew his patterns, habits, and intonations as any partner would after many intimate years.

Another long delay ensued before the voice continued, "Most know me as Mary Magdalene."

"Mary Magdalene!" Rochelle said with skepticism. "The one from the Bible?" The words flew out of her like an alarmed wild animal rather than a curious human being.

"Yes, the very one," she said. "I realize this may be difficult for you to understand, but you are speaking to her soul."

Her soul? How could her soul be with them in their modern world? Rochelle reflected. Had they slipped through a portal to another time, or was it a dimensional shift of sorts, the kind you can't explain but know is real?

As she scanned the deck, narrowing in on anything and everything familiar, she saw that their surroundings looked the same. Through the glass doors to their sitting room, she gazed at the often-played Steinway piano and the books lining the left wall. The dark wooden bookshelves were jammed with so many titles she knew at least one of them mentioned Mary Magdalene. She took a deep breath and pinched herself to ensure she wasn't dreaming.

"How did you get here?" asked Rochelle and then let out a long ummm . . . . "I mean, how arrre yooou . . . ?" Then, her words trailed off like someone in shell shock. "What is happening to Angelo right now?" she stammered, struggling to compose herself, now more concerned about her partner than the mystifying exchange.

"He is, you could say, observing. His energy or soul is off to the side, allowing me to come through to speak," came the response.

"Off to the side? What does that mean?" Rochelle asked.

"I can't be here unless he permits me to be," she said softly.

"I don't understand," snapped Rochelle. "I'd like my husband back."

Within a few minutes, Angelo's head began to shake, regaining consciousness in the physical world Rochelle had never left, *or had she?*

"I'm okay," he finally said to her. "I don't understand what just happened, but I was in a blissful state the entire time, observing, watching, and listening, as if I was one with this being's energy while removed from it at the same time."

"How did that happen?" she asked, perplexed.

"I don't know," he replied. "I truly don't know, but her energy was very peaceful. It's as if she has more messages for me. For you. For us."

As they reflected under the stars, they had an innate sense they had just connected to a place and time beyond their known world.

Four days after Miriam's visit, they were in their blue sitting room. Their favorite room was teeming with art, statues, books, indigenous drums, and ancient relics. Incense was burning, and they were sitting cross-legged, eyes closed while relaxing to meditation music over an evening pot of tea, Angelo's hands resting in front of him. Opening her eyes slightly, Rochelle put her right hand on his leg when she suddenly saw Angelo's head tilt back, similar to earlier that week. She gulped, unsure what would happen next. Would Miriam's soul be coming back?

As if reading her mind the voice said, "It is not Miriam. This is Yeshua, although most know me as Jesus."

"Uhhh, you mean the soul of Yeshua or Jesus or . . . ?" she said, stumbling over her words in shock.

"Yes, in a way," he said. "Do not be alarmed. Mary Magdalene was my partner over two thousand years ago, and we have a deep connection with you both."

"A deep connection," Rochelle repeated, and thinking he must be mistaken, she added, "You don't understand, we aren't religious," not knowing what else to say.

"Let me explain," Yeshua responded. "We aren't who you think we are . . . "

"Clearly," she interrupted, her tone turning slightly cynical. "This is ludicrous. Illogical. Impossible." Suddenly catching what he had just said, she paused before asking, "Who are you *really*?"

"I say we aren't who you think we are because you can't truly understand how the soul works. But our souls inhabited the bodies once known as Yeshua of Nazareth and Miriam of Magdala, who once walked the planet. We are no longer who they once were as we are now in spirit form."

"Where are you now in your . . . spirit form?" she said, still confused. She was shaken up in a myriad of bizarre and profound ways, but perhaps it was just all a lucid dream of sorts. Yes, maybe that's what it was—a lucid dream.

"I realize you may be feeling as if you've traveled back in time, but there really isn't time as you think there is," Yeshua said. "You may have heard of the space-time continuum from your scientists, which is beyond humanity's linear constructs."

We aren't who you
think we are because
you can't truly understand
how the soul works.

Rochelle's eyes were bulging as she scanned the room. She was sure their physical bodies were still in the twenty-first century for she recognized their prized possessions scattered around the room.

How was this possible? Not only was she undergoing a mind and heartaltering shift in her consciousness, but she also sensed they were about to take a leap so monumental they might just be escorted into a world far beyond their comprehension. Or were they already there?

Lost in thought, she couldn't have heard Yeshua's words if he were to deliver them. Her mind splintered in a million directions. How could Miriam and Yeshua connect to their time and dimension and speak through Angelo's larynx? And more important, why?

Yeshua had told them on that mind-blowing evening that both he and Miriam weren't religious either. He must have felt the need to address her shock at his unexpected arrival into their lives when she uttered in disbelief that neither of them was religious. Truth be told, they were both exposed to religions as children, but the experiences had been more ceremonial than anything else. Rochelle had been baptized under so many different Christian denominations she ran from the litter of dogmas when she reached high school. Angelo chalked up his connection to the Catholic Church as cultural, a response he used when Rochelle asked why he had a cross on his kitchen wall when they first met. It rattled her a bit, but he merely laughed when he said, "All Italians have crosses in their homes." She wasn't sure, but she knew she wouldn't be drawn into a belief system that embraced a constricting, outdated narrative.

"You're both paradigm shifters," Yeshua relayed on that unforgettable spring night under the stars.

That felt true, thought Rochelle as soon as he said it even though she didn't fully understand it. He was taking them both into unknown territory. Part of her was excited by the prospect, and another part of her wanted to run.

Resonating with the language he used, Rochelle speculated: Was it not their mutual thirst for philosophy, science, and history that had ignited their interest in the mystical world? That said, their esoteric knowledge and experiences were a far cry from the profound otherworldly visits with Miriam and Yeshua from ancient times.

After that encounter with Yeshua, Rochelle, and Angelo spent the next two weeks second-guessing their experiences. They both had so many questions beginning with how and why? Foremost amongst their questions was: How was it possible they could speak to the souls of two crucial figures in history long gone from physical view? Just as perplexing was the question: *Why them?*

On Tuesday night of the third week, Miriam returned and continued to visit almost daily. Occasionally, Yeshua would step in to add something to the conversation. It was as if Rochelle and Angelo crossed into another reality as Miriam and Yeshua crossed into theirs.

Nightly, they questioned the nature of what was real versus illusion even if they couldn't find definitive answers. How does one decide what is real or not real? What is reality itself? Rochelle and Angelo began to see how a set of belief systems condition us to perceive reality in a limited way, only to discover later in life there's another, more expansive way to look at it. Could the same be true of history? Of spirituality? They had been conditioned and taught to understand reality only as the tangible one their eyes could see and the audible one their ears could hear. They never imagined they could communicate with non-physical beings. Could souls communicate from the past and enter into a current timeline?

Rochelle asked Angelo one night, "Do you think we are traveling to their dimension and time or the other way around? Or do we all meet somewhere in the middle?"

"All I can say is that it feels like I am floating in a dream-like state, but I'm aware I am awake, not asleep," Angelo responded and then added, "I can feel, see, and hear their presence, but it's also as if I'm observing their visits while they are here. It's as if they are tuning into me energetically and connecting to me . . . actually connecting to both of us."

"Connecting to *both of us* energetically?" Rochelle asked, confused by the word *us.*

"Yes, in a way," he replied. "I can see and feel them connecting to energetic fields around our bodies and then merging with us somehow."

"Then, why don't I feel them like you do?" asked Rochelle even though at times she felt shifts in the room, ringing in her ears, and trembling in her body when Miriam and Yeshua first entered their world. But these sensations didn't resemble what Angelo experienced in his altered state. She wondered what was really happening when Angelo talked about merging.

"I don't know entirely," came Angelo's response. "It seems as if the more often they come, the stronger that connection becomes, almost as if they're fine-tuning the connection like someone would toggle a radio dial to get a clearer signal. It's as if their regular visits strengthen and fine-tune a signal between their world or dimension and ours."

They knew the experience was real, but how could they ever communicate to anyone what was happening to them? Far from mere science fiction, Rochelle and Angelo felt their dimension was overlapping with Miriam's and Yeshua's daily, and down the rabbit hole they went into an alternate reality each time. As their connection to Miriam and Yeshua strengthened, their journey with them started to become more real than the appliances in their kitchen and the flowers in their garden. They began to take on a sense of wonderment that stretched far beyond where most people would dare to go, shaking the very foundation of reality itself.

It's almost as if they're
fine-tuning the connection
like someone would
toggle a radio dial
to get a clearer signal.

One night while they were preparing dinner, Rochelle said to Angelo as he was tossing vegetables in their favorite wok, "It makes me wonder, was it only Tolkien's imagination that made him a creative genius and storyteller, or was there something more to it? Did he see a reality beyond what we physically see, beyond the veil of our five most known senses? Could these rich accounts of alternate realities that keep us glued to pages in a book or our seats in movie theaters be the extension of a human transcendental experience, each with its unique flavor, layers, and textures? Maybe transcendental realities are a way to explain how meetings with other souls can take place beyond a space-time continuum as Yeshua was alluding to."

"You know Rochelle," Angelo said as he looked deeply into her blue eyes, "I have a feeling our experiences can happen and do happen because we already have a connection to them somehow . . . a soul connection, although I can't really understand it. And because we are curious and open to new ideas and ways of looking at the world. In other words, it's not random."

"What do you mean? We invited them here without consciously realizing it?" she asked.

"As odd as this may sound, Miriam's energy unlocks an inner knowing of sorts, a knowing that we're truly connected to the universe and everything in it," Angelo replied. "So, in that context, it feels more like a reunion with both of them, not a meeting for the first time."

Rochelle felt the same way even though she didn't fully comprehend it. It was as if the four of them had begun to weave together an ever-changing tapestry that included empathy, gratitude, ancient wisdom, feminine and masculine balance, and love. After each interaction, a greater sense of remembering emerged although not in the traditional way. It was more like an inner knowing from something the four of them had experienced together before this life.

After a couple of weeks had passed, they were savoring a 2016 bottle of Bordeaux one evening when Rochelle asked Angelo, "How do we know it's not just our imagination? Or is imagination actually a path to a higher reality?"

Before he had a chance to answer, she added, "You know, Carl Jung wrote that 'the psyche creates reality every day.'"[4] After a pause, she reflected out loud, "In other words, creative thinking and imagination elevated beyond mere make-believe." Picking up a book lying beside her, she opened it to a bookmarked page and began to read:

> The only expression I can use for this activity is *fantasy*. Fantasy is just as much feeling as thinking; as much intuition as sensation. There is no psychic function that, through fantasy, is not inextricably bound up with the other psychic functions. Sometimes it appears in primordial form, sometimes it is the ultimate and boldest product of all our faculties combined. Fantasy, therefore, seems to me the clearest expression of the specific activity of the psyche. It is, pre-eminently, the creative activity from which the answers to all answerable questions come; it is the mother of all possibilities, where, like all psychological opposites, the inner and outer worlds are joined together in living union.[5]

Rochelle speculated, "Maybe imagination is a tool of the psyche. For example, the psyche serves as the source of a higher reality of unity versus our restricted perception of separation and duality. It makes sense to me."

"Agreed," said Angelo. "I believe we all have senses we are either unaware of or don't know how to access although I seem to be tapping into them now as if it's the most natural thing in the world. I think of shamans and sages who have used other senses for thousands of years to heal in ways even modern doctors and scientists can't fully understand. It seems likely to me Yeshua used those unseen, non-physical senses and forces when he taught and healed people long ago just as other ancient mystics did."

Rochelle and Angelo wondered why more people didn't question how history had been shaped, especially given that the perspectives were largely dictated and passed down by men who changed the narrative to whichever one supported their position of power at the time.

After some contemplation, Rochelle speculated, "The fact that more people are looking outside of conventional science and religious dogma for answers must mean major shifts are occurring. Antipathy toward politics also suggests a migration from old paradigms and ways of seeing possibilities."

"It appears that way," said Angelo.

Absorbed in making sense of their transcendent and extrasensory experiences with Yeshua and Miriam, Rochelle had to probe deeper. She ached to better understand what was happening to them.

"What actually exists outside of our senses and perceptions? Is it imagination, fact, fiction, fantasy, psyche, or dream-state experiences?" she asked.

"Perhaps they're all the same in a way, meaning our perceptions create words to describe whatever experience we are having," said Angelo. "We merely attach whatever word we feel most comfortable with to that experience so it makes sense to us. It becomes *true* to us but may not be true for someone else because they haven't experienced it."

"If we can't make sense of it, then we lose meaning, and when we lose meaning, we lose our "known map" to the world around us which ultimately throws us far outside our comfort zones. Or worse, we begin to think we're crazy," Rochelle concluded with a rueful grin. They both laughed, realizing how preposterous and even implausible their nightly experiences would sound to a random stranger or a family member. Even those in their spiritually-minded circles would have a tough time processing the interactions they were having with Miriam and Yeshua.

In a prime example of creating a paradigm of perception, Miriam asked Rochelle one afternoon, "What do you think your soul is made up of?"

Rochelle thought about all the disparate and overlapping ideas Plato, Aristotle, Descartes, and Spinoza came up with to explain the soul. Although she had read countless books and theories, she still didn't know—did anyone really know for sure? While Miriam didn't explain the soul that day, her question urged both of them to rethink everything they've ever known about humanity's existence.

Miriam and Yeshua had shared that they were neither a she nor a he but merely energies manifesting themselves two thousand years ago as female and male within this earth realm. Miriam had only broached these topics and they both sensed more was to come. Much more.

Meanwhile, Rochelle and Angelo examined what they had already read to find hints about the soul that might explain what they were experiencing with Miriam and Yeshua. For instance, they wondered what the Vedas, the oldest known Hindu scriptures, would say about their experiences. If the Vedas could communicate as a collective consciousness, would they suggest Rochelle and Angelo's encounters with other dimensions are normal for those who are awake? What would the enlightened spiritual masters who scribed teachings over millennia say? It seemed as if they would find in them only the most recent example of humans accessing non-physical realities.

If that were the case, then the ancient wisdom from Miriam and Yeshua could surely teach humanity today about these deeper levels of consciousness as an untapped power for all of us. Or would the Western emphasis on intellect and science continue to create too much resistance?

As if answering her own thoughts, Rochelle saw an opening in Western thinking.

"Psychological and philosophical theories, history books, and ancient Eastern texts repeatedly point to the mind's power and how it notoriously gets in the way of creation and manifestation," Rochelle said. "And famous musicians, artists, and spiritual teachers have always known the creative power of getting out of their heads. So why couldn't others do the same?

"Why does such a notion have to be so esoteric and far-reaching in people's minds? Or is it so deeply embedded into the fabric of our conditioning that we need to become vigorously aware of these pattern-creating ideas—on a daily basis—to actively de-program them?"

As soon as she asked these questions, Rochelle realized she was also asking herself and Angelo why they were still holding onto old beliefs and keeping this profound wisdom at arm's length.

Angelo piped in, "We're so wired to plug into a deeply rooted collective consciousness with a narrative that is no longer our own. Take a global culture that has been conditioned to believe in a certain way for thousands of years and then ask them to think on their own; it's a bit like taking away milk from a baby when he's thirsty or a tree away from a bird when that's where they have always made their home. It's all they've always known." Then he paused and added, "How we've been culturally conditioned is all we've always known until our travels. And until now."

"Yeah, how can you create anew when you're so influenced by and in some cases glued to what others have said or done?" Rochelle added. "And how do you create an entirely new way of governing when you merely try to improve upon a worn-out system? Collectively, we keep unhealthy ways of living alive by refusing to update our thinking. Fear throttles entire societies and the aftermath is destroying people's morale and faith in a better world."

"We can borrow from the fanciful and far-fetched to improve our lives *here*," Angelo said. They both looked at each other as if to say, "Do we even know what and where *here* is anymore?"

"Think of the movie *Avatar*," Rochelle said.

"Right," Angelo interjected. "While the world of Jake Sully may not be real in the dimension we wake up in every day, how can we irrefutably know it doesn't exist in another dimension just as real as our own, merely unseen by human eyes?"

"I suppose people need to experience the shift, not just learn about it," Rochelle replied. Had she not felt transported to other dimensions, she would never have believed that they existed . . . could exist.

Lost in thought for several minutes, Rochelle then suggested, "Perhaps we're like seeds. Just as the meeting of Miriam and Yeshua planted a seed that blossomed into a paradigm-shifting relationship, they planted a seed in us that will lead to shifts in our consciousness."

It was getting late, but they were wired. She filled their glasses with what remained in the bottle of Bordeaux sitting on the table. After taking a sip of her wine, she said, "The seeds are taking root in us—as ideas and experiences combined—and although we haven't a clue how the seeds will grow, grow they must, right? That's what seeds do. Grow."

"A seed is like an intention," Angelo said. "An intention creates a ripple that leads to a field of infinite possibilities where the seed of manifestation takes root. But we are dealing with layers of disbelief people have held onto so tightly that they've been unwilling to let go of old paradigms and see the marvelous process of creation, not by God, but by us. We are all creator beings, co-creating and manifesting in each moment."

"I know," Rochelle chimed in. "It's as if *holding on* to old paradigms shields light from entering someone's field of awareness, light which could turn their perceived impossibilities into possibilities. And yet, we too are still resisting the idea that multiple dimensions exist and the notion we can access them whenever we wish. As profound as the messages are and as bright as Miriam's and Yeshua's lights shine, much of what they say opposes what we have learned."

Likewise, as Rochelle and Angelo knew deep down, indigenous elders have always received visions of profound knowledge that counter much of Western thought. Even if they didn't use scientific language to describe it, these elders have always known of multiple dimensions, all existing in harmony with the planet. They honor the earth, looking to her for wisdom because they understand we are not separate from her. Some of the oldest cultures still integrate nature into their daily lives, and the wisest realize Gaia's breath creates life for us. It always has and always will, for we are not separate from the life-sustaining land we walk on and the air that fills our lungs. Rochelle and Angelo thought about how this oneness thinking and way of living were a far cry from the self-alienated and disconnected way much of humanity has been living for far too long.

As they were considering humanity's resistance, Angelo's head went back, and his breath slowed down. "Really?" Rochelle blurted out. "Now?"

It wasn't long before Miriam joined them again as if she was tapping into their thoughts. Or did her soul simply know when to merge with them? Perhaps their intentions or emotions—even if unaware—brought her through and into their dimension, into their world.

"Did you know we were talking about you? And trying to make sense of the innumerable dimensions that exist?" Rochelle asked as soon as the signal became clear enough for Miriam to speak.

"In the words you shared, you were connecting to Gaia," Miriam responded, "or at least imagining you were. This too creates a connection to me."

"Why is that?" Rochelle wanted to know.

"Yeshua and I are one with Gaia just as you both are, and it is in this earth realm where we have strong cords . . . together," she said.

"So, this bond we all have with Gaia reunites us in a way?" asked Rochelle.

"It's more complex, but it is one useful way to look at it," Miriam replied. "When you connect to Gaia, you do so from the heart. Similarly, we connect to your heartfelt emotions, not your intellect. You see, love is the glue that binds humanity together with the entire planet, and even the particles and subatomic particles in the void your physical eyes can't see. Love, God, Source, whatever human beings want to call it, is the message we taught over two thousand years ago and bring anew today."

"So, if we are love, then we are also the glue?" asked Rochelle.

"Yes, you are both the love and the glue," said Miriam. "You are truly one with the universe, but most of you don't see it that way. There is no separation, and one gesture, intention, or action has a ripple effect on everything else. Each word and every sound has an impact too. The primordial AUM of creation in your universe continues for billions of years after its initial vibration, and you are one with it. You are the particles, and yet you are also the whole. You are the void or the nothingness and the everythingness all at the same time."

Rochelle considered what she had read about AUM and its infinite nature. The breath of creation. She recalled that the Indian Vedic Upanishads had about a dozen verses dedicated to AUM. She thought of it as the totality of All That Is, the Fully Realized Self, the Whole Self, the Authentic Self, the God Self. But what about the science behind the vibration of AUM? What synchronicities had to dance together to rouse our universe into being? Was its birthing more of a gargantuan breath followed by a primordial sound? Perhaps the illustrious AUM was the first song sung, and its harmonics seeded what would become organic life.

Much like the paradigm shifters in science and quantum physics, Miriam had extraordinary boldness and courage, thought Rochelle.

It had been a while since their first encounter, and Rochelle couldn't help but warm to Miriam as if she were a sister, if not in this lifetime, then perhaps in a past one. But why did she feel so connected to her? When she first appeared to them, she had barely heard of the woman's name until they began researching her past, and what they learned left them incredulous at times and disturbed at others.

The rejoining of four souls turned into a life-altering encounter for Rochelle and Angelo. At first, it was abrupt but then Miriam and Yeshua slowed down;

the pace had to be gradual for them, not just to grasp the profundity of their dimensional-shifting experiences, but also to accept them. As they continued to feel a presence of divine love they had never experienced and received such illuminating teachings, their resistance slowly took a back seat. They began to surrender to a different way of looking at history, one beyond linear explanations.

Their understanding of history wasn't the only thing about to be capsized. It appeared Miriam was trying to show them that it wasn't just their four souls that were divinely intertwined, but also every living thing in their universe. But before they could move into such lofty realities, information they least expected was about to come their way—the intricate details of her life.

• • • • • • •

CHAPTER 3

A WOMAN'S ROLE IN ANCIENT JUDEA

The day will come when men will recognize
woman as his peer, not only at the fireside, but
in councils of the nation. Then, and not until
then, will there be the perfect comradeship,
the ideal union between the sexes that shall
result in the highest development of the race.
—Susan B. Anthony

Rochelle was fidgeting around on the floor in their New England colonial sitting room as she watched Angelo's breathing patterns alter. Sometimes his breathing would slow down so much that she'd move next to him, lay her head upon his chest and hold his hand. At his side, she connected to his consciousness which was moving into another dimensional realm beyond the only one they had known to be real.

Meeting regularly since their first encounter with Miriam and Yeshua, they were becoming accustomed to their energy. Although the visitations began to feel more familiar as time passed, their extraordinary impact on Rochelle and Angelo raised questions about their reality. Were they simply an illusion? Or a heightened reality—distinct from, yet linked to—their fully waking state? Could Miriam's soul pass through a veil of sorts and communicate with them, making Miriam's world as real as their own? Were they being transported into an alternative timeline, and if so, how did it happen? Rochelle and Angelo had asked how and why again and again, but they still didn't have digestible answers.

At first, Miriam would come through to convey a few isolated messages, and Yeshua would do the same, albeit less often. They didn't stay for long, nor did their messages have much structure. Angelo's body shook when one of them appeared, and his head would tilt back as if he was in a trance or altered state just as it had happened the first time. Even though they couldn't fully grasp it, they felt energetic shifts in their physical bodies and often in the room itself. Over time, the shifts became more seamless.

As they became more comfortable with their nightly visits, Miriam would ask Rochelle questions about her day, and Rochelle would ask Miriam in a variety of ways: "How are you able to merge with and speak through Angelo?" She would respond with variations of: "It is possible because of a melding of sorts, as if his soul becomes mine and mine becomes his."

In the beginning, Miriam's statements were somewhat muffled, almost as if the connection wasn't strong enough to receive a lengthy, coherent message, a bit like a telephone signal can be when interrupted by electrical interference. In some ways, it reminded Rochelle of the early Internet days when people had to dial up manually to check their email, and the hissing sounds of the modem would continue until the connection was complete. If every organ has its own unique electromagnetic field,[1] then were Rochelle and Angelo somehow acting as energetic base stations and conduits for messages from another world?

Rochelle remembered reading something that Harvard-trained psychologist Dr. Gary Schwartz said: "Consciousness exists independently of brain activity. It does not depend upon the brain for its survival. Mind is first, the brain is second. The brain is not the creator of the mind, it is a powerful tool of the mind. The brain is an antenna/receiver for the mind, like a sophisticated television or cell phone."[2]

Neurosurgeon Dr. Eben Alexander echoes that sentiment, explaining, "I was taught that the brain creates consciousness . . . The truth is that the more we come to understand the physical brain, the more we realize it does not create consciousness at all. We are conscious in spite of our brain. The brain serves more as a reducing valve or filter, limiting pre-existing consciousness down to the trickle of the illusory 'here and now.'"[3]

Maybe we are all just resonating at different frequencies, playing out as a swirling dance of sorts, thought Rochelle. Tuning into this spectrum of frequencies seemed to be the key, and Angelo ostensibly had the ability to do it. She noticed the connection to Miriam and Yeshua appeared to come when his mind was incredibly still, in the midst of or after meditation when he was in a pure flow state. During those moments of stillness, something happens—it's as if an unseen antenna on his head is greeting cosmic information from the universe, tapping into its AUM primordial sound and merging with the moon, the stars, and the anonymities in the void. And somewhere along the way, he synchronizes with Miriam and Yeshua beyond our earthly space-time.

They were far from scientists, so their speculation of the connection mystery was purely intuitive. To them, it felt like Miriam's soul came through regularly to strengthen the signal between them so she could speak more fluidly. And Rochelle and Angelo gradually became better attuned to these signals. Whatever was happening, transmissions were coming through much louder and clearer as the weeks progressed.

One warm New England night, Rochelle asked Miriam, "Why are you *really* here?" The signal between their two worlds was so clear that Miriam's response surprised Rochelle. Usually, there was a pause before an answer, but Miriam replied instantly that evening.

"I am here to tell you both my story."

"Your story? You mean the story of your life?" Rochelle asked in disbelief.

"Yes," Miriam responded, "but it's not just the story of my life but also the story of your life with Angelo."

"What does your story have to do with our lives?" she asked. Why on earth would she want to tell her story to them? It made no sense, but neither did her ability to communicate through them. Miriam's response was far from what Rochelle expected.

"In your female form, you have had lives that have pushed you beyond your limits, as have I," she replied. "Many of us have even died for our convictions. While I didn't die in my lifetime as Miriam of Magdala for my convictions and beliefs, I have in others, and so have you. It is no accident I come to you now."

"So, you are here to tell your story to us?" Rochelle repeated as a question and then added, "But for what purpose?"

They sensed they were about to uncover Miriam's once-shrouded imprint on history with fresh eyes and ears. Later, they would discover Magdalene's eagerness to share her journey was because humanity had been misguided for far too long. But her motive would go beyond merely correcting the narrative or recounting her life, as she initially implied.

"There will be more . . . much more," Miriam said, "but let's start here, shall we? It will make more sense in time."

"You mean now? Right now? You want to tell us your story *right now*?" Rochelle stammered.

"Yes, of course," Miriam said. "As a woman in this lifetime, haven't you ever wondered what it was like to live as a woman over two thousand years ago?"

Rochelle reflected for a few minutes. Certainly, she was well aware of the grief she felt whenever she watched a movie or read a novel depicting women as *less than* men or as victims of rape and violence, or . . . didn't the list go on? Hadn't she traveled around the world and witnessed women who had been beaten or murdered but never received justice? Hadn't she seen mistreatment even in her First World generation but on a lesser scale?

She recalled times when her father would yell at her mother who was poised and confident when he wasn't around. Oftentimes when he entered the room, her mother's courage and strength evaporated, and she sank into the background like a squashed ant. She knew of women who had been raped, and because the men were never found guilty, they remained emotional victims. Playing the memories over and over again like a broken record, they carried the stories throughout their lives. She herself remembered shrinking in a board room meeting, where she had been the only woman and feared speaking up when she saw unethical decisions that would impact thousands. She winced when she thought of the male entrepreneurs she had witnessed or worked with over the years who didn't care about anything but profit, often at the peril of others. So yes, she was more than a little curious about Miriam's story, her pain, and her journey—if she was indeed Miriam of Magdala.

As Rochelle and Miriam's connection strengthened—woman-to-woman—more questions about why she and Angelo were the recipients of her story began to fall to the wayside. It was as if each session was a rekindling of old souls with a shared history. It wouldn't take long before she and Angelo would become acutely aware of a reality obscured by centuries of deceptions, a reality Miriam and Yeshua were seeking to once again bring to light, this time in a modern world.

And so, on that exceptionally humid evening, Rochelle cozied up in one of their soft plush chairs, covered in cloth the color of a cloudless sky at dusk with hints of azure and sapphire almost as deep as she imagined the unknown void far beyond their sight. As she sipped her tea, she noticed Angelo's voice and the color of his eyes changed slightly. Then, his eyes closed as if he had left their dimension and was with Miriam in another one Rochelle couldn't see with her human eyes. Yet, she felt Miriam's energy as intensely as she could feel Angelo's breath on her neck when they spooned at night. In a husky whisper at first, the mesmerizing Miriam of Magdala began to recount her journey.

Miriam Speaks

"My name is Miriam of Magdala, although most of the world knows and refers to me as Mary Magdalene or Mary of Magdala," she began.

"Magdala is the place I was from . . . my hometown, you might say in modern terms. It was common to refer to people by where they lived, such as Yeshua of Nazareth or Yosef of Galilee, and there were many Marys and Miriams in what you refer to today as the Holy Land.

"Why am I bringing you this message now, over two thousand years after I once walked the planet? You could say the world is ready to comprehend the message in a way it has never been able to before. I must speak the truth of the woman I once was and what Yeshua taught humanity because this timeline is critical for humanity."

Rochelle thought about her choice of the word timeline and wondered what she meant by it. And why was it critical? But she assumed Miriam would cover it eventually.

"We will also speak to it in my story," Miriam said as if reading Rochelle's mind. "My hope in sharing the wisdom we once taught, but in new ways, is that we will awaken people ready to hear the message, and in turn, they'll be able to awaken others to comprehend our true teachings *then* and *now*. And through my story, you will also discover who I actually was in flesh-and-bone and what Yeshua truly represented as well."

As Rochelle sank deeper into her chair, she was riveted by every word as they flew across the room like swarming butterflies filling an empty and lifeless space.

"Let's begin with my physical appearance," Miriam said, which surprised Rochelle, so much she let out a small laugh.

"There's a reason I wish to start here," she said. "There are many inaccuracies about our lives and who we once were, so why not start with my appearance?"

Rochelle laughed again, and simply replied, "Sure, why not?" Recalling some of the paintings that depicted Magdalene's voluptuous body and her often bare white shoulders, Rochelle added, "I have to say, I'm more than a little curious." Other paintings showed her with red hair and a small nose, neither of which seemed to match the physical features of what is now known as the Middle East.

"Unlike the way I have been represented in many images over the millennia, my skin wasn't milky white," she continued. "There was no sunscreen back then, so our skin inevitably became brown and weathered, especially given our lifestyle of walking from village to village. So why would I have soft creamy skin?"

Rochelle sensed she was annoyed by the notion anyone would think so. What's more, Miriam's forthright manner countered other images that showed her glancing up circumspectly as if she were too timid to look straight ahead. Rochelle had even seen her portrayed similarly to the also inaccurate light-skinned, blue-eyed images of Mother Mary.

"My most distinct feature was my nose which was strong and larger than average, and my fingers were long and narrow," Miriam went on. "Both Yeshua and I were slightly taller for our time—in your current metrics, he was roughly five feet eleven or so and my height was around five feet seven inches. Yeshua had a lanky body, for we did so much walking that our bodies remained slender.

"The popular pictures of all of us do not fit the reality of our challenging lives in Judea. Why would people represent Yeshua, Yeshua's mother, and me with pure white skin? To be more like them? To fit some idealized saintliness? That's not who we were."

Those images never made sense to Rochelle and Angelo either.

"What about the hygiene of the time?" Rochelle asked her, momentarily forgetting Angelo was Angelo. It was as if she were addressing Miriam directly, sister to sister.

"Naturally, we didn't have deodorant and showers, but we had oils and perfumes," Miriam responded. "We would go for days without bathing when we traveled to different towns teaching, so we often used perfumes. Whenever we had access to water, we bathed ourselves with both salt and fresh water—salt was exceptionally purifying, so we used it often. Salt water healed abnormalities on our skin and helped with infections."

The popular pictures of all of us do not fit the reality of our challenging lives in Judea.

Rochelle recalled Mary Magdalene's connection to perfumes and oils, especially the oil she used to anoint Yeshua, so she was about to ask a question when Miriam changed course.

"I was always drawn to the mystical world like my mother, so we didn't follow the traditional ways, something my sister never truly understood about my mother and me. It was also something I shared with Yeshua's mother, Mary, whom some of the religious amongst you refer to as the Virgin Mary.

"Yeshua did not result from a virgin birth; however, Mary did see visions and receive messages, traditionally called *visits from angels*. I suppose you could say she had what you refer to in your modern world as clairvoyance and clairaudience, intuitive senses I developed as I grew older. I also had clairtangence, meaning I could sense things and receive messages simply by touching something. These visions or messages came to Mary mentally, unlike how you and Angelo connect with our energies today."

"Connect to your energies today?" Rochelle asked, perplexed. "It almost feels as if we've gone through a portal, where illusion and imagination appear to be the only plausible explanations when nothing else fits or makes sense. Can you elaborate?"

"We will get to that," she responded. "Be present to where we are now, and it will be revealed in time."

I was always drawn
to the mystical world
like my mother.

Rochelle wondered how long "in-time" meant, for she and Angelo were growing impatient. Still, she knew that the best stories create the fabric of a rich and deeply lived life where each word carries its own unique thread, color, and texture. And stories and teachings like these take time to unfold. She released a sigh of acceptance as she readjusted her pillows to get a little more comfortable while Miriam continued her tale.

"Mary knew Yeshua had unique gifts from childhood, and both she and Yosef realized Yeshua was a man of God. Yeshua's father ran a carpentry trade that mostly focused on making furniture, a skill Yeshua learned as a boy. Even though our family was wealthier than Yeshua's, his family was far from poor.

What made Yeshua's father so esteemed was his religious affiliations with the Jewish people. Yosef was connected to what you would refer to today as the Orthodox Jewish community, which held a great deal of power and respect at that time. He had a positive standing with them because of his ethics and the trust the Orthodox community placed in his work and words, a reputation that naturally brought him more business. Yosef's abilities extended beyond carpentry, for he also had a brilliant business mind. He sold his furniture and building designs to others although they didn't call those sketches architecture in those days.

"Like his father, Yeshua became a talented carpenter. You see, it was common for sons to follow in their father's footsteps and help them with their businesses or ventures, so it should be no surprise to discover Yosef wanted Yeshua to become a businessman like him, or take on a respectable profession for the time, such as a philosopher or a lawyer. Today, you distinguish these disciplines, but back then they often overlapped.

"Mary had many intuitive abilities and innately knew Yeshua was headed on another path. In many ways, despite what Yosef might have wanted, you could say both his parents knew he would become a spiritual teacher . . . a man of God."

Rochelle piped in, "Did Yeshua have any siblings?"

At this point, however, Angelo's head began to move back and forth as if he was reading something before him Rochelle couldn't see in the physical realm. Because he was in an altered state, Rochelle realized she couldn't interrupt the process. He was no longer in her world, no longer in her dimension, and certainly no longer in her reality, or so it seemed until Rochelle began to receive visions and messages. She initially dismissed them but eventually saw a connection between them and what Angelo verified later on.

"What is happening to Angelo? Where is he now?" asked Rochelle.

"Some people are aware of the Akashic Records or, as others call it, the Akash, a depository of information of every memory, imprint, or experience that has ever existed on the planet," Miriam responded. "In other words, not only does it carry the memories of past lives and experiences, but also the energetic memories of all living things, including plant life, animals, and the earth grid itself."

That evening, their connection to Miriam and her world was so lucid that Rochelle oscillated between disbelief and a willing scribe. While Angelo's eyes were darting side to side as if he was reading a massive library of books at the speed of light, Rochelle asked, "Is he/are you accessing the Akashic Records from your life as Miriam?"

"Yes, in a way," she replied and then added, "You might say we are there together. Remember that I am not in a human body now as Miriam of Magdala, certainly not the one that once housed my soul when I was living on this planet. All memories are stored in what you could call an energy database where I access information from this timeline. Energy carries information, and because you are energy, you too carry information. Put another way, energy, and physical form or matter (a denser energy) comprise information. Because you think in linear ways, it is difficult to explain how information is stored in and accessed from a quantum field, but know I can access this information just as you can in your human form. There is no difference between you and me, for we are connected outside of time and space. But we will discuss this in depth later."

More confused than ever, Rochelle wanted to go deeper into this alternate reality; however, she stopped herself from derailing Miriam who seemed to be on a roll. She was also worried she'd lose track of a chronological narrative if she interrupted her, so she let Miriam continue.

"Naturally, there were siblings," she said, picking up an earlier thread. "Yeshua had several brothers and sisters; however, Mary was not the mother of all of them. Yosef's first wife passed away. One sister whose name was the same as her mother Mary also died from an umbilical cord caught around her neck during childbirth. She was given a burial and rite of passage as was typical for the time. Early deaths were not unusual for us since untreatable physical conditions or disease plagued many."

"In historical writings, it seems there were many Marys," Rochelle said.

"Yes, it was a common name, and this is why it became normal to refer to people from the place where they lived. Remember we were a people of tribes, and these place names were considered holy and sacred to us. If you were a family of means as both of our families were, you didn't venture far from your community when you married."

"My father was a man of law, so he spent much of his time arbitrating conflicting issues amongst people. Religion and law were combined at the time, so there was no difference between them. My father never accepted the path I needed to walk, so he was never proud of me in the way Yosef was of Yeshua. Yosef recognized his son's gifts and understood the necessity for Yeshua to study extensively, including learning about teachings outside our own tradition.

"What you refer to in your contemporary world as Yeshua's lost years was the time Yeshua traveled to Asia. Yosef stayed to maintain his status in the local community while Yeshua was away in India. It was typical for people who had money to travel to other places to be educated and expand their knowledge."

"Did Yeshua incorporate what he learned in India when he taught?" asked Rochelle.

"Yeshua spent twelve or thirteen years learning in India's southern and northern regions," Miriam replied. "He studied with sages who spoke to him of the sacred caduceus and chakras although they didn't use this language back then. They didn't understand how to explain light bodies or what quantum meant, but they understood intentions and thoughts could become reality and materialize. They taught Yeshua how to go inward, meditate, and access fields of consciousness that allowed him to become one with his spirit and then connect it to God or Source. Reaching this higher consciousness was mainly done through meditation, prayer, and repetitive mantras, something he instilled in the apostles and me in the early days of his work in Judea. These practices were also part of the teachings with his cousin John the Baptist whose work was collecting momentum at the time.

"Mary understood Yeshua even more than Yosef because she shared some of his spiritual gifts. She had a great deal of faith, but not just the conventional faith customary in our community."

Rochelle quickly realized she was about to learn new things about the sainted Mother Mary.

"Mary combined her Jewish faith with what was later referred to as the teachings of Isis, taught underground specifically to women," Miriam explained. "In the Isis teachings, there was more respect for women than in traditional patriarchal society since they were considered equal to or above men. In Egypt, where the Isis movement was most dominant, they treated women in higher regard than in Judaic society or Roman-controlled areas.

"During this period, women started to lose their status and my family followed Judaic patriarchal dictates. As harsh as this may sound, women were treated like cattle, sold off by families to be married. Men decided who would be the best suitor for each daughter, as my father tried to do, and Yeshua was not part of his plans.

"If I married into a wealthier family, more money would pour into mine, which would increase their standing in the community. When a woman married into wealth, the other family received an endowment. This came in the form of cattle, a home, livestock, or money, and is why women often didn't have a choice about whom they would marry."

In considering women as bride trade, gifts, or barter, Rochelle wondered how long such a tradition had been commonplace, for this act in itself devalues women's opinions and personal rights. What contributed to its acceleration? She read about ideas others have put forward over the years, such as anthropologist Claude Lévi-Strauss who suggested that "once men began to think of women as commodities, men began to appropriate women's power."[4] Modern feminist historian Gerda Lerner proposed that the decline and ultimate demise of the Goddess was the result of the creation of archaic states which led to centralized authority and a tendency to encourage the alpha traits of the male.[5] Yet Leonard Shlain posited in his best-selling book *The Alphabet Versus the Goddess: The Conflict Between Word and Image,* that "misogyny and patriarchy rise and fall with the fortunes of the alphabetic written word."[6] Rochelle also observed that Shlain noted two other important points:

> Around 1500 B.C., there were hundreds of goddess-based sects enveloping the Mediterranean basin. By the fifth century A.D. they had been almost completely eradicated, by which time women were also prohibited from conducting a single major Western sacrament. The Old Testament was the first alphabetic written work to influence future ages. Attesting to its gravitas, multitudes still read it three thousand years later. The words on its pages anchor three powerful religions: Judaism, Christianity, and Islam. Each is an exemplar of patriarchy.[7]

And as Gerda Lerner explained in *The Creation of Patriarchy*: "The very process of class formation incorporated an already pre-existing condition of male dominance over women and marginalized women in the formation of symbol systems." And later she wrote, "The exclusion of women from the creation of symbol systems became fully institutionalized only with the development of monotheism. Hebrew monotheism conceptualized a universe created by a single force—God's will. The source of creativity, then, was the invisible, ineffable God."[8]

Clearly, layers of complexities led to the downfall of the feminine in society, shifting from cherished and respected to suppressed and subjugated. But over time, horrific habits and patterns not only emerged but endured.

"Most men during our time only saw women's importance for creation and death," Miriam went on, bringing Rochelle back to her story. "You see, women didn't only represent creation but also death since they can birth life but also take it away. She was truly a creatrix even though the depth of this feminine power was rarely understood or respected."

"A creatrix," Rochelle repeated in awe under her breath. She tucked the word away, eager to learn more. Meanwhile, Miriam changed direction and moved on to her relationship with Yeshua.

In the Isis teachings, women had a higher standing than in traditional patriarchal society since they were considered equal or above men.

"When Yeshua and I first felt a connection, it wasn't just his energy or physical presence; I also resonated with his teachings and wanted to be part of his work. Let me ask you this: If you decide to run off with a teacher/rabbi whom others called the *Son of God*, how do you think a respected family in the community would treat you?"

Miriam didn't wait for a response although her question stirred something in Rochelle who thought to herself: Miriam and Yeshua were not just rebels in their teachings, but they also lived life from their hearts. They didn't let societal norms dictate their path, an astonishing choice for their time.

Rochelle thought back to her college years in London. A friend from Asia told her once that when she returned to her country after graduation, an arranged marriage was waiting for her to provide financial stability, solidify family and social ties, and ensure emotional support. Although she had fallen for a fellow student from Connecticut in her Anthropology class, Rochelle remembered her friend saying one late night, "It's best for our family."

Miriam interrupted Rochelle's memories with the consequences of her rebellion.

"I was only in my late teens when I ran off to follow Yeshua's teachings. Even though I received no support from my father, my mother was strong-minded and figured out a way to support me from afar when we taught in villages, seeking shelter at each stop.

"Female and male relationships during our time were important, but only in fulfilling Judaic law, where the purpose of women and men's union was to create offspring. I would love to say the act of procreation was divine for them, but it wasn't. Sex for them was about increasing the numbers of the tribe; the larger your tribe, the more power you had in society. This motivation is one reason why the feminine was unequal to the masculine. You see, the only importance women had was to bear children like a cow that gives milk; keep the cow in constant lactation, and it will continue to provide milk."

Her tone was austere, thought Rochelle, as if Miriam was remembering the oppressive and limited state of affairs for women.

"Far from being equals, we were considered property so we could produce children," Miriam continued. "Do you know capital comes from a Latin word that means head? The more heads you had, the greater your wealth. The more daughters you had, the greater your wealth. As harsh as this may sound, a man could simply sell them off as potential breeders. This is the foundation of what it was like to be a woman during my time. Yeshua and I broke all the rules because we demonstrated feminine and masculine equality by example."

"By example?" Rochelle asked.

"Yes, by how we lived and showed up for others," she said. "And through our teachings."

Her response made Rochelle recall something she had stumbled on about Mary Magdalene from an abstract on the Baha'i Faith. Abdu'l-Bahá spoke of her (he references Magdalene without the e) as a "veritable lioness." He wrote: "My hope is that each one of you may become as Mary Magdalen—for this woman was superior to all the men of her time and her reality is ever shining from the horizon of Christ."[9]

The lioness description made Rochelle think of courage and resilience. Miriam wasn't a woman to hold back, Rochelle thought, wondering what else she would learn about this woman of relentless force, always moving toward what she believed in as Yeshua had done so many years ago.

"You are breaking the patriarchal rules and religions by writing down my story of who I really was," Miriam observed, "and many more things I'll share with you people might not want to hear. But now, the four of us have an energy sequence together, so there's no turning back."

A bit startled and confused by the language, Rochelle couldn't help but intervene, "The four of *us*? An energy sequence *together*?"

"Yes, Angelo, you, and our souls have an energy sequence together—we have integrated our frequencies into your auric field so you can act as pure vessels for us to tell our story and heal others."

Trying to wrap her head around Miriam's explanation, Rochelle probed even further, "Integrated our frequencies?"

"We are all energy," she replied. "And as energy, even in material form, we can be expressed or described as a spectrum of vibrational frequencies. But each soul has a unique signature."

Rochelle didn't understand the terminology, but it made Rochelle think of our life force energy that the ancients spoke of, relating everything as energy, vibration, and electricity even if they didn't necessarily use those words at the time. As far back as the 6th century B.C., the Upanishads spoke of the Nadis as energy centers that move throughout the body.[10] As intrigued as she was by her words that moved them beyond her life and esoteric wisdom, she sensed that Miriam wanted to carry on with her story.

"At least you're no longer labeled a prostitute," said Rochelle, shifting the subject back to Miriam.

"This is true. However, I didn't create a feast day to honor me; humanity did. I didn't ask to be worshipped, yet now some people worship me," she responded.

Rochelle had to add, "But isn't it wonderful to have a day honoring what you represented when you were once in human form rather than the dark clouds hovering over your name for so long?"

"Yes," she said, "I suppose it is, but I am not an idol to be worshipped, nor is Yeshua. I am not a skull you should have, nor did I hold a skull of anyone."

Rochelle thought of her time devouring art museums in Europe where she saw Mary Magdalene portrayed with a skull in religious paintings from the sixteenth and seventeenth centuries, some of the same art depicting her with auburn hair and ivory-colored skin.

"What do you think the skull means?" Miriam continued. "Does it represent death? Our human perception sees our skull as death because when the flesh rots away, the only thing left are the bones. But this is not what the skull signifies—the skull represents rebirth and the liberation of the soul, or you could say, the rejoining of the soul with Source. You're not bound by the human form of flesh and bones, and in the moment of what you call passing, you are free to become your Authentic Self once again."

"Authentic Self?" questioned Rochelle.

"Yes," Miriam replied. "Your Authentic Self is who you truly are. The soul you. The energy you. The infinite you. The immortal you," she added, and then returned to her previous thread since she clearly wasn't finished speaking about the skull.

"Some who painted me with the skull knew the higher meaning of transcending the human body to become one with God or Source, and some didn't. While a few understood it, most were simply imitating other masters, without understanding it themselves."

Knowing the distinction between truly grasping and merely parroting, Rochelle nodded, thinking of how often she saw replication in technology and music as two prime examples. Passed down imitations. The same holds true with beliefs. Rather than going inward to access their own innate genius, some merely repeat another's "gospel," which keeps prior conditioning in place generation after generation as the *only truth.*

"You have had your own experiences," Miriam said. "Remember the exchange you had with a group of women? One didn't believe you could connect to or communicate with Mary Magdalene. Even if it were true, she said Magdalene wouldn't have chosen a man to speak through. Do you recall that day, Rochelle?"

She had indeed, for it was an uncomfortable moment. She was apprehensive about sharing their experiences with others since even the most open-minded amongst their friends questioned the validity of the visitations.

"You wonder why I am so direct and blunt at times, perhaps because of what you expect of me and of women generally. It's your history and conditioned perceptions that have portrayed me incorrectly. I need you to write my truth, not what you think it is, but what it truly is. With the strict rules of our religions and cultures at the time, women were not presented as important, valid, intelligent, or powerful. It's just how it was, and even though I was strong and smart, men depicted me as they wished with their own patriarchal biases.

"In the beginning, when Yeshua and I spent time alone, the male apostles didn't like me. Today, do you not have women in government whom men hate? There are young women whom men call names publicly on your television networks; it was no different for me during my time. Why should we silence this message now? Women could not speak their truth back then. In fact, they couldn't speak at all, for they were not even human in the eyes of many, so some chose to escape. During that turbulent time, even my brothers didn't protect me. With Yeshua gone, who would control his message, teachings, and efforts? It certainly wouldn't be a woman, would it?"

As Miriam spoke, the energy she felt from Angelo was different from the energy she had come to know; it was more tender and sympathetic as if Miriam intuitively knew everything Rochelle was feeling as a woman at that particular moment. Rochelle sensed not just frustration but also a touch of anger, albeit controlled. The intense reaction felt like accumulated emotions from what Miriam had experienced long ago.

"I want you to feel what I am saying to you, Rochelle," she continued. "Feel it. I want you and all women to become as dynamic and strong as I had to be in my life as Miriam of Magdala. I want you to become relentless like a mother with her cubs so you can protect the truth of who you truly are. Your mother would be proud of you, wouldn't she? Mine was proud of my strength and yet my father never was. Be resilient in this lifetime, Rochelle. You've shed enough tears and so have so many women you know."

Rochelle didn't feel as weak as Miriam was perhaps suggesting, but she innately understood what she meant. Countless times in a business setting she didn't speak her truth out of fear of being judged, or worse, because she felt she wasn't smart enough to comment. Rochelle also knew that sometimes she was afraid to ask for a raise or hesitant to offer advice in a family setting dominated by men. Sure, she had shown a warrior spirit throughout the years, yet she recalled situations where she had retreated when she should have asserted herself. Most of all, as she listened to Miriam, she was aware of the times she had sunk into the background when she was afraid to step on stage or into the limelight. Certainly, she had seen threatened men disparage strong and effective women time and time again.

"I have always been a warrior, not with fists, but with my heart and words," Miriam said fervently. "Many people don't want to see a warrior in Mary Magdalene, for they only want to see a woman of love. I am that too—you cannot heal alongside Yeshua and be committed as I was without being of love. The female apostles also poured their hearts into their work, and like me, had a great deal of faith. They made significant contributions despite their status as women who were treated like goats and cattle.

"Today, institutionalized sexism, racism, and the rules around them make women hide their beauty and truth. Women have become brainwashed this is something they must do, so they cover their faces, hair, and shoulders. In some cultures, killing a woman is acceptable if she's caught with a man other than her husband. Some people won't like or accept my words if I express myself with frustration or anger at times, but I have the right to speak my truth now. Women have learned to be quiet and humble in the face of violence for hundreds of years."

It made Rochelle think of Frederick Engels' work which pointed to the "overthrow of the mother right" which he asserted was the "world historical defeat of the female sex."[11] That defeat led to centuries upon centuries of enforced patriarchal views that over time, it simply became the norm for both sexes.

As Gerda Lerner points out, "Women have for millennia participated in the process of their own subordination because they have been psychologically shaped so as to internalize the idea of their own inferiority."[12] She also reminds us that for over 2,500 years the God of the Hebrews was addressed, represented, and interpreted as a male Father-God," and with it came the "meaning which carried authority and force." That "meaning became of the utmost significance in the way both men and women were able to conceptualize women and place them both in the divine order of things and in human society."[13]

This psychological distortion became so cemented in place that women learned to be seen, not heard. To stay in the home because it was her place to do so. To speak softly and be gracious even when her values weren't being honored or her truth wasn't being heard. Occasionally, she might find that she could open up to another like-minded woman who was a maverick in the shadows. Truth be told, this internalization of inferior status takes its toll over time. It naturally leads to wanting to take a back seat but only because she's known no other way, and her psyche tells her there's punishment in store should she create any waves . . . should she have the courage to speak up or take charge. Being conditioned in a world where women have been devalued and demeaned for so long, they've simply learned to mistrust their own opinions, considering them less valid than those of men. Rochelle's mind was racing as she considered how much of the ancient, reinforced programming rolled over into modern times, including her generation.

Yet the ancient religion of the Goddess was once revered, thought Rochelle. But Miriam was on a roll, so Rochelle collected her thoughts and returned to Miriam's words.

"Look at what the women in Afghanistan have gone through. Men dictated what they could and could not do, when they could leave the house, and why," Miriam continued. "They threw acid on women who misbehaved. After a brief period of hard-won freedoms, the Taliban returned to deprive women of freedoms once again. In such a society, women are much better seen than heard, aren't they? Although less brutally enforced, isn't that what you learned even in your own life, Rochelle?"

Institutionalized sexism,
racism and the rules
around them make
women hide their
beauty and truth.

She nodded, for it was true. She felt the heaviness of Miriam's words as she pondered the cruelty of years gone by. The dictates have been in place for so long, that it felt as if they'd never be challenged, at least not seriously. Many scholars and historians assumed that men have always played a leadership role and have been the only inventors of significant ideas.

Few people know the history of the Goddess as an ancient religion. Egyptian Goddess Isis who goes by many, many names wasn't just adored and worshipped by women but also men in ancient Judea, Egypt, Greece, Italy and the surrounding areas. She has been referred to as the Mother of the Gods, the Queen of Heaven, the Lady of the Mysteries, and countless other references. Isis was said to have initiated men into the mysteries, but it didn't stop there. People could turn to Isis' profound wisdom, resilience, and bravery to overcome their own obstacles and trials in life and prevail over even the darkest of challenges.[14]

The impact of Isis stretched far and wide, beyond Egypt, Judea, Anatolia, Persia, Babylonia and ancient Greece. Although Isis was so powerful that she crossed myriad borders, Goddesses have been worshipped by countless societies in the world, all representing various manifestations. Although the Goddess was relegated beneath the Pantheon of Gods over time and later squashed under the monotheistic Yahweh, She continued to be relished, albeit subversively.

And let's not forget, thought Rochelle, that outside of the Abrahamic religions and Western traditions, the Mother and/or the Goddess was a universal figure of power, central to people's beliefs, myths and stories in the ancient world across cultures. She epitomized fertility. Flow. Sensuality. Creative Spirit. Life itself. She was the Queen of both Sky and Earth. She was considered the Creatrix for what she birthed but also the force that governed death.

As Rochelle reflected on the transition to a patriarchal worldview, Miriam marched on, bringing her back to the present moment as she so often did.

"I couldn't speak my truth back then but have earned the right to speak up. I can express myself now as I once was and won't be silenced for fear of being stoned to death. How would you like to grow up in a society that treated women as nothing more than sex objects? Angelo has no knowledge of what I went through as a woman, but I can now speak out because he allows me to do it, and so do you since I come through both of you. It's long overdue that my truth comes forward. We as women have the right to call out any of our abusers and will no longer be silenced as we had been for so many years.

"Humility doesn't mean sitting back, allowing yourself to be verbally abused, and saying nothing. You can meditate in silence, but you also have the right to stand up and say, 'No more, I am *not that*, and I will not accept your labels.' We will no longer be humiliated, bashed, and subjugated to a male-dominated society. I need people to see that I'm a fighter and that I've always been a fighter during my time on this earth plane. It's not so much about setting history straight as it is about the rebalancing of men and women. It's about elevating women again to their legitimate place in society and the world."

Rochelle wondered if Angelo would later remember the words pouring through with such force, conviction, and resolve.

"What does it truly mean to be humble?" she asked Rochelle. "Know when to say nothing and know when to say something or everything. All women have a right to say everything, and I'm here to empower them to regain their voices. Do you have any idea how hard I struggled to become the woman I became, or you could say, the woman I have become?"

"You mean as Miriam of Magdala in that lifetime?" Rochelle asked.

"Understand the future and past don't exist as you think they do. I am Miriam of Magdala. I am the Magdalene, not the Magdalene of the future or the past, not even of the present. There is only existence. There is only a presence. I need you to understand this."

She didn't understand, but Miriam went on.

"This is an exceptionally difficult path to follow, and copious times you and Angelo have died for standing up for your beliefs. Some who are reading this text now have also died numerous times for standing up for their beliefs. We're here to tell people to let go of their fear, step into their Authentic Selves, and speak their truth. It's time."

And with that packed oration, she was gone. Magdalene's energy had come through like a tornado and left the same way. When she came in, Angelo's body shook, his head tilted back, and he released long deep breaths of air. When she stepped back from his auric field, his arms and hands twitched as they often did.

After such a direct and penetrating dialogue, Rochelle and Angelo's rendezvous with Miriam appeared to be over for the day.

"What do you remember from our encounter with her this evening?" Rochelle asked Angelo.

"Everything and nothing," he replied unexpectedly.

"What do you mean?" she probed.

"She gives me images. She takes me to places beyond time as I have always understood it. I become everything and nothing all at the same time. Her personality and the intensity of her messages blend with me as if I am her, yet I am observing her at the same time. Throughout, I can feel her fire and passion as she speaks about being oppressed as a woman. I can feel what she felt then and the conviction she possesses now. There's an urgency for us to capture her story, and I can feel it."

"Yes," said Rochelle. "I sense an urgency too. It's as if she's been waiting for a critical time to tell it."

They stayed in silence for several minutes before Rochelle asked again, "What do you mean when you say you remember nothing?"

"It's like her soul blends with mine but uses energy from both of us . . . from both of our energetic auric fields," he responded. "When this happens, I am acutely present and can only describe it as a feeling of being one with the Divine or one with God. It's hard to explain. I sense, feel, and see things, but then after she's gone, the details fade. It has been like that since her first visit. If you ask me tomorrow or the next day to tell you what she said, I won't remember the details. The feelings and sensations, yes, and even her intentions, but not the details."

"Wow," said Rochelle. "I remember everything she says the next day as if it were from a movie I've seen fifty times. I'm so captivated that the words wash over me like a stream of water on a hot day, and the intensity of them remains with me. It's as if her words wake something up in me, and they refuse to leave."

He grabbed her hand, and she cozied over to him, resting her head against his shoulder. Surrounded by candles, they remained sitting on the floor, sipping their tea, and waiting for the Frankincense to finish burning.

• • • • • •

CHAPTER 4

AS A HEALER & YESHUA'S PARTNER

I am not afraid.
I was born to do this.
—Joan of Arc

Rochelle sat cross-legged with her elbows propped up on a slate-blue wooden table etched with symbols: Infinity. Elephants. Kuan Yin. The Tree of Life. The table was so low she could barely fit her legs underneath it, but it was long enough to hold a set of eight Tibetan singing bowls they picked up during their travels. When Rochelle struck the rims, the vibration created such a calming effect she could sit silently with Angelo for hours. Sitting in stillness allowed them to be in the present moment together, bringing a sense of inner peace that lifted their spirits after a long day.

Focusing on Miriam's messages earlier that week, Rochelle began to ruminate on what she must have felt as a woman under strict Jewish laws during harsh patriarchal times. She had lived before electricity, plumbing, or any of the other modern conveniences Rochelle and Angelo were accustomed to in their day-to-day lives. It was also a time when men led the way in all aspects of society. Men dictated societal behavior and norms because they were in charge of politics and had authority over moral conduct, ethics, social privilege, and marriage laws. They also inherited thrones and controlled property. It's no wonder Miriam's reputation was thrown into the prostitute's den to decrease her importance not just as one of Yeshua's apostles, but also as a partner who taught and healed alongside him.

These two historical figures understood and embraced gender balance two thousand years ago—what might the consciousness of our society look like today if others had followed suit? At least the world was showing renewed interest in Miriam, which was bringing Magdalene's name back to the world's awareness, not as a prostitute needing to be cleansed, but as Yeshua's partner. The intrigue in her life gave rise to the mystery behind this long-silenced and misunderstood feminine voice.

Rochelle and Angelo realized the timing of Miriam's story was no accident, for they were living during a time of great turbulence and transition. Gender definitions were changing in profound ways and people were struggling to make sense of and give meaning to gender roles. They knew this period of change presented an opportunity for everyone to show up in the world differently, and to be kinder and more empathetic to others. In less than a generation, Rochelle and Angelo saw society go from His and Her toilets to a host of new identities modern teenagers know as the norm. Transgender, gender-neutral, non-binary, pangender, genderqueer, two-spirit, and third gender are now part of the societal vocabulary. They wondered what these new identities would mean for the next generation in how people would view each other. Would everyone be seen as equal regardless of what sexual orientation they most identified with? And with new lenses of individual identities, how will we show up as partners?

It became clear that Miriam's story was more than just her journey. Miriam and Yeshua were here to push them beyond their conditioned linear thinking . . . far beyond. Rochelle's head was often buzzing during the day, especially after an evening with Miriam. Did Miriam plant all these feelings, emotions, and memories into Rochelle's auric field? She often wondered where her insights came from, often crucially timed before or immediately after an important teaching. How are imagination and intuition influenced by another energy field?

Roughly a week had gone by since Miriam's last visit. On a rainy Thursday night after dinner, Rochelle was standing in the kitchen boiling the tea kettle. Waiting for the whistle to blow, she could hear Angelo's breathing change in the adjacent room. Although he was at a distance, she could tell his consciousness had shifted. She quickly filled her cup and scurried into their sitting room where she noticed several lit candles and burning incense. Did Angelo proactively plan the evening encounter they were about to embark upon, or was it Miriam's decision? Or was it a merging, a collective *calling* of sorts?

Soon, Rochelle could feel the energy of the room change and hear ringing in her ears. As she watched Angelo's head fall backward, Miriam came for a visit, greeting Rochelle as if she were an old friend coming over for drinks.

"It's nice to see you, Rochelle," Miriam said cordially.

Rochelle smiled as she grabbed Angelo's hand and squeezed it as if making a physical connection at that moment was the most important thing in the world. Even though she felt divine love when Miriam and Yeshua visited, she missed Angelo's presence and the sarcastic wit and goofiness she found annoying at times.

"Partnership," began Miriam. "Not all your modern relationships understand the importance of a soul connection, but you and Angelo do, don't you? You recognize the value of having a solid union. You've both been through a lot and now appreciate the lending hand of the other, the comforting hug at the end of a long day, and the loyalty and love when things are tough. Yeshua and I had such a connection together, but it wasn't easy given the path he was on and the likely outcome."

Rochelle didn't feel like running upstairs for her laptop, so she grabbed a pen and pad of paper from their Asian table's top drawer to capture Miriam's words.

"You're going the old-fashioned route tonight, I see," said Miriam.

It was clear she wanted to speak more about Yeshua and her relationship with him, something Rochelle knew had been particularly controversial within various circles. It was hidden behind the canonical portrait of a repentant prostitute until the Gnostic Gospels suggested a much bigger role and the Catholic Church elevated Mary Magdalene to the Apostle of Apostles. Now was the time to go deeper.

"While Yeshua taught me new things he experienced during his years in India, he also learned the teachings of Isis from my work," Miriam continued. "I will explain more about this movement later. But here, I want to note its importance as a place for women to bond, grow, and learn together. As I mentioned, Yeshua's mother, Mary, was part of this group, and so was my mother. I developed strong bonds and friendships with women on this path of esoteric learning, which wasn't for the weak-willed. We brought each other strength and supported each other.

"We are truly beyond your comprehension, and I don't mean to sound aloof or distant when I say this. People don't understand what Yeshua was here to do. He was a man of profound love, but he was also here to change the world, and our energies have shown up in the auric fields of others who desired to do the same."

Hmmm, thought Rochelle. She had to know more before Miriam moved on. "Can you give some examples of people you have worked with through their auric fields?" she asked, trying to decipher exactly what "through someone's auric fields" really meant. Perhaps like they were doing with her and Angelo?

We are truly
beyond your
comprehension.

"We have worked with and through those whose message was about peace and love. Your Gandhi and Martin Luther King were here to change the world," Miriam replied. "Your modern Amma, Yogananda, and others of their ilk who represent and teach about love show up in this realm to change the world, not to create little ripples in a lake. We were not here to create little ripples, a message many do not want to hear."

What a strong force she is, mused Rochelle. A hot torch. A hand grenade. A tornado. Miriam was a bit of all of them and without apology.

"We are here to create waves as we did two thousand years ago," she said. "We are speaking as one now through you and Angelo even though your perception is that we only speak through him. We are your shadows, the very thing you fear the most. Angelo fears us too."

Rochelle didn't like the sound of this, so she had to interject. "What do you mean?"

"You both fear the message," Miriam replied. "You've always run far away from religion and anything associated with it. While we were not religious in a traditional sense, nor was our message, you still associate Yeshua and my name with the Catholicism of your youth."

Rochelle wouldn't call what she felt fear, but it was true she didn't want to be associated with religion, and she had experienced discord in her great-grandmother's Lutheran church, her grandmother's Methodist church, and her other grandmother's Episcopalian church. History through the so-called holy books and other literature certainly did a number on Yeshua and Magdalene. She grew to distrust anything connected to the Catholic Church with its rules and dogma. She recalled her time at a private Catholic school and how much she felt confined by the nonsensical world around her. Rochelle clearly remembered the dress protocols and list of rules she could never follow, so she could only imagine the world Miriam of Magdala had to face over two thousand years ago. Full of shoulds and shouldn'ts. Loaded with rights and wrongs. And there was no shortage of judgment and polarity. She would never let the image of Eve—set in motion by the Old Testament—be her image of a woman.

Miriam continued.

"When you show up to help humanity, it sometimes requires making waves and being bold. It was certainly needed back then for the male and female apostles and us. We had to have faith and trust the journey."

"Female apostles?" asked Rochelle, noting Miriam had mentioned them before in passing but without any details.

Miriam was audacious and quick in her reply as she posited the question, "Do you truly think Yeshua only had male followers and apostles? Those in power in the Christian churches would have liked the world to believe this notion, so it was the message they passed down . . . from one corrupt man in charge to another."

Rochelle tried to digest both the message and Miriam's growing frustration. It was as if she was able to relive the painful emotions from the Akashic Records—the unified field of memories including her own.

All of the Abrahamic religions were male, thought Rochelle. And although Judaism, Christianity, and Islam "may have differed about what sacrament to take when or which day was actually the Sabbath, they were in complete agreement on one subject—the status of women. Females were to be regarded as inferior creatures who were divinely intended to be obedient and silent vessels for the production of children and the pleasure and convenience of men,"[1] as Merlin Stone offered in *When God was a Woman.*

While it may sound harsh to read such a blatant statement, in *The Victorian Woman*, Duncan Crow shares some of the strict laws prohibiting women's rights, such as the fact that men could legally use physical force to ensure his wife didn't leave home until 1881 and up until 1884, a woman could go to jail if she refused sex from her husband. He also talks about the pivotal roles that Christianity and Judaism played in keeping women subordinate.[2]

Rochelle's great-grandmother lived during that time, and she had heard some of the horrific stories. It made her heart ache to think of the restrictions placed on women when Miriam walked the planet.

Finally, the voice and tone settled a bit. Although Rochelle was eager to learn more about the female apostles, she sensed Miriam wanted to change the topic and she did.

"People think their souls are one—one entity—but this is not the case. Many energies make up a soul for I am not just one energy. I am many, and the same holds true for Yeshua, you, Angelo, and everyone else. This multiplicity is another reason why I said you cannot comprehend who we are; the quantum portions of what makes us up as human beings are hard for you to understand. We will get more into the soul later. For now, I want to address the layers of religious and institutional duplicities and practices which have clouded your vision and closed off your heart to a deeper understanding of the truth."

Rochelle shifted her body to find a more comfortable place to sit as the intensity of her message appeared to be rising.

"You have lost faith in Source, God, Godde, Universal Consciousness, or whatever name you wish to give it because you have all lost faith in yourselves through your religions. You moved from an innate knowing and understanding of your power to obeying the script of another. Tell us, Rabbi, tell us, Monk, tell us, Buddha, tell us, Priest, tell us, Prophet, tell us, Spiritual Master, tell us, Guru: What should we do? Should we eat pork? How should we behave? Please give us the answers teacher, for we will follow you."

Miriam's sarcasm made Rochelle smile, for she was beginning to appreciate her down-to-earth and fearless approach. The torch was lit, and it wasn't about to fizzle.

"But when the time came for people to attest that they were followers of Yeshua, they renounced him since they feared being thrown to the lions as he had been, metaphorically speaking. In modern times, will you be thrown into the lion's den?"

Rochelle had hoped not as she took a deep breath and tried to relax while Miriam carried on with her story. Serenity was certainly not the tone Miriam had created, and Rochelle could sense her unrelenting passion and need to speak her truth.

"After a few years of expanding our knowledge, teaching, and healing, Yeshua and I grew closer and closer," she went on. "The apostles knew this, for they saw us spend much time together and often alone. I taught and healed with him wherever he went and followers grew as did disbelievers.

"Although a lot of Yeshua's parables and teachings fell on deaf ears, many supported us. Knowing people could only digest the teachings within the parameters of certain reference points, we had to teach using language they could understand. Even so, our teachings were misunderstood by so many. Still, word of Yeshua's healings and what you today call miracles spread, not just in Judea but in the surrounding settlements and even into your modern-day Europe. News traveled through fishermen who journeyed from coastal towns to ports where they traded goods.

"Remember we lived before the Catholic Church was established, and several early religions were polytheistic, so we used terms from their beliefs and understandings. Even though we used familiar terms, we didn't teach that there was only one path or belief system, and we don't teach it now as we work through both of you and others on this planet. Religious paths often dictate only one way to reach the Divine and that you are separate from God. In contrast, the message Yeshua and I gave focused on the unity with God within you—all you need to do is look inside to find divinity. Of course, any path leading you to know the Omnipresence of All That Is, God, Goddess, Source, or whatever it is for you can be enormously healing.

"Back then, this concept of the Divine within was hard to understand because, as I mentioned, many believed in varied gods or held quite a different idea of God. For example, people could understand terms like the Father, which is why we often used it in our teachings. This is also why Yeshua saying, 'You can't get to the Father until you go through me,' was highly accepted. While the apostles understood paradise or the kingdom was here on earth, they knew most people wouldn't understand this concept. People believed salvation came after the body died and that the Father or God was beyond this world. You see, it was a hard life back then, so it was difficult for common people to see heaven as something before them, within them, or as part of their present reality.

All you need to
do is look inside
to find divinity.

"I was called to heal with Yeshua and realized it was my purpose. When I was in my human form, I preached and healed but wasn't acknowledged for I couldn't speak my truth as a woman. But now, I will speak up and encourage all women to do the same. Yeshua will sometimes refer to himself as Yeshua of Miriam; he does so to honor the divine feminine force I was during our lifetime together, something others didn't respect.

"You see, they would say Miriam of Yeshua or Mary of Yosef as a way to denote which man the woman was married to or belonged to, so when I speak my truth now, free of those patriarchal prescriptions, it may be inconvenient for many," Miriam added, her tempo accelerating with a sense of urgency. "I know you and Angelo doubt my words at times too or don't always like what message comes through; however, please convey my journey as it comes forth in its raw form."

Rochelle nodded as Miriam continued.

"I was part of these teachings with Yeshua and the apostles. Even though history doesn't report it, I was always by his side, teaching, healing, and even leading. The Bible doesn't tell you this, and academics won't tell you this either unless they give credence to the Gnostic texts. When we healed together, Yeshua modeled the balance of the divine feminine and divine masculine to show there was no difference between men and women. He tried to demonstrate that this balance led to *becoming one* with God again. Because it was such a patriarchal society, even the male apostles had a hard time understanding it and certainly didn't accept it, yet Yeshua did what he could.

"In a man's world, as it has been for so long, my story will insult some people's ears, but let it be so. I was Yeshua's partner, and there was a significant amount of love between us even though the path was far from easy. Spiritual life isn't for the cowardly and we certainly had our fair share of trials. We learned from and supported each other as we faced numerous challenges along the way. Not everyone accepted my role next to him, and harsh words found their way to me often. We were extremely out of balance as it was an antiquated society devoid of respect for women.

"Humanity has been confused about masculine and feminine energies for quite a long time, which is why the imbalance remains on your planet. Currently, the collective consciousness is moving toward oneness. Those here to elevate consciousness will not be killed for doing so, for the movement has gathered too much momentum. In light of all I am telling you at this time, it is also true that everything you do, see, and experience is a perception, an illusion, or as some on your planet call it, maya. Does this mean you're not real? Does this mean what you feel isn't real? No, but don't fear death. This too is an illusion, for your human death is simply an expansion back into the Universal Consciousness of All That Is, but again, we'll talk more about these matters in time."

"Ahhh yes, illusions. I want to hear more, especially how you and Yeshua taught it," Rochelle piped in.

"We will expand upon the teachings but remember during our time they couldn't understand such things," reminded Miriam. "Using parables was one of his ways to reach people despite the fact many couldn't decipher them. That part of your history is correct."

Rochelle smiled warmly as Miriam spoke of Yeshua's parables, noting the tenderness in the voice. Then she asked, "I know Yeshua studied in India, and much of your spiritual knowledge came from the Isis teachings, but did you ever study more formally together, or was this simply not an option for men and women at that time?"

"We shared what we knew with each other and had learned before meeting up again when he returned from Asia," Miriam replied. "Later, we studied with others, and healing and purification were part of that knowledge. You will learn about this chapter of our lives when we next speak."

And with that forecast of the next topic, her energy was gone, though not like a tornado as so often occurred when she appeared and disappeared. This time, Miriam slowly stepped back. When she did, however, Rochelle wanted to call her back and say, "Miriam—no, don't leave yet."

The evening's message was far too short, and she wanted more details. Patience was a virtue Rochelle knew she had to strengthen, for she saw and admired it in Angelo. As a therapist, life was never a race for him and he often joked that he resonated with the tortoise not the hare as a child, and he lived his life the same way as an adult.

Perhaps Miriam was trying to teach her patience that evening. She remembered hiking in her early twenties on the Annapurna Circuit in Nepal with a group of people she didn't know. Athletic from childhood, Rochelle had always been out front, whether it was biking, hiking, running, or playing a group sport. Not one to sit on the sidelines, she often led with vigor and passion in everything she did, including physical exercise. On this particular hike, however, her calf flared up, and she was in so much pain that she had to stop and sit down. The rest of the group moved forward without her. Frustrated by her inability to join them, she felt weak, yet she physically couldn't continue. In about an hour, a remarkably gentle man with memorable Himalayan features appeared from nowhere. Although he didn't have a bag with him, he pulled a small bottle from his pocket filled with an ointment made from local herbs and plants she could use for her leg. Before the naturally taciturn man left, he said to Rochelle in the quietest of voices, "Life is not a race. Patience, grasshopper, patience." And then he was gone as mysteriously as he had appeared.

Yes, patience was needed at this time as Miriam and Yeshua needed it back then, Rochelle reflected. She was lost in thought as Angelo's awareness returned to their reality, so he grabbed her hand to make it known he was with her. Still wrestling with her impatience, she turned her head and looked into his eyes.

"You know, I really wanted her to expand upon her relationship with Yeshua," she said to Angelo. "Why does she always get to decide when to come and when to leave?"

"Sometimes, it appears that way, but there are moments when I think of her or Yeshua, and they'll come through if my intention is strong enough," he responded. "At other times, they leave because they're aware of what my body needs."

"What do you mean?" she asked.

"When my physical body is tired, they know," Angelo said with a long yawn.

She smiled since they often joked about how she needed much less sleep than Angelo did, and he was forever reminding her to slow down and not take so much on in a day. Lesson noted, she thought. "Patience, grasshopper, patience."

It was as if both the kind, wise Nepalese man and Mary Magdalene were there together, reminding her that life wasn't a race . . . that the sweetest things in life can't be rushed. The most profound things in life can't be rushed either, and Miriam's story was certainly nothing short of profound.

• • • • • •

CHAPTER 5

LIFE WITH THE ESSENES

Purity of speech, of the
mind, of the senses, and of
a compassionate heart are
needed by one who desires
to rise to the divine platform.
—Chanakya

In learning about Miriam's and Yeshua's lives, Rochelle and Angelo discovered they may have had a connection to the Jewish sect known as the Essenes, often associated with the *Dead Sea Scrolls.*[1] Angelo had read about them, and they both had watched a documentary about some of their beliefs and importance in history. The scrolls were discovered amongst other Judaic manuscripts and writings in the mid-1940s with more unveiled in 1956. These scrolls led to a different interpretation and understanding of some of our so-called holy scriptures. Angelo and Rochelle had talked several times about their interest in visiting the caves near the Qumrān Ruins where they were found.

If the scrolls were written around Judean independence when governed by Jewish high priests and Hasmonean Dynasty kings, Rochelle mused, maybe the purported authors, the Essenes,[2] worried these scrolls would be destroyed by the Romans whose strength was mounting at the time.[3] After all, it wasn't uncommon to annihilate another culture's writings and knowledge as a way to assert power. What often followed was a new doctrine of beliefs everyone had to abide by or face the consequences, usually imprisonment or death. Occupiers and tenants of our past have often held us back from empowering ourselves to find the truth.

Rochelle and Angelo were starting to see parallel messages between some of these texts and the Gnostic Gospels. They all seemed to paint a divergence from what humanity has been led to believe through the traditional Bible's canonical texts.

Historically, more was known about the Pharisees and Sadducees of the time than this mysterious group known as the Essenes.

The Pharisees strongly believed Oral Law was passed down to Moses from God and they should adhere to it in their daily lives. Oral law was later recorded in what is now the Talmud. The Pharisees were amongst those who believed a Messiah would shepherd in a time of peace. In contrast, the Sadducees, an elite, aristocratic group, were committed to following and maintaining the Written Law of the Torah. Believing these two sects had corrupted Jerusalem and the Temple, the Essenes apparently rejected both, lived a reclusive way of life in the desert, and created their own strict rules.[4]

These three groups differed in specifics, but an overarching principle was the need to abide by certain rules and laws, something Rochelle felt Miriam and Yeshua saw as a barrier to the teachings of love. In other words, laws and rules often got in the way of the purity of the teachings.

The Essenes were lesser known largely because their activities and teachings were more private. Although Rochelle and Angelo had a tattered version of the *Dead Sea Scrolls* on their bookshelf, they hadn't yet scoured the text as they had with so many other books. It was time to dive deeper.

One drizzly afternoon, Rochelle headed to the library for a change of scenery and to do some digging. While she realized she could find nearly anything digitally, she was curious what deeper probing might uncover. Unlike the solitude of their sitting room, their local library was housed in a turn-of-the-century building on a congested street. One couldn't escape from the traffic horns and splattering of puddles on the wide avenue through the slightly ajar windows. Inside, she could also hear the creaking sounds of the antiquated chairs when someone moved. It didn't look like the furniture had been updated in decades.

Opening her laptop, she began rifling through online pages of encyclopedias and articles, cross-referencing information from other sources. The information flew off the pages on the screen as fluidly as if an ancient sage were telling her the story himself around a crackling fire. She learned that the Essenes flourished in Judea from the 2nd century BCE to the 1st century CE, the time Yeshua and Miriam walked the planet.

Both Pliny the Elder and Polish scholar Jozef Milik wrote about the simple and modest lifestyles of the Essenes.[5] On the other hand, historian Flavius Josephus proposed that the Essenes also married and lived in cities and more urban areas.[6] Rochelle also noted that scholar James Tabor commented that the Essenes followed the solar calendar, a departure from the more traditional Jewish lunar calendar.[7]

Awe-struck by what she had read and seen, Rochelle wished she could have been a fly on the wall during those times. She couldn't help but feel that perhaps a former version of her actually was there, for some of it resonated and sounded oddly familiar. Were they part of an Essene community in a past life? What was their connection? Why was she mesmerized by their history, almost spellbound by each apparent fact she dug up? And yet, all those rules were disconcerting.

Upon further delving, Rochelle discovered more evidence pointing to their strict rules and constrained lifestyle. Living communally, possessions and wealth were shared with all members. Water baptisms and a clean diet engrossed them. Simplicity and purity were the order of the day, as evidenced in their white clothing[8] and the fact they didn't anoint themselves with oil, a practice common amongst the Jews of the time because the Essenes regarded oil as tainted.[9]

Rules, rules, rules, thought Rochelle. Laws, laws, laws.

It was a lot to absorb. She couldn't help but wonder how religion would have been shaped had women been part of leadership across all of these sects.

Rochelle could see the rain subside outside the library windows; however, the cloud cover remained opaque and ominous. It was a good time to head home since it looked as if a downpour was coming. On her way, she thought about the Essenes and wondered what Miriam and Yeshua thought of their teachings. Images of this group from long, long ago filled her head as she darted around puddles.

Although Yeshua didn't subscribe to or teach strict codes of behavior, some have suggested Yeshua may have been an Essene. Hadn't Rochelle read somewhere that Yeshua's mother Mary may have been an Essene as well? Were Miriam and Yeshua Essenes or did they simply know and walk amongst them?

The Essenes, Rochelle learned, did not concern themselves primarily with whether Oral or Written Law was supreme, but rather with strict purification rituals. They saw them as key to reaching God, so it was necessary to follow their rules around purification if you wanted to be part of their group. These rituals included bathing several times a day, wearing white, eating a regulated diet, and abstaining from sex.

Then again, notably, many spiritual masters in other parts of the world have taught about the importance of purification as well as pranayama, the art of breath control. She remembered reading about *niyama* (religious observances) in Yogananda's autobiography, as the second step in the Yoga system of Patanjali: "The *niyama* prescripts are purity of body and mind, contentment in all circumstances, self-discipline, self-study (contemplation), and devotion to God and guru."[10]

Rochelle knew the word purification created triggers for so many today, especially because of how it has been used to exclude women for epochs. For example, women were deemed impure when menstruating and often treated as outcasts. She was deeply moved by Anita Diamant's novel *The Red Tent* which shared how women were required to sit in a separate tent away from the rest of the community each month during their menstrual cycle.

She wondered what purification rituals Miriam and Yeshua might have practiced together. Rochelle was dead set on asking Miriam about purification relative to their teachings on her next visit. She also wanted to learn more about their connection to the Essenes. Several days later, when they merged dimensions once again, Rochelle had her list of questions ready.

"Did Yeshua learn about purification in India?" Rochelle began.

"Yes," Miriam responded quickly. "Yeshua traveled extensively. Where do you think he studied so much at such a young age? He learned certain rituals and meditations from ancient sages and masters. Not unlike today in many ways, traveling to broaden your knowledge wasn't uncommon if you were from a learned and well-to-do family."

"Of course," said Rochelle, recalling Miriam's stories during their early encounters about his younger years.

"It wasn't just in India but also in Persia and our homeland," Miriam added, picking up an earlier thread. "You see, purification has always been seen as an important aspect of spiritual practice across cultures and throughout time. This was the case with the Jews as well, especially amongst an ascetic group called the Essenes."

"We will speak of the Essenes," Rochelle posited, half as a question and half as a statement, excited they were moving to the Essenes so quickly.

"You have read about the Essenes, and we should talk about them since they were part of our lives," Miriam said.

Rochelle wondered if Miriam knew the Essenes had been on her mind and she had been doing some research at a nearby library. It seemed as if both Miriam and Yeshua were always in their heads.

"For roughly eighteen months, we worked and lived with the Essenes, who were seen as outliers of their time," Miriam professed. "Because we lived in their community, some people think our main teachings were from them. We did work with them to expand our knowledge and learning, but our teachings were not rooted in their beliefs. Strict in how they lived, they had a stronghold long before our time teaching on the earth. Today, they are connected to and many consider them to be authors of what your historians call the *Dead Sea Scrolls.*"

Rochelle settled into her chair and grabbed her cup of tea. She sensed Miriam was about to go into depth and share what they had learned from this enigmatic but powerful group.

"They had their own interpretations of God's laws, and their ways were not always ours," Miriam continued. "However, the Essenes were more inclusive of women than other communities at the time. You see, women could be teachers and healers within the Essene sect, so in this regard they were equal to men. That said, their strict rules about purity and devotion that governed behavior made the Essenes exclusive. You might say they created equality but only amongst themselves."

"Amongst themselves?" asked Rochelle.

"Let me explain," Miriam replied. "They were Orthodox and respected by many, but certain things set them apart from other Jewish sects at the time. They adhered to their laws and wouldn't allow anyone with an illness to be part of their group. If you couldn't heal yourself, you called upon those who practiced the sacred arts of healing and medicine to help you get better. They believed God brought on sickness to those who were impure, so you could no longer live amongst them if you didn't heal."

"For those who healed quickly and easily, did they take it as a sign from God they were the holiest amongst society?" asked Rochelle.

"In a way, yes," Miriam responded. "Utmost cleanliness was such an integral part of their daily routine and lifestyle—inside and out. In some ways, they were similar to Buddhists since they were vegetarian and adhered to strict diets. And like Pagans, they lived according to nature, becoming one with it. Even though they had great teachings, some of which we shared, they were zealots in many ways we could not adopt. For example, they had many constricting rules including abstinence from sex. While homosexuality was frowned upon by Jewish populations, the Essenes didn't pay much attention to it, largely because sex was excluded from their life altogether. You might say their lack of interest in or concern with homosexuals was a byproduct of their celibacy; however, this also meant they failed to see their value as a result."

They believed God brought on sickness to those who were impure.

Recalling her childhood, Rochelle thought about how hard it had been for some of her friends who feared "coming out" about their sexual orientation, especially in high school, where it was filled with judgment and pressure to conform. She and Angelo had marched alongside their friends during Gay Pride, and Rochelle celebrated with friends on the San Francisco City Hall steps the day same-sex marriage was solidified. Contemplating her own experiences with discrimination today and trying to imagine how hard it must have been over two thousand years ago, she simply nodded, keen for Miriam to unravel more of her story.

"I traveled with, taught, and healed with Yeshua for about two years before we became part of the Essene community," Miriam resumed. "They knew who Yeshua was, and there was mutual respect while we lived amongst them.

"White was considered the color of purification, and their white clothing was how you recognized them in society. There was a sense of duty and pride. If you were an Essene, you were acknowledged as one with high status because of their pure and holy ways.

"Many of them also studied in what is now Egypt and India; they were what we would say back then 'learned people,' whereas other Orthodox Jews knew and adhered to only one way—their way. The Essenes weren't religious as much as they were highly spiritual beings. Even so, their high status was not shared by everyone since they were seen as an ascetic and reclusive group. As I mentioned, their many severe rules around cleanliness, knowledge, holiness, and purity made them exclusive too, but they appeared so clean that other groups made fun of their ways.

"Yeshua and I were two of the few accepted by the Essenes although we left their community when we felt we had learned the necessary wisdom to integrate into our teachings and move on."

Rochelle welcomed the pause that followed. Imagining the Essenes living on the outskirts all dressed in white, always clean and pure, she tried to absorb it all.

"Remember Yeshua and I rebelled against any structured religious sect or group," Miriam finally said. "In many ways, we were the new agers of today or the hippies of your generation. We lived on the outskirts of society and felt as if we didn't belong to any specific group, a bit like you and Angelo have always felt during your lifetime."

Then, Angelo's head went back as his arms and hands started twitching. Miriam later explained this might happen when a shift in energy or frequencies occurs. During a long silence, the "match" seemed turbulent, suggesting a new energy was coming through to speak. Rochelle sat on the floor in awe as Angelo's body moved around with his eyes closed. A voice began to speak, and it wasn't Yeshua or Miriam, so the abrupt change in energies gave Rochelle a jolt.

The Essenes Speak

"Let us give you an understanding of who you are," the voice said. "We are who you know as the Essenes."

"The Essenes?" gasped Rochelle, half choking on her words. "You are speaking as a collective? How are you coming through to our dimension? How does this woo-ork?" she stammered and then composed herself. Still, she wondered: How could they speak as one?

"You have cleanliness and purity in you, through you," the collective voice said. "Purification is not solely for the physical body but also for mental and spiritual cleansing. Through purification, you will develop the ability to connect to other realms and dimensions. You call them hidden realms, but they are not hidden to all humans, just those who have not developed the ability to see, feel, and hear the frequencies in those realms. You have unique frequencies, just as energy beings in other realms do. Some, like you and Angelo, can connect their frequencies in this lower vibrational dimension to others in higher dimensions, or perhaps it's more accurate to say faster vibrational dimensions.

"These were hard concepts to understand for those within the Jewish groups back then. As Essenes, we didn't use the language you use today to describe transcendental experiences taught by the ancients. And of course, we didn't have the advanced technology you have today, but we experienced spiritual transcendence through our practices. An important part of our teachings focused on purification, seen to be severe by other groups. One form of purification we used was water and wine; cleanse the body with water and the interior with wine. We speak of wine because it was considered sacred and seen as the blood of humanity, which is why it was used in many of the sacrifices we did not subscribe to in ancient times.

"We were vegetarians and didn't accept the flesh or blood of animals; however, eating healthy or, as we used to say, clean, is only one part of purifying the physical body. As Buddha also taught, you must *think clean,* so the ego dissipates, steps back, and doesn't dominate your decisions and behavior. Sitting, meditating, and praying are a few ways to cleanse the auric field. When you calm your breath and focus on God, you become one with light. These physical purification rituals were included in the teachings Yeshua gave to his apostles and followers. But he also taught through stories and parables to allow people to understand a deeper meaning of the wisdom."

"Were Angelo and I part of the Essenes in a past life?" Rochelle asked them, curious to know. Why else would the Essenes cross into another dimensional timeline and speak to and through them?

"You could say your souls were part of the auric fields of people who lived as Essenes during a time, but do not try to understand this, for your linear analytical way of thinking in your human form will distract you from the message and true learning," they responded and then added, "We want you to stay focused on the message we are communicating to you now.

"We were always seen as straight and narrow. For this reason, many people didn't understand or like us," they went on. "We were similar to the traditional Orthodox Jews of the time in following restrictive rules; however, our ways were much more esoteric. We were, in fact, more liberal than Orthodox Jews because we accepted other belief systems than they did, but you had to be a *learned being*—as we said back then—and of purity to become part of our group. You have organizations similar to this kind of exclusivity today, such as the Illuminati or the Freemasons. Still, we accepted men and women were of equal status, for there were Priestesses who would teach as well as Priests, a rarity back then."

"The Essenes really treated women as equal to men?" asked Rochelle in disbelief.

"Yes and no," came the response. "They were treated more equally than in other Judaic sects, but it's all relative to that period in history. You wouldn't think so in your contemporary world, but we truly saw no distinction between male and female energies when it came to being a teacher of our ways. Through the balance of energies, the spirit and the physical body can become one.

"At the same time, we didn't allow those who were what you call in modern language homosexuals to join our group, for we didn't see their value. You see, we didn't understand the energies of a soul are both masculine and feminine, regardless of sex. In our limited perspective, we could only see the masculinity of the physical body and the femininity of the physical body, a mistake in our understanding and teaching. It is not about the physical body; rather it's quintessentially about souls exchanging their energies to be in balance and merge as one."

Fascinating, thought Rochelle, envisioning what it must have been like to be amongst them over two thousand years ago. The collective voice continued.

"Yeshua and Miriam accepted those with the same sexual orientation because they saw love in all things and people. We didn't understand this concept during our time in history, for we saw fault and deficits with those who didn't adhere to our teachings and rules. Understanding the purification process was one of the main teachings Yeshua and Miriam came to us for; however, their teachings went beyond ours—they were of pure love."

Without warning, Angelo's eyes repeatedly moved from left to right quickly as if absorbing the objects in the room for the first time. Then, no words came for several minutes as if they were digesting the colors and textures in all directions.

"It has been a while since we have been able to step forward and express ourselves through a human body because we have been in spirit form for eons," they continued. "We are in awe of the process and of seeing and feeling skin again. It is quite emotional for us in spirit form to have this human experience as we don't feel emotions as humans do. Understand this. We will bring back Miriam of Magdala now."

Their teachings went beyond ours—they were of pure love.

"Wait," said Rochelle. There was so much she wanted to ask them. But the Essenes stepped back and within five minutes or so, Miriam returned. Rochelle was astonished by what was unfolding before her eyes. Magical and mystical certainly but also unbelievable to most. Miriam began to speak once again.

"They were stern teachers, but we learned a great deal from them—meditation, sacred stones, sacred rituals, prayers, mantras, and purification," Miriam said. "The Essenes knew about the prophecy of Yeshua even though they didn't always agree with his ways. There was discord frequently since Yeshua didn't subscribe to how they treated others outside their society and teachings. Still, we trusted them, so many of our teachings were left with them for we felt they were safe there. More of our life's scribed writings and teachings will be found in time."

Wow, thought Rochelle, eager for Angelo to return to see if he had experienced any other visions to explain their connection a bit more. She didn't want just to know more about their time studying with the Essenes but also to hear about the arguments they might have had with Yeshua, for he was a force who wouldn't step back from his convictions. Rochelle also wanted to know more about the scribed writings that would be found in the future and when. Would these writings be discovered in their lifetime? If so, where and by whom?

Although she wanted to probe deeper, it became clear that Miriam and the Essenes were done sharing. After they retired for the evening, Rochelle's dreams were so vivid; it was as if she had been transported back to that timeline and walked in the shoes of an Essene woman.

Was it a dream, or was it a flashback to another life? Did her consciousness take her there, or did Miriam and Yeshua take her there? Maybe it was a combination of both.

• • • • • •

CHAPTER 6

ON FEMININE & MASCULINE BALANCE

Male and female represent the two sides
of the great radical dualism. But in
fact they are perpetually passing
into one another. Fluid hardens
to solid, solid rushes to fluid.
—Margaret Fuller

The more time Rochelle spent with Miriam, the more she felt empowered by her energy. It was as if Miriam was the female Martin Luther King of her time. Yet she also sensed she couldn't step into her fullness or completeness as King had because of the male-dominated society that maligned her and controlled everything.

Time and time again, it has been said, "Behind every great man, there is an even greater woman." She and Angelo knew that even under patriarchal rule for thousands of years, the importance of yin and yang working as one has shown up in one way or another. Despite the fact we haven't yet embraced true equality, ancient masters have forever taught that the balance of masculine and feminine energies is not only critical to the life force of our human existence, but also in nature as well as in the harmonious flow of all systems in the universe.

Rochelle and Angelo discovered Yeshua's soul would visit when he wanted to add a unique perspective or share an experience from his life as Yeshua of Nazareth. Above all, it seemed as if his shares were fundamental to illustrating his support for Miriam's wisdom and authority. His messages revolved around the notion you can be one with the Divine, one with your Higher Self, one with Source . . . or one with the purest essence of God. Only through patience and witnessing their teachings did Rochelle and Angelo understand the importance of feminine and masculine balance.

One full moon, as they dined outside under their old oak tree, Yeshua's arrival surprised both of them. Even more surprising, he only shared a few words before leaving.

"Only through the combined divine feminine and divine masculine energies can you truly reach God, for both energies form a sacred whole in the eyes of God," he began. "One cannot create without the other, for they are equal and complementary. This necessary balance was one of the most difficult messages for people to receive back then. They could not see that men and women could be equal in the eyes of God when women were not treated equally in society. They would say: 'Who are you amongst us to say these things?'"

Rochelle started to reflect. Albeit true that European and American women have more freedoms today than they do in other parts of the planet, they had both witnessed a male-privileged world playing itself out in politics and society through issues like birth control, abortion, wages, and career opportunities. Through this lens, it was easier to digest the response of those who weren't ready to embrace the equality of sexes, especially as a way of reaching God or as they often referred to Him, the Father.

Still somewhat dazed from Yeshua's brief appearance, Rochelle remained in deep reflection when suddenly she entered a different timeline and was able to experience the patriarchal society from over two millennia ago, including the emotions they once had. Within her mind's eye, she could sense Yeshua's energy off in the distance while Miriam's energy got brighter. Rochelle had to pinch her arm to bring herself back to their earthly reality. What just happened? she wondered.

After another ten minutes or so, Miriam showed up to expand upon the rituals and rules in the male-dominated world during her life.

"In your modern times, you are more familiar with what you now refer to as Orthodox Jewish culture for those who follow strict rules," she remarked. "The Pharisees' reliance on Oral Law to interpret the Torah during our time ultimately became the foundation of Rabbinic Judaism. Their obsession with rules about how to do things, rather than love, faith, and justice, put them in conflict with Yeshua's teachings. Just as troublesome were the Sadducees who corrupted Temple practices to make money, clung to their social and legal power, and didn't believe in life beyond the physical body. You can imagine from within their conditioned frameworks why both groups were not just unhappy with what Yeshua was teaching but also refused to accept it.

Suddenly she entered a different timeline and was able to experience the patriarchal society from over two millennia ago.

"Unpopular were his words, 'There is no difference between men and women in the eyes of God.' Such language was modified and redefined through a patriarchal lens, establishing an unequal hierarchy that became the law through the holy books of our times. But in truth, only through both the divine masculine and the divine feminine—together and equal—can you connect with God completely. Combined, they allow a deeper awareness and consciousness that truly connects you with Source. You see, Yeshua was aware at this time that women were unequal to men and not treated with respect, so he taught all were one and equally worthy of connecting to God. That no difference existed between men and women in *all ways*.

"Although not in the Bible, you may have heard Yeshua say to you both during one of his visits, 'What comes through me comes through the Goddess. What comes through the Goddess comes through me.' He uses modern language to demonstrate a point. While patriarchal orthodoxy posits a contrasting message, Yeshua's words illustrate both sexes are equal. The male apostles didn't understand equality between the sexes since they did not see it in the society around them.

"If he said something along the lines of, 'What you do to her, you do to me,' the apostles didn't understand, so Yeshua would use terms they could more easily comprehend. For example, he would speak of *God the Father* as working through all of us equally. Then countering a patriarchal conception of the Divine, Yeshua would often say to the apostles and his followers that God is love, gratitude, and joy; give thanks and thanks will be given to you.

"He also told them they could reach God through love. Even more radically, he said, 'To know me is to know God, but in me, see you, for there lies the treasure. There lies the true God.' He was trying to explain no separation exists between himself, God, and you, for you are the treasure, and you are God.

"It was awfully difficult for his apostles and followers to understand when Yeshua spoke to them in these ways because they didn't understand the unity of God and themselves. Similarly, the Holy Trinity is all in one, but back then, they didn't see themselves as part of the unity. You see, they could only see themselves as separate from God.

"For you, we can summarize our teachings as emphasizing these truths: the divine masculine and divine feminine working as one; no separation existing between God and us; the kingdom of God residing within; and the importance of practicing purification, which clears the way to God—the latter we mostly learned from studying with the Essenes. Much of the teachings about the divine masculine and divine feminine working together in harmony came from what I learned through the ancient Isis teachings and from what Yeshua learned in India about the energy centers running through our bodies. Today, you refer to these energy centers as your chakras."

Precipitously, as Angelo's head fell back, Miriam left and Yeshua stepped forward. His breathing became slower and slower as he moved into a deep theta brain wave state. Angelo's eyes completely closed when Yeshua came into their dimensional reality to speak.

"I would often use stories and examples to teach the apostles and other male followers about the power of both males and females," he said. "You call some of my teachings parables. I once shared this analogy with the apostles: 'The male seahorse carries the infants given to him from the female. Both take an equal part in creation.' That was one of my lessons. I would tell the fishermen who were eager to listen. You see, the male seahorse cannot create without the female. They are equal in creation, and so are human males and females. It truly takes both to create life."

Yeshua decided to use another illustration.

"The male birds are colorful, so the females are attracted to their feathers. The male attracts the female with his colors in order to bring about copulation. It is the female who chooses the male, so it is the female who is truly in charge of creation. Now you understand the real essence of female energy. The male dances with his beautiful feathers but make no mistake: the female is in charge. Does she choose to create with this male or with another one? Both must dance together for creation to occur. If she does not like his dance, she will move on to another male until she makes her choice."

Then Angelo's head tilted back again and Rochelle waited a long time before his body shifted. When it did, Miriam's energy came through as Yeshua's stepped back, and she began to add more texture to the teachings.

"Manifestation occurs through both the divine feminine and divine masculine—one cannot create without the other," Miriam said, continuing Yeshua's thread. "As above, so below. All creatures know and respect this order, but human beings tend to resist this balance time and time again.

"Unlike my personality, Yeshua was a bit like a turtle. Sometimes, he'd get upset or frustrated with people's lack of understanding. As he meditated more, the anger dissipated into the ether, and over time, he became gentler and more peaceful.

As above, so below.
All creatures know and
respect this order, but
human beings tend to
resist this balance
time and time again.

"Despite countless messages, the apostles and our followers still didn't always comprehend the message. It has taken many people over two thousand years to wake up to his teachings. It is now easier to understand because your physical bodies are, what you might say, more *enlivened* at this time. When you cast light on the unconscious shadows—what we used to call demons and what ultimately create your belief systems and thereby your realities—you can release them from your auric field. If you choose not to believe in those shadows, you don't give them energy and they cannot manifest without energy. It sounds so simple, yet it's hard to put into practice because of the ego.

"You don't pay attention to superstitions in the same way humanity did over two thousand years ago. Back then, people felt that if others didn't follow norms, demons possessed them. Today, you have evolved to a point where you no longer give credence to these archaic beliefs as you once did.

"You have read in your Bible that seven demons were cast out of me, but they were simply ego shadows perceived as demons because they were so potent. In your modern times, you know we all have shadows; by learning to accept them, we can transmute their power. They are merely part of any spiritual path, an idea that is much more accepted today.

If you choose not to believe in those shadows, you don't give them energy and they cannot manifest without energy.

"How we communicate through you is unique because Angelo hears us through waveforms and frequencies in real-time, a remarkably sacred event. Before I leave for this evening, I will bless the wine as a symbol to mark the sacredness of this exchange."

Miriam had obviously noticed the 2015 bottle of Bordeaux sitting on the table under the oak tree. Rochelle and Angelo had opened the special bottle earlier in the afternoon to give it time to breathe.

"With wine, you have heard it is the blood that has been shed for you to erase your sins," she said. "The wine is nothing more than a representation of all our blood, and our common humanity represents that too. While wine represented the blood, the body was the bread; we were both the bread and the wine. Remember, we were instruments to show no difference exists between you and us. We are the body and blood, but you too are the body and the blood. When you embrace and truly understand this unity, you also become one with God.

"Perhaps this explanation dwells in the old paradigm and terminology of our time. Modern language might translate this meaning to *do as we do.* In other words, you've done the work and faced the shadows that bring suffering. People have gone through many traumatic and stressful experiences and reached what you call a low point.

"Humanity sometimes uses the language *dark night of the soul.* Today, the idea of shadows is symbolic of internal conflict rather than the literal possession of demons, as many believed during our days. But it's a similar dynamic. Some might still refer to it as karma, whereas others might call it shadows or shadow work, notably your trauma practitioners.

"We can't conquer our shadows, so we must rise above them and flow with them. We must shine light upon our shadows because the more we resist them, or leave them in the dark, the bigger they become. As many great Buddhist masters have said, 'What you focus on, you reap more of, energetically and materially.'

"We wanted the apostles and others to see themselves in us through the sacred bread and the sacred wine, but they couldn't see it. They stayed captive to their shadow side, always feeling separate from each other and themselves. You see, the sacredness of bread and wine stems from their representation of humanity's oneness, including oneness with Source, and it always will."

Rochelle had to ask, "Did any of the apostles understand this message? What about Judas?"

There was a pause, and then . . .

"I loved Judas, as he was one of the more caring souls amongst them," she replied. "He did understand, so much so that he gave us his own life in remembrance of Yeshua. He knew Yeshua was the true essence of what God and humans are together, but he was looking for a miracle, which is where he failed. The true miracle is not in the miracle itself but in the faith, trust, and love of whom you are as divine beings."

"What about Thomas?" Rochelle interrupted. She was intrigued by his gospel, discovered with other texts in Nag Hammadi. "Were the words from *The Gospel of Thomas* really his?"

"Yes and no," she responded. "Transcribers and translators changed the words over the years. That said, they didn't change so much that they became corrupted as the canonical Gospels did, where there were so many translations and agendas that the subsequent copies deviated from the true message.

"And with this, I'm going to take leave. I am in awe of your ability to record my journey, but more so to be able to comprehend it. No scribe could understand the message back then."

Rochelle laughed, thinking of how often she and Angelo discussed an evening with Miriam and Yeshua after they left, wondering if they ever fully understood their messages.

"I will leave now so you and Angelo can rest. This is Mariam, and these are my words."

"Mariam or Miriam?" Rochelle quickly asked, noting the difference.

"The pronunciation of my name was more Mariam than Miriam, but in your modern language, it seems easier for you to use Miriam. It is not exact, but the emphasis of how people would say it differed slightly back then. For example, also Mariamne or Miryam. It is the same with names that changed into more English-sounding ones, such as Joseph, which was much closer to Yosef.

"Although people would often use your name in the context of where you were from as I mentioned earlier, they would also use your name related to another, such as Miriam of Yosef, meaning the daughter of Yosef, or Miriam of Yeshua, so people would know you meant the partner of Yeshua. Someone might ask: Which Miriam are you speaking of? The response might be: 'I am speaking of Miriam of Yeshua.' It was common to use this language back then."

And then Angelo's head went back, and her energy was gone.

The next afternoon, Rochelle and Angelo were sitting under their oak tree reading Eastern philosophies, mostly about the importance of masculine and feminine balance. It was a topic of great curiosity to Rochelle; she ached to better understand it because it was an integrative part of all living things.

A soft breeze and birdsong from the above branches echoed across their yard. They had a large birdbath and several water fountains, all of which the birds flocked to as if the space was truly their home. Rochelle loved to think they felt that way and nurtured the garden to make them feel welcome. A few dozen birdhouses hung from their tree, some of which were used by their feathered friends for a short respite. She smiled as she watched a pair of finch crossbills fly past her.

"I wonder if birds think about the future and plan for it, or if they merely stay in the present moment and let that present moment guide them to the next action, whether it's to find food or fly to a warmer climate as the seasons change," Rochelle said to Angelo. Before he could answer, his body started to shake and his head tilted back. As he was on his way to another dimension, Rochelle looked up at a few wrens above her. Then a cardinal unexpectedly flew past when she sensed Miriam's energy returning.

"I see what you're reading, Rochelle," Miriam said. "To find the true nature of God, one must find the true nature of herself. Both masculine and feminine divinities reside within each one of us. With millennia upon millennia of experiences, the soul has a better understanding of the true nature of both the divine feminine and divine masculine energies than your mind does. An awakening is occurring now on your planet of that imbalance between these energies and the need to restore it. That balance cannot happen until people can reconcile the feminine aspect of who they are in human form. To do this, he must release fears, surrender, and let go of the ego. If she does not, then a full awakening will not ensue."

Rochelle began to see patterns of communication emerge the longer they spent time with Miriam and Yeshua. Changes in Angelo's energy or a period of silence, sometimes with no message at all and other times with a request to wait "a few moments please," often meant new energies or souls were coming forth to speak. When this was about to occur, a long pause allowed frequencies to adjust, shift, and become accustomed to Angelo's humanness. In this instance, Yeshua came for a brief visit.

To find the true nature
of God, one must find the
true nature of herself.

"As I said before, only through the balancing of divine feminine and divine masculine can you reach God, wisdom I am trying to convey in myriad ways. The divinity of a grape is like Mother Earth, which springs forth the blood of humans intertwined in a dance that is forever connected. Divine Mother, Divine Father as one blood. These are my words. I am Yeshua."

Yeshua only spoke for a minute before Miriam returned, a precipitous change that frequently made Rochelle dizzy. She was starting to get accustomed to sudden adjustments and fluctuations, but sometimes it was a wild rollercoaster ride. As Angelo became more attuned to these shifts, the frequency-match became smoother and tighter, like one who is learning a new language becomes more fluid in their ability to stitch sounds and meanings together and express them more seamlessly.

About Yeshua's most recent share, Miriam said, "These are the types of parables he used with the apostles. He gave them visual aids to understand his words more easily; however, because they were often so stubborn, even the visual aids didn't help at times. It is hard to get blood from a stone, so to speak.

"The balance of divine feminine and divine masculine was central to our teachings. It was a key precept one must follow to reach enlightenment and a profound connection with Source or God."

And then she too was gone and Rochelle returned to her book, jotting some notes in the margins. It seemed as if the sudden changes in their energies to convey a message and then step back was to show the beautiful and fluid dance between the feminine and masculine. Energy becoming solid form and then energy once again, demonstrating the circle of life . . . the oneness of life.

The divinity of a grape is
like Mother Earth, which
springs forth the blood of
humans intertwined in a
dance that is forever connected.

Angelo got up after centering himself, walked over to the hose on the fence, and began to water the garden before filling up the birdbath. She was glad he connected with birds as much as she did, for they genuinely had become part of their family, just as Miriam and Yeshua had. What a beautiful cosmic dance with All That Is in every moment. We just need to be aware, awake, and alive enough to see the miracle in each exchange.

. . . . . .

CHAPTER 7

SACRED SEX & RELATIONSHIP

Whatever our souls
are made of, his and
mine are the same.
—Emily Jane Brontë

On Miriam's next visit, she announced, "Tonight, we will speak about sex—sacred sex." The topic took both Rochelle and Angelo by surprise. Why, they didn't know, since sex is part of everyone's life, and shouldn't be excluded if a life story were to be truthful and complete. With sex comes the birth of beauty and new life. With it comes love, affection, and a bond. And with it comes excitement and play.

Growing up in New England, many considered discussions about sex faux pas, whether you were conditioned by religious doctrine, or your parents simply brushed it under the carpet. Generations passed down that suppression until the attitudes and patterns became calcified. Not until they had both lived in Europe did they realize how conventional and limited their upbringing was around sex. In Catholic and Jewish circles, they had been conditioned by dogmas that suggested sex was immoral and shameful, the "original sin" if you like, especially before marriage. Rochelle read about patriarchal origins and the ancient goddess religions to better understand how these beliefs had been formed and why they stuck around for as long as they have.

Consider history and our societal conditioning as a result of what we were fed in schools, churches, synagogues, and other institutions. Turn back the clock not that far and sex was only permissible for a woman when she was a man's property. Anything that deviated from this hard rule turned her into a harlot, which was punishable by death. This of course led to centuries of brainwashing about what was acceptable and holy versus what was evil and ungodly.

Although sexual customs of the "older religion" embraced women's sexuality rather than shunned it, how could anyone even reconsider it as an alternative option with cultural norms that countered it everywhere you turned? "Older religion" was the one Merlin Stone referred to as the one that worshipped the female deity, which had been practiced for thousands of years before patriarchal religion took root and led to biblical references that justified male dominance in nearly every aspect of society. Sadly, these became the values that the three Abrahamic religions embraced, fearing the angry, jealous God they had become consumed by for well over millennia.

Squashing the ancient goddess religions had become vital to male domination in politics, religion, and social affairs, including property ownership which used to be passed down through the matriarchal lines. With such deep-seated rules and laws that defined morality, it's no wonder so many have a hard time talking about sex openly . . . even fear it. But it wasn't always that way. As Stone reminds us, "In the worship of the female deity, sex was Her gift to humanity. It was sacred and holy. She was the Goddess of Sexual Love and Procreation."[1]

Historians and archaeologists have known about sexual acts and customs in ancient temples for years, but bear in mind that most of them in early contemporary times were men who often minimized these traditions as primitive, symbolic, and even related to magic. They were programmed by the same literature and holy books as the rest of society and so the "male story" strengthened. The more accurate history of goddesses and the rituals surrounding them remained in the background and to some degree, still does today. Rochelle was thrilled to see it re-emerging in various pockets around the world.

Neither one of them had heard sacred and sex used together before Miriam visited them in their sitting room on that enchanting evening to speak of it. Sacred sex was a highlight of Magdalene's life, and as such, it was part of her journey and truth to be told.

Miriam's and Yeshua's narrative led Rochelle and Angelo to think about sex differently and reframe it—as a combining of masculine and feminine energies to create balance within and without. When you think of sex as a sacred energy exchange, you begin to venerate sex as you would all special energetic exchanges, such as purification rituals as a path to connecting with Source or your Higher

Self. Rochelle learned through Miriam that when you treat sex as sacred, you manifest a sacred experience. Our perception creates our reality of every experience we have, including sex. When you unite that sacredness with relationship and love, a special kind of alchemy occurs.

Rochelle and Angelo knew the world might not be ready to hear Miriam's message about sex. Much to the chagrin of most religious groups, particularly those who hold Magdalene on a pedestal or worship her as a saint, she loved to speak of sex, especially in the context of her relationship with Yeshua. Contrary to Miriam's views and practice, her world at the time prescribed sex solely for procreation. Rather than being raised believing intimacy, sex, and love could co-exist harmoniously, masculine rules and repressive doctrines—often based on fear and control—were the order of the day. The patriarchal church and social and economic institutions in power didn't want people to know you could become one with God through the sexual act and intimate unity of both partners. This structural ignorance led people not to trust themselves, nor to allow themselves to be open with their partner. Conditioning was far too strong of a force for people to practice sacred sex as a pathway to transcendence.

When you unite that
sacredness with
relationship and love,
a special kind
of alchemy occurs.

Over time, Miriam learned to shine a light on such restrictions and disparagements to rise above, flow with, and ultimately move beyond them. She was essentially trying to say: Regardless of whether you experienced the deleterious effects of this imbalance as a man or a woman, uniting masculine and feminine energies and destigmatizing sex can dissipate pain and transform it, healing the wounds and scars resulting from such rigorously negative conditioning generation after generation. This unity is one powerful illuminating path to freedom.

It wasn't an easy journey, as Rochelle would soon learn from Miriam. She began to notice Miriam's energy would sometimes come through like a cyclone and, at other times, more slowly, with purpose and an agenda. She wondered whether the explosive energy connected to Miriam's favorite topics and passions, while the more concerted and slower energy centered on important things she had to teach but was perhaps less interesting for her. One thing she knew for sure: It was hard to predict what the feisty Magdalene would do or say next.

When Miriam turned to sex, it happened to be a warm evening. Rochelle poured herself a glass of Pinot Grigio because it seemed more fitting for the topic than a cup of tea. Looking out through the glass doors, her reflection was more prominent than the natural wonderland of the yard although the branches of Maggie, the oak tree, were within her sight. Smiling, she recalled how often she spent time sitting on the grass under her, lying in the hammock tied to her sturdy branches, or leaning up against her strong, thick trunk. Her, *not it*, mused Rochelle. The tree always felt like a *her*, for she stood tall, yet her branches swayed with the wind, ebbing and flowing with life's daily changes. Immovable yet also yielding. Exuding such a graceful stance yet stalwart and beautiful. There was barely any wind that evening, but she opened one of the glass doors to feel whatever breeze might come as the night wore on. Yes, the oak tree was definitely a *her*. The branches were like her children and the leaves like her grandchildren, all playing a role in the interconnected web of life. It made her think of Miriam's messages about the importance of connecting to Mother Earth to stay grounded. As if on cue, Miriam began to speak.

"Women and men came together to create children as part of Judaic Law, and that procreation was really about numbers," Miriam reminded Rochelle. "The message of sacred sex was not one our Jewish brothers and sisters could readily digest because of the social norms and hard-coded beliefs.

"As I said earlier—but worth repeating—having more children, especially within a powerful family, increased your clout. In a society where women were reduced to breeding and treated like cattle, it was hard for most women to feel a sense of worth without a connection to a man or his family. Sex served as a way to bring children forward to increase worth, wealth, and power, not as a path to a holy and sacred union. This cultural practice made it even more difficult to teach the importance of divine masculine and divine feminine balance and the equality of women and men in the eyes of God.

"Yeshua and I taught the act of sex was not only for procreation; rather, its highest nature was to connect with the Divine, a view not accepted amongst our Jewish brethren. By bringing each other to orgasm, we taught that copulation was sacred sex, a divine act of God. It was a demonstration of the most expansive love for our partner and love for God.

"Sacred sex, of course, is also part of what you could call a sacred relationship which begins when one is vulnerable to the other. This connection starts when both partners join with their partner at the soul level, igniting the connection and communication with Source.

"When you become vulnerable, your wounds surface. To heal them, you need to explore them and meet them head-on. People didn't have the necessary tools or support back then, so this healing process was difficult for people to see, understand, and even more importantly, do. Vulnerability is one of the most important parts of a sacred relationship because opening up to your partner involves opening up to Spirit and trusting in your Higher Self.

"There's a beautiful wholeness piece to a sacred relationship. You must understand the aspects and powers of yin and yang—both partners must be equally evolved *and* involved. Each partner must be willing to grow equally with the other partner and be similarly engaged with and committed to enlightenment and connection to Source as part of the relationship. It doesn't matter whether this intimacy involves a man with a woman, a woman with a woman, or a man with a man. We will speak more about the variety of coupling shortly. With any couple, if discord or a mismatch exists, an imbalance exists as well. With an imbalance of masculine or feminine energies, or if one is spiritual and the other is not, the couple will never reach their full potential in a sacred partnership. Yeshua and I were able to reach our full potential in this inspired lifetime and timeline we shared. Like what you and Angelo have together, we are what some people refer to as twin souls, so we were often able to incorporate the same energy bodies at the same time in other lifetimes."

Confused, Rochelle asked, "What do you mean?"

"One example is Martin Luther King," she replied. "We came together in a way where our energies were able to interact together in his body's auric field. In his lifetime, parts of our souls infused his auric field, but he also had other guides and souls assisting him. Usually, when a great master incarnates in a human form, numerous souls incorporate into the body's energy field to assist. I know such an integration of soul energies will be hard for your scientists and academics to believe. Indeed, I realize this may also be hard for you and Angelo to comprehend; however, it is paramount to understand that we combine our frequencies so that the blend of both masculine and feminine energies can balance each other and allow divine love to lead in the teachings."

Aha, Rochelle thought. Miriam's energy often reminded her of a female Martin Luther King. Joan of Arc also came to mind, but her words were flowing rapidly so Rochelle chose not to interrupt her.

"You will find parts of our souls in many human masters who speak of love and peace, from sages and saints to healers and individuals such as you and Angelo. We work with those who are open to us and not afraid to be wounded in some way. You see, you have both become accustomed to our energies, so our frequencies don't create confusion for either one of you anymore."

Rochelle thought to herself, You're kidding, right? True, they had learned to discern variances in energies, but she felt the complexity of energies required much more than telling one energy from another. They were forever peeling back onions, teasing out riddles, and piecing together puzzles. Miriam carried on.

You will find parts of our souls in many human masters who speak of love and peace.

"When you explored meditation and yoga, you both had experiences you couldn't explain, right?" Miriam asked, and Rochelle nodded recalling the memories. "Angelo felt a jolt of electricity run through his body which caused shaking. Some people on your planet call this Kundalini awakening. Rochelle, you had other vibrational sensations, but not as intense. Both of you felt our energy through the ringing in your ears when we first came through to connect. But in the balance of your energies, you both allow us to filter the energy which makes it easier for you to manage our frequencies. This balancing and filtering are why both of you are essential to our transmissions."

Rochelle and Angelo had indeed undergone mind-bending experiences as they dabbled in things over the years, from meditation and yoga to life on a kibbutz and in an ashram. Even so, it wasn't as if they had traveled around the world studying with gurus. However, it seemed as if Miriam was telling Rochelle that she and Angelo had created a sacred relationship, a balancing of masculine and feminine energies critical to the four of them working together. Rochelle looked at Angelo, wondering how he was feeling at that moment and squeezed his hand. After a few minutes, Angelo's facial expression changed, and she could sense Miriam wanted to move in a new direction. Any more reflections on their specific lives in partnership would have to wait.

"Let's now speak of homosexuality," said Miriam. "Of course, they didn't use your modern terminology; however, they had their own version of it in

Sumerian, Aramaic, and ancient Hebrew. And it was frowned upon amongst the Jewish population."

Then, Miriam threw questions Rochelle's way.

"Was homosexuality considered a sin? Was it against God? The Jews didn't approve of it, not because it was a sin although they would make it appear to be, and you would be persecuted if you practiced openly or were discovered. In our homeland, they saw homosexuality as unacceptable first and foremost because a man with a man and a woman with a woman couldn't produce offspring to maintain or expand the tribe. Without making this purpose explicit, if you were homosexual or lesbian back then, they would say this: 'It is against God's law; therefore, it is considered heresy, and you should be punished for it.' So, if you were homosexual or wanted to express yourself this way, you had to go underground and out of the public eye.

"This repressive view took root in Islamic and Christian beliefs as well. Now you understand why homosexuality was considered taboo in Jewish society during our lifetime as Miriam of Magdala and Yeshua of Nazareth. If something can be corrupted, human beings seem to find a way to do it. Some debate whether the Bible forbids homosexuality as a sin, but in truth, they implied a ban simply by saying it doesn't benefit human procreation, a cultural precept. The question is truly this: Is it against God's law? How can it be against God's law when we are all God, and God is within us, part of us, one with us? Many species on this planet are considered same-sex creatures, such as some of your monkey families who have sex with each other to quell arguments and socialize. It's actually not uncommon for species to have a bi-sexual nature.

"The more you evolve, the more you will become bi-sexual as a species. Feminine and masculine energy in balance is how you can truly come to know God or Source or Oneness with the All—whatever your belief system happens to be. This balance can occur within each human being and between human beings. We are not suggesting there is one path or an either/or choice. Think of feminine energy in the left hand and masculine energy in the right hand; see them come together in unison with Universal Consciousness. Even your Eastern traditions speak of this connection but merely use other phrases.

"As forms of femininity and masculinity evolve, they will slowly come together and create a species of light energy in origin," she continued, focusing on balance. "You are on the precipice of uniting your energies together female and male merging to become one. Your bodies will become lighter, but this process will take thousands of years. Several millennia may sound like a long time, but it really isn't in the context of hundreds of thousands of years.

"Although a man with a man and a woman with a woman cannot pro-create in the traditional manner, they can still give their physical bodies to each other in a way that leads to divine balance. The true nature of sacred sex is the communion of both male and female energies, regardless of gender, and the ability to give to each other from a place of love. As your species evolves, not only will bisexuality emerge as a species norm, but skin colors will slowly fade as your body becomes less dense. When this happens, you will become more and more conscious."

Mind-altering, thought Rochelle. She tried to imagine humanity's skin colors fading away. Fading away into what? As she listened to the message, she loved how direct and bold Magdalene could be. If it needed to be said, regardless of how awkward or in-your-face she sounded at times, Rochelle knew Miriam would speak her truth without holding back. And without apology.

As your species evolves, not only will bisexuality emerge as a species norm, but skin colors will slowly fade as your body becomes less dense.

Rochelle wasn't surprised by Miriam's and Yeshua's support for homosexual relationships and sacred sex because they were the rebels of their time, and their teachings were inclusive, not divisive. Adopting a corrupt dogma to create power over others was not who they were. Since their wisdom was ultimately about the oneness of divine love, it was natural they would support all people regardless of their skin color, religious affiliation, belief system, or sexual orientation. The surprising part was moving from basing inclusion on the principle of oneness to a conversation about the evolution of their species.

"Do you know why your auric field looks like a rainbow?" Miriam asked her. "Your chakras and auric field are colorful because of the astounding diversity of your DNA from so many unique species. All colors blending is yet another aspect of true resonance with masculine and feminine energies, which in turn is the true resonance of God—all frequencies coming together and vibrating in one beautiful pattern."

Our DNA as an evolutionary rainbow, Rochelle mused in wonderment as Miriam went on.

"In that lifetime, Yeshua and I were teachers, healers, and lovers, and I cherished every moment. We don't always get to be together in a lifetime, especially on the earth plane. Right now, there's important work to be done here, and we are coming through to share the knowledge of love, light, balance, and healing to help the human species evolve.

"To this end, it's important to remember the Isis teachings were designed for women. Part of the teachings included understanding the art of sacred relationships and sacred sex for men with women but also for women with women. You see, sacred sex occurred within the Isis teachings between women because men didn't understand or embrace the intimacy and vulnerability required of them. Unfortunately, it was always about men and procreation, never about mutual pleasure.

"Even though Yeshua and I had sacred sex, most couples never imagined or experienced it. The Isis teachings started thousands of years ago, so others knew of it beyond our followers. Today, you can think of the Isis energy as expressions of your truth, sexuality, sensuality, femininity, and everything this encompasses. But when I walked on this planet as Miriam of Magdala, women couldn't express themselves, so we hid it. When we gathered as women in the Isis group, we learned how to pleasure ourselves and then pleasure each other. It was much safer for women to have this tender sexual pleasure amongst themselves than to find a man in a strange place they couldn't trust. This sensual physical contact wasn't necessary for me, but many of the younger women needed to be held and fondled.

"I'm not telling you this because it was the most important part of our lives. However, it helped us to feel connected to each other physically and honor the divine feminine energies within us. I share this part of my life because it shaped me as a woman. It is something I also shared later on with the female apostles, and it became part of all of our lives long after we left our homeland. I will stop here, and we will continue soon."

Then, with little effort, less than it normally took her to leave, Miriam's energy stepped back abruptly, and she was done for the night. Angelo shook his head back and forth as he came out of his trance and then scratched the back of his neck as he often did when one or both of them hung out for a long evening.

A bit bewildered by the rapid departure, Angelo said, "It felt as if she was going to speak of something with much more gravity but appeared to change her mind." The next day, they both learned why. A more serious topic requires time and more sleep than they had the previous night.

• • • • • •

CHAPTER 8

YESHUA'S RESURRECTION & ILLUMINATION

When he shall die, take him and
cut him out in little stars, and he
will make the face of heaven so
fine that all the world will be
in love with night and pay
no worship to the garish sun.
—William Shakespeare

Rochelle and Angelo knew at some point the topic of Yeshua's Crucifixion had to come up since it was such a significant and life-changing event in Miriam's life. Beyond her life, it has deeply shaped history. On the one hand, they were eager to hear her perspective and experience, yet they weren't looking forward to the visuals accompanying them.

The day came when Miriam announced she was about to speak of Yeshua's death and Resurrection. After settling on her mother's antique silver pot, Rochelle filled it with lapsang souchong tea leaves and boiling water and settled into a yoga back chair in their sitting room with her laptop. It turned out to be a drizzly day, and although there wasn't much wind, Rochelle closed the glass doors and watched the raindrops spatter onto their back deck. Rosemary was growing wildly on her left and basil and cilantro on her right. She thought about the hot sunny day they planted them and how much her favorite herbs had grown since then. Rochelle's gaze was brought back to Angelo on the floor the moment she heard his breathing change. Soon, Miriam was once again with them in their dimension.

"People think of Yeshua on the cross . . . " she commenced. She didn't finish her sentence; instead, she moved on to describe her account of that horrendous day.

"So many are fixated on the Crucifixion and, of course, the Resurrection because they are what your religious scholars, academics, researchers, and theologians have written about most. It was a terrible death for me to see in my human form as his beloved, but it was not the end. In essence, you could say his Merkabah body or simply his Merkabah became *actualized* or *illuminated.* Let me explain. His Divine Self became present again but without the physical body. The term actualization means actual or present, so you could say that he became present again in a new way, an illumination for all of us.

"Everything is a perception, but I will try to make this account as accurate as possible for both of you. Angelo has no idea what I am going to say right now. He needs to get out of the way while also becoming part of me, so the message can be as clear and pure as I can make it."

Angelo twitched, and his breathing became even slower before she moved forward. Rochelle was always wondering: Was he in both dimensions simultaneously? Even though Miriam tried to explain it to her, she couldn't wrap her head around the multidimensional nature of our being, and it was hard for Angelo to translate his experience.

"Remember I must access all the emotions I encountered when I was human over two thousand years ago," Miriam noted. "I do it by *willing it* to happen. Put another way, I manifest it and create it. I can also access the data of my life from that timeline."

Rochelle asked, "Do you create it in a new reality—meaning our reality—or the old reality, meaning your lifetime and timeline?"

"The reality in which it once existed," she responded. "Before I continue, I am sensing some discomfort from Angelo. He doesn't know where they put the metal rods—through his wrists or his hands. I listened as they were debating where they wanted to place them. What would make him suffer more? I remember them discussing it, and it was truly wrenching. Should they tie him to the cross as they did with the other two, making the suffering last for longer, or should they let this one die faster? They knew who Yeshua was. They also knew he had been wrongly accused and traded for a common thief convicted of murder and thievery. The other two who hung next to him on each side were convicted of crimes against humanity; however, that was not the case with Yeshua. You see, it was not the Jews who put him to death but the Romans because he was seen as a political threat."

Of course, Rochelle reflected. But surely the Pharisees and Sadducees saw Yeshua's teachings as heresy, and therefore a threat as well, especially given the crowds Yeshua drew. For those who subscribed to strict rules and laws, Yeshua's actions and words were perilous since he not only broke the social and religious norms of the time but the Sabbath as well. As the masses grew, all wanting to be healed by his touch and hear his teachings, certainly both sects would also want to put a stop to his mounting popularity. Yeshua's ability to gather a flock so easily must have been deemed dangerous to the powerful Jewish sects as well as to the Romans. After all, some saw him as the king of the Jews whereas others believed him to be the Messiah.

Rochelle's heart grew heavy as she contemplated the crushing rigidity of the dictating patriarchal thrones that did everything in their power to dwarf independent thought and personal empowerment. Despite the fact Yeshua wasn't decorated with gold trimmings of a king, his words held great power. His humility and unique ability to touch so many with his teachings and healings stirred up crowds, threatening peace, at least in the eyes of strict Jewish sects and Roman leaders. Once seen as a non-threatening, hippie-like prophet, they suddenly deemed him to be a rebel and revolutionary, no doubt a concern for the Sanhedrin as well as the Jewish ruling body at the time. It didn't help that he arose during a period of tenuous relations between the Jews and Romans. At a time when threats to their safety riddled Jews with fear on one side and the Romans quelled anything and anyone threatening their dominance on the other, the proverbial cross inevitably became Yeshua's to bear. Little did either side know how much the upwelling support for Yeshua and the violent response would change history.

Despite the fact Yeshua wasn't decorated with gold trimmings of a king, his words held great power.

Rochelle was lost in thought when Miriam's directness about the progression of events brought her back to the present.

"The metal rods went through his hands, but they decided to tie him up anyway, to make sure he wouldn't fall off the cross," Miriam finally said. "They placed the rods through his hands, not so he could suffer more but so he could suffer less. You see, he would bleed to death, which would be faster than hanging by ropes alone. They could have just tied his feet up, and they did, but they also placed the rods through his feet. And then, after they added the rods, they lifted him into the position where he would stay.

"What usually takes about fifteen to twenty hours to die by ropes alone only took around seven or eight hours with the rods. The Romans went even easier on him. They punctured the right side of his ribs and his lung, causing him to die relatively quickly. The death occurred through a combination of his lungs collapsing and his bleeding to death. Afterward, they left the body to the mourners."

"Who was there? Were there many?" Rochelle asked, trying to imagine the harrowing scene.

"I was there, as was his mother Mary, Thomas, Andrew, Peter, and the female apostles," Miriam replied. "The rest kept their distance, and Judas had already hung himself. After Yeshua died, the Romans took the spikes out of his feet and his hands and cut the ropes. Your modern movies and stories show a thunderstorm or rain. They wanted a perfect ending to the horrendous scene, but there was no storm. Rather, the skies grew dark from the sunset, dissolving the day into an evening of sweltering heat and enveloping everyone in a wave of profound peace. As I remember, he died around 8:30 or so in the evening. Once we removed his body from the cross, we cleaned the blood off his body before wrapping him up."

"They allowed it?" Rochelle asked, feeling the agony pouring out of her raw account of such tremendous suffering.

"Yes, of course," Miriam responded with a stinging directness, more an expression of grief than a rebuke. "They allowed us to do our sacred ceremony because he was dead. They didn't care what we did with the body after it was dead since they had no respect for life. I know you see things in your timeframe as brutal, but this is because humanity has come a long way. You have more respect for life than they did back then, especially the Romans. He died on the top of Golgotha Hill, a common place to crucify people. Torturing and crucifying people high on a hill where all could see was a way of making examples of people, and of course, this is what they did with Yeshua as well.

"Mary, the female apostles, Andrew, Peter, Thomas, and I carried the body down the hill to the town below it. We took his body to a friend's house where we often held meetings and gathered as a group. It was a friend of an apostle; people may not know this, but we had many friends in various places to hold meetings. People would take us in when we traveled and give us a space to teach and stay. We knew where his body would go and already had the cave prepared."

Rochelle interjected, "How did you know? Why did you decide on a cave?"

"Caves back then were like your mausoleums," she responded. "Although we didn't have them as you know them today, we had little alcoves or caves where we would entomb the bodies, as the Egyptians did. Besides caves, people often placed bodies in burial rooms inside a building. Those who didn't have a room, alcove, or cave to place the body would burn or bury the bodies in the ground. In our case, this cave was the closest thing we had to an enclosed space. Before we could place him in the cave, our Jewish custom dictated that we prepare Yeshua's body."

Rochelle probed deeper, "Did he tell you how to prepare him?"

"Yes, of course," she replied curtly as if it was a ludicrous question. "We had to prepare Yeshua for the ascension process, which started with cleansing the body. All bodies must be completely cleansed when being prepared for burial. You do that now. If you opt to view a body, various steps are followed to preserve it. We knew that Yeshua's body didn't need to be preserved, but we were following his requests, and cleansing the body was part of the process. Yeshua had stated how he should be prepared to some degree."

"What do you mean?" Rochelle then asked gently, recollecting Miriam's brusque reply.

"Well," she explained, "Yeshua told us he would return after three days during his ascension process and to look for him. Do you know how hard this was to believe for people back then?"

Rochelle sat there thinking to herself: Do you know how hard this is to believe now? But she said nothing as Miriam moved on.

"We considered most of what he had said had come true, so why would this be a lie? Remember we had also seen him perform what you call miracles, so we respectfully followed his requests. At the same time, we observed our Jewish law which dictated we cleanse and prepare the body for burial . . . for the heavens, so to speak. So, it was simply part of the process. Yeshua's body was cleansed and perfumed and then wrapped in white linen. It almost appeared to be mummified, which was not uncommon at the time. His body lay flat with his arms down along his side, and white linen was wrapped around his entire body, even his head. As I said, his body was perfumed, and after the linens were wrapped around him, the outside was also scented. As the body decays, it rots and begins to smell, so the perfume helps with the odor. The cave where we planned to place his body the next day was not far outside the town. As you can imagine, many tears were shed during this period."

Miriam paused at this point, taking deep breaths through Angelo as if reliving the experience. Her soul was seemingly able to do that in their dimension through a human host, or perhaps she was actually in both her dimensional reality and theirs at the same time. Angelo closed his eyes while his breathing became severely labored, and then she resumed her account.

"The cave's opening was so small you had to bend down to get inside. In your depictions, you might see it as a giant opening where you could walk upright; however, this was not the case. You couldn't stand up completely erect in the cave."

"Why did you choose this particular space?" Rochelle asked, wondering if there was something particularly sacred about the cave. Miriam's voice sounded a little pained through Angelo's tightened voice box.

"It is what he requested," she replied. "Perhaps two people could fit into the cave at one time, but it was also quite narrow. These caves were considered sacred burial sites, to be used only for this purpose; however, some people broke the rules and went there to pray or meditate. Heavy stones were placed in front of the cave as a deterrent.

"I believe somewhere in your history, it is reported the Romans stood guard and placed a wheel in front, but it isn't true. The Romans didn't care what we did with Yeshua's body once he died. A prophecy said Yeshua would rise after three days passed, and the Romans knew this too; however, they didn't really believe it. They had their own problems to worry about and this wasn't one of them. You might say they simply left it up to the Jewish community to bury our own based on our belief systems.

"We worked together to place the stones in front of the tomb, and then we all took turns sitting in front of it. I know this may sound bizarre; however, we were all on guard to ensure no one would steal the body, pillage it, or take the sacred cloths off him. We followed a mourning period, which can last up to seven days or longer, depending on the family's tradition, but following Yeshua's instructions about his ascension process, we stayed for three. Some stayed as a team of two or three during the night, and then they were released. For three days, we changed every four or five hours over each twenty-four-hour period, including me. I didn't stay there the whole time for I was needed with the women apostles who were also in mourning. When women sat in front of the tomb, men always remained with us for protection. The Romans didn't show up as has been written in some of your books."

"So, what happened during those three days?" Rochelle wanted to know.

There was a long silence; it felt like an eternity as Angelo stared into space, clearly outside the dimensional reality Rochelle was in at the time. Yet, she felt energetic shifts in her body and the room even though she couldn't explain it. Finally, more words came from Miriam.

"I stayed in front of the cave from the second night until the early morning of the third day, and in addition to Andrew, Thomas, and Peter, some of the other apostles were there as well, knowing this would be the day of Yeshua's Resurrection. We all took care of each other during this painful time as it was draining and agonizing for all of us. Yeshua came to me on the second night, and although it was the first time this had happened, it was not the last."

Then, it seemed as if Miriam was leading Angelo's consciousness into an unseen field of data, where memories in all forms existed of her life from long ago. When his head moved rapidly from side to side, as if reading, Rochelle realized he was in the Akashic Records with Miriam. He seemed to be in this state for quite a while before Miriam's story moved on.

"The words that came to me were clear and the voice said, 'Your Isa is no longer here. He is amongst you. His body has risen. His physical body is gone.' I said, 'My master, Rabboni, my love, is that you?' And he said, 'Blessed are you who do not fear the sight of me.' I first experienced this vision as a dream."

As if contemplating, Miriam stopped briefly before continuing.

"You see, I called Yeshua by several names, and Rabboni was one of them, which translates to teacher. It wasn't uncommon to use this name at the time as it was a sign of respect, but my favorite was Isha or Isa, a name he picked up during his time in India.

"On the third morning, there were several of us at the tomb; however, the others were sleeping when he appeared to me at the break of dawn. At first, the image I saw was a man who resembled a shepherd, not a gardener as your books suggest; I don't know why a gardener would be there before dawn around a cave. He looked like a sheep herder, but when I looked at him, and he looked back at me, I knew. I said, 'Rabboni, Isa, my love, is that you?' Again, as in the dream, he said to me, 'Blessed are you who do not fear the vision of who I am.'

"This was the second time I received the vision, but then I was awake, so I went to him because I naturally wanted to embrace him. He said, 'Do not cling onto me as I am still in my ascension process . . . but in time.' Of course, I wanted to know how this could happen, so I asked him, 'How would this be possible?' He said, 'It will not be the physical body, but you will be able to feel me.' At that moment, I could feel his warmth and love; over time, I felt it often. I could feel his spiritual body as it washed over me; however, it's not the same as the flesh—it can never be the same.

"That morning was the first encounter, or you might say, the first visitation from Yeshua during my waking state. Because the others with me were asleep, they didn't hear or see what I experienced. Our encounter lasted only five minutes or so before he said, 'Go back to the others, and I will return.' I asked him, 'Isa, where are you going?' He said, 'To the Father' as this was the terminology we used back then. I walked back to the tomb, and his Merkabah, which had appeared to me, was gone. Somewhat shaken by my experience, I returned to the others and woke them."

I could feel his spiritual body as it washed over me.

Recollecting Miriam's momentous account with a sinking feeling, Rochelle sensed her face wash into a shade of murky gray. The cloudy skies outside seemed to mirror how she felt, but she braced herself for more details from that tragic, historic day.

"On the third morning, the female apostles were not present because we wanted them to be safe in case the Romans or thieves would come by," Miriam continued. "With the male apostles, I shared what I had seen in my dream and also physically what I experienced after I woke up, and this time, they believed me. I will explain. Often, they questioned my visions of Yeshua as they persisted, but this time they did not challenge me. I will clarify this for you in time."

"This seems significant. Why not now?" Rochelle asked. Bluntly, Miriam came back with a response that surprised her.

"Okay, I will elucidate now then."

Angelo seemed to be staring out into space randomly again; however, Rochelle was learning that nothing was purely random. She witnessed a great deal of belabored breathing and contemplation. When energies shifted and Miriam and Yeshua took Angelo deep into the Akashic Records, things slowed down even more. His Ujjayi breath was evident, the very breath yogis and Taoists use. Rochelle had read it was sometimes called the ocean breath, and Angelo could move into this breathing and state of awareness seamlessly. When he did, Rochelle felt energic shifts around her, but it was always calming.

Although they glimpsed how Miriam and Yeshua worked through their humanness, it didn't make it any easier to grasp or digest. Multidimensionality wasn't a concept either of them grew up with, so getting their heads wrapped around it was next to impossible. What they did know was that when Rochelle and Angelo would venture on a journey with Miriam and Yeshua, gratitude, serenity, and humility often followed.

The importance of divine masculine and divine feminine working together formed a core part of their teachings. The various shades and textures of the teachings intensified in Rochelle's consciousness as Miriam spoke about Yeshua's Resurrection. She was not only more sensitive to the energies coming through to speak but also felt attuned to them in a multidimensional state, even though she couldn't explain why or how. It was as if Rochelle's heightened awareness was popping up like bubbles ready to burst as Miriam picked up where she left off.

"Many visions of him came to me in my dreams, especially early in the morning; you often refer to them now as lucid dreams. This isn't unlike people having the energies of deceased friends and relatives coming through their auric fields with messages in either a waking or lucid dream state. The main distinction between how you, Angelo, advanced shamans, and Eastern sages connect to us and how I connected to Isa is that my intuitive abilities simply presented themselves differently—I could see Isa's Merkabah when he appeared to me in my waking state, but other times, visions and messages would come to me in my sleeping state.

"These types of visions happen to people all the time, but many people to this day avoid language that might unfavorably label them. There's still a stigma around the word channeling, but ultimately everyone channels in their own way, from musical composers and landscape artists to athletes and software engineers. And everything in between. You feel more comfortable calling them heightened or altered states of awareness, but everyone has these abilities. Because your society has come to reject or gloss over these experiences, those who have had these visions have learned to suppress their intuitive gifts, or at a minimum, remain quiet about them publicly."

Rochelle simply nodded because she knew of the stigma and avoided conversations about their otherworldly experiences with Miriam and Yeshua, except with a few friends who were curious enough to probe deeper without judgment.

"Back then, it was not uncommon for people to speak of messages from angels, but if you used language that stretched beyond the scope of what people could accept based on their religious laws and upbringing, they might see you as someone possessed by demons," Miriam observed. "You had to tread lightly, and this was the same for me. Amongst the apostles who had witnessed his miracles and were followers of his work, I had more support, but not from all of them.

"Following the days of his Resurrection, Yeshua came to me in visions and stayed with me everywhere I went. Because I received visions often in those early days, many of the male apostles questioned the validity of them, especially Peter and Andrew. Remember this was also a time of turmoil, chaos, and stress for all of us."

Rochelle contemplated that tragic time as Miriam spoke of the grief she felt in those first few days and weeks following his death.

"I would pass stray dogs and women heading to market, small children on their backs, but I'd stroll by them as if they were ghosts. If I had to interact with someone, I'd respond in an automatic way but stare past them as I did, not remembering a thing that parted my lips. Sometimes they'd try to engage in a dialogue, and I'd gaze back at them as if I were deaf or they were speaking a language foreign to my ears. What was once vibrant and alive was now empty. Darkened doorways. Shadows regardless of the time of day. I was devoid of prayer during that time."

Using Angelo as a vessel, Miriam stared out the windows into the dark wet night for some time. It was a period of reflective disquiet but also inner calm, Rochelle felt.

"I can re-see and re-feel all of it again through you and Angelo," she finally said. Rochelle wondered if Angelo could feel the knot in his throat Miriam had to be feeling by remembering all of it. Days where her heart and the apostles' hearts were pierced and their tears emptied with little solace.

I'd gaze back at them as if I were deaf or they were speaking a language foreign to my ears. What was once vibrant and alive was now empty.

"Not only were we grieving, but there were severe implications if we made ourselves too public following his death, and we all knew it," Miriam went on. "As such, we spent time in our grief as it was necessary for all of us, including his mother. My faith in my path even waned for a time. I think it did for many of us. Remember, I had lost my husband, my partner, my Rabboni, my teacher, my Isa. In those early days, I had even lost faith in God; we were all deeply challenged in our own ways during this transition."

Listening to Miriam's heart-wrenching words pour out, Rochelle imagined her despair . . . their despair.

"There were times I would writhe on the ground, clutching my heart asking, 'Where is God now?' It was something I felt often in the subsequent days. In my sorrow, it was hard to see the bigger picture although my faith was strong. It did return."

"Did you seek comfort in each other?" Rochelle asked her.

"Some would gather discretely; however, I needed time alone to absorb the shock of the chain of events from the previous days. We were all in a mourning process, but bear in mind, we also feared for our lives."

Rochelle interjected and asked, "Did the Romans come after you?"

"We had to lie low as you say in your modern tongue, so they wouldn't look for us," she replied. "Because of our love for him, we all wanted to go out and preach what Yeshua taught us, the *Good News*, a term we used to describe his teachings. We wanted to prophesize he would be resurrected in three days, but how could we go out and talk about the *Good News* after they had just crucified him? What would they do to us? Yeshua wanted us to testify that the body would ascend, but we were in no mood to preach his wisdom."

Trying to process that wretched day, Rochelle remembered how her heart ached when she lost her parents and grandparents and couldn't imagine losing Angelo or a child, especially under such gruesome circumstances. She recalled other unthinkable stories from their modern-day: Mexican women being raped by cartel leaders while trying to escape the violence in their once-safe villages and Ukrainian women enduring many hardships when the Russians invaded their towns, taking up weapons to protect their families. She thought of the Afghan women possessing no rights on the land where they were born and the Holocaust survivors living with haunting memories of gas ovens extinguishing family members as they looked on. The Rwandan genocide. The heinous violence in Iraq. The sex trafficking of children. The list of horrors went on.

Turning back to Miriam's memories, Rochelle piped in, "How close were you to Yeshua when he was on the cross?"

As soon as Rochelle asked the question, she wished she could retract it, for her mind was darting from one atrocity to another, internally weeping for the crimes of humanity, wondering why we couldn't come together as a species. An increasingly somber mood swept over her.

"Why can't we learn from history's carnage and horrors?" Rochelle asked quietly under her breath; however, Miriam answered her first question.

"Close enough to hear the sounds when they pierced his body, feel his torment and pain as he writhed, and see his eyes sink deeper and deeper as his death grew nearer," she responded.

Rochelle didn't want to hear anymore, but she regained her composure and shifted her mind to more neutral thoughts as she waited for Miriam to continue.

"Together, we became strong because we had to, despite the circumstances. When Yeshua did rise, and his Merkabah appeared to me on the third morning, I didn't recognize him at first. But why should I? Although I was hoping to see him as I did in my dreams, it was still difficult to believe his body would rise again when you saw it put to death in such a chilling way.

"After I had told the apostles I had physically seen him with my eyes, they wanted proof, so they removed the rocks blocking the cave's entrance. Yeshua told us he would rise on the third day and that we would see him again, but he never said his body would disintegrate. In truth, his body didn't rise from the dead. You see, it disintegrated or rather it actually disappeared. How does a body disappear into nothingness in three days? We didn't know; however, it happened that quickly."

Rochelle tried to fathom a body disappearing, but if the physical form was merely a perception or perhaps a projection, then wasn't anything possible? She was eager for Miriam to add more, and she did, underlining Yeshua's spiritual power, the same power available to all human beings.

"When we removed the rocks and entered the cave, his body was gone," Miriam repeated and then went on. "The linen materials we had wrapped the body in were still there, but the physical body was gone. How is this possible? How does a dead man levitate and disappear? How do human beings produce miracle cures? How? How did your less-known spiritual masters from the jungles of South America, in the mountains of China, Tibet, and other places across your planet bilocate, raise the dead, and perform what you deem miracles? Yeshua wasn't the only one in your history who did these things, but he is one of the most known and misunderstood.

"Those who were cured by your prophets and mystics had faith. Those whom Yeshua mysteriously cured believed he could cure them, and he did. In the case of your João of God, unfortunately, he couldn't heal himself because he lacked faith in his humanity and those who were assisting him. When you lack faith, you are not one with your Authentic Self, and your human ego self begins to drive and lead again. It has happened to many of your great spiritual teachers and healers. Rest assured, João of God wasn't the only one, but he garnered a lot of media attention because of what transpired on his property."

"Yet for many years, he performed miracles," Rochelle said, even though she was sickened by what she had read.

Miriam quickly countered, "He didn't perform those miracles, his Higher Self, his Authentic Self . . . did."

Rochelle took a deep breath and let her continue.

"Remember, you're not writing this story—we are. But you and Angelo must both have faith you're in a creative process with us and as such, it's a collaborative effort. Healing is like that too. You must have faith in the miracles you are going to perform. Miracles come in many ways—it's not just about raising the dead or curing cancer.

"Shifting energy to release emotional trauma and enable a person to experience joy, faith, and love again is just as powerful. Humans don't see this, however. The miracles, as you call them, Yeshua most enjoyed were when he saw people waking up to their Authentic Self, more so than when he cured the sick and those with leprosy. To him, the real miracle was when people understood they were Spirit and not separate from God. Is this not a miracle that the words of Miriam of Magdala and Yeshua of Nazareth are coming through your auric fields to tell a story of two thousand years ago, right here in your home? You sit on your chair or floor and listen to us nearly every night. Is this not a miracle? You have grown accustomed to our energy, so you do not see it this way. You're not going to raise the dead just yet but have faith."

Miracles come in many ways—it's not just about raising the dead or curing cancer.

Perhaps she sensed Rochelle's shock since her words softened and slowed down.

"You and Angelo doubt each other because you doubt yourselves," Miriam said gently. "This is how most humans are—they doubt their power, they question their intuition, and they mistrust their own truth. Yeshua and I are here to remind you and others you work with not to doubt yourselves. I'm here to bring both of you together again as I came together with Yeshua. You are divine feminine and divine masculine . . . here as a means to balance these energies again on this earth realm and to share our life.

"The story I am telling you isn't easy. My journey wasn't easy. While there's been an attempt to recount this historical time in a panoply of ways, it has been corrupted and converted into something it's not. But the simplest version is this: As you and Angelo get out of the way, you are allowing our words to come forth with our version of the story, our version of what once was, our version of how we felt during those times with the apostles and followers of Yeshua, our version of Yeshua's true teachings and his truth. And my truth of our time and experience long, long ago.

"We knew what Yeshua could do because we had seen him perform wonders before our eyes, and this news spread far and wide. While it was significant for our time and certainly mind-bending, there are human beings today who can do the same thing. Look to your India, your Brazil, your China, your Peru. Many people can perform miracles, and many can channel. You see it around you more and more now as people are waking up to who they truly are. And because your modern world is beginning to accept ideas they couldn't over two millennia ago, and many more are embracing the call to their inner truth.

"There's less fear today about speaking publicly about things considered heresy and witchcraft in our day, like energy healing, channeling, Kundalini awakening, and so much more. Despite this greater freedom to speak up, many are asleep, but back then, many more were asleep. Your global consciousness is shifting now. For those leading the way, it won't be easy, but it will be far easier than it was in our time as Yeshua and Miriam in human form. Perhaps this comparison between then and now will shed some light on how and why we could believe Yeshua when he said we would see him again. We had a great deal of faith, not just in God and Yeshua's teachings but in the Rabboni himself.

"Of course, we didn't understand things like energy body or auric fields at that time. We didn't understand the form he would present himself, but in your current times you have seen evidence of this form from many masters and sages."

As Rochelle pondered this information during an unusually long break in her story, she could feel the severity and intensity of this experience for Miriam. It was hard to imagine how torn her heart must have felt and how fragile she must have been. As a woman, she must have carried a great deal of sadness and loneliness during those days. That and the fact she didn't have the support of all the apostles as a strong feminine voice at a time when society treated women like cattle. Objects. Breeders.

Rochelle had to ask the question, "What were you feeling after you saw his Merkabah but knew you couldn't embrace him?"

"I think I was feeling every emotion a woman could after losing her partner, and I also had the torment, as some others have had, of having to watch the brutality of how they killed him," she replied. "I was pregnant at the time as well, but didn't know right after his death, or more accurately after he transcended from one dimension to another. So yes, it was wrenching despite my faith in God and my faith in Yeshua. You must have faith."

No more words came and Angelo remained peaceful on the floor. She peered out of the glass doors and watched the rain, now falling heavily. It looked as if it was going to teem down all night. The gravity of what Miriam shared that night began to settle.

Rochelle grabbed a blanket from the back of the couch. Angelo's breathing was becoming more normalized, so she lay down next to him and took his hand. Like clockwork, he turned toward her and snuggled close.

The candles on the table were still lit, but suddenly they extinguished on their own, as if Miriam willed it from afar. Or not so far. They both fell into a deep sleep until the morning sky and birds woke them at dawn.

• • • • • •

PART II:

BEYOND KNOWN WORLDS

CHAPTER 9

VISITATIONS FROM YESHUA

Oh, bird of my soul,
fly away now, for I
possess a hundred
fortified towers.
—Rumi

Faith is the word Miriam ended their last meeting with, that five-letter word that challenges most human beings whether they're spiritual or not. Faith is about apprehending and believing in something beyond proof, whether demonstrated through mathematical language, measured with instrumentation, or observed directly. Faith is trusting in the unknown and in the process without foreclosing possibilities. Faith is about going with the flow, and it is also about surrendering the ego's protective need to control what happens or doesn't. When faith doesn't align with divine wisdom, including divine timing, struggle will follow. Your journey unfolds seamlessly when you don't try to force a square peg into a round hole.

Rochelle innately knew this wisdom yet fear sometimes interfered with trust. Although she understood fear was the very thing holding so many people back from realizing and stepping into their true potential, she also knew it was a normal human emotion everyone feels from time to time. She had to know how Miriam and Yeshua both felt about fear. When Miriam next came through, it was the first question Rochelle asked.

"Of course," Miriam responded. "Yeshua had fear, for remember he was living a human life through Spirit. Many spiritual masters have experienced fear because they are living a human existence too, but Yeshua also had great faith and was able to overcome fear. With his faith, he could do what few in the earth realm could do. As a prime example, Yeshua could separate his Merkabah from his so-called physical body. This is a technique some of you call time travel. Not many on your planet can dematerialize and then rematerialize into what appears to be the physical body yet isn't."

Rochelle asked, "Do you mean bilocation?"

"In a way, yes," Miriam replied. "Bilocation is when you can separate from your physical body and shift to another place. The soul can split itself, so when this happens, part of your soul can bilocate to another physical location and manifest itself as YOU. With the Merkabah, people can see a physical image identical to you although it is not physical. Today, you have modern witnesses of monks living in remote locations who can bilocate, and other spiritual masters who can do the same. Time travel is similar to bilocating. Both are possible because, remember, there really is no time. Yeshua could move himself to other locations within the same dimension and time. Even though few can do it in a conscious awake state, when you sleep, your soul is always bilocating and trilocating."

Rochelle thought of how Angelo recalled his dreams more often than she did, but occasionally she'd remember one, and the details were always vivid the next day. Did 3D perceptions of time become irrelevant in other dimensions and frequencies, whether in dream states or otherwise?

"I had a dream a few nights ago," Rochelle piped in, interrupting Miriam's flow. "What made it so odd was that I looked similar to what I see in the mirror today, but with darker hair, deep green eyes, and higher, more angled cheekbones. Still, it felt like the me I have come to know in this lifetime. The next thing I remember was returning to a regal home I shared with others. It seemed as if we were preparing for a trip, and I ended up leaving the house wearing a dark purple leather coat with Matisse-like designs, something I'd never wear today.

"Was I bilocating? Was the dream merely reflecting my unconscious desires, as Freud suggested? Or was it an expression of the collective unconscious that Jung advocated was at play during dreamtime, a layer or *state* that allows all human beings to access universal symbols, ideas, myths, and cultural archetypes that may have special relevance for an individual psyche?"

"This is one idea that is universal to humans," Miriam responded. "We all have access to what we could call universal energy or the collective consciousness. You are part of it, and yet you are all of it at the same time."

Miriam then moved to Rochelle's questions about dream states.

"Trilocation and bilocation in dream states happen all the time. It's hard for humans to understand they're having many experiences simultaneously, which is the quantum aspect of your soul. Consciousness doesn't need your physical shell to exist. However, we were speaking of bilocation in the earth realm in conscious states as well as unconsciously, such as dreaming. Bilocation occurs when you're able to take your physical body along with your soul and relocate to another location concurrently. Yeshua learned how to bilocate from Indian masters, but that is not what he was doing post-Resurrection. You see, following his Resurrection, he was missing his physical body, which was the *conscious portion* of his body."

We all have access to what we could call universal energy, the collective consciousness. You are part of it, and yet you are all of it at the same time.

"What do you mean by the conscious portion of his body?" And how does the physical body relate to the Merkabah?" asked Rochelle.

"The conscious portion of the body is the perception of the physical body," Miriam explained. "The physical body includes the Merkabah or the soul itself. Yet the physical body is separate from the soul. When the conscious portion of the body and the soul come together, you perceive yourself to have a physical body. In other words, you perceive the physicality of humanness. At this moment, you're having a perception of consciousness, and it is a perception of your physical body along with your soul."

Miriam began to touch Rochelle's hand while she was typing the messages coming through. "You're feeling my consciousness now, my touching you now, which is quite a fine perception," she said. "And you, Rochelle and Angelo, allow us to feel humanness again. It is because we combine our souls with you *as consciousness.*"

Rochelle remembered reading about the Merkabah as a chariot when she dove into ancient books on Jewish mysticism like the Zohar and the Kabbalah. It was almost as if it could be transported to other dimensional realms. What occurred when Miriam and Yeshua visited them in their realm? Were they taking them to their dimension in a way? If so, how was this happening during their waking states? Or were their waking states more of an illusion than their dream states? What did it mean to share consciousness?

When the conscious portion
of the body and the soul come
together, you perceive yourself
to have a physical body.
In other words, you perceive
the physicality of humanness.

Miriam then expanded on the relationship between the soul and the body.

"The Egyptians referred to the soul and the physical body as being one. They used the term Ka Body, which they saw as a combination of the Merkabah and the physical body together as one. They simply didn't distinguish between them. Now you can see how assorted cultures understand and process spirituality in their own unique way."

Angelo's body shifted and his breathing slowed down even more.

Rochelle squinted, puzzled by her explanation. "So, the Merkabah is like an energy form with memories?" she asked. "I'm still confused."

"The Merkabah is actually the soul itself," Miriam responded. "The Merkabah or soul is nothing more than a stream, which goes back to Source or the All That Is. The physical experience or incarnation gets recorded in the Akashic Records, data in the quantum field that is always accessible. The Merkabah also has the recording of that physical experience. You see, the Merkabah or soul carries an imprint of each recorded experience as well."

Rochelle nodded, trying to follow along, but her linear conditioning was getting in the way.

"You must remember something Rochelle, and this is the difficult part," Miriam cautioned. "You are perceptions of your own making, of your own agency. This body is memory, without the soul," she added, touching Rochelle's arm. "I am not here to make your life difficult but to illuminate you again. I am also not here only to give you historical facts, but to teach you who you are here in this lifetime."

"So, this is not really about what happened in your lifetime or ours; it's about the nature of the soul," said Rochelle. "Is that what this story is really about?"

"It is my story and my truth, but it is also yours," she replied and then added, "History is not so much a set of facts as you have come to believe, but countless perspectives on a narrative. Now, you're starting to feel your Jewishness more and more. You see it showing up in our connection, your interests, and also what emerges in your dreams. The problem with understanding your Authentic Selves in this lifetime is that you begin to doubt the information coming through us. This doubting has been expected as part of the process, for nothing comes as a surprise."

You are perceptions of
your own making, of
your own agency.
This body is memory,
without the soul.

"This doubting has been expected," repeated Rochelle. "What does that mean?"

She closed her eyes and deeply reflected on Miriam's words as if each word was somehow deeply bound to her. To Yeshua. For a while, there was silence until Rochelle opened her eyes, and a small tear dropped from one of them. She felt an expansion in her heart and a profound love, not just for Miriam and Yeshua's presence in their lives, but for humanity itself. It was as if her Merkabah was one with Miriam's and she could even sense and feel her pain as Miriam was reliving her life long, long ago. At the most tender of times, Miriam skillfully managed to weave new textures and layers into her story, perhaps as a way to illustrate or amplify the teachings.

"Rochelle, you asked me earlier what my emotional state of mind was like at the time of Yeshua's Crucifixion," Miriam finally said, changing the subject. "My faith was constantly being tested. The grief made its way into my bones, and it felt like a weight I would always carry in my limbs as much as in my heart."

Reliving the memories with her, Rochelle could feel her energy and see the past as vividly and real as the books on their shelves. In her mind's eye, she could see Miriam walking alone in the hot desert as a way to escape the memories, including the sights, smells, and sounds of the day Yeshua was crucified. She saw her remove the shawl from her head, which normally acted as a shield from the sun's scorching rays. As Miriam sat unprotected and the heat beat down upon her, the middle of her scalp where her hair parted burned from the sun, minor pain compared to the physical agony Yeshua must have endured during his final hours.

"Following the Resurrection and for the subsequent two months, I received visitations from Yeshua to prepare me for leaving the land of Judea," Miriam went on. "What do you think it is like to leave your home country for a destination you know nothing about? Today, before you travel thousands of miles to a location, you know something about it through pictures, brochures, your Internet, and videos. We had no home to go to and scant knowledge about where we were going. Naturally, we were unsure of how we would survive when we arrived.

"The visitations from Yeshua helped us become comfortable with the journey yet to come. You see, Yeshua could manifest his Merkabah with his soul in something physical mediums refer to as ectoplasm. Usually, the soul needs a physical being to manifest ectoplasm, but Yeshua did not. This is also why when I first saw his Merkabah, he said, 'Do not hold onto me, don't cling to me.' Because he was still in transition from the physical earthly realm to the spiritual one, it was dangerous for me to touch his energy field at that time. Since the body was pure ectoplasm, it could have cut or burned me if I touched it when he was in that state. When he said, 'Do not cling, do not hold onto me,' I didn't understand the message then, but I had to trust it. There's a period when the soul is separating from the physical body. Put another way, his soul wasn't fully separated from his physical body yet. Despite not having transitioned thoroughly, Yeshua could appear in the earth realm before the transition was complete."

Rochelle asked her, "How long did it take for this transition to happen?"

"It took seven days," Miriam responded quickly.

The preciseness of her answer floored Rochelle, so she asked, "How did you know this?"

"He told me," Miriam said. "During those first several days, he only appeared to me."

"Because of safety?" Rochelle asked.

"Yes, that was a big part of it," she replied. "He appeared to me when I was alone, but I still couldn't touch him. He would remind me not to touch him as he was fully integrating and transitioning himself into his Merkabah, not because I was impure or a sinner, as your holy texts suggest. Such a disparaging explanation was a way to make women undeserving of Yeshua, and of course, it was also a way to create separation from your Authentic Self and the Authentic Self of Yeshua or between your Authentic Self and God. I had to remain silent for seven days, so I isolated myself. The others saw this as a grieving process therefore they perceived it as normal when I didn't appear publicly."

Rochelle then asked her, "When he appeared to you, how long was the visit?" She found herself wanting more details so she could better understand what Miriam experienced at the time.

"Each day, he would come to me for an hour or two," she responded. "We talked about what I was going to do and where I was going to go to be safe. We would also talk about where the apostles would go to teach and how they would prepare for their own journey. I am speaking to you in the twenty-first century, and some people may read this and think my account sounds implausible or even crazy. During my time, they would have thought we were demons or possessed by them. If I were to tell the Orthodox community I was communicating with Yeshua regularly, they would have stoned and burned my body. The spiritual path takes time, faith, and patience, and it wasn't easy. Remember, so far, I have only given you the first seven days after the Resurrection. Much more occurred.

"After Yeshua's Merkabah resurrected, he would often visit his masters in India; however, he would also search for places he thought would be safe for the female apostles and me to live. Those who accepted our teachings the most were the nature-loving Pagans, some of whom lived in what you know now as southern Europe. There, I could live in freedom and be safe without persecution because no one there knew of me, Yeshua, or what had happened in our homeland, even though some knew of his healings. The Romans had not yet spread everywhere, so Yeshua deemed Gaul, what you now know as France, a safe location for the sisters and me. During this period, I had visits with him almost daily.

"I felt secure knowing the man I deeply loved was caring for me even after he left his physical shell. It took time for us to establish a relationship of a more spiritual nature. I had to adapt to sensing and feeling where he was so I could get used to speaking to him, similar to what you and Angelo do when you connect to us now from this realm. When we speak to you and Angelo, we talk to you in different ways. We also work with and through you when you're typing at your keyboard, and you receive what you call downloads in your modern language. You feel us and know our presence, and of course, Angelo feels us more directly and physically."

Rochelle looked over at Angelo and saw he was in a deep meditative state with his eyes closed as her story was pouring through him, relaying a tale from over two thousand years ago that dumbfounded both of them. One might call it an otherworldly journey few would believe and even fewer would understand. Yet it seemed Miriam and Yeshua thought that now, many more might believe and understand.

"During this time, I had to get used to my body's feelings, sensations, and vibrations to discern when Yeshua was near me," Miriam went on. "In the evenings, when I was alone, he would manifest his Merkabah, and we would sit together. Over time, I could even touch his Merkabah. Although it wasn't the same as touching his physical body, it provided comfort.

"I am trying to liken it to what you might experience on your planet today. For example, when you go out on a hot day, you can feel the heat in the air. I could feel the intense heat from his Merkabah. At first, the warmth was uncomfortable, similar to when Angelo first felt our energies and you too, Rochelle, but in a different way. Contemporary people might call it "opening up to Spirit," but we could call it opening up to other dimensions and vibrations, and when you both first attempt this, you might feel a lot of heat. Angelo feels that heat often when he first connects to our fields, and you and Angelo have had to learn how to adjust to our frequencies. It is similar to what I felt when I was adjusting to Yeshua's frequencies."

When I was alone, he would manifest his Merkabah, and we would sit together.

Rochelle knew what she was talking about because Angelo often spoke of heat, so much so that after a session or visitation with Miriam and Yeshua, he would shower to cool off and sleep with his feet hanging out of the covers at night. When Miriam came through, Rochelle felt an alignment and connectedness as if she was one with her energy, but when Yeshua would visit, her body always felt a bit hot. She couldn't understand it, but she imagined it had something to do with shifting dimensional realities or realms. Perhaps a linear example might be when a person would physically travel from Alaska to somewhere hot like Fiji although she realized the quantum explanation would likely differ from their densely physical reality. She was no physicist, but she knew enough that what they were experiencing was far beyond the scope of linear thinking.

Miriam expounded on those early days.

"Touching his Merkabah was like touching an invisible force field," she said. "I will tell you this: Oftentimes when you focus on your chi running through your body, you can feel it in your hands. Energy practitioners and Reiki healers know this feeling, except it's much, much stronger. It is similar to the forceful polarity of a strong magnet. My energy would bounce off his, so it wasn't the same in that I could never be with him like I used to be. His Merkabah was so powerful that Yeshua could see, feel and touch me, and I could see him, but I still couldn't physically hug him.

"These meetings happened for roughly two months which helped my grieving process. Although we could not embrace one another, we could sit next to each other and look at each other's visual image, which is more of a projection in this realm.

"Even though I shared some of my visions, I didn't discuss these experiences with the male apostles. After four or five weeks, I began to tell a few of the female apostles I trusted the most. I also told them they were going on a journey with me, and we would not return. None of them were married, so they had no children; some were only in their late teens and early twenties. It was best they were not married, but it was unusual because they were with us."

"Why weren't any of them married?" Rochelle asked.

"They were similar to me because they had left their families, and most of them were quite young," Miriam replied. "You see, some were orphaned because their parents either died from illness or were killed. It wasn't uncommon to have parents die young of famine, disease, or war during those times. A simple virus could kill you; back then, we didn't have hospitals. If something serious emerged, you died, so unlike today, the death of a loved one was an integral part of life for us we learned to accept.

"My news of Yeshua's visitations made its way to all the female apostles in time. One-by-one, I made them all aware of the fact we were in contact and that he had located a safe place for us to live in the southern part of Gaul where we could live out our lives in communion with his guidance and where the people would accept our teachings.

"I was supremely devoted to the female apostles, and they were devoted to me. Why would they stay with the male apostles who would not treat them with respect? It was part of the culture and society at the time, so it wasn't a good idea for them to stay with them, and quite honestly, it wasn't safe for us to be visible in Judea either.

"None of us—the male apostles included—went out to teach early on. Because of the circumstances, we kept a low profile. You don't go back into the den of wolves after they have eaten one of you, so we didn't. It took time to adjust. Many of us experienced something like PTSD or what you called shell shock during your world wars, but we didn't have people to help us with emotional trauma back then. Truthfully, we never slept peacefully until we were completely away from the strife we left behind, but at least we survived. As you say in your time, what doesn't kill you makes you stronger.

"Despite the shared trauma, I couldn't tell the male apostles Yeshua was visiting me regularly, for they likely wouldn't believe me and never had much respect for me as a woman. Now you understand why the Church that emerged after this period was patriarchal, not unlike the male-dominated Jewish religious orders. As we spoke of earlier, the Essenes were much more equal although they too were zealots about rules. Both male and female Essenes were allowed to teach at a time when the Orthodox groups would never have permitted it. Although things are shifting in some groups, your Christian and Islamic religions are branches of the same male-dominated tree.

"Certainly, structured religion is one way Source can work through spiritually-minded people to get them to understand their true identities, but this imbalanced male domination and the mostly unyielding adherence to old dogma corrupted it over time. Even to this day, it is still corrupted. Instead of growing into a living truth, your calcified religions are starting to become obsolete. Sure, courageous individuals are seeking to help their church evolve into a living truth, but overall religious institutions are not progressing much. Their strength, dependent on hierarchy and various exclusions, is diminishing because the idea of equal sovereignty in spirituality, including a direct connection to Source, is becoming more accepted and adopted.

"During the week following Yeshua's death, his Merkabah also visited the male apostles to strengthen their Merkabah bodies. His visitations prepared them for their journey without him and, of course, without the female apostles or me. As a result, their strength became increasingly potent over time, and they brought Yeshua's words to people throughout the land."

And then, the energy shifted, and Yeshua came through to speak.

"Miriam was not merely there to serve me or oil my feet when they hurt," he began. "She was there to make me a better man. People with preconceived ideas of who I was as a holy man or prophet don't wish to hear that Miriam was my wife, lover, other self, or partner. Miriam was there to strengthen my Merkabah so I could go through a death I didn't want to experience. Initially, I was unwilling, which is something many may not wish to hear. Remember I was human, so the journey did not come without some fear and hesitation. Does anyone want to be sentenced to death? I knew the process of being put to death would be excruciatingly painful but wouldn't last long. I hung on the cross for hours, not days, as others who hung on crosses endured, so in this context, my physical pain was much less than it was for others."

The outcome seemed inevitable given the pattern of crushing anyone with opinions that contradicted the authorities who dominated the land. How did we get from preaching words of love and truth to dying on the cross to save humanity's sins? thought Rochelle. Saving our sins was a far cry from what would appear to be a much more likely account—people acting out of fear over the revolutionary message of love and oneness with Source that threatened power structures. Undoubtedly fear was an all-too-human but mistaken basis for creating belief systems.

"You might say my soul already planned my death, meaning how I would leave my physical body," Yeshua resumed. "I will emphasize this again: Your conscious portion of your body and what you perceive as your physical body are one and the same, and your chakras are part of it."

Yeshua ceased speaking, and a long gap followed, but Angelo's eyes remained closed. Rochelle shifted positions on the floor of their sitting room. She picked up the hand-painted teapot she had purchased in London and poured more tea into her cup. Soon, Yeshua recommenced his thread.

"Now, I want you to write this down, Rochelle," he said. "I did not die for humanity's sins but for what I believed in—my beliefs and my truths about God and love. I was a bit like your modern-day activist who rebelled in the belief that I was speaking of truth, light, and love. I didn't die because of the sins of men and women, for humanity was never born into sin. People were only led to believe they were of sin; however, sin is a distorted perception of who you are in this lifetime. But you know these things already, don't you? We have been preparing both of you since you came into this dimension. And you Rochelle, it's no accident you were born at 11:11."

Preparing both of us, Rochelle repeated to herself in wonderment. What did he mean by that? She found it fascinating that he referenced her birth time, something she only discovered shortly after she and Angelo met. Rochelle had an incredibly intense dream one night where she had visions of 11:11 in a murky blue sky, followed by multiple copies of the number spinning around in circles and another image of them flying around a triangle. It was so evocative it woke her up abruptly. She knew the dream was profound even though she didn't understand its significance. Why she went toward the locked box that housed her birth certificate once awake, she didn't know; it was as if her body was on autopilot. There, next to the line for the time of birth, was written 11:11 am. She had never known the time of her birth before, but she had never had a reason to know. Only later she learned that the number had a significant meaning amongst spiritual teachers and seekers, apparently a message indicating support or direction from Spirit. Rochelle and Angelo both knew numerology and sacred geometry address the hidden meanings behind numbers, shapes, and symbols, such as the Tree of Life, Metatron's Cube, the Triangle, and Platonic solids; however, these topics were relatively new to their awareness.

Yeshua went on, but only briefly.

"Let this be part of the Magdalene story as well. Blessed is the man and blessed is the woman who listens to their spiritual intuition," he said. "You are both becoming stronger every day. You now sit here often with Miriam and me, and she comes through both of you. She also comes through strong women because they represent who she once was in her human form."

What a strange thing to say, thought Rochelle. Wasn't Miriam connecting through Angelo? But hadn't they also said they connect first through her auric field and then into Angelo? How could this be, and how did it work? She felt so aligned with Miriam it was as if they were interconnected. It was as if they were truly one spirit, or one soul, or one . . . ?

"Rochelle, you are not afraid to voice what you believe in—your truth," Yeshua continued. "You have strong convictions, and you even look like Miriam. Above all things in this universe, you must be ready for what is coming your way. I bless both of you with all I am. Take what I say for what it is—a blessing, a saying, a suggestion, maybe a covenant of sorts.

"I am still your Rabboni because I am a part of the ascended masters. May love be with you both. May peace be with you both. Share these things with others, for this is how you truly heal yourself and the world. I am Yeshua, and these are my words."

And with that, his energy was gone.

• • • • • •

CHAPTER 10

LEAVING HOME

A journey of a thousand
miles begins with one step.
—Lao Tzu

Miriam seemed ready to move on, and frankly, so were Rochelle and Angelo because of the heaviness of Yeshua's Crucifixion and the sorrow that followed. Although neither Miriam nor Yeshua saw it as death since the soul is eternal and returns to the Universal Consciousness of All That Is, an end to physical life is still difficult for human emotions to process as Miriam also acknowledged.

Looking at the callous cruelty of Yeshua's Crucifixion, Rochelle thought of the political corruption and oppressive enforcement of the time. Yeshua's teachings challenged both Jewish and Roman power, inviting harsh punishment, which often meant death. Despite reading about this pivotal time in history, Rochelle found it deeply disturbing to hear how many were hung on a cross atop Golgotha's summit for minor crimes and incidents. Even though it was profoundly moving to listen to the perspective of the woman Yeshua loved, the visual images her accounts conjured in Rochelle's and Angelo's minds were heart-wrenching.

Uncovering countless hard realities for both Yeshua and Miriam, their stories drove home the growing realization that life wasn't easy in ancient Judea, and after the Crucifixion, it was also much more dangerous as well. And so, Rochelle was relieved when Miriam appeared one night and announced she would speak next about their preparations to leave her homeland. Rochelle knew this couldn't have been easy for a woman to do over two thousand years ago, yet she also understood implicitly the departure was necessary for the group's safety.

One Saturday afternoon after they returned from a leisurely lunch in Rockport, Miriam began to speak of their lives in the immediate aftermath.

"Following the Resurrection, Yeshua strengthened the energy of the disciples' spiritual bodies to prepare them for what lay ahead," she commenced. "Regardless of how many times they were shown and told men and women were equal, it was still too difficult for them to deliver that message. They wanted to be accepted, so they taught using more forgiving language for the times. His apostles didn't want to cause any problems that might result in their own death, so some of the teachings were modified or softened.

"During the next two months, we prepared ourselves for our journey. Toward the end of this period, I knew I was with child. Although my pregnancy wasn't obvious yet, I wore fairly loose-fitting clothes to avoid scrutiny. However, it was only a matter of time, and my pregnancy put me in even greater risk of being discovered. I knew I had to leave, and so did the other seven female apostles. I never wondered whether I would see my parents again because I knew the first chapter of my life would be over the moment I left Judea. There would be no turning back.

"Near the end of that window, it was time to tell the male apostles that the female apostles and I were leaving. While they didn't respect me equally because I was a woman and we had shared some tense moments, we also had developed a kinship given our mutual love for and connection with Yeshua and his ways. We had become like a family in that we could sometimes be loving and at other times somewhat abusive. Of course, I didn't tell them about the baby—I could never tell them I was pregnant with Yeshua's child.

"Remember, most of them couldn't accept I was Yeshua's wife and partner because, in some ways, they still saw him as the *Son of God*. Yeshua tried to explain that all men are sons of God and all women are daughters of God in their own right; however, they didn't see or understand this since they didn't feel it or see it in themselves. Sometimes they were like children, so it was easier not to tell them everything because they would over-worry and stress about things. They were concerned for me and expressed it in their own ways; no one wanted to see harm come to any of us.

"The journey we women had committed to wasn't for the faint-hearted, and we were all intimately aware of the strength it took to carry on as outcasts, which is what we had become. While we made preparations for our departure to Gaul, I had no idea how the trip was going to manifest itself. How would I, as a pregnant woman, travel hundreds and hundreds of miles by foot and boat to a place

I knew nothing about? Do you understand how difficult this was for a woman then? Rochelle, it seems as if you are sensing fear, and that's exactly what fell upon me. Fortunately, I was constantly reassured by Yeshua's visitations that he would provide comfort for our group."

Rochelle nodded in affirmation, clenching her teeth as she considered their challenging voyage ahead.

We were all intimately aware of the strength it took to carry on as outcasts, which is what we had become.

"Roughly two weeks before we left for Gaul, Yeshua appeared to the female apostles and me to share the things we would have to endure and to remind us he would be there for us," she continued. "His words provided a great deal of support for what would otherwise have been an exceedingly daunting and arduous journey for eight women to make on our own, especially during this epoch. We knew leaving the only way of life we had known in pursuit of freedom and safety was our only choice. After we said our goodbyes to the male apostles and our families, we headed north, away from the corruption and tension. We had traveled some distance north before with Yeshua, so we knew people who would give us a roof over our heads at night."

"Do you remember the location?" Rochelle asked eagerly.

She had collected physical maps from her travels, so she ran to their den where they were stored in a large crate. She fished through the pile until she got to the map of Israel she had saved from her time living on a kibbutz. When she returned to their sitting room, Angelo's hands reached for the map, and it was as if he could read it energetically somehow, a bit like blind people using other senses or even intuition more deeply because they don't have their physical sight. Put another way, Miriam used Angelo's eyes and touch to read the map. Rochelle also pulled up a map of Israel on her laptop, zoomed in on an area in the north, and waited for Miriam to speak.

"The names would not be the same as they are here, but this was roughly about as far north as we went," Miriam said, as Angelo's finger pointed to an area on the map, northeast of Nazareth. Miriam seemed less interested in the names and more in sharing why they went this route in the first place.

"We decided to go north one last time before heading to the coast because it was an area where we had taught with Yeshua when he was still alive. You see, we had supporters and friends there," she said, pausing as if recalling a vivid memory.

"It was arid and dusty most of the time, and although we mostly made the trek on foot, we occasionally had assistance from donkeys," she noted. "We retired early, sometimes sleeping on a packed dirt floor, and rose before the sun did, often leaving without breakfast. Getting an early start was critical to be able to travel as far as we could before the sun would envelop us—at times, the heat beat down on us with the force of a hailstorm. Common happenstances included scorpions on our path, dehydration if we didn't get enough water throughout the day, and blisters on our feet from hours of walking.

"We used scarves and coverings over our heads to protect us from the heat. Inland, it was much wilder, and at first, I needed time to process the scale of the land since it was not developed as it is in modern times. I felt its expansiveness, yet I also felt connected to *all of it*—the dirt and trees and the birds, lizards, dogs, mules, sheep, and goats. Life was much different than it was along the coast where ports brought in foreign goods for trading. It was more provincial, not unlike today's smaller towns and villages. This was all we knew. That last journey north was significant for us because we knew it would be the final one that we would take in our homeland."

Before Miriam resumed her story, she looked at the map through Angelo's eyes again and seemed to be reflecting for several minutes. Eventually, she commented, "After our time up north, we headed west. Once we hit the coast, we headed south where a boat would be waiting for us near what you know today as Gaza."

Miriam's story elicited images that made Rochelle think about her own travels to the Gaza Strip. When she was only eighteen, she had lived and worked on a kibbutz for nine months. She recalled celebrating her nineteenth birthday with Israeli friends before leaving for England in December. Rochelle remembered hitchhiking up and down the coast to visit friends in nearby towns, catch a movie, or buy items not readily available at the kibbutz store. She learned how to hail a ride safely and always had fascinating conversations. She knew to look for environmental clues that the turn to Kibbutz Chokmâh was near, such as familiar cows in a pasture, since named signs were absent back then.

During this chapter of her life, Rochelle learned humility. She held several diverse jobs on the kibbutz, from washing dishes, picking oranges, and milking cows to raking hay and packing foam in a factory. Everyone rotated through the various tasks that needed to be done. The accountant of the kibbutz performed the same jobs she had to ensure everyone understood and appreciated even the most menial task. Kibbutz life was about the collective interest and well-being of everyone there. Children lived amongst families, and everyone looked after each other. She had always felt every American should experience this way of life. While individuality has no shortage of merits, she often saw the ego-self create an imbalance of excessive self-interest. That imbalance often gets in the way of helping and serving others as a way to understand the benefits of collective concern and egalitarianism.

Neither Rochelle nor Angelo was raised Jewish, yet they always felt a pull to Jewish culture and traditions, including food and ritual. Rochelle's great-grandmother had Jewish roots and often deflected many of her childhood questions about their family history and the past, including why they changed their surname. Angelo's connection to history, culture, and literature led to his love of ancient texts and chanting. They both felt a connection to and growing curiosity about Judaism.

Nostalgia filled Rochelle's head and heart as the memories of her own journey through the Holy Land came pouring forth. Just as Rochelle's emotions surfaced, Miriam began to speak again.

"The names are not the same today, but we left from a port a little south of Gaza. We had to walk great distances to get to our destination although we also rode on camels and donkeys. In those days, people often traveled in groups of thirty, forty, or even more, for there was always more safety in numbers. At times, we would join others, riding on their carts, wagons, and animals.

"When we arrived in a town, we would break bread with people, for sharing food with others was an important and integral part of our culture. It was a hospitable part of our society and something we were proud of since it also broke down communication barriers when you entered a new community. It wasn't uncommon for people we were traveling with to stay in a town because they wanted to find work there, and then we would continue without them.

"There were many plantations and farming communities inland and fishing villages dotted the coastline. Visuals became a blur after a couple of weeks: A mangled donkey, women preparing food around a fire, the eight of us huddling on the floor eating nuts, bird song at dawn, and feeling the chill cover us at dusk. It was the same after we left land.

"As the boat would come closer to shore for a stop, I'd look up at the sky to watch the gulls swarm lower. I would marvel at their beauty and lightness and envy their simple existence. They moved toward food when they were hungry and stopped to rest when they were fatigued. These beautiful gulls floated above the chaos and brutality of the human world. I ached for their freedom at times."

A lull in the conversation followed Miriam's recollection of her long and onerous journey, and Rochelle lingered on the anguished tone in her voice.

"After we left Judea, it took a while to get to the next sizable coastal town because of a storm; however, when we arrived, funds had arrived to pay for our voyage," she continued.

These beautiful gulls floated above the chaos and brutality of the human world. I ached for their freedom at times.

Surprised by the reference to finances, Rochelle asked, "Where did the money come from?"

"Mostly from family members; however, the male apostles assisted us as well," Miriam replied. "I don't know if they assisted out of grace or because they were happy to see us go. That said, they did care for us, and naturally, they were concerned for our safety. We always had plenty of provisions, a place to sleep, and food to eat along the way.

"Remember my family was well off, connected, educated, and an important part of the political and religious communities. My mother always found money to send us through people she trusted. It was my inexorable mother, not my father, who never gave up on me. At this time, my father didn't know I was leaving our homeland. After I ran away to be with Yeshua, he didn't want anything to do with me since he felt my nomadic ways brought utter shame to the family. Although our families knew each other and were friends, Yeshua's untraditional ways made some people uncomfortable, including my father.

"It wasn't long before my pregnancy became more obvious, and my discomfort grew. The boat we took was a sailing ship, unlike modern ones with motors. It was large enough for about a dozen people, but you couldn't sleep comfortably. Ten were on board—me, the seven women apostles, and two men who captained the boat. Back then, it was dangerous to travel by night, so sometimes we stayed on the boat, and other times we stopped for the night and slept on the beach if it was warm and safe. It wasn't an easy journey even though we hugged the coast most of the time. Since the men who captained the first boat couldn't take us all the way to Gaul, we disembarked at the furthest port they could travel, a place in what is now northwestern Italy. Remember, Italy, France, and Spain did not exist as you know these countries today."

"How did you know when it was safe to get off?" Rochelle asked her.

"The seasoned men we traveled with knew those waters well and relied on established connections with people up and down the coast," she responded. "They made a living by trading with people in various ports, so they were familiar with the route. It was not uncommon to travel on the boat for ten to fourteen hours a day. When we arrived in port towns, we purchased staples such as vegetables, rice, and grains. We found ample goat and sheep, as was common back then, and fish was bountiful along the coast. Even though goats were plentiful, we had more fish, grains, olives, nuts, and fruits. As our nomadic lifestyle dictated, we ate when we were hungry, or could find food, not at designated times.

"Every night, when I gathered the women together, the two men either stayed on the boat or went into town. Sometimes, I would try to remember my mother's voice, the times it was tender toward me, but it soon faded into distant memory. The uncertainty of the voyage and the grief of Yeshua's death enveloped me so tightly that there was no space to mourn other losses. His visitations helped me tremendously during those tenuous weeks on the boat.

"Yeshua came to us in his Merkabah during our evening gatherings only when we were alone, so it wasn't possible every night. His presence gave us the support and encouragement we needed to maintain a positive attitude during the trip. Remember, this journey required great endurance, patience, and faith, but we had Yeshua's messages of comfort to keep us going. Yeshua's spirit penetrated all of us, creating a swell of hope that settled in our tired bones. Although he wasn't with us in the flesh, the familiarity of his energy thawed the parts of us that might have remained hardened otherwise. We felt guided, and it was powerful since we could see his Merkabah. Evidence of this will be found in time."

Rochelle couldn't help but wonder: How and in what form would they find evidence of that?

"Because of the small size of the boat, we took the longest route along the coast, where we could see land," Miriam resumed. "Hugging the coast week after week took a lot out of us, especially for me as I was pregnant. The journey was harrowing at times. Even though we didn't venture too far from the coast, our days were not without heavy winds and occasional storms. A few times, we clutched a part of the ship and lay low as if our lives depended on it.

Yeshua's spirit penetrated
all of us, creating a
swell of hope that
settled in our tired bones.

"Along with my mother's voice, the memory of the arid desert land I had always called home began to fade from my grip. I tried to recall the fonder moments of my time in Yeshua's physical embrace, and yet they too were eradicated from my mind, almost as a way to keep me focused on the present moment and the safety of my unborn child.

"Fortunately, as I said earlier, Romans were not prevalent everywhere we went since they tended to stick to larger towns where there was more money. In your contemporary world, it is similar. Consider that most of the United States is made up of little towns, and just as people of power and wealth reside in your big cities today, those with power and wealth did the same back then.

"Sometimes, other sailors and merchants would join us on the boat; however, they would come and leave at various ports rather than remain with us for the entire journey. Luckily, the gracious and kindhearted man who owned the boat supported Yeshua's message. He also knew about my relationship with him, so he took on the role of guardian and protector, ensuring no harm would come to us on our route.

"As is the case now, abundance comes in a cornucopia of forms; the same was true for us. Why did you spend years traversing Europe, Asia, and the United States, Rochelle? You've traveled countless long road trips since you have always loved learning about new cultures and languages, and Angelo does too. We hugged the coast because it was safe, of course, but we were also there to learn about new customs, food, and other people's ways on our journey.

"As you know from your travels around the world, more knowledge and experiences lessen your fears and inhibitions. But you must tolerate some discomfort at first. Naturally, this was the case for us as well. We were learning to become comfortable with being uncomfortable. Every spiritual journey also starts with being uncomfortable; after a while, you become comfortable with and trust yourself. Over time, you begin to love yourself more and more and realize that love is abundant, so you extend it to others with ease and grace."

She went on to speak of love. "Love comes in many forms, too, doesn't it?" Miriam asked Rochelle without waiting for a response, something she did often. "You know from your own experiences traveling on your own and with Angelo that love expressed in Japan differs from love expressed in Peru and love expressed in Fiji differs from love expressed in France. This is exactly what we encountered on our journey—love in many forms. Not everyone back then had malice in their hearts despite the stories you have read in your history books. Many were incredibly caring and giving, just as you encounter today, and often that generosity happens in places where you'd least expect to find it. Most people on this planet are loving, even if they don't consider themselves spiritual since love is the moral and ethical basis of humanity. Would you not say that your family members are caring? They may not always express themselves in a nurturing way or understand your lives, but they love in their own way."

Miriam always seemed to know how to trigger hot buttons with Rochelle and Angelo, pulling at the things that most tugged at their hearts. Rochelle first learned about trudging through the muck of life as a teenager when her mother died, and Angelo also experienced family trauma after losing a sister. They both went through many dark chapters in their lives and took similar inward journeys when they weren't aligned with their life purpose.

Rochelle and Angelo knew people could learn how to rise above these *dark nights* by first going through the pain and distressing emotions around the trauma. These are the shadows we must not bury, avoid or ignore. We cannot pretend they don't exist, or they will only penetrate us more deeply. No. We must learn how to dance with all emotions and people's energies, including those who understand and embrace us for who we are and those who don't. Sadly, family members often fall into the latter category, and Rochelle and Angelo knew this was the case for many.

As Rochelle let these ideas percolate, she thought to herself: Resisting is futile. Learning to let go of pain and move through it allows us to find that inner peace regardless of what or who comes into our path. Often, Miriam would refer to parts of Rochelle's and Angelo's lives to draw parallels between her journey and their own, experiences which to varying degrees reflect everyone's journey in life. The language and states of mind humanity encounters along the way may differ; however, regardless of our culture, race, skin color, or sexual orientation, we all grapple with the same issues as energy beings having a human experience.

We must learn how to dance
with all emotions and
people's energies, including
those who understand and
embrace us for who we
are and those who don't.

Miriam brought Rochelle back to the boat trip.

"At each port, we filled up on provisions, found a place to bathe whenever we could, and talked to people, but our overarching mission was to reach our final destination," she said.

"Was safety your main concern?" Rochelle asked.

"Yes, safety was always on our mind," came the reply. "We didn't want to call attention to ourselves, so we spoke with people, but we didn't spend a lot of time in each port. You could say we were a bit like your modern-day nuns in keeping to ourselves, praying, and meditating, mostly at dusk and dawn. Often Yeshua would appear to tell us about our journey so we would continue to feel safe, and our captain's embrace of Yeshua's wisdom also helped us feel supported along the way. Many had faith in Yeshua and his teachings but would not admit it for fear of being persecuted. Do you fear being persecuted for what you believe in?"

"No," Rochelle said. Then Miriam turned things around.

"Okay, in terms of today's world, let's change the word persecuted to ridiculed."

Rochelle didn't need to think for long, of course, since she knew plenty of people who would either ridicule or outright disbelieve she and Angelo were being taken into other dimensional realities with the souls of two individuals who no longer walked the planet. Rochelle and Angelo were both rooted in the tangible despite the many esoteric encounters they had experienced in their lives. And many others were as well. Ridiculing what you cannot see or understand would happen, especially without scientific evidence or direct experience to back it up.

This perception of two realities made Rochelle think of the film *The Matrix.* When Neo took the red pill, he discovered a startling new reality, one which was a far cry from the one he had been living but now appeared illusory. If he had chosen the blue pill, he could have continued his same old life or, you could say, the status quo, a restricted or asleep existence.

Miriam and Yeshua were asking them in multiple ways: Do you stay asleep or decide to wake up to a rich and colorful world where countless probabilities and multiple truths exist? In an awakened state, there is no external God; rather, God lies within. In an awakened state, there is no evil, and there is no death. If you live in the equivalent of the red pill's world, you'll no longer fear anything because you'll see life in an expansive way, beyond your physical shell, your human life infused and led by your energetic self which continues to exist long after the shell falls away.

"The experience of two realities was similar for us since many people ridiculed us, but there were also many who believed in our unconventional message," Miriam continued, as if reading Rochelle's thoughts. "Some people saw us as fanatics who were against the Jewish religion, and although they didn't use the description of spiritual anarchists back then, this is how some people saw us. Depending on the group, we'd be called heretics or blasphemous.

In an awakened state,
there is no external God;
rather, God lies within.

"Other people's resistance, amounting at times to rejection, is why you must be firmly grounded when connecting to other dimensions, including the one you are in now when you speak to Yeshua and me. You must also be securely grounded in your beliefs and in everything you do. You will both bring science and spirituality together in your teaching and healing with others. Your work won't be just to ignite people's chakras and auric fields as some spiritual teachers say of their purpose and offerings, but you'll be doing the spiritual work to become your true Authentic Selves again and demonstrate this possibility to others."

Wondering how and where they would both be doing this, Rochelle asked, "Isn't everyone doing precisely that as teachers and healers in unique ways?"

"Yes, of course, but we give you a lot of hard-to-digest information because we feel you're ready for it," she responded. "I must give you a wealth of knowledge so you can share it with others who will listen; however, most will not be able to accept this information all at once. Some may accept it only partially or not at all. For a handful, the understanding will come in stages, but for others, the teachings may be too far out for them to comprehend, or even if they do, perhaps they simply can't accept it.

"Why do you think we're coming to you nearly every night now? You're learning a new language, and it's actually a language of love, even though you may not see it that way. We attempted to do the same in our lifetimes as Miriam of Magdala and Yeshua of Nazareth, but our language and teachings were much more basic because of what people could digest back then."

Rochelle considered her explanation and thought to herself: It's not as if they're teaching anything new; they're merely using more expansive language to impart a deeper understanding of what their message has always been. She wanted to hear more about their day-to-day experiences.

"Were there any special encounters along the way where you wished you had more time to connect with people?" Rochelle asked her.

"Occasionally, we would stay in a port for about two days," Miriam replied, "but it wasn't very often, and that decision was based on practical issues more than anything else, such as whether we needed to purchase more food, if we had to wait when a merchant wanted to invite another merchant or sailor on board, or if the weather was bad. Our captain always vetted who joined us when it became necessary to bring on additional sailors to help navigate the boat. When we dropped off a sailor or two in one port, it would sometimes take a day or two to find new men to join us because the captain would only approve those with whom we all felt comfortable. He understood the responsibility of eight women on his boat for a lengthy and toilsome journey. Since the trip needed to be rapid out of necessity, we didn't linger unless we needed to do so and don't forget I was pregnant.

"Hygiene vastly differed as we didn't have access to things like your current-day toothbrushes and towels, but we had other materials to clean our bodies.

It wasn't always pretty or comfortable when you had to defecate in a pot or off the side of the boat. We also didn't have sanitary napkins back then, so we used a type of towel during menstruation. Often, we separated ourselves from others when we menstruated so we could let the blood come out."

"Where?" Rochelle asked.

"Sometimes, it would come down our legs."

Rochelle asked, "Onto the floor?"

"You mean, onto the dirt," she replied.

The tone was very direct and sharp as if to underline the basic conditions in which they lived.

"It wasn't very ladylike nor especially easy for any of us," she explained. "We used basic towels we cleaned afterward, and they'd be used again and again. Modern underwear wasn't part of our time, and the undergarments we wore didn't securely hold towels in place. This made it difficult when we had to walk many miles under the hot sun and work the land."

Rochelle thought about heavy women depicted in paintings of old, and almost as if Miriam was reading her mind again, she said, "Heavy was considered sexy, but more for the wealthy and elite. Most people in our circles didn't eat high-calorie food and remember we were on the go and walked a great deal. We didn't bleed as heavily or as long as many women do today. Of course, it depended on various women's natural cycles as it does today; however, we grew accustomed to it as all women have had to do."

Angelo's head suddenly tilted back, and his gaze moved to the ceiling. As his breathing changed, Rochelle saw a bolt of energy running through his legs and arms.

"During the voyage, I would come through energetically—both seen and unseen—to comfort them," Yeshua said after a stronger connection had been made with Angelo. "My Merkabah often appeared to them in the evening during dinner. They could obtain wine from several places, so sometimes wine was part of their meal. It was a big commodity back then as it is now, though, for other reasons. Because it was cleaner than the water, it not only tasted better but was considered sacred and healing in many ways. Miriam would make it known when I would come to visit, so the seven sisters could be prepared for my energy. There were also times when I would visit Miriam alone as I was well aware she was carrying our daughter Sa'rah at the time.

"Apostles of Apostles, they all were to me. Their job was much more difficult than the male apostles because they were women, so I sent them to a place where women were more accepted as healers and shamans than in our homeland. In

Gaul, there were many women healers and shamans who were one with the land. Blessed is the womb of Miriam, the Apostle of Apostles."

Yeshua spoke very slowly while Angelo's head repeatedly moved from left to right, as if reading or seeing information from another reality. Rochelle sensed Yeshua was in the Akashic Records accessing more information from his life in that timeline, but she couldn't be sure.

"Blessed are you and Angelo, for you hear my words," he continued. "You sit with me. You feel and see my true essence. No one gets to Source or God unless they see themselves as me, as one with God themselves. This is why I said, 'No one gets to the Father except through me.' You must see yourself as me, in me, as you. There is no difference. That's what I meant back then."

Rochelle asked, "What would you talk to the women about?"

"I would tell them to have faith, not just in me, but in each other, for they are the true protectors of humanity. They are the source of life and the givers of life. And they are the true healers of *all*."

Rochelle had to know, so she inquired, "What would you speak to Miriam about when you came to her alone?"

Yeshua replied, "I would tell her my ascension wasn't possible without her. I would tell her my journey wasn't possible without her. I would tell her I could not fulfill my mission without her. It was through Miriam I could express my true essence of God as Angelo can express it through you, Rochelle. Now you understand the importance of divine feminine and divine masculine coming together as one. These are the words of Yeshua. Joyful are those who hear them."

His energy left effortlessly, and Miriam's energy came back the same way. Rochelle could see the energy shift immediately. Yeshua's energy was softer in a way . . . gentler. This is not to say Miriam was abrasive and unloving, but her communication style was much more direct than Yeshua's. It could be harsh when tough love was needed, and Miriam wasn't afraid to give it.

"You want to know something special, Rochelle?" Miriam asked her. "The way you both bring Yeshua forth often brings tears because Angelo can bring Yeshua's essence through as he once was. And there's another thing we haven't shared with you and Angelo yet."

A long pause ensued before she explained, and Rochelle's breath tightened, unsure what Miriam was about to spring on her.

"There was a woman amongst the seven sisters whom Yeshua spoke through, similar to how you connect to us today," she expounded. "It was a rare gift at the time, but his energy came through me and into her so she could bring forth or, you might say, channel his energy and teachings although we didn't call it channeling. This connection wasn't immediate; however, it happened more regularly after she stepped into her true essence and allowed the energy to flow without fear and resistance."

"I see," said Rochelle, not expecting that addition.

"We will talk about the seven sisters and their names later," Miriam said. "The names may not be exactly as they once were because the nuances, accents, and dialects were markedly different than they are today, but I will do my best to get them as close as I can. You also know the name Jesus came later, right? In our time, he was Yeshua or Y'shua—pronounced between an s on its own and the sh. In India, many called him Isa, but I would often call him Isha with a sh sound. Yeshua would do the same with me, often shortening my name to Mari, as you would say in Italian or Spanish today.

"Over time, when Yeshua came through to the sisters, sometimes it was in his Merkabah form, and other times, it was the presence of his energy alone to provide healing and comfort. Yeshua spoke more directly through the sister I just mentioned, which I'll talk about more in time. You could say that our entire journey was planned."

"What do you mean?" Rochelle asked.

"What I mean is this—unpleasant surprises were few," she replied. "We knew all the ports and towns where we would stop to rest and get provisions because the captain knew this route well from traversing it many times. Others knew who we were through our teachings which had spread, and we stopped in towns that were friendly to us where they provided food as well as a place to stay and clean ourselves. Word traveled, even back then, from port to port and from sailor to merchant about a man who heals and speaks as one with God.

"Bear in mind too that Yeshua spent time in India, so people heard about this remarkable man who made the long trek to learn under other masters and returned. This is not to say he had followers in all these regions, but many knew him as a spiritual teacher and healer. It was also not a surprise for others to hear he was crucified. Sadly, it wasn't uncommon for spiritual teachers and healers to be killed when their wisdom created conflict with those in power. This obliteration was especially true if their teachings didn't align with the ways and laws of the land and opposed what the governments stipulated.

"Our journey was difficult enough, so we were fortunate to be given free passage when we docked at certain ports."

Word traveled, even back then, from port to port and from sailor to merchant about a man who heals and speaks as one with God.

So, they had connections, thought Rochelle. Although words, money and other help may have traveled slowly, the female apostles received assistance as they made their way from ancient Judea to a new and foreign land. Of course, this journey wasn't what Rochelle or Angelo had imagined, but then again, how did they learn the story of Yeshua and what happened after his Crucifixion anyway? The story they learned barely had Mary Magdalene in it, and nothing about the female apostles at all.

What they knew had been passed down through historical accounts, but only officially sanctioned ones, and even those were not without interpretations from those with biases and agendas, dogma, or varying language translations, all of which served those in power in a patriarchally driven world.

Rochelle and Angelo thought about how many authoritative agendas have rewired us as a global society for millennia. We have so much more awareness of corrupted power now, yet still so few challenge their belief systems based on that awareness. Rochelle loved how *A New Republic of the Heart* author Terry Patten described this conditioned consciousness, referring to it as a "consensus trance" and a "mass hallucination." He suggests that we can transcend with a deep "moral intuition."[1]

Rochelle and Angelo hoped more courageous souls might start to ask more probing questions to break free from that trance. Isn't it long, long overdue?

• • • • • •

CHAPTER 11

BECOMING OUR BELIEF SYSTEMS

If I do not believe as you
believe, it proves that you
do not believe as I believe,
and that is all that it proves.
—Thomas Paine

They were housesitting for friends in Virginia—it was a small cottage on a serene lake filled with ducks and surrounded by flowers that attracted a copious number of hummingbirds and butterflies. Early mornings were filled with canoe rides and trail walks consumed their late afternoons. In between, they worked remotely from their laptops. On a calm evening, when sounds of nature filled the air, Rochelle was sitting alone on the dock with her feet dangling in the water.

Nostalgia about her shoestring travels continued to sweep over Rochelle after Miriam's last transmission. How many times did she not know where she would lay her head at night? She had stayed with strangers in Israel, Europe, Central America, Southeast Asia, and the South Pacific, yet she rarely worried. It was always a journey of discovery into the unknown during her nomadic phase; however, Rochelle realized she had lost some of her fearlessness over the years. Had her views and beliefs changed? She didn't think so, but the spark of adventure wasn't as bright as it once was in her youth.

Over the next several days, Miriam was not to be found. Toward the end of the week, Angelo's energy was softer and calmer, and Rochelle noticed he was more meditative and reflective, but she didn't question him about it. Later, they knew why. It was the gentler spirit of Yeshua who would fill their next few evenings.

"Hear my words, Rochelle," he began. "Do you think I would have allowed the women to make that journey alone without my support? Here I am, speaking through you and Angelo, and I am just as much Yeshua now as I was over two thousand years ago. I am human in the flesh of another man. What makes you both so unlike my apostles? Do you have more or less faith than they did? I know you feel my energy and love, but I also know there are times you don't always believe I am coming through in the flesh now—why would you? Who will believe you? Do you believe in Miriam's story, the one coming through both you and Angelo at this time?"

Rochelle nodded but then bowed her head down, hoping he would move on. It's not every day one has a dialogue with the soul of Yeshua of Nazareth. It's not every day that the soul of Yeshua of Nazareth asks you direct questions, expecting direct answers. At times, she wondered how much understanding any of it in a logical way even mattered. Rochelle had never been one to follow the status quo and plug into a mainstream narrative anyway. And yet a part of her wanted more clarity. Expected more clarity. Was that her ego self?

"Do you believe Miriam's energy runs through you and is part of your soul in this lifetime?" Yeshua asked and then added, "You're *becoming her* as your earth roots are slowly fading away."

The last comment was a horse of a different color, thought Rochelle. She found herself thinking: Are you kidding? When Yeshua asked questions, she discovered they were purposely designed to push her buttons. They were designed to encourage her to go inward, reflect and open her heart.

"You're changing now, meaning the prime energy running through you in this lifetime is changing," he went on. "Miriam was much more earthy than you are in this lifetime since she couldn't adorn herself the way she wanted even though she understood its value. Blessed is she. Blessed is he. Blessed are you. Blessed are they. Blessed are we."

"It seems as if there's more to these visitations than sharing Miriam's story, isn't there?" Rochelle asked, wondering if these teachings would somehow link back to her boat journey from Judea to Gaul.

"The main reason I am here is because of you both," he responded. "Why are there great leaders in your world? Why do they continue to work for what they believe in? When you were little, you had quite the imagination. You created your own divinations. You generated magic in the basement of your house where you mixed potions and dreamt of healing people. As a child, you were connected to Spirit, Earth, Water, and Sky in a significant way. Back then, you didn't speak to prophets, spiritual teachers, indigenous masters, or Yeshua, but today, you can.

"People may ask Angelo, 'Are you Yeshua?' What they likely won't expect is this response from me: I am a part of Angelo, and he's a part of me. I am a part of you, and you are a part of me. Miriam is a part of Angelo, and he is a part of her, and Rochelle, you are a part of Miriam, and she is a part of you—her energy runs through you. I had Christ Consciousness running through me when I was Yeshua, and you both have Christ Consciousness running through you today. Many on your planet incorporate the Christ Consciousness energy. You could say they are waking people up and igniting people's consciousness."

"Christ Consciousness?" asked Rochelle.

"It is simply an energy of pure, divine love," he quickly replied. "It has no religious undertone or implication. Other cultures and belief systems may call it something else, but it's an energy many embody, including you and Angelo."

As Rochelle breathed in his explanation, he asked, "Why are you all afraid of becoming what I once was? Why do you separate yourself from who I once was?" Not waiting for a response, he went on, "You are all connected, yet humanity has made me into something I was *not* in that life. I simply wanted to show people that God was in me as God is in all of you, but all they could see was me as a god, while those who didn't believe saw me as a blasphemer. You have so many problems finding the balance . . . finding your true Authentic Selves. It's one or the other for humanity since people are more glued to a set of belief systems than they are to being free."

Rochelle cut in, "Yes, look at what has happened to many of our structured religions. They dictate what we should believe and how we should think, which then harden into tools of exclusion and judgment. If we become those beliefs, it is all too often out of fear. Many embrace the dogma without truly understanding it and lose their way."

Affirming her observation, Yeshua said, "To use one example, Islam is a great religion, and Mohammed who was of love guided people to a positive, loving, and enriching place. But it didn't evolve, and the same is true with so many other religions. Everything else evolves, so why shouldn't your religions? Because they aren't, your religions are slowly dying or, you could say, phasing out. The more you understand you are Spirit first, the less need there is for religion or a set of beliefs and rules. I am Yeshua, and these are my words."

People are more glued to a set of belief systems than they are to being free.

Yeshua left, giving Rochelle time to reflect on what he shared. Structured religion isn't the foundation of people's lives as it was for the previous two generations. Miriam and Yeshua were teaching them to stretch their minds beyond their previous limits, including expanding their minds about God and their souls as Universal Consciousness and the idea that human beings are far from being the only living beings in the universe. Rochelle and Angelo also learned the importance of not subscribing exclusively to any one belief system, refraining from taking yourself too seriously and staying humble.

They wondered, if they are made up of particles and subatomic particles, then surely, they are nothing but a grain of sand in an expansive multiverse. If this is the case, why does what we do matter at all? In this context, it sometimes felt as if their lives weren't even *real.* Spiritual masters speak of the illusion or maya of our lives and have for thousands of years.

Countering the implication of meaninglessness or insignificance, Rochelle thought about the *butterfly effect* from Chaos Theory, which suggests one small change in one state can change a state somewhere else in the world or even in the cosmos itself. For example, a butterfly's flapping wing can affect the timing or the path of a tornado a thousand miles away.[1] If this is correct, then perhaps even our words and actions are significant because the ripple effect matters a great deal in a quantum universe. This idea of interconnection led theorists to an even grander idea of multiple worlds, which suggests that an infinite number of universes exist and that perhaps we're even folded into or part of other universes we simply can't see, as we affect these other universes and vice versa.

Trying to get their heads around multiverses using linear logic didn't get Rochelle and Angelo very far, nor did attempting to understand Miriam's and Yeshua's explanation that the soul is made up of countless frequencies and energies. Over and over again, Rochelle thought about Magdalene's words: "You can't begin to comprehend who we truly are."

In an effort to deepen the new insights pouring in from Yeshua and Miriam, their bookshelves expanded and their questions quadrupled. After Socrates,

Aristotle, Plato, and Galileo, they turned to Confucius and Constantine. Next came Isaac Newton and other Renaissance innovators. Then they devoured the Vedas, Kojiki: Records of Ancient Matters, the Bhagavad Gita, the Bahir, the Tanya, and the Torah. It was all extremely dizzying. Belief systems were simply too diverse, but at least they could affirm Miriam's and Yeshua's teaching that there were only perspectives, not one truth.

When Miriam appeared the next day, Rochelle decided to continue the thread on how we choose to believe or have faith in something or choose *not* to believe or have faith.

"Belief systems dictate so much of our life's reality, including our financial well-being and health," Rochelle began.

"Of course. Let me give you an example," Miriam interjected. "Yeshua and I worked amongst the lepers, but we did not contract leprosy. Why not?

"First, you must understand how leprosy spreads from one to another. It is often passed on from blood or through infection, so naturally, we took precautions. They had open sores, so we had to be especially careful. Although we didn't understand everything about leprosy back then, we knew it wasn't a good idea to mix fluids with lepers.

"We also both had a great deal of faith. Put another way, we felt we would be okay no matter what happened. Even with that faith, our beliefs were grounded in knowledge. By this, I mean that we understood we were not entirely immune from getting a disease, just as the most faithful in contemporary times are not immune from contracting modern viruses. Yeshua lived by faith, not fear. He taught faith and love, but he also used the heart's intellect and common sense. Blind faith doesn't serve you, so practical judgment and precautions to protect your body are both necessary to live a balanced life.

"Some did not believe they could contract the virus during your modern pandemic. People may not use this analogy but consider Yeshua who walked amongst lepers. We spent time with those who were ill but didn't catch their conditions, illnesses, and diseases. Leprosy didn't spread through the air like some of your viruses do today, and we also didn't spend much time with individuals who were deathly ill either. When people read from their holy books and tell you Yeshua went to see lepers and didn't get leprosy, it is true, nor did I. But remember, we didn't act from faith alone; we took safety measures and realized that we too could contract a disease and die.

"Now you understand why the Essenes kept themselves impeccably clean and why some of their teachings were useful to us as we walked amongst the sick.

We healed people to the best of our abilities; however, our primary role was to teach those who were poor, desperate, desolate, and infirmed. If you have a positive attitude and a strong immune system, can you still contract a virus plaguing your planet? Yes, of course you can, but it doesn't mean a resilient immune system and a positive mental attitude aren't helpful, for they can help you recover more quickly or reduce the severity of an infection.

"Some spiritual healers believe they are untouchable and immune to disease from faith alone or because they are doing divine work, but remember all human beings are prone to illness and disease. If you believe you can heal yourself, you can. If this is a true statement, then can you believe you can't get a virus, and let that be true as well? Some people have a stronger immunity to a particular virus, which is why some don't get sick while others do or even die. Many factors play a part in fending off an ailment or catching a virus.

"To put it another way, your genetics and environmental factors affect your biological and chemical make-up which play a part in your immunity to a viral infection, and your belief systems also factor into it. It's important to stay humble and never believe you are invincible. When you start to believe you are more powerful than you truly are in your physical body, you start to lose your humility and run into problems. This happens when your message and work become corrupted by the ego."

"Ahhh, yes," Rochelle piped in. "Falling into the ego's belief systems versus serving as a vessel for your Higher Self's wisdom."It made her think of what happened to a renowned yoga teacher.

"Belief systems obviously play a part," Miriam agreed. "As does biology. However, another reason some people have more immunity to a virus is the strength of their auric field. When what you see as your physical body is kept healthy, it affects your auric field because they're interconnected. This doesn't mean you shouldn't be cautious; however, each time you connect with us and stay in our field, we strengthen your energetic fields. The faster you vibrate, the more you become one with all of us and Source."

The faster you vibrate? What on earth did she mean by that? Rochelle thought to herself, but Miriam moved on.

"There's a fine line between having faith and being in denial, and each of you must discern the distinction. Yeshua said, 'If you think you can heal, you can heal.' This idea belongs to the quantum world you are discovering now. Although we were unaware of such things as quantum healing, we understood that the soul was responsible for what people saw as a miracle. We knew we were simply the vehicles or vessels by which Source energy worked through us for the healing to occur."

"So, in healing, shifts in consciousness and miracles become a reality if the frequency match is seamless between two souls and both sides agree?" asked Rochelle.

"Each person who connects to an alternate dimension for messages or knowledge has their own unique spectrum of frequencies, so they will interpret things differently as a result," came her response. "By interpretation, I mean their perception and acceptance of healing will vary. What is healing for one may not be for another. Each soul, or what is more accurate to say, all the frequencies that make up a soul, will have various perceptions of reality. Is one right and one wrong? No, they're just different perceptions of the same thing.

There's a fine line between having faith and being in denial, and each of you must discern the distinction.

"The data you access in the Akash depends on the soul's combined sets of experiences and knowledge, so it is like a paintbrush stroke of one artist compared to another. Even if the same master trained them, their perception and representation of an image or idea would not match each other. For musicians, the same holds true, so why would connecting to other dimensions be any different?"

Rochelle rested her head on her hand as Miriam went on.

"The more you start to understand quantum realities, the more you will realize there is no singular truth, only a truth related to your perception of a particular reality or set of realities. The countless realities within your quantum field can't be easily explained right now. What happens when you shine a light through a prism? It breaks up into a beautiful array of colors you call a rainbow. All of the unique frequencies of light are channeled through one prism, yet it's coming out in an array of colors and frequencies. Each person sees colors and frequencies as they desire to see or understand them."

This explanation made Rochelle think of all the ways she had heard colors as frequencies explained, from art and photography classes in college to science books. Rochelle's mind went back to a radio segment she listened to once in her car about the color red and how colors aren't as real as we think they are; there are only frequencies interacting with our nerve cells in the optical nerve of our eyes. Within this interaction of frequencies and nerve cells, we interpret and give a name to what we believe we see—in this example, the color red.

The more you start to
understand quantum realities,
the more you will realize that
there is no singular truth,
only a truth related
to your perception of it.

"So, if color isn't real . . . " Rochelle jumped in, but then paused, thinking of her cousin David who was color blind and had to learn to interpret red as the same red his friends and family members around him described as red. He had to train his mind to understand red in the context of other colors, without the physical ability to see it the same way.

"Hmmm, so light waves have distinctive frequencies. It sounds as if you're suggesting we interpret how light hits an object as one color over another, right?" Rochelle asked, suddenly aware they were still discussing science.

"Your brain interprets light in different ways," Miriam responded. "When light hits an object, some of the wavelengths from the light get absorbed and some of them get reflected. Cells communicate information from the light waves to the brain through electrical signals. To take it a step further, some cells deliver information about things like shapes and motion while others process color. You feel, sense, and perceive color based on information that cells transmit to your brain through the optic nerve. It is merely one way to convey how human beings interpret and perceive things around you, including a color you call red or blue."

Rochelle turned her thoughts to processing what Miriam just said and how it might also connect to belief systems.

Even if I understood the science behind color, thought Rochelle, would I not see red as red and blue as blue because the collective consciousness of humanity all validated the colors over time? Miriam brought Rochelle's racing mind back with another example.

"If you think of one of your Persian carpets in your home, there are many threads or realities that make up one piece of fabric. Didn't you speak to an artist who feels my energy coming through when she makes jewelry and pyramids? Why aren't you both relaying information about gemstones from me? It's because it's not your reality or your purpose in this lifetime. Yeshua and I work through others in timelines they can understand based on their unique soul streams and experiences."

Rochelle tried to take Miriam's last example in, reflecting on her words . . . "it's not your reality or your purpose." Miriam and Yeshua's teachings resonated with both of them although they experienced them differently. Shifting into other dimensions and timelines, Angelo went into an altered state that affected most of his known senses, whereas Miriam and Yeshua seemed to work through Rochelle's inner knowing, sensing, and feeling as well as through her hands when she wrote, painted and typed. Words poured through Rochelle in ways she couldn't explain to people in a digestible way. Equally important, what came through extended far beyond her imagination, for they validated some of the information Miriam and Yeshua shared they wouldn't have known anything about otherwise. Rochelle wondered how all of this new knowledge was shifting their prior conditioning and belief systems in ways *yet to be seen.*

Her body jolted as Miriam picked up the thread again.

"You and Angelo create a bridge between science, spirituality, and consciousness. We have been giving Angelo these messages since he was a small boy—everyone is connected—and we have done the same through you, Rochelle, whenever you spent time in nature.

"What will you tell people about all of these realities? We first must speak about various stories and belief systems. What and who is true and not true?

"Let's take one story as an example: Some people have an image of me living in a cave for thirty years. It is the reality for some from the Catholic Church and certain communities, but it is not mine. Others who have received messages from Yeshua and me have spoken about strengthening his Merkabah as an internal alchemy to prepare him for what was about to come his way. There are also messages about our training in the ancient Egyptian Isis teachings of magic including the ways of sacred sex. Some of this I have conveyed to you."

Miriam was silent for several minutes, and then Angelo's eyes closed for about ten minutes or longer before she started speaking again.

"I am going to give you a visualization," Miriam finally said. "Imagine you and Angelo are in two separate spaceships. You see Angelo's spaceship enter a cosmic portal, yet you don't realize another reality exists on the other side of the portal. In other words, time and space are different for Angelo, but you're on the other side of the portal, so you exist in an alternate time and space from him. Angelo waits for you to come through the portal for fifty years. Finally, you return through the portal to his dimension and are joined together again; however, Angelo is fifty years older, and you're the same age. What was fifty years in time for Angelo was nothing more than five minutes for you in your reality on the other side of the portal."

From light, photons, wavelengths, and frequencies to vibrations, spaceships, alternative realities, the void, and portals, Miriam managed to take them down the wacky and surreal quantum rabbit hole again. Then she was gone and Angelo slowly regained consciousness in their more commonly experienced reality.

Before he had a chance to stand up, Rochelle asked him, "Did Miriam just talk to us about portals to different realities? What do you recall about her story?"

Angelo scratched his head and said, "It is less what I remember about her story and more what I recall her showing me. She took me on a journey into a portal as if I was part of and connected to it. On the other side was another reality, just like it is another reality when she visits us now. In this case, she showed me aging while you stayed the same. I kept seeing circles and circles in the cosmos. Maybe this is the quantum aspect of who we are, yet we are not fully able to comprehend it at this time."

"Why is she now taking us through portals in the cosmos to convey a message, a message that seems to be part of or in some way connected to her personal journey?" asked Rochelle.

"Perhaps simply to suggest that some things are far too vast for us to completely understand, just as Yeshua's healing people instantaneously with a touch is difficult for most people to digest. His miraculous healings. The ability of ancient prophets and sages to bilocate. Yeshua's Merkabah reappearing. All of these things," Angelo responded.

"Maybe she's trying to make a connection," Rochelle said. "A connection to how our belief systems are formed and how often they become solidified without experience, and often even after we have new experiences that are not aligned with those beliefs. Beliefs are passed down from one person to another, and for many, one person's or one group's beliefs can become gospel for them."

"Yes, just look at our own upbringing," said Angelo. "When we studied literature, history, science, and philosophy in school and later in college, it didn't occur to most of us that a teacher's set of beliefs could bias the teacher's presentation of knowledge. The same holds true for religion, medicine, and quite frankly, all professions."

He took her hand as they snuggled on the couch. "We know this," added Rochelle, speaking not just of themselves but of friends in their circles they've had similar discussions with over the years. "While our later experiences may challenge certain belief systems, by that point, they have taken hold of us, sometimes so tightly it's hard to believe another way. Often, when someone dares to speak their truth, people they love such as a parent, sibling, or boss may avoid them or in some cases disown them. It may not happen as frequently as it did two thousand years ago, or the reactions may include ridicule instead of physical harm. Regardless, at least people are bolder now about speaking their truth. Look at the strength and courage of women in Afghanistan and the Ukraine."

Rochelle thought of friends and people she had met on her travels who had the courage to walk their own paths despite the challenges to gain the freedom they sought. She witnessed women leaving dysfunctional marriages where their husbands either verbally or physically abused them. Many years ago, she met a man on a train in central Europe who fled his only known world, a racism-riddled small town in the American South, simply because he couldn't live another day with the divisiveness. A woman from India she had met in London wanted to marry a French man; after having the courage to stand up to her family, she never heard from them again. Then there was a Canadian woman Rochelle studied dance with whose mother still treated her as an outcast because, twenty years before, she had divorced her husband and left a religion with so many rules and restrictions she felt like she would suffocate if she didn't escape. These chains and constricted belief systems were global and made their way into all living rooms.

Rochelle and Angelo fell asleep leaning up against each other until the soft sounds of rain woke them up; however, it was not enough to cool things down over the next few days. By the next afternoon, the temperature had climbed up to a rare 111 degrees. They closed all the doors and sat on the cottage living room floor. With no air conditioning, they turned the floor fans on high and prepared iced tea.

Over dinner, Rochelle and Angelo spoke about what Miriam, Yeshua, and the apostles must have endured when they walked from village to village in the blazing sun, shade under a tree providing their only relief. Later that evening, the energy in the room changed and Rochelle could feel her ears ringing. In a few minutes, Angelo's head tilted back, and he was off to another dimension, energetically bringing Rochelle with him, at least part of her.

I wonder what direction she'll take us tonight, she thought to herself while her ears continued to buzz and her head started to shake. She could sense a dimensional shift in a way she never had before, so she closed her eyes and held Angelo's hand, feeling the energy exchange between them. It took a while for Miriam's signal to connect, but once it did, she popped through as if they had been expecting her.

"Where were we?" she began as if no time had passed since her last visit. "We were talking about beliefs and how they are shaped. We were talking about how your beliefs create your realities, and so often, you think your realities are the only ones. You also think your timelines are the only ones."

"Timelines?" asked Rochelle, taking a sip of iced tea and then adding, "It's still hard to get my head around them." She wanted to go deeper, so she could better understand them in the context of Miriam's teachings.

"Time is a construct. The time continuum of one reality is different from the time continuum of another reality, and wormholes are like portals or tunnels between time and realms, yet another quantum aspect of your realities," Miriam responded. "No human being enters the same timeline, but the messages are often pretty close because these timelines intersect."

"So, one person's reality or truth is based on the timeline they're accessing information from? And once that information comes through *for them . . . to them*, they see it as the only reality and truth," Rochelle said, half as a question and half as a statement. She wondered what timeline they were in and whether Miriam and Yeshua had the ability to access all timelines. Could she and Angelo access all of them too?

"I do not wish to be the bearer of bad news, but one of your challenges is to present to people on your planet in this reality the truth of our existence—if there is a truth—and that is this: Our teachings were and are first and foremost about love. Love is the most important message you are here to convey. You're not here to focus on the world of quantum realities or healing although both will be part of your work as a natural extension."

"Part of our work?" asked Rochelle, curious why she kept referring to their work as if their current professions were not what they were on the planet to do.

"You will share the messages we are bringing forth with others. You will teach as we did. When you get lost or feel deflated, just remember the core message of our teachings—your teachings— is Love."

Following a long pause, Miriam interposed, "Do you understand what we are attempting to say?"

Trying to take it all in, Rochelle blinked. She could feel the room's energy shift in ways she couldn't easily describe if anyone were to ask. Angelo was still in front of her, his eyes closed, his head back, his breathing as slow as molasses as it always was when Miriam and Yeshua were present. She grabbed Angelo's hand for reinforcement. It was hot as if energy was flowing from it, releasing into her hands and into the room itself. Pushing her fingers into his now sweaty palms, she felt her body shake and then give way to a sense of inner peace and calm.

"Okay. Yes. Love. This is what it's about and what it's always been about," Rochelle responded quietly. Nestling up to Angelo in a state of serenity, she felt the oneness of everything around her.

Miriam confirmed Rochelle's insight, "It's so simple, it's hard, isn't it? It's only hard if you choose it to be hard. This too is a perception. As Yeshua and I taught over two thousand years ago in our human forms, and we teach through others on your planet to this day, the fundamental message is the same: Love is the strongest force in the universe and the glue that connects all living things."

The moment felt pivotal and uplifting. As they spent more time in Yeshua's and Miriam's dimension, they became a bit like family. The visitations were incredibly profound and even intoxicating at times, never more so than at that moment. It was as if all their energies were divinely interconnected, and there was no separation amongst the four of them. This experience—this feeling of divine love—felt sacred. Wanting everyone to experience this awe-inspiring interconnectedness with all living things, Rochelle wondered why some people felt it, and others didn't.

Moved to delve deeper, Rochelle asked, "You've both been explaining we are united and we're all intertwined, but what did Yeshua mean by becoming an energy you take on?"

Love is the strongest
force in the universe and
the glue that connects
all living things.

"What he's trying to tell you is that when you take on the energy of an ascended master or another energy, you become that energy," Miriam replied. "Early on, when we open people up to our energy, they may first think they're crazy, but then over time, some might believe they are an ascended master or one of us. As they continue to do the work, they realize they are not the incarnated master so much as they are one with the energy, for we are all one with each other as we are all one with Universal Consciousness and God or Source energy. What is the message for humanity, then?

"The message is to take on the energy you wish to become, and you will. Now, do you understand what we were trying to do back then? We were trying to show people they were all God and not separate. None of us are separate. Become the energies you truly are in this lifetime, for when you do this, you will create your own truths and perform your own miracles."

"I believe everyone can do this because we are all interconnected if humanity could only see it," Rochelle interjected. "I think some people sense the interconnectedness of everything, but many don't see society making decisions coming from a place of oneness. Left without social support, they model leaders available to them who may not have humanity's best interests in mind. Not everyone has the courage to step into their truth alone."

"People don't need to lead in a traditional way if that's not their soul's purpose," Miriam suggested. "For example, what you *perceive* as leadership is only one way to lead. There are quiet, more subtle ways to lead and speak your truth which can be just as potent. Demonstrating love in your daily life has a ripple effect that can help many in your wake. Put another way, assisting someone in your community or family can have powerful ramifications you may not see in your lifetime, but your words and actions matter—all of them. Being of service and love is enough, don't you see? When people get so set in their ways, insisting on only one belief, truth, and reality, life doesn't flow with ease and grace as it naturally should."

"Yes, human beings are so conditioned by the belief systems of their parents, teachers, siblings, and others," Rochelle added. "Even when we think we live on our terms, we are often robots or slaves to other people's beliefs."

"I say this unto you: Make sure you believe in love and your truth comes from your heart, because if it doesn't, then it doesn't have Source energy coming through you," Miriam said. "When Source works through you, it is pure love, and there are always miracles."

There was a lull as Angelo's body moved around and his breathing slowed down even more.

"You know what else is a miracle?" Miriam asked Rochelle with emotion. "I can look up at the sky and examine the stars from your dimension. I can see the sky in your earthly realm through Angelo. I am having a sensory experience through him because you both allow me to have that experience. I can enjoy beauty again on this planet tonight because you allow me to do it. I see a night so serene that God herself couldn't create such perfection, and yet here we are. Now you understand why you feel much more at peace living within nature. Simply put, spending time in nature expands your consciousness.

"You've become one with nature now, and because you've become one with nature, you've become one with the universe. Sacred geometry is always at play. Fractals exist everywhere in nature and even in your food. They are ubiquitous and when you breathe into them, you will understand the interconnectedness of us all. Everything is a repeating pattern, and you even have mathematical equations for them. Beauty is beauty, and it repeats itself—you simply have to be awake to see it."

Rochelle looked up at the stars, noting Angelo couldn't do the same with her because his eyes were closed. The sky was magnificent, and she could see the mirror effect on the lake that was so calm and peaceful she felt the same. The sounds of ducks in the distance and a woodpecker suddenly broke the silence. Was the woodpecker interrupting the serenity or just adding its unique spectrum of frequencies to the orchestra of nature's sounds? Wasn't it really just a contribution to the landscape of All That Is? Instantly, she felt gratitude in her heart and in awe of the sky that expanded into a universe she knew was far too vast to understand.

Beauty is beauty, and it repeats itself—you simply have to be awake to see it.

"How can I describe to people who are reading my story?" Miriam asked her. "How can I describe how I feel when I can manifest myself as a physical being and integrate all the sensory activity on the human plane once again? It's hard to explain this to people, but in your world, it's like being a child who tastes ice cream or sees a rainbow for the first time. It's rich, vibrant, and magical all in one."

Remembering a movie with the same physical power, Rochelle piped in, "And possibly like the scene from *City of Angels* when the character Seth (an angel) accepts falling into human form.[2] He feels the hot water of a strong shower pelting his skin, capturing the intensity of a human experience he had never felt before."

Miriam concluded, "I can now soak up all of these sensory experiences you as human beings take for granted once again. I absorb and take them into my being and can do this because you and Angelo have allowed it. You give me this precious gift of humanness again, and you do the same for Yeshua's soul."

Then, Miriam's energy left.

It was nearly midnight when Yeshua made an appearance in their dimension. Rarely would Yeshua or Miriam visit so late at night, but sometimes they would show up with a lesson after Rochelle and Angelo had watched a relevant movie or read a poignant passage in a book. Rochelle happened to be nose-deep in a series of philosophy books, and she had just finished a chapter when Yeshua popped through. Sometimes this kind of visit felt as if Yeshua was there simply to relay a brief message or insight; other times, a longer visit would nearly knock Angelo out as if he had physically left their earth dimension. In those cases, it felt more like she was having dinner with just Yeshua, and even though she could physically see Angelo's face and body before her, it was as if the merging of their souls was so united and deep at times she could see little difference between Yeshua and Angelo. This particular visit was more of a popping-through, so she assumed he wasn't planning to stay for long.

"You spoke of truth, belief systems, and perspectives with Miriam earlier," Yeshua commenced. "What is perspective? What is a belief system? If you become another person's belief system, are you free to choose your own? In other words, are you free to select what your Higher Self is innately guiding you to do or how to show up in the world?"

"Go on," said Rochelle, eager to hear more.

"There truly isn't one belief or one truth since it all depends on one's perspective," he said. "You and Angelo have started reading about quantum mechanics and the laws of abundance and manifestation. If your consciousness desires something to be true, then it becomes true. If you pay attention to it over time, the ripple you put into the universe moves a desire into material form—it becomes a reality, and each reality and truth is different. Within this dimension, there are multiple realities, and believe it or not, you're only just a hair away from other realities. What you do in this realm affects everything else in the other realms and dimensions."

"By multiple realities, do you mean the result or outcome of the multiple probabilities a soul chooses to take?" Rochelle asked him. "Does that boil down to truth itself not existing? Is the idea of truth an illusion?"

If you pay attention to it over time, the ripple you put into the universe moves a desire into material form—it becomes a reality, and each reality and truth is different.

"As we said before, the soul isn't made up of only one energy," Yeshua responded. "Your chakras resonate at many different frequencies, and the soul too is made up of varying frequencies. In the complexity of these frequencies, there is truth, and there is no truth or no one truth. So, if people ask you whether this story is true, you can tell them this story is true and it's not true since it all depends on your perspective. At the same time, I can say within this earth realm and dimension and within the aspects and spectra of frequencies that make up the soul of Miriam of Magdala from millennia ago, this story is true. It is her truth, and it is long overdue."

Yeshua and Miriam had spoken to them about the soul's vast range of frequencies before, and both Rochelle and Angelo had yearned to better understand it. That night wasn't the night though because his energy was gone as quickly as it had arrived. Then again, they were both spent, so when Angelo's energy and presence returned, he and Rochelle soon fell into a deep sleep.

• • • • • •

CHAPTER 12

THE MULTIDIMENSIONAL SOUL

Do not ask me where
I am going as I travel in
this limitless world where
every step I take is my home.
—Dōgen

Although Rochelle and Angelo had a thirst for knowledge, they weren't sure whether going down the quantum rabbit hole even further would quench that thirst or take them deeper into a maze of confusion. Nonetheless, they had to know more about the soul. If the soul was many, they were eager to know if the soul lived multiple lives simultaneously. And if it does, how does the propagation of these frequencies and energies benefit each of us?

From Miriam's and Yeshua's perspectives, Yeshua's so-called Merkabah not only continued beyond the death of his physical body but also could materialize before Miriam and the female apostles. His Merkabah also seemed to be able to appear in India and in multiple realms, dimensions, and timelines concurrently.

Rochelle and Angelo wondered whether humanity was ready to accept the notion that there's much more than our linear brains can understand and science can prove. They realized no matter how hard they tried to find logic in the information Miriam and Yeshua shared, many of their teachings were as mind-bending as *The Matrix* and as otherworldly as *Alice in Wonderland.*

The more Miriam and Yeshua showed up, the more Rochelle and Angelo found themselves reading everything they could get their hands on, from ancient teaching in holy books across cultures and materials on yoga, meditation, and bioenergy healing to information about the chakra system and discoveries in integrative medicine and quantum physics, all in search of possible corroborations and explanations.

They knew the material world they interacted with every day was in the infancy of quantum discoveries, and string theory was only one of many ideas that scientists debated. As their knowledge expanded, the more they realized how little they truly knew about the universe in which they were living. They had enough to manage in their day-to-day lives without adding the complexity of cosmology and quantum soup to the mix.

Then again, even if they somehow managed to comprehend Miriam's and Yeshua's multidimensional explanation of the soul, would anyone agree? After all, humanity has been trying to understand matters of the soul across cultures for thousands of years. On one hand, despite the decline in traditional religion, its dogmas and fear have endured. On the other hand, new understandings and beliefs were emerging. If you were to throw artists, scientists, novelists, poets, biologists, anthropologists, psychologists, musicians, and philosophers in a room, the debate would be never-ending.

Besides, didn't Miriam and Yeshua just teach them there is no one truth, only perspectives? What's more, they went far beyond contemporary ideas of relative truth with explanations of multiple lives occurring simultaneously and countless probabilities for each life experience.

After another long week of Angelo in a deep contemplative state without a peep from Miriam, Yeshua came through unexpectedly one evening for a visit.

"You wish to understand the soul," Yeshua began as if he had heard their earlier discussion.

This teaching called for a serious bottle of Bordeaux thought Rochelle, so she grabbed one from their wine cellar and hurriedly returned to settle into an evening discussion about the soul. She sat on the floor against a yoga back chair, lit a candle and some Frankincense, and began to record Yeshua's transmission. He was ready to take them into new territory.

"We only exist in a timeline, but how thick or thin is that timeline?" he asked after she got settled. "It's nothing more than the hair upon your head, but people wish to see themselves as so much more than a strand of hair. Think of each strand as a potential path you can take. We are all faced with daily choices and each one leads you in a specific direction, which creates a unique experience. Consider the vast number of probabilities the soul can experience, and all these choices are not as random as you think. Remember, however, that one piece of hair matters since it is part of the All—you are part of all things, and what you do influences the other realities in the universe. How you think about those decisions and experiences creates your reality—or rather *what is real to you*—in every moment."

It made Rochelle think about something she read by a physicist on synchronicity: When we expect synchronicity and flow in our lives, "then instead of focusing on our regrets for the opportunities we missed, we can see how life has supported the things we *did* choose." From that frame of reference, we can feel at ease when we realize the cosmos has our back and is supporting us.[1]

Of course, you can decide you don't matter at all and not make the effort to connect with the All, but you decide, we don't," Yeshua added. "No God or master judges you."

Rochelle agreed, for she never believed in or understood the concept of an almighty ethereal being who played traffic cop and judged every decision a human being made.

"Here's another analogy," Yeshua offered. "Think of the soul as a large tree, and each branch on it is its unique expression or energy that shows up in a human or some other energy form again and again. Put another way, see each branch as a past life or experience, including the personality that came with that life. Consider the leaves on those branches as the unique skills, abilities, and wisdom we learned during a particular life experience."

You are part of all things,
and what you do
influences the other
realities in the universe.

Rochelle interrupted, "The branches and leaves on a tree are a useful analogy of the soul's complexity. It helps me conceptualize it in a material, 3D way."

"Now, imagine all of these aspects of our souls as an immense spectrum of frequencies expressing themselves in unique ways, like the way one musician strums a guitar or cello string versus another," Yeshua elaborated. "They all share a similarity in that playing the D note is always a D note, but how it gets played and what gets added to the piece makes it unique in its individual expression. All of these branches and leaves on a tree include various aspects of who and what your soul is made up of—individual expressions as part of the tree, but also the whole tree. The tree (or the soul) and all of these branches (lives) and their leaves (our experiences, expressions, personalities, and talents) create a distinctive spectrum of frequencies as a combination of *all of it,* just as an orchestra does when it integrates all of the musicians and their instruments."

"As a musician, this makes sense to me," Rochelle piped in although she had never personally played in an orchestra.

"Back to my tree analogy, each soul has its own journey it decides to take in a life, or you might say, in a timeline," Yeshua continued. "When you don't show up to do the work, meaning to make a difference along the way, it's because of fear and lack of faith in yourself, in us, and in the All. We truly are connected to the All as an integral part of it, but we are also the All in its totality—we are not separate from it, nor are we separate from God, Godde, or the Goddess.

"In a way, where you live is a perception, but who you are is also a perception. You each comprise many aspects and expressions, yet you see yourselves as one. In this reality, more than just your soul occupies your quantum field; you have spread or rather extended your energies (and soul) out to the universe and beyond. Think of it like this: You are currently having an experience in this human body in this dimension, but it's temporary and just one of many experiences and timelines you are having simultaneously."

"So, I guess all four of us are having other experiences in other realms, perhaps even in this one?" Rochelle asked.

"Even your soul is in communion with many others while it is also in communion with Yeshua of Magdala and Miriam of Yeshua in this dimensional reality, what you see as your present life," he responded.

Where you live is a perception,
but who you are is also a
perception. You each comprise
many aspects and expressions,
yet you see yourselves as one.

Rochelle remembered Yeshua using these references before, and sensing her curiosity, he added, "I am using this description to demonstrate that there is no difference between Miriam and me, Angelo and me, you and me, Miriam and you, or masculine and feminine, for they truly are all one and the same. We are each part of the All, and one with the All. It is also a way to honor the divine feminine because, during our time, it would only be said, 'Miriam of Yeshua' as a way to denote the woman he was married to."

"You mean, belonged to," said Rochelle under her breath, considering this clarification would likely have been Miriam's response to underline the exclusive masculine power of their time, but Rochelle stopped there, so Yeshua could finish his explanation.

"There are others who work within the energetic layers of your auric field. As we come into your and Angelo's dimension, you are starting to realize we aren't separate from you. When we speak through his auric field, Angelo's soul may also individuate if it chooses. Those who are asleep believe they are only individuals, not a collective. The souls who are awake know they are a part of and connected to everything, although they may express themselves in unique or individual ways. When I speak through you and Angelo, you see it as one voice and one soul, and you have the same perception when Miriam comes through to speak, but we make up many just as you and Angelo make up many."

Suddenly, Miriam's energy came through effortlessly as if both she and Yeshua were seamlessly flowing into each other in a similar way that Tai Chi practitioners demonstrate their subtle and fluid movements. What a beautiful example of non-duality, Rochelle thought. It was as if the balance of masculine and feminine energies flowed together naturally like water running down a stream, over the rocks, around the boulders, without resistance. It was as graceful as the moves of a Qigong master when she shifts energy to create harmony and balance.

"I too have many energies that are part of my soul, just as Yeshua does and just as all of you do," said Miriam. "Doesn't your brain acquire knowledge over many years? What do you do with all that knowledge? It gets stored in a way, like data you offload to the cloud in your modern-day terminology.

"Similarly, the soul gathers a lot of knowledge; however, this information is not only stored but is always *active* and *accessible.* What I'm trying to say is this: Think about your brain gathering intelligence and skills from the various people you have met throughout your lives—the people you have touched and who have touched you, the books you have read, the movies you have watched and the numerous experiences you've had. The soul not only has accumulated diverse knowledge from all its individual life experiences but also knowledge from all the energies (the souls of others) who have given it that knowledge. It has access to that as well: the soul is already born with this vast, rich knowledge because it is born with Source energy. That said, you lack the experience in the physical body upon each reincarnation to know how to access it.

"When I walked your planet as Miriam of Magdala, I had multiple energy sequences, frequencies, and fields in me, as well as timelines, just like all of you do. It's important you understand we each are not a singular energy but more of a collective one. Your mistake is you think you're just one soul, and you are in one sense, but your soul is also made up of countless frequencies that stem from multiple timelines, as we've said before.

"For example, the personality expresses itself in a particular way specific to the realm and the timeline. My personality is being expressed now as it once was during this earth realm and in the timeline when I was Miriam of Magdala, and in that lifetime, I was an astoundingly strong feminine woman. You see, personalities change depending on the time the soul expresses itself."

"The time the soul expresses itself? Can you elaborate?" asked Rochelle.

"Let's provide a real-life example from this current timeline," Miriam said. "The energy of your deceased mother Irene can come forth to speak to you like we do now. She can express herself with the personality she once had. Why is that? It is because you wish to experience her as she once was, and your intention matters. Rochelle, would you want to see her as she is now in her spirit form? No, not really. You don't want to see her countless frequencies within one because you want to connect with the energy and personality you knew as your mother in this lifetime."

"While we are in physical form, we have memories of our relationships and with them, all the emotions that come with a human connection," Rochelle said. "I suppose the grief we feel from the loss of a loved one is something we don't feel in our spirit form?"

"I can feel the emotions I once had as Miriam of Magdala through a human energy field now," Miriam replied. "I am not accessing another strand of hair or leaf on a tree—other manifestations and expressions of my soul. Do you understand?"

Rochelle bowed her head as she brought her right hand to her heart because she knew Miriam was right. She missed Irene and although she was curious about other manifestations or incarnations she may have taken, Rochelle wanted to sit once again in the presence of her mother's soul's expression of the Irene she knew in this lifetime.

"What I'm telling you now goes against most spiritual teachings, science, and other ideas about human nature," Miriam added. "As Yeshua and I have explained earlier, one soul is made up of vast soul streams or strands, expressing itself as one strand when it reincarnates into a human body, and it will take on unique traits and personalities it wishes to experience in a particular lifetime. As I speak through both of your auric fields now, I am projecting myself to you as a strong woman because this is who I was when I lived as Miriam of Magdala. When your father disowns you as mine did, you need to be strong, and so I was.

"Although some question whether we even existed, we did live in this realm and that timeline long ago. From a quantum perspective, there are multiple realities and timelines, and we lived in more than one. But this realm and that timeline was one of them, a very important one, I might add.

"You see, this story is being created not just by one soul, the one you think of as Miriam of Magdala, but all those in this combined auric field now. We keep coming back to the soul since your linear minds have difficulty processing what is occurring now as we speak and work through you.

"My soul is made up of countless energies, not just one energy, and Yeshua's soul is bounteous as well. If you hear us repeat this idea multiple ways, it's because it's crucial that you process it . . . understand it. Infinite energies which make up our souls are working together to narrate this story. Even though my soul is part of *the many*, I can access the information and memories from my life as Miriam of Magdala."

Then as smoothly as the last transition, Yeshua returned to further elaborate on the soul. Rochelle was starting to witness how he taught through parables so many years ago, but now with a modern flavor.

"Think about the soul as a telephone book," he said. "You have your phone number, but the entire telephone book is accessible to you. Then, think about your access to all the phone numbers in the United States and then expand to Canada. Now, expand that database of numbers and information to South America and then to the rest of the world—you have all this data and these memories accessible to you and far beyond. Truthfully, the soul's complexity is beyond human comprehension, but I am using this analogy as a place to start."

Trying to wrap her head around Yeshua's examples, Rochelle sensed what was coming through was deeply profound wisdom. While she was pondering her physical, massive database, indeed with names from every continent, Yeshua stepped back again, and Miriam's energy came forth. Rochelle wondered why they were making these rapid transitions. Perhaps they were teaching them about the fluidity and expansiveness of the soul. Flow. Yes, it must be about feminine and masculine flow, as effortless and invisible as the movement of air and energy, she thought. They were also demonstrating flow as a byproduct of oneness.

"I only need to think about a situation or person, and they come to me because they are part of my soul," Miriam said. "I am individualized, but I am also part of everything else. You might say I have the names of everybody available to me if I choose; however, they're not names to me as you know them in your human form. Instead, I see and know them as energies and frequencies. It's not easy to connect in this way, but it can be done—intention, belief systems, and energy have a great deal to do with it."

Then Miriam augmented her last analogy with another one.

"Imagine your computer and all the information saved on it. You gave it a name as most people do when they first initiate the setup. So now, think of the computer as individualized with a name, but it also has a significant amount of content you can access whenever you choose. You might consider the data stored there as inactive, but it is easily accessible whenever you think of it or push a button to retrieve a file. You can see the name you've given your laptop as the soul but don't think about all the data stored on it as dormant. Rather, the information is always alive and active, so it's far more than data just stored in a hard drive or RAM. Also, all this information *has consciousness,* so you don't have to press a button to access it. In this context, you simply think about it, and it's accessible to you. This is really who you are as a soul."

I only need to think about a situation or person, and they come to me because they are a part of my soul. I am individualized, but I am also part of everything else.

Soon Yeshua's energy was back, and although Rochelle was having a hard time keeping up with the shifts in energy she could feel and sense, she tried to accept that perhaps it didn't matter, for the seamless flowing of energies seemed to be part of the teaching. If she didn't worry about keeping up and stayed in the present moment of the unfolding miracle, she could simply marvel at the flow and the distinctive energies. Yeshua's energy tended to be softer, and he spoke more slowly, whereas Miriam's energy often came through like a spark of fire ready to blaze across the room. Once she was done with the room, it felt as if she'd take on the house, the country, then the planet, and finally the universe itself.

"As your light within your soul changes, so do the guides surrounding you as well," he said. "Because you are not one energy of a soul but numerous energies within one soul, you can tap into and *become* your Authentic Self. Put another way, a spectrum of energies within your soul will become enlivened and ignited again like we are doing with you now. Imagine the immense power you can tap into when you realize you can access the collective unified field of consciousness any time you choose."

Rochelle had to know so she asked him, "Are you part of my soul?"

"I am part of your soul, yes, but I am also part of all souls," Yeshua replied. "You are all interconnected and part of each other *if you choose* to be; you just think you're separate, but we'll get to this perspective in time. You have a brain with trillions of neural connections, and all these synaptic connections are lighting up simultaneously to create a new experience or you could say, an action. That's what we are—those myriad neural networks creating new experiences or actions, and you and Angelo are allowing us to do it.

"You are a living entity, so don't think of yourself as just a computer because you haven't been programmed like one—you have free choice. Then again, human beings are creating computers, programs, and robots that will become self-realized. You're nearly there now. The question is this: Will that computer program acquire a soul?

"More importantly, will it have a consciousness that matches a human one?" Rochelle asked, thinking of the latest developments in artificial intelligence (AI).

"Imagine living spacecrafts that interact with occupants of a ship, an interaction which allows them to travel through time and space instantaneously," he responded. "They're here one moment, and then they're gone. This is the true essence of who you are as human beings. You're starting to see science and spirituality merge again, which translates to this: If you can imagine it and dream it, you will become it."

It made Rochelle think of all the empowering voices she had read over the years, many of whom remind us that traditions across cultures married science and spirituality in significant ways we have displaced in modern times. She loved one of Jean Houston's examples of the interconnectedness between realities when she spoke of the ancient Egyptians who danced between the Divine (theocentric) and Humanity (anthropocentric). She wrote:

> Man was a model of the universe, and the universe was a model of god. When he understood himself fully, he could also understand the universe: its laws of astronomy, astrology, proportion, mathematics, geography, measure, medicine, anatomy, rhythm, magic, art. All were linked in one dynamic scheme. One part could not be understood if separated from any other part.[2]

Rochelle was lost in thought and several minutes passed before he continued.

"Why do you need robots?" asked Yeshua. "One day, you will even outgrow your current science and no longer need ships or planes to travel. Robots are nothing more than an extension of your consciousness. It's not that you need them; rather, you're able to create extensions of yourselves because of what you can do as human beings. From this context, robots will simply become part of humanity."

If you can imagine
it and dream it,
you will become it.

Rochelle kept wondering who would believe she and Angelo had daily encounters with Miriam of Magdala and Yeshua of Nazareth not just about their lives over two thousand years ago, but also about the impact of AI, the nature of the human soul, and the existence of multidimensional realities.

As Rochelle breathed it all in, he began to speak again.

"Humanity thinks if they encounter a new race, it will automatically want to conquer them as if dominance and control would be the only motive. That is your perception and reality in this lifetime and this particular realm and dimension. Change your perception, and you change your vibration. Your own shifting is how you transform things and the consciousness of the All."

"There is no shortage of fear on this planet," Rochelle said. "We can become the consciousness we wish to see in others. We can radiate it through our words and actions."

"Yes, and by *being love*," Yeshua said.

"Do you know that we know everything?" he then asked, which suddenly felt out of context. "Not because we're omniscient, but because we can read all the timelines that can exist in a field of unlimited probabilities. We can access all the dimensions; we're actually part of all those dimensions right now. For example, there are infinite dimensions, and we can view those most pertinent to your reality, which is how we can affect situations and convey information to you."

Rochelle changed positions and looked down at her notes. She wondered how his reference to unlimited probabilities related to the idea of multiverses and parallel lives in other dimensions.

"If you were to slap my face, what would I do?" asked Yeshua, changing course again. "I obviously wouldn't want you to hit me; however, would I defend myself if you hit me? No, I wouldn't because I'm a pacifist. This is one way I'm different from Angelo; however, I can work through his auric field to change his consciousness about this kind of situation as well. Old paradigms die over time because they no longer serve people. Your religions are dying too because they're antiquated and don't change. They must evolve if they are to have any life. Language evolution is an example of what needs to happen to religions. The conditions for speaking Latin changed with population and geographic expansion, and over time you saw Latin morph into new languages. Everything evolves."

Rochelle asked, "Violence and anger will move on too?"

"You can't live by fear for the entire life of an evolution as a species," he responded. "You must move on. If you live in fear, you will perish, so you must learn to live from and by love. Love was my message two thousand years ago, and it is still my message now. This was the message Miriam and the female apostles delivered when they moved from village to village, and my male apostles also shared this message as they traveled. This will always be my message regardless of what form I take in any dimensional realm. My teachings have always been the same—non-violence, peace, and love—because it works. You understand, don't you? These principles allow humanity to live in harmony and flourish."

Addressing Rochelle directly, Yeshua then delivered a poignant message: "Angelo will fight back since he was wired to fight in this lifetime but let him find the balance of masculine and feminine energies, and there, he will find himself, his true Authentic Self. You didn't think you would hear so much about and from me when Miriam first came through to speak to you, did you? And yet, I am sitting in front of you speaking through Angelo in your sitting room. I told you and Angelo there is no separation between Miriam and me, and no separation between you, Angelo, Miriam, and me as energy beings working through you and being in your auric field. These are the words of Yeshua."

In a few moments, Miriam returned.

Rochelle said to her, "Sometimes, I feel like I'm on another planet when you both come through to speak to us. We were talking about the soul's ability to have access to information that is always alive, active, and accessible. Then we moved into technology. And naturally we talked about fear, resistance and ultimately the need to evolve, but I'm still struggling with how our soul can tap into the vast power of the All."

"Let's expand on this," Miriam said. "We can merge and speak as one, but we can also individuate, which is what Angelo's soul does when we step back from his auric field. But that information and knowledge are always available to the soul, and as you just reflected, it's not stored but always active and alive, as is the data in the Akash."

Rochelle asked, "Don't you need permission to access information about someone else?" Hadn't she read about Akashic Records protocols somewhere in her travels?

Miriam's response was immediate and direct. "No, that is your concept, not ours," she replied. "But we won't go into it now. It's best to give ideas to you so you can learn little by little about the spiritual realm and how it works. We don't want to overwhelm you."

"It's too late for that," Rochelle said as she let out a light-hearted laugh.

"Perhaps we should return to the *we*," Miriam suggested.

"Ahhh yes, the soul as *we* . . ."

The Soul as We

"When I say I and when I say we, I have to use your language to speak as one, but I'm not one," Miriam said. "You will notice that Angelo fluctuates between saying we and I because I am showing him many as one. All your lifetimes are aggregated and make up your soul, and as we explained with the computer analogy, all your lifetimes are alive. I'll say this again: All your lifetimes are *alive* and a part of who you are. Now, this has many implications.

"All the positive lifetimes and all the negative lifetimes are alive within you at this time. This is what I mean: When you enter a *dark night* or a shadow period in your life, your Higher Self is becoming aware of itself and has awakened to the fact that you are many, not just one. This step of awakening is a terrifying event for the soul, and remember *you are the soul.* When you do what you call shadow work, you cannot eliminate your negative shadows; you can only rise above them.

"What does that truly mean? To rise above your shadows means focusing only on the positive aspects of all your lifetimes as an aggregate, which brings light to all the negative ones. As you likely know, this takes a lot of practice and patience. It means *not bringing attention to* what some see as karma, shadows, or traumas. Although they exist as part of an aggregate in your auric field, if you don't bring attention or give energy to them, they'll simply sink into the background and no longer drive your decisions or thinking.

You cannot eliminate
your negative shadows;
you can only rise
above them.

"Many times, Yeshua and I were both at risk of becoming ill and sick, especially when we went to heal those with infectious diseases like leprosy. We didn't believe our health was impermeable because we could manifest healing. Just because we became aware of our Authentic Selves—who you are at a soul level—didn't mean we thought we were above the common man. The idea was to show humanity each person could discover who they truly were and become their Authentic Self.

"If we lost our humility, we would have become like the religious orthodox who thought they deserved the power to control messages and through them, the masses. On your planet today, there are religious people and lightworkers who see themselves as more authoritative than they truly are and have lost their modesty as a result. Since your spiritual journey began, we've told you often to stay humble. When you lose your humility, you lose your Authentic Self.

"Yeshua didn't have to be crucified, and it was not something he chose. He didn't elect to martyr himself; he simply chose to stick by his values which stemmed from his belief he was one with Source and that we are all one with Source. Many Christians confused his rebellion with martyrdom; however, they are two separate things. Why do I tell you this?

"You have both embarked on a deeper spiritual path now and as such, you are stepping into and becoming your Authentic Selves. You are both starting to understand who you are at a soul level. And you are both starting to comprehend the complexities and rich texture the soul is made up of as well as the importance of sharing it with others, but this awareness doesn't mean you need to martyr yourselves. With a deeper understanding of your soul, you will no longer give in to the fear of karma and shadows dominating your lives. Without attention, energy and belief, the so-called karma and shadows can no longer *manifest.* Don't give these notions oxygen or merit. Without energy, they cannot exist. You see?"

"Yes," Rochelle said, "what you focus on is where your energy goes, which only strengthens those beliefs. Where your attention goes, or rather I should say, flows, is what ultimately becomes your reality."

"In each and every moment," Miriam added.

Rochelle thought of people who constantly complained and had a negative attitude about life. It was so draining being around them. Sometimes she wondered about those who intentionally wished ill on others.

As if reading her mind, Miriam said, "You're probably thinking: What about negative or darker energies that may want to toy with human beings and their emotions? The energies that are of the light call forth energies of light, and those who are dark energies call forth the energies of the dark. Like attracts like.

"You must change your mindset that some things are not of the light, not of Source, or that karma follows you, and you must pay back those debts. If you're going to be true teachers and healers of Spirit, then you must focus only on love and light since similar energies attract each other. As you know from your studies and personal experiences, it's how the natural laws of the universe work."

With a deeper understanding of your soul, you no longer give in to the fear of karma and shadows dominating your lives.

Rochelle had to ask, "So, have our souls worked with your souls in some capacity before?"

The question had to come up, didn't it? Rochelle thought. Why else would the souls of Miriam of Magdala and Yeshua of Nazareth keep popping into their home night after night to speak to them? They had even shown up when they were on airplanes, in hotel rooms, and at restaurants.

"Yes, but in other capacities," Miriam responded. "Both of your energies were in many of us, so let's use an analogy you can relate to about humanity and our souls. Think of our souls like incense, and each human being lights itself. Now, think of your body as the incense stick and the smoke coming from it as your soul. Where do you desire to go? Right now, you and Angelo are continuously burning yourselves, directing your energies into the energy-verse. The critical question is this: How do you desire to burn? What will you smell like? You see, human beings can choose to burn themselves slowly and judiciously in order to learn, experience, and give themselves to others."

"How are you experiencing both of our souls at this time?" Rochelle asked.

Miriam's response made Rochelle laugh. "Fascinating. Joyous. Enraptured in beauty and elegance."

"How are you sensing and experiencing that?" Rochelle added.

Miriam replied quickly but with a soft voice. "I hear it. Listen. I can see it through both of you. Observe. I can see it through the smoke. I see the colors. I can smell it. I can feel it. Through your human sensory systems, I can see, touch, and sense everything; what I am experiencing now is nothing short of divine. You and Angelo project a state of blissfulness; continue to live in this state so you can continue to do divine work."

Rochelle nodded as she breathed in Miriam's words, becoming one with them. A merging of their combined strands of hair and leaves on countless trees. A merging of incense smoke. Of multidimensional souls . . .

"Grain-by-grain, we are getting there with my journey. We are slowly building a mountain that will reach the sky and heavens. We cannot work through you unless you give yourself the gift of allowing us to do so. God does not furnish you with gifts—you do. Chaei'el, one of the female apostles, gave herself the gift of being a vessel to receive and transmit Yeshua's teachings in my lifetime. You will learn more about her in time.

"Chaei'el worked alone, but you joined forces. Do you see how your abilities are interactive and blend as one? We first come through you, Rochelle, and then into Angelo to speak—we work through both of you. Do you think Angelo could do this alone, Rochelle? Don't underestimate yourself. I'll say to all reading this: Don't underestimate yourselves, for you are all true creators of your being."

She certainly is a spark of fire who sets the world ablaze, thought Rochelle. That's truly who Miriam is and always was—a giant spark igniting everything she touched with the power of love. Even more astonishing, she/he/it/they continued to do it through others in this timeline and reality. Angelo's voice seemed to get gentler as Miriam went on.

Don't underestimate yourselves, for you are all true creators of your being.

"We told you the soul is made up of immeasurable frequencies. But there were more ancient ideas of the soul I will address briefly. It was believed that the soul was made up of the soul, the nous, and spirit. And these three aspects attach themselves to the physical body."

"The nous?" asked Rochelle, immediately thinking of the *we* pronoun in French, but hadn't she once read that Aristotle referred to the higher nous as the *immortal aspect of the soul*?[3] And didn't she also read about the nous somewhere in the Gnostic writings as well? Yes, it was in the *Gospel of Mary*. She needed to know more.

Miriam said, "It is part of your history; however, Yeshua and I will take you beyond these teachings. The nous refers to the mind in Greek but also where the seat of our intuition lies. You can see it as your divine heart and divine intellect combined. I simply convey this to you as it is mentioned in your Gnostic texts, and it was the language once used to attempt to make sense of such things at the time. This is largely why I share it with you now; however, you are ready to expand far beyond these ideas at this time in humanity's evolution. For example, ideas such as the soul having an infinite number of frequencies and inhabiting an infinite number of vibrations. A thread or aspect of your soul is inhabiting this vibration you call the earth, but there are multiple vibrations of the earth as well which we'll expand upon later."

Although the modern and developed description should have excited Rochelle more than the terminology from Gnostic texts, she wanted to hear more about the older references. The definition of the soul with only three aspects or components based in part on ancient concepts seemed a bit easier to process than an infinite number of frequencies on tons of earths, so Rochelle pulled out Jean-Yves LeLoup's version of *The Gospel of Mary Magdalene* from a nearby bookshelf, and she found the reference to nous from the index, flipped to page 31, and began to read aloud:

> . . . There where is the nous, lies the treasure. Then I said to him: "Lord, when someone meets you in a moment of vision, is it through the soul (psyche) that they see, or is it through the spirit (pneuma)?" The Teacher answered: "It is neither through the soul nor the spirit, but the nous between the two which sees the vision . . . "[4]

Then she flipped open *The Gnostic Bible* by Barnstone & Meyer and found the same passage in *The Gospel of Mary*, which she read aloud as well:

> I said to him, "Lord, how does a person see a vision, through the soul or through the spirit?" The savior answered, saying, "A person sees neither through the soul nor the spirit. The mind, which lives between the two, sees the vision . . . "[5]

Even though the language differed slightly, the concept remained the same.

"Yes," said Miriam. "It truly is divine. You see, the nous is a bit complicated to understand, and a number of your philosophers have attempted to explain it in multifarious ways, including as far back as Plato. You can see it as your divine ego if you like, a collaboration between the seat of your knowledge and the seat of your heart. It is also the seat of your intuitive abilities and your Authentic Self, which is why Yeshua said the treasure is with the *nous*."

Miriam then went deeper into the teachings.

"As we said earlier, upon the death of the physical body, the soul separates and goes back to Source. The soul is made up of endless frequencies and experiences, or to use the earlier analogy, many hairs on a head versus one individual hair, the one you experience in a particular life. This one strand of hair is recorded within the Akashic Records in the earth's crystalline grid."

Crystalline grid, mused Rochelle, wanting to hear more.

"We told you several times the conscious portion of your body is your perception of a physical body, the part you see as dying, but you don't really die—you live on as energy, specifically the memories and records of who you once were," Miriam continued. "You see, the soul continues on. When your soul separates from this body—and experience—it is only one of many because your soul is having multiple experiences. We have told you many times that the soul itself is made up of countless energies, not just one, and as a result, you can have numerous experiences simultaneously. We repeat it often so it sinks in. We also want you to better understand it. Now, we're telling you why it is."

Miriam decided to use another example.

"Remember when you both went to see how cigars were made in the Bronx?" she asked Rochelle. "The way cigars are made is complicated because so much goes into the process, and chemical reactions occur when you light one. Even though we have already used several analogies for the soul, you can also think of the soul as a cigar. It's much more complex than you think, and everything is alchemy when you think about it."

This cigar analogy made Rochelle laugh since she so wanted to understand alchemy from a spiritual perspective better, but being more of an artist than a scientist, it still felt beyond her grasp. It seemed as if Miriam and Yeshua were forever looking for new analogies to make it easier for them to process. She was not quite sure the cigar analogy made it any easier, but it brought a smile.

Everything is
alchemy when
you think about it.

"You know Rochelle, when Angelo brings my or Yeshua's energy forth, we give him projections of what we're going to say, in the form of sounds, pictures, and colors, all indicating what's going to be said beforehand," Miriam said. "It's often only a second beforehand although right now I am showing him nothing but a forest. With only isolated visuals, it makes it hard for him to comprehend since he doesn't know what will be said at this time."

Rochelle asked Miriam, "So, where does the information come from? I assume it's the Akashic Records?"

"Yes," she replied. "It's coming from the earth's Akashic Records and mine. When he lets go of the fear and doubt, then I can work through both of you more fluidly."

And with that, her energy dissipated, and Yeshua's energy didn't return. It appeared they were done for the evening.

After Miriam left, Angelo came out of his multidimensional state, and Rochelle asked him, "What did she mean about the forest?"

"Before they speak—think of it as a nano-second before they speak—they also show me pictures of everything as a way to convey the concepts and their meaning," Angelo responded. "I have to get out of the way, for if I don't, they won't be able to convey their message and story in a pure way. I must let them speak their truth without influencing any of it. I have no idea what they'll say next, but let her journey continue through us."

Rochelle felt peaceful, calm, and serene as she often did when Miriam's and Yeshua's energies were present. It's as if they raised them both up to their field of resonance, where the vibration of divine love worked on and through them, and their energies lingered for long after they left, almost like residue. She knew they could choose to have that vibration of love linger forever or for only a short window—human beings are always responsible for choosing their realities.

Both Rochelle and Angelo also realized they didn't have to plug into the vibration of negative shadows, traumas, and memories within their souls unless they chose to do so. It's a choice. It's *always* a choice. Our choice. She likened it to selecting a movie from the collective cloud's always-active data file. Do you choose one filled with violence, hate, and destruction or one filled with love, compassion, and oneness? Rochelle knew which file she would choose, just like Neo knew he had to take the red pill.

Human beings are forever manifesting, *buying into* what reality will show up in every moment of their day. Few realize their power, which is precisely what Miriam and Yeshua were trying to teach them. Rochelle and Angelo would try to live by example, by making decisions that harmonize, by selecting words to nurture others, by eating organic food, by choosing loving and supportive relationships, and by reading consciousness-expanding books not fear-feeding ones.

In all of these decisions that made up their daily lives, she and Angelo were beginning to see they were creating a ripple in the participatory universe around them. Miriam's and Yeshua's messages were quite simple when it came down to it: Choose the vibration of love, and know you are love. You are God. You are Universal Consciousness. You are one with the All.

How could humanity have gotten it so wrong for so long?

• • • • • •

PART III:

THE SOUL'S QUEST

CHAPTER 13

ON MOTHERHOOD

This otherworldly place where
great transformation happens
is the sacred space of birth.
—Britta Bushnell, Ph.D.

When Miriam next came for a visit, Rochelle sensed she was planning to change direction; however, it wasn't a new topic but a story about another soul—her daughter. Yeshua's daughter, Sa'rah. Before Miriam launched that chapter of her life, she recounted their arrival in what is now France.

"When we landed in southern Gaul, the main landmark was a group of islands across from the port," Miriam began. "There was a beach, but within a hundred meters inland lay an abundance of trees. Gaul was mostly forest back then, filled with small towns and villages where clans of people lived."

Rochelle pulled up an old map of Gaul to see if any light bulbs went off, but of course, when you're accessing information from the Akashic Records, she wondered how much a visual would matter. That said, how do you convey complex topics like thermodynamics, a language using symbols rather than letters, or aviation mechanics if the person you're communicating through has no knowledge or concept of it? In other words, if Angelo didn't know ancient Gaul, would he be able to convey precise details in Miriam's story? If no framework exists to translate the transmission into something meaningful, then maybe other words and visuals might be helpful. In this context, a map would surely be useful. Then again, she had no idea whether or not it was anything close to an accurate representation of that time.

Rochelle looked at the map and then shoved it under Angelo's eyes so Miriam could see it, or so she assumed. Most prominent were the islands across from the port town of what is now Marseille in France.

As Miriam recollected their arrival, the main images she gave Angelo were of trading. It was a major trading route where merchants brought items to sell and trade, especially spices. Nostalgically, she spoke of those early days.

"Approaching the bustling port of your present-day Marseille, I remember looking out at the sea, for it was my view for many weeks. Realizing I might not see it for a while, I breathed in the salty air, feeling it dance across my face. It was nearing dusk, and the dappled blue horizon began to change. Soon, the sky was laced with soft oranges, yellows, and muted pinks. The gulls sang. Everything felt alive at that moment. I knew we'd never look back, and a new chapter for all of us was about to begin. It was exhilarating and terrifying at the same time.

"With the sisters by my side, however, I felt safe and knew I could give birth in this foreign land with their help. Many women back then were instinctive midwives. Part of what I had absorbed from the Isis teachings was to assist women in any way possible and helping them birth children was simply part of it. All women who became shamans and healers learned to become midwives as well. It was a natural aspect of who we were in that environment, so I wasn't concerned about delivering the child. I also didn't worry since Yeshua's Merkabah visited us often after we landed. When he came, we would drink wine and break bread, and then we'd pray and meditate.

"Emboldened by visitations from Yeshua, we found solace and strength in our work. You see, he often appeared to me in my dreams, and we became the voices of Yeshua and his *Good News,* the gospel of the time. We started to teach others who would listen to us because we knew we wouldn't settle there permanently, yet it was a way to build relationships with people who lived near the port."

"Why not?" Rochelle asked. "Why not settle near the port, where there's plenty of trading, goods, and easy access to food?"

"We needed to continue for the same reason I come to you and Angelo—we were being guided by Yeshua to move forward," she replied. "We did our best to complete his mission, for he knew we would be more accepted further north with the Pagans. Nature and earth lovers, the Pagans lived in the forest and prayed to the land. They gave homage to the sky and the stars and connected with everything. You see, they sat outside around a fire under the stars at night, and the moon became both friend and guide. The moonlight was more luminous when it was full, and those who were one with the land became one with its mystery and magic, even if they didn't always have words to describe it.

"The Pagans felt an intrinsic oneness with the skies, stars, sun, and moon above them and the soil, roots, and herbs beneath them. At dawn, the forest rang with birdsong, the grass shined with dew, roosters roamed about on farms waking communities with their morning calls, and the leaves on the trees glowed in various shades of colors as the day marched on. Here amongst the forest, the Pagans would embrace us.

"But before we ventured further north, we spent time in the town now called Marseille. We taught and healed amongst the townspeople who gave us food and occasionally money. Locals saw us as your modern-day nuns, preachers, and healers."

Rochelle probed deeper. "What was your message?" she asked.

"Love, of course. Being one with the Father, one with Yeshua, and one with the divine feminine," came the response. "Not everyone could handle the message of the divine feminine, and those who couldn't, moved on.

"Many merchants came to this port to trade jewelry, food, furs, metals, spices, and materials. We decided to remain there for a while, even though it wasn't our final destination since I was well on my way in my pregnancy and had no more desire to travel. Still, we didn't stay there for Sa'rah's birth even though we had a place to stay in Marseille. When I was about three weeks away from giving birth, we moved to a new host in a smaller town a few miles outside Marseille. We didn't want to bring attention to the birth and knew it would be calmer away from the hectic commerce and trading center.

"The sisters traveled ahead to places where they knew we would be welcomed. The women would tell them I was pregnant and didn't want to give birth around the buzzing port. What you see as being impossible was possible for us. Some couldn't conceive of being eight months pregnant and walking a few miles to set up a temporary base in a stranger's home to give birth. Think about how people would respond to accepting outsiders into their homes today; however, it was much more common back then.

"Rochelle, you remember this from traveling through rural towns and villages in Africa, Europe, and Asia in your twenties, where random people invited you to stay in their homes, and you did. Your nomadic traveling for so many years prepared you to understand what I am telling you now. Given your experiences in this lifetime, being accepted by strangers doesn't sound as unusual to you as it might to those who grew up in a city or small town and feared traveling to unknown lands."

Miriam's reference to Rochelle's personal travel experiences brought back memories she hadn't thought of in quite a long time. It was true people would take her—a stranger—into their home, and it happened so often it became normal for her, something her friends couldn't fathom. Family members saw it as dangerous. Truth be told, she experienced it as enriching, stimulating, and expansive. She was humbled by such kind generosity during those gypsy years of her life. An adventurous soul, Rochelle jumped at any opportunity that moved her out of her comfort zone, from hitchhiking in the Middle East and riding on elephants through tall grassland in northern India to working on a greengage farm in New Zealand and driving from Cape Town to Malawi.

Looking at those days with renewed eyes, she could now see that perhaps her Higher Self had led the way although she would have never described it that way. If there was an opposite to her Higher Self, maybe it was the small self or the ego. She was sure it wasn't the latter making decisions in her youthful years as she explored foreign lands with enthusiasm, curiosity, and gratitude, and without fear, uncertainty, and doubt. Didn't she lead from her heart and trust in her intuition? Her visits to small villages around the globe—as Miriam and the sisters had done in ancient times—were about faith and trust, for both were necessary to travel this way. Rochelle chose not to focus on fear. Whether the quantum universe merely played out the sequence of events as the natural laws dictate, or whether she was simply lucky, no danger came to her. She was welcomed with love and generosity time and time again.

Sure, her college years were inspiring; however, she always felt they were a poor substitute for embodying life experiences. Angelo's time living in Europe and learning languages also expanded his awareness and understanding of the world in ways no textbook ever could. Their travel adventures shaped their belief systems. If it weren't for those experiences, she wondered whether either of them would be drawn to books on philosophy, science, and esoteric studies today or would have surrendered to nearly daily encounters with two souls who walked the land of ancient Judea over two thousand years ago.

Miriam and Yeshua seemed to know how to pull at both of their heartstrings, and Rochelle usually saw a purpose in their choices, but not always. Sometimes it appeared that it was to move them both into a higher vibration of love or as HeartMath speaks of, heart coherence,[1] to receive their messages fully. Other times, it was simply to demonstrate no difference exists between Miriam and Yeshua and Rochelle and Angelo, or between them and the rest of humanity, for everyone and everything truly is interconnected. As they so often told them, each person has unique life experiences; however, each one also has access to other frequencies, vibrations, and wisdom that exist outside the construct of space and time. We are each an individual strand of divine expression making up a collection of frequencies. And the combination of all of our frequencies creates one symphonic dance, meshing, melding, and flowing in elegant harmony as one.

Seeing Rochelle's attention was elsewhere, Miriam pulled her back in so she could talk about her early days in Gaul shortly before Sa'rah's birth.

"When we arrived in the small town a few miles north of Marseille, I knew my delivery was close," Miriam continued. "Our hosts were a couple with a little girl, and they all witnessed her birth. The eight of us stayed in one room of the house, something you might not be able to imagine. You see, life was very simple for us. We slept together as sisters, which united us, and that closeness and proximity to each other made us family. We cried together and kissed each other goodnight. We looked into each other's eyes and could feel the love and divinity coming through us, creating a tight bond that only grew stronger over time.

"Remember, we were accustomed to sleeping on the floor as we didn't have mattresses as you do in modern times. We'd sleep on things filled with hay, grass, and sheep's wool. Basmat, one of the sisters, suffered from nightmares, so we had to comfort her often. As a little girl, she witnessed gruesome scenes of Roman cruelty, including situations where children were killed, and innocent men were tortured. The times and people were harsh, so death was always upon our minds.

"When it was time to give birth, a water bath was prepared for me to stand in and blood came down through me as part of the process. The umbilical cord is attached when the baby comes into the water and this was seen as a purification ceremony for us. Remember, when the baby is inside of you, it receives oxygen through the mother's umbilical cord. When the baby is passed through the womb and vagina into the water, it is a natural and gentle process, with the child moving from the waters of the womb to the warm waters of the bath, and that's how Sa'rah was born—in water. We baptized her with the Holy Spirit."

"Were all of the sisters in the room with you?" Rochelle asked.

"Yes," she replied, "and the couple was there as well. It was an easy birth, and everyone was around me to assist. The couple who gave us their home never forgot this birth. You see, when you offer your home to others, you never know what's going to happen, do you? When you give from your heart, as they did, experiences transform how you look at the world, which occurred for all of us.

"Even more remarkable, my Isha was there as well. During the birth, he spoke through Chaei'el, and it was exquisite. If you could see a real wonder, then this was it. Imagine seeing divine light around all of us as I gave birth to Sa'rah. His presence was truly a miracle."

As the story came forth, tears poured out of Angelo's eyes. Somehow Miriam was able to revisit the experience and emotions accompanying them through Angelo's auric field and through the humanness she felt from this visit to the earth dimension.

"We all took turns holding Sa'rah, swaddling her and praising her as mothers naturally do," she went on. "Consider that she had eight mothers to care for her, not just one. Don't you have an African proverb that says: 'It takes a village to raise a child?' This was certainly the case for Sa'rah. It would be the only birth I would experience in my lifetime, so it was a significant event for me. You understand, don't you?"

Before Rochelle had a chance to respond, Yeshua suddenly came through to speak. Although brief, his message was poignant, direct, and emotional.

"Through Chaei'el's auric field, I could convey messages and have a physical experience again in the way I can through you and Angelo," he said. "I could feel my child through Chaei'el. I could smell my baby. I could gaze into her eyes, and I did. I could touch her and see her. It was something I couldn't do in my spirit form."

Yeshua left, and Rochelle sat there on the floor in their sitting room, trying to process the magic of it all: Sa'rah's birth in a bubble of divine light and the ability of Miriam's and Yeshua's souls to convey the emotions of a story from two thousand years ago through a physical body in the twenty-first century. Short and sweet were Yeshua's words but also powerful, raw, and pure. It's hard to imagine, isn't it? How could she possibly explain this interdimensional and intertemporal experience to others? Miriam once again interrupted her thoughts to resume her story.

"Yeshua stayed for approximately an hour of your earth time after she was born. There was no Frankincense and no little drummer boy," she said. Miriam laughed through Angelo, which was a bit strange to witness since it didn't feel or sound like Angelo's laugh Rochelle knew so well.

"There were no three kings and no star of David, nor was there an explosion of a Supernova, but there was God. God was present in all of us during the birth of Sa'rah. Chaei'el could perceive when Yeshua was coming through even before he came so we would know in advance. You might say she was like the forecaster of the weather because she always announced his arrival. Her body often shook when Yeshua's energy came through. Her shaking could be likened to a Kundalini awakening, which manifests a little differently for everyone; however, in Chaei'el's case, her face would start to change, and then her body would shake, even illuminate, with his energy. She took on the energy of Yeshua similar to the way Angelo takes on the energy of Yeshua when his energy steps into Angelo's auric field—it comes through as pure love and nothing less."

Rochelle thought about her words "steps into Angelo's auric field" and wondered how Angelo was feeling at that moment.

"Perhaps you now understand why Yeshua decided to connect to us through one of our sisters," Miriam said. "I had to be a teacher, leader, and healer through him. We needed another who could bring him into our dimension so the sisters could see, experience, and witness it. It was also a way to demonstrate that others could do the same with faith and love, as Angelo and you do together today."

Rochelle asked, "Could the couple hosting you see Isha's Merkabah too?" She realized that she had used Yeshua's Indian name and sensed Miriam found it endearing.

"Yes," Miriam responded, "They could see it because they also had faith. Seeing him in spirit form gave them even more faith, a deep faith you cannot fully comprehend in modern times. Their faith was unshakable like the sisters and I had also come to have. You must have such unshakable faith that even the death of the human body doesn't scare you; this *seeing through faith* is why I always tell you and Angelo to let go of your fear. It's wonderful to watch it leave inch-by-inch over time.

"Basmat cut the cord during the birth since she was the most experienced amongst us in delivering babies. Cutting the cord was more difficult because we didn't have things like scissors, so we'd use a knife, which meant there was a lot more blood. Part of the cord was shoved back into me, and then it would slowly disintegrate through and out of me; that's how it was done in those days. What your body doesn't need, it releases in blood or waste. Basmat was serene and collected as she cut the cord, and the sisters kept plenty of warm water and towels nearby to clean the baby.

You must have such
unshakable faith that
even the death of
the human body
doesn't scare you.

"As was tradition back then, Sa'rah was put on my breasts after the birth so I could hold her, and then they wrapped blankets around both of us as mother and child together as one. This was done to keep the baby warm against the mother's body and continue the bond. As you likely know, the bond continues outside the womb, and there was never a separation, but this doesn't always happen at birth today, does it?"

Rochelle thought about how mechanical birthing had become in the West. While some hospitals have created home-like birthing rooms and encourage immediate breastfeeding as Miriam had done, c-sections have become much more common, and too often, they are done not out of necessity but convenience or to protect the hospital from possible complications of natural childbirth. Hopefully, as more women voice their truth in the world, they'll realize they have more choices about how to birth children.

"We ate, drank, and celebrated the birth of Sa'rah," Miriam recounted joyfully, "and Yeshua came forth to teach us. For one thing, he blessed the family for allowing us to give birth in their home. They were not a Jewish family but Pagans; however, they had heard stories about Yeshua and had faith in his messages."

Rochelle smiled as Miriam shared her memories of that emotional day.

"Sa'rah was an average size baby as we were not large people back then, and she was born with light blonde hair with dark streaks. She had brown eyes, like my own. After a while, her hair became light brown. Believe it or not, Yeshua's eyes were blue, and I say this because there were so many things history has gotten wrong about who he was, but his eye color is correct.

"She was quite an easy-going baby and suckled my breasts for an appropriate amount of time, even after the baby started speaking. Mother's milk provides nutrients to assist the baby's immune system. We gave milk from our breasts, and while some mothers still breastfeed today, it isn't universal. Breast milk contains natural immunities the baby needs for disease which is often a disruption in Gaia's divine plan. Human beings often interrupt that divine plan. I daresay this, but human beings are the cause of their own disruptions. You may certainly quote me on this one."

Rochelle loved her bold, provocative spirit and felt a stronger connection to her over time.

"I was never short of hands and help since all the sisters were there to assist, as was Yeshua," she continued. "Perhaps you're wondering: Could he really hold the baby in his Merkabah? No, he couldn't, but we could put her in his resonance field where he could feel her. And through Chaei'el and her senses, he could have a more direct experience of his daughter, like what Angelo gives us through his auric field right now."

Rochelle assented, squeezing Angelo's hand to let him know she was there with him.

"As women, we were as fierce as Amazons, physically and emotionally strong," emphasized Miriam. "We didn't rely on masculine energy back then—there was no need for it. We spoke of sexual encounters earlier. Does a woman need a man to please herself? Enough said. Simply put, we satisfied ourselves when we needed it. We were not lesbians in the way you think of in contemporary times; however, it was common for women to please themselves and other women. And it wasn't uncommon for men to take a male lover either.

"Although the Isis teachings started in the region of the world you now call Egypt, they were taught throughout ancient Judea and the Mediterranean as well. Truthfully, spiritual people were everywhere, and it was common to be connected to both the land and the sky during my time."

Rochelle asked, "How long did you stay with this family?"

It wasn't as if Rochelle wasn't curious to hear more about Miriam's views on sex, the women's encounters, and the Isis teachings, but she was also eager to learn where they would be heading when they left the coast and how they would be accepted.

"After the baby was born, we stayed for nearly two months, and then it was time to move on. You have no idea how resilient a baby can be, especially when so many are providing care. She was also in the resonance of Yeshua's love. You're both protected because you're in our field. We have spoken about staying in a higher vibration resonance field, for this strengthens your auric field, which is intricately connected to and impacts your immune system."

"Protected?" asked Rochelle.

"We're not suggesting you can't get sick or die; we're merely saying when you're in our vibrational pattern, it is less likely you'll contract a disease, and this is what it was like for Sa'rah," Miriam replied. "She was far less likely to succumb to a viral or bacterial infection, which was comforting since many children died young from infections and diseases.

"Even though you and Angelo tend to take a more holistic and natural approach to medicine, never deny science completely. We say this since science is progressing exponentially in potent ways, so ignoring it denies incredible advancements that can truly help people. However, many who work in traditional medicine have gotten lost because they only focus on science and not on their intuition or integrating modern medicine with holistic approaches. It doesn't have to be either/or, this or that; however, incorporating both into your life doesn't mean you shouldn't make smart choices. In other words, not all medicines are the same; not all vaccines are the same; not all procedures are the same; not all products are the same; not all food is the same; and not all water is the same.

"You know this already, but having discernment means drinking clean alkaline water, imbibing the highest quality wine, and eating the best quality food. Combine this great wisdom and smart judgment with keeping your body healthy through exercise and staying in the highest vibrational light, and you will find balance. Here, you will also find serenity and love. Good night dear souls, be well and love each other. Be of love and have no fear."

Angelo's head tilted back, and his hands started shaking as they often did when Miriam and Yeshua came through for a visit or when they went back to their realm.

When Angelo's individuated consciousness came back, he said, "Wow, she showed me something new tonight as they left. It's as if they're white lights on a Christmas tree, and then it's as if their lights dim and my light as Angelo gets brighter. It's more like they're dimming the auric field of who they are, and then strengthening and brightening my light or my soul. Their light is so bright that mine becomes softer when they're here, so it feels like I'm dimming or going offline, floating into the background, or to use their technology example, hanging out in the cloud. When their enormous light becomes dominant in my auric field and their consciousness takes over my individualized consciousness, I am still one with them, delivering their messages and visions."

Rochelle tried to imagine the melding of their four souls through the imagery of photons and other subatomic particles. The dance of one, then two, then three, and then four. Ultimately, that dance of four becomes the dance of the universe and then a solo performance or expression again. After our shared circle of human life, our souls continue to dance in oneness without end. We surrender to the nothingness in the void, or you could say the vastness of God's quantum soup.

They both knew it would take time and patience to fully process this new awareness and the shifts occurring. It was as if two or more realities were merging, and the multiverse was active and accessible to them whenever they called it forth. Perhaps humanity didn't need to take Morpheus' red pill to move into an expansive quantum reality—perhaps they just needed to wake up.

• • • • • •

CHAPTER 14

THE FEMALE APOSTLES REVEALED

Every great dream begins with a dreamer.
Always remember, you have within
you the strength, the patience and the
passion to reach for the stars
to change the world.
—Harriet Tubman

Rochelle could tell Miriam was excited to introduce Angelo and her to the female apostles, the ones the world had never heard about. It was clear Miriam was frustrated and angry that both holy and academic books omitted so many powerful women from history. The fact that Yeshua's female apostles were amongst those on the list was something she was adamant about fixing.

On a cloudy Saturday afternoon, Miriam announced it was time for Rochelle and Angelo to meet her sisters. She began in a way that surprised them.

"You know what my name Miriam means?" she asked Rochelle. "One who goes against the grain and is rebellious. Some who revere me today have an exalted image of who I was while others have a diminished one. Both images are wrong. I was neither a saint nor a small and meek woman who stood on the sidelines. I was a tall and loud woman who spoke my mind and did as I pleased. People like to paint me as a saint, but it's not who I was, so don't paint me with a halo around my head."

The fire, passion, directness, and resolve of Joan of Arc, thought Rochelle.

"Many books depict me in a way that elevates me into something I wasn't, just as so many did with Yeshua," she went on. "I don't come to you so you'll create a chapel for me, worship me or turn me into a Goddess, and I'm certainly not here to be made into a saint. I am here to give you my story, my truth, our truth. Those with ears will hear it, and those with eyes will see it. Those with brains will understand it, and those who deny my words will never know me."

Rochelle realized Miriam was using her name's meaning to counter the idea of worship that had replaced her long-time reputation as a repentant prostitute, but this idea equally distorts her real character.

"I share this clarity so you can understand what I represented in that lifetime," Miriam continued. "I will attempt to do the same for the seven female apostles who traveled with me.

"Although I was strong-headed and went against the grain, I also understood the need to work collectively to fulfill our purpose and mission: to disseminate Yeshua's teachings and build a community. The female apostles, whom I have also referred to as the sisters, were instrumental in carrying out our mission. They worked with me to build a community of followers who not only understood Yeshua's wisdom but began to teach it as well. And they also had names whose meanings echoed who they once were.

I am here to give you my story, my truth, our truth. Those with ears will hear it, and those with eyes will see it. Those with brains will understand it, and those who deny my words will never know me.

"You've been briefly introduced to Basmat, the most advanced midwife amongst us, who cut my cord at Sa'rah's birth, and we spoke about young Chaei'el, who acted as a vessel to bring Yeshua's messages to us as a group. My journey . . . "

Her voice trailed off as she waited for Angelo to shift into a deep meditative state with his eyes closed. When she began sharing the names of the female apostles, everything slowed down. It felt like hours before Miriam began to speak again. Usually, when Rochelle was taken into and through a dimensional shift, it felt like seconds to her but not today. Time seemed to move at a snail's pace. It was as if the image of Angelo before her turned into a slow-motion video replay.

As Miriam spoke and worked through Angelo, he began to draw letters in the air. They appeared to be shapes of some kind, perhaps Hebrew, since he was directed to write from right to left even though Angelo had no knowledge of Hebrew or Aramaic. Remember Hebrew as the world knows it today existed in an earlier form two thousand years ago, which made the experience even more amazing. This *air writing* took hours because her energy needed to match the frequency of that timeline with shapes of Hebrew letters, followed by letters of the Latin alphabet to aid Angelo in making sense of them in English and then use the linguistic connection to figure out the sounds of their names. Even with the Latin alphabet, Angelo and Rochelle struggled since neither of them was familiar with ancient names nor this period in history.

Gradually, the names came forth through Angelo, speaking and showing shapes one letter at a time. It was painfully slow, so much so they had to work on bringing through the names over several days. Between the spelling out of each name, Angelo seemed lost in another dimension; Miriam appeared to be showing him more shapes of Hebrew writing and Latin letters, none of which was an exact match to the names and their spellings from her time.

"Their names will be an approximation to simplify the process of receiving the names," she explained. "It will be far less complex than saying this name is Sumerian or old Hebrew and that name is Aramaic and so on. If you research, you may find variations of these names from regional dialects, or the name spellings may differ a bit. But this aspect is not what is most important with my sharing the seven sisters' names and their lives. Rather, the names will help create a better understanding of the diversity of who we were as a group. And that variety will demonstrate how we complemented each other and provide some insights into how our community grew, evolved, and continued the teachings of Yeshua.

"You know Rochelle, names are not random. As I said earlier, Miriam means someone who rebels, which is who I was back then. Rochelle, your name means rock, and Angelo's name means messenger, so names connect to the soul in some way."

Rochelle thought about their individual journeys as well as their path together. She always had to be a rock, even as a child, and Angelo certainly was a messenger in this lifetime. She was beginning to see they would both be strong and resilient and share messages with others as well.

"Earlier, I mentioned Basmat," Miriam continued. "A variation of her name might be Bassat, which means spicy or sweet-smelling. As befits her name, Basmat performed wonders with herbs and oils from nature. You might call her an alchemist, but she also incorporated teachings from the Isis group, which is where we met. Nevertheless, her true gift was in healing, using the purest ingredients from plants, flowers, and even bark from trees."

Rochelle was suddenly transported back to a misty forest, with cloud cover Gaul had during long winter months. She could even feel a cool breeze as she gazed through the thicket just after dawn, the sun pushing its way through the fog. Dew lay on leaves and there within the haze, she felt one with the trees, one with the land. In her mind's eye, she saw Basmat preparing oils and ointments from certain herbs to assist an old woman who needed healing. She could smell the wood of a fire as well as cinnamon, lavender, and other dried herbs. Rochelle could see and smell it all. Then, Miriam's commanding voice brought Rochelle back to her description of Basmat who used Gaia's plentiful flora.

"We went to this sister for healing remedies made from trees and plants growing in rich soil," Miriam continued. "In her late twenties, she was a powerful midwife, and I was thankful for her assistance with the birth of Sa'rah. She combined her alchemical skills with holistic nursing.

"Through Basmat, I met Chaei'el. I was drawn to her immediately because, like me, she came from a family of means but received no support from them except for her mother. She also received criticism for following her unconventional path rather than the dictates of her family."

"It seems as if this was the case for so many women," Rochelle said.

"It wasn't an easy time to embrace your intuitive skills, for our world was riddled with superstition and fear," Miriam said. "The more advanced your abilities were, the more you needed to hide them. Chaei'el was a bit complex because of her strong esoteric gifts. Perhaps only twenty-one years of age when we left Judea, she was highly psychic, even more so than myself despite all of the inner visions and messages I received from Yeshua. With such gifts, is it surprising that her name means God's voice or the voice of God?

"Similar to what you and Angelo do now, she could connect to Yeshua, but with her gift came a price. Except for her mother, her family didn't understand her abilities. Not unlike today, these skills were misunderstood, but even worse, they were shunned. If you weren't considered a prophet or holy man, you were seen as possessed or a sorceress, and if you could channel prophets or God, it was blasphemy, especially if you were a woman."

Rochelle nodded, for she understood and could feel the collective pain of all the sisters as Miriam's story unraveled.

"As a result of these realities, Chaei'el didn't express herself or bring Yeshua's soul through when she was in public; she only allowed the energy to flow through her to heal others or convey a message. As someone who could be seen as possessed, she had to maintain her composure and learn how to ground all the energies desiring to connect through her. Chaei'el was simply a vessel for Yeshua to bring messages of divine love, but this idea wasn't something people could relate to or accept over two thousand years ago.

"As Yeshua's Merkabah showed up during our private gatherings, her demeanor would change. She glowed with the radiance of Yeshua we could both see and feel. Chaei'el allowed Yeshua to come directly into her auric field, something she practiced every day, especially early on."

"It sounds like she had the most difficult time of all the sisters," Rochelle chimed in.

"Yes, she did," Miriam replied, "but fortunately, she was surrounded by support which made it easier. Sometimes you have to look at your unique abilities not as a curse, but as divine gifts given to you by yourself; however, it took her many years to realize her soul had both received and chosen these innate skills. Ultimately, bringing Yeshua through in the way Chaei'el did was a gift and a curse simultaneously, similar to what is occurring today in my work with you and Angelo.

"Do you think everything you're writing down will be believed or accepted by others?" Miriam asked her. "Simply focus on love as we did to overcome the ignorance of those who don't believe that connecting to and communicating with another dimension is possible. This is why you're both here . . . to shine light upon ignorance. And light is love. Gandhi knew this, as did other spiritual masters in history."

As Rochelle's eyes widened, Miriam expounded on her message.

"Shining our light in the world manifests in multiple ways. The contributions of Meyra, whose name means *giving light*, illustrate how the seemingly humblest work can also shine brightly. A generous soul, she volunteered to do whatever was necessary for the group's well-being. If someone needed to be cared for, if food needed to be made, if clothes needed to be mended, if our space needed to be cleaned, she stepped in and helped. The rest of us either didn't have the time or energy for these necessary chores, so it was useful to have a younger sister around who exuded that lively enthusiasm.

Simply focus on love as we did to overcome the ignorance of those who don't believe that connecting to and communicating with another dimension is possible.

"Meyra was both giving and innocent in her ways, but her generosity and innocence drew us to want to take care of her. Isn't there always a pleaser and giver amongst every group willing to do what it takes to bring a cause forward? One with pure ears and eyes but who supports everyone else?"

Rochelle smiled, thinking of all the Meyra personalities she had encountered in her own life.

"She was not only the quietest and youngest amongst us but the smallest as well," Miriam went on. "You might say she was a child to us since she was perhaps only sixteen when we left our homeland. While she handled many of our chores, the sisters took turns looking after and guiding her. Remember women had to grow up quickly back then, and it wasn't uncommon even in your grandmother's generation to give birth at seventeen or eighteen years old.

"Meyra's softhearted innocence contrasted with the playfulness and free-spirited Ruthu'ah. Already in her mid-twenties when we landed in Gaul, her curious and carefree temperament was endearing. More of a gypsy soul, you'd likely see her as a hippie in your current day. Her vivacious personality lit up every room she entered. If there is an archetype for her, it would be a blend of entertainer, actress, gossiper, and storyteller. She had zest and loved to tempt men and let's just say that they easily fell for her charm."

This made Rochelle laugh and she longed to meet Ruthu'ah in person.

"When the air amongst us became too serious, Ruthu'ah began to sing a song to brighten the mood," Miriam added. "If someone was depressed, she'd dance or tell a story to cheer them up. Ruthu'ah is an ancient name, but your modern-day Ruth, meaning companion or compassionate friend, stems from it. Ruthu'ah fulfilled these meanings by raising our spirits when we most needed it.

"As a tutor and mentor, Ruthu'ah was very strict about her meditations and prayers, a habit she extended to those who became part of our community. Ruthu'ah ensured they learned Yeshua's wisdom and all the techniques, meditations, and prayers from the Isis teachings. Knowing our students well, she recommended when they would elevate to the next level. Befitting her joie-de-vivre, when students moved forward, she always hosted a fiesta or party for them. In building a community, it's important to have someone who not only can be serious about the teachings but can also lighten the ambiance when times get tough. Over the years, Ruthu'ah transformed into a Goddess who radiated her light, as all the sisters had.

"Despite Ruthu'ah's bubbly presence, perhaps the most striking, larger-than-life personality belonged to Shallu'ah. One of the things that made her so unique amongst us was the lightness of her hair and skin. Her eyes were a piercing green, and her skin was so light you might think she was from the northern Europe of today rather than the Judea we had left. The oldest amongst us, perhaps almost thirty by the time we landed in Gaul, she was also stocky, tall, and muscular. In today's world, you'd call her an athletic type. When I wasn't around, she took on the role of defending the sisters, and since she was tough, she stood up to men, spoke her mind, and sometimes even used harsh words if a situation called for it."

"I could use a few women like her in my life," Rochelle said, smiling as she marveled at Shallu'ah's resilience and perseverance during a tenuous time in history.

"Strong and opinionated was how she showed up in the world, so she felt the need to protect all of us," Miriam continued. "With her build, she had no difficulty lifting heavy objects and prided herself on her strength, especially since we had to carry buckets of water and wood. Well-read, her intelligence made men uncomfortable because she could argue with the best of them. Full of vitality and drive, Shallu'ah wouldn't allow anyone to quit. She'd pick you up and put you back on your path if you lost your way. When people were crying, she held them tight, enveloping them as your modern-day Amma does."

Rochelle thought about the time she met Amma, feeling her embrace, her love, and her resolve.

"Do you see in Shallu'ah the dichotomy of both the warrior and the lover, flowing together as one to become a warrior of love?" Miriam asked her, not waiting for a response. "Her hair grayed first; however, she wore it as a privilege amongst us. She may have had big hands and feet, but her heart was even bigger.

"Shallu'ah was biased toward the female sex, although today, you would call her bi-sexual because she didn't exclude men. Your contemporary labels for sexual orientation tend to divide and exclude, and yet as energy beings, it is more natural than you have been conditioned to believe to enjoy physical pleasure with both sexes. Some of you know, accept, and embrace it, whereas others either hide from it, ignore it, or even condemn it. As these labels fade, you'll find more oneness in each other as we did as sisters back then."

In a sense, Rochelle thought, Shallu'ah's bisexuality mirrors the balance of the divine masculine and divine feminine central to their teachings.

"Who doesn't want a Shallu'ah amongst you who embraces love, truth, and wisdom as well as emotional and physical strength?" Miriam added.

"I couldn't agree more," Rochelle affirmed. Sensing Miriam wanted to move on, Rochelle didn't expand upon her thoughts even though she wanted to know more about Shallu'ah's past to better understand what shaped her.

"Almost the opposite of Shallu'ah, Sa'rah made just as large an impact albeit in a much quieter way," Miriam continued. "In her mid-twenties and another Isis sister, Sa'rah was as introspective as Shallu'ah was active and outward-looking. Although ever pensive, Sa'rah always had a smile on her face, which warmed my heart. Of course, it helped that she carried my favorite name, the one I had chosen for my daughter. The name's meaning, princess or noblewoman, emphasized the special light of her spirit."

"Like your own Sa'rah?" Rochelle asked.

"In some ways," Miriam replied. "The sister Sa'rah was a bit of what you'd call today a systematic thinker or even an analyst. In contrast to the healer Basmat, the industrious Meyra, the sprightly, outgoing Ruthu'ah, the vociferous Shallu'ah, and the inward mystic Chaei'el, Sa'rah was the thoughtful, analytical mechanic amongst us. Often reflective, even preoccupied, she was also grounded and tranquil, so it was a joy to be around her. She had the greatest amount of faith in our mission, largely because she could rationalize everything and think through any problem."

Sa'rah reminded Rochelle of her friend Celia who seemed to find a solution to any problem or issue. Not only did she find the perfect sink for their bathroom, but it was made with sustainable materials as well.

"Forever tinkering with things, it was this sister we all went to when broken things needed fixing," Miriam said. "She had the patience to figure things out when the rest of us didn't have the endurance or the gift. Sa'rah was also quite good with numbers and calculated distances for us when we walked to new villages.

"We also felt comfortable speaking to her about our emotions and feelings, but it was since she exuded authenticity and love without judgment, so people trusted her. Even if someone has a rational mind, is technical, and often in their head doesn't mean he can't be loving. It's important to remember this since artistic and creative people tend to show love differently than accountants, scientists, and engineers. When you and Angelo spent time in Asia, you saw love demonstrated in other ways than what you're accustomed to in the West. I add this here only to encourage you to consider people like Sa'rah in your own lives and view their acts of love with new eyes."

Rochelle thought about their travels to the East and how love was expressed in a more formal way than with Angelo's loud and passionate Italian relatives. Miriam moved on.

"Then there was Tirah who was an honorable and reliable container for our confidences. An impressive listener at only 25 years of age when we arrived in Gaul, she acted as a counselor of sorts, a bit like your modern-day sociologist or psychologist. Like Sa'rah, she had the patience to handle the sisters' problems and shared her insights selflessly. I too asked her opinions on certain issues.

"Except for Shallu'ah, we were all quite thin; however, Tirah was particularly slender and tall with long, dark brown, flowing hair, and glowing skin. Using a modern reference point, she had the features of a model, and we often marveled at her enticing eyes, smooth face, and high cheekbones."

Miriam's words transported Rochelle back in time, and the sisters felt as vivid and alive as her friends from her timeline and dimension. Had she once walked amongst them?

"As you can see, each woman had unique characteristics and skills, and we were all educated in that we could not just read and write but also speak more than one language," Miriam continued. "If you were part of the Isis teachings, as most of us were, you needed to be able to read and write in your first language and have some knowledge of Greek."

Rochelle imagined the women based on Miriam's descriptions, wondering what they wore and how they presented themselves. She could see them as priestesses performing rituals together as part of a daily practice and as mystical goddesses in Gaul's forests, breaking bread, and drinking wine with the Druids.

Miriam then shifted her focus to how they worked together as a group.

"My journey with the seven sisters was filled with adventure, joy, and hope. Using present-day parlance, you would call us a sorority. We kept nothing from each other and that bond kept us all safe and healthy. Since we each had unique gifts that contributed to the whole, we worked together as a unit, serving as protectors of one another.

"After Yeshua's physical body was no more, we all knew—both the male and female apostles—what we had to do: teach and heal. In today's language, you might call us spiritualists, evangelists, energy healers, sages, and mystics all wrapped up into one. The sisters and I shared our fears, wants, desires, hopes, and aspirations. Remember, we moved to a new country we knew nothing about and lived in an unfamiliar environment—very foreign compared to our homeland. As strong as our faith was, we had reservations. It helped that Yeshua came through every few nights to speak to us as a group, providing both hope and inspiration to empower us on our journey."

Rochelle nodded and smiled as she captured Miriam's words.

"Even though Yeshua couldn't eat or drink with us, he always blessed the food and wine," she reminisced. "The bread, lamb, and vegetables would all be blessed. We were on a holy mission, a mission to create, not destroy. Yeshua strengthened us in that mission with his ongoing blessings.

"My mother sent money to help us on our journey as did the male apostles, and we had other connections. Money flowed to us from several families so we could continue our work."

"But your father never supported you, did he?" Rochelle asked, knowing about his disapproval of her unconventional life.

"No, he did not," she responded quickly, "but women hid money that men brought home and sent it to us through trusted merchants who regularly traveled those routes. Sailors used messengers from ports they stopped at to trade goods, which is how letters were delivered and also how news of our teaching and healing spread from Judea to Gaul and beyond. We also sent messages to our brothers—the male apostles—through these merchants, sailors, and messengers."

"Your news made it to the male apostles?" Rochelle asked.

"Perhaps not all of our messages made it through, but some found their way to them eventually," Miriam replied. "Several of the apostles were indeed fishermen; however, others were more educated, and one was even a lawmaker. Back then, you could be a woodworker and carpenter and still be of high status in society because of your family's influence or learning. As I mentioned earlier, if you knew people in higher places and your religious connections aligned, it brought clout to you and the family. Your associations were highly valued since they could bring in wealth. In many ways, your society is similar today, especially in politics and business."

Miriam then changed course.

"This next part is hard for me to say because Angelo must let go," she stated matter-of-factly. "I will wait until Angelo gets completely out of the way so I can share something he will find hard to speak about; however, the difficulty exists only because of how conservative you have all become as a species about sex and relationships."

So true, thought Rochelle, especially in New England where they grew up. After a lengthy pause when it seemed Angelo had indeed gotten out of the way, Miriam moved on.

"Purification was part of our rituals, and although we couldn't bathe daily, we did what we could to cleanse our bodies. Since we were so close as sisters, not only did we share everything, but when we slept, we nestled up close together like children. It was a way for us to feel safe, provide each other comfort, and stay warm.

"We also practiced some of the Isis teachings, including physically pleasing each other. Today, you have labels for women who partner with the same sex, just as you have labels for men who do the same. We viewed sacred sex and relationship very differently than the modern-day buckets and silos you have created for sexual orientation. Just because you chose to please another woman physically didn't mean you wouldn't find a man physically desirable.

"Even though I have said this many times in numerous ways, it merits saying again: Most men didn't treat women with respect and sex was more about procreation than intimacy and connection. This aspect of our lives was an important reason why the Isis teachings and group were such a support for so many women. There, we felt safe and could be our free selves, sharing, learning, expressing, and connecting. There, we could receive sexual pleasure in a safe environment without being persecuted or wronged by a patriarchal society. And there, we had intimacy in a way most women didn't have with men if they were married and wouldn't have at all if they didn't have a partner. This practice may be hard for your contemporary minds to comprehend but pleasuring another woman was not uncommon back then, and the same was true with men who wished to be with men. They would, as we would, be private about it because it was not something any of our religions, governments, or those in power supported.

We viewed sacred sex and relationship very differently than the modern-day buckets and silos you have created for sexual orientation.

"We didn't feel we had a voice during those times, but we all felt the power of love within us. Feel the power within you and stand up for what you believe in, for this strength is what I represent. You are always in conflict at this time in your human evolution, so it will come your way even if you don't invoke it. Don't shy away from controversy.

"Who came before you and Angelo? Who were your teachers? Who were those who took risks before you? What did people say about them? From the 1930s to the 1980s—who were they? They were the hippies who believed in love and unity. They were the holistic healers who practiced at a time when it was only deemed pseudoscience. And they were the mystics and séance holders who paved the way for the spiritual movement. You are here because of them since they weren't afraid to bring messages forth and deliver them with courage. They made it easier for you so you cannot throw away the gifts which have been given to you."

And with that jam-packed exhortation, she was gone.

• • • • • •

CHAPTER 15

FROM VILLAGE TO VILLAGE

What is important in life is
life, and not the result of life.
—Johann Wolfgang von Goethe

Miriam seemed eager to share her life in the villages. It was plural because they took their time reaching what would ultimately become home. This recollection came when Rochelle and Angelo were staying in a family cottage in the Adirondacks, and the entire week had been dreary. And so, on one rainy afternoon, over a massive pot of Earl Grey tea, the story of Miriam's trek began. It wasn't a journey Rochelle and Angelo expected, but then again, it was difficult to imagine a day in the life of Miriam and the sisters over two thousand years ago in rural villages set amongst Gaul's trees and hills. Without electricity. Without plumbing. Without insulation. Without a lot of things that have made their lives comfortable. It seemed as if Miriam especially wanted Rochelle to not only understand what it was like for women but *feel* what it was like.

Rochelle brought her mug to her lips and bathed in the warmth of her tea and the solace it provided on that drizzly day. Although the skies were filled with cloud cover and the habitual birdsong was absent, their fireplace was blazing in the background and the stillness of the day was comforting. Rochelle settled deep into her coffee-colored yoga back chair as Miriam recounted the time she and the sisters ventured from village to village.

"When we landed, it was toward the latter part of the summer," she commenced. "The days were still warm and mild, but the evenings were cool. In southern Gaul at the time, we didn't feel the presence of the Romans, so if they had their grips on the area, we didn't notice. Over time, the Romans became fierce in their rule over people. The cruelty would stun you if you could see what many in our circles witnessed during those days."

"I suppose you were relieved not to be looking over your shoulder everywhere you went," Rochelle interjected.

"Yes, we were," Miriam replied. "Before we set off for the first village, a group of women and men who knew we were coming met us along the coast to discuss our journey."

"How did they know you were coming?" Rochelle asked.

"Word traveled we would be coming and, with us, the presence of Yeshua," came the response. "News spread—by boat, camel, and horseback—of our arrival, but we had to be discreet since we didn't want Roman authorities to hear about us or our teachings. Gaul was dominated by rural villages fending for themselves, so it was a safe area for us, and also the reason Yeshua guided us there. Trees were abundant, and houses were built into the hills and mountains, all of which contrasted sharply with our arid homeland. The further we traveled north, the colder it became, and we didn't have warm clothing."

Angelo's head went down, and his breathing got heavier. It was as if he was either viewing the Akashic Records with her or accessing a timeline to gather more information about what to convey next.

"In your lifetime, there's a new awakening, and things are shifting as you and Angelo are experiencing directly," she went on. "Although we had an era of awakening as well, it wasn't anything like what is occurring today. That said, hope was in the air, and Yeshua was that hope for many. We were there to spread the *Good News* if you like, that all could have paradise here, which brought comfort to those who could understand the message. We told people to believe in themselves as divine, but most people were too much into duality back then, so they couldn't comprehend such words. Today, such a message is possible.

"Am I not shaking your foundation right now by telling you I am not one soul, but many, and the same is true for you, Angelo, and every human being? You might say we did the same thing back then. We shook the foundation of their traditional beliefs because what we taught went beyond what they had ever heard or thought was possible. In your current day, we are shifting your thinking in other ways. Remember, you're not separate from any and all energies, and I don't just mean one giant God but everything around you—the trees, the fish, and even the Buddha on your front porch. You're connecting with all of it on a subatomic level.

"We needed people back then to understand they were part of one giant God, one system, but we obviously didn't use modern words like Source or consciousness. At a time when we were limited in how we could present the teachings, belief in Yeshua was a way to shift their views. We defaulted to *God the Father* since it was through the Father you would find salvation in a patriarchal society. And the presence of the Divine in a flesh-and-blood man also helped them believe they could be saved. Everyone was looking to be saved, not unlike today. The religious talk about the second coming of Christ, and the non-religious want to be rescued from their daily grind or from their ego, from traumas, from unhealthy scripts in their heads, or some such way."

"What about the unconventional thinkers who are open to updated understandings of spirituality and reality?" Rochelle asked, thinking of herself, Angelo and some of their friends.

"You are the visionaries and teachers of today who believe in non-duality and understand its implications," she replied. "You both understand oneness consciousness now, and others are incorporating it in their own unique ways. People should also start to view karma in a new light. Oftentimes, karma is seen as a wheel you're on and around you go, again and again. It is really a belief system of your own experience. In other words, karma is a perception because you give credence to it, and if you perceive it to be true, it *becomes* a truth for you. Karma is another pathway to higher consciousness, but don't get stuck on the wheel since it is merely a perception.

"Rather than choosing to embrace either spirituality or science, as has been the case for far too long, you should combine your spirituality and science once again, for they really are one. You see, what you share with others now is a modern version of what we taught in Judea with Yeshua and from village to village in Gaul long after his death."

Rochelle considered her own understanding of karma and the cross-cultural versions of it she had encountered. The idea of karma was certainly floating around during Yeshua's and Miriam's time, for it was noted in ancient Hindu texts in roughly 1500 BCE and found again later in other sources, including the Upanishads (c. 800-300 BCE).[1] In ancient Judea, karma was equated to sin; however, Yeshua said sin could be cleansed and forgiven with repentance.

In letting go of ego separation and becoming one with Source again, you were no longer subject to the consequences of sin or the karmic wheel.

Karma is another pathway
to higher consciousness, but
don't get stuck on the wheel
since it is merely a perception.

She also reflected on history, when science and spirituality were embraced by the same people until they weren't. But the "big divide" was all fairly recent in the long arc of history. A nuanced history would likely show a more complex relationship between science and faith, but a simplified picture of the divide started in the sixteenth and seventeenth centuries, at the height of the Renaissance. On one side, you had Galileo's scientific method and his support for Copernicus' heliocentrism, and on the other, the Church's geocentrism, or a belief that the earth was the center of our solar system. The division intensified in the middle of the nineteenth-century when Darwin's theory of evolution countered the Church's creationism. This was when the conflict expanded beyond church authority and a few scientists into the general populace. People on each side alienated the other; it was as if those who supported Darwinism were enemies of the church, and the religious faithful were enemies of science.[2]

Reflecting on the past made Rochelle think of Yeshua's words, "Everything evolves." How true, she thought. People and ideas evolve. Products and services evolve. Science and technology evolve. Even art and music evolve. Why shouldn't religion evolve?

Suddenly Miriam picked up her story, bringing Rochelle back to ancient Europe.

"The southern part of your modern France was not as you picture or have experienced it today," she went on. "Because it was primarily dense forest spread amongst mountains and filled with little towns, I needed to feel strong enough to travel as we knew the trip wouldn't be easy. After Sa'rah was around two months old, it was time to continue our itinerary northeast."

"Did you go on foot?" Rochelle asked.

"Of course, by foot," she said with an edge, suggesting there was no other way. "As directed by Isha, it would be quieter and safer further north in the mountains where the Druids and shamans of the time lived. Today, you might call these people light workers, medicine women, sages, mystics, and healers. You wouldn't find Roman legions in the mountains, for how many taxes could they collect in this sparsely populated and rough region compared to the busy towns and cities? It wasn't worth their time to trek into the mountains, so they stayed away from more remote rural areas.

"Sometimes our days were uneventful; other times we'd encounter surprises in the forest. Even though there were days when it felt like we were walking on autopilot, we couldn't afford to be complacent. One day, we might see wild boars and other animals, and then for several days, we'd engage with nothing at all but dirt, trees, grass, rocks, birds and sky. Given these conditions, it shouldn't be surprising to hear we needed help to navigate the terrain for parts of our journey. Sometimes we had people to lead us."

"How did you find the right people to assist you?" Rochelle asked.

"Many had heard of us through our teachings," she responded. "Word started to spread throughout the Mediterranean of a spiritual teacher who performed healings. The common languages of Greek and Latin facilitated that spread."

Rochelle was surprised by her answer. "Even in Gaul?" she asked.

"Yes, Greek and Latin were spoken," said Miriam. "There was no French as you know it today, nor did English exist, until it developed within Britain into what you might call Old English."

"What was your primary language?" Rochelle asked.

"Mostly Aramaic, Latin, and Coptic, the latter an Egyptian language but written using the Greek alphabet, and a common language spoken amongst Isis initiates and adepts," Miriam replied. "My knowledge of Coptic, Aramaic, an old form of Hebrew, and Latin was immensely helpful in our travels. It isn't uncommon for people who border another land to know the neighboring language, which was also the case back then. It was customary to speak two or three languages, four if you were studious and five if you were a scholar. If you pursued higher education, your studies were always in Greek. Remember, whoever was in power dictated the language that flourished. Latin was the preeminent language of power and Greek was the prominent language for education, including literature and philosophy.

"Some of the sisters could speak Greek and Latin and were able to write in Coptic. Despite the fact we didn't know Gaul's language or dialect, locals also spoke Greek and Latin which helped us integrate. We could communicate what was necessary to get by, especially in towns with merchants. They typically spoke at least three languages—how do you think they managed trading and commerce? The more languages and cultures you knew, the better you would fare, and the merchants knew this advantage, of course.

It was customary to speak two or three languages, four if you were studious and five if you were a scholar.

"It is highly beneficial for us to tell our story through you and Angelo because you are both travelers, linguists, and culturalists—your diversity of knowledge and experience makes it easier for us to connect to and through you. We can only work with the knowledge you have, including language, so the more diverse and extensive your knowledge is, the more we have to work with as we try to convey messages with meaning and relevance to those we are communicating through in this realm."

Rochelle began to fidget, not because she was bored but because Miriam's last comment diverted her attention. Although it had become common for them to have lengthy visitations with both of them, she still found it astonishing that two ancient but not forgotten figures in history were telling such a profound story *through* them. Here they were on the front porch of an Adirondack cottage chatting with the souls of Miriam and Yeshua. Despite receiving deeper hints of why, they hadn't stopped asking themselves: Why them?

"We were lonely during this time too, similar to how many felt during the pandemic that hit your earth realm," Miriam continued. "The pandemic touched everyone around the world as people discovered they weren't untouchable. Something once affecting people in a remote country impacted every country and region, which ultimately brought you closer together. Some people who felt deep loneliness put the need for connection above common sense and physical safety. But I will say this about fear, especially around illness or death: do not turn to fear; if you become ill or die, you will always go back to Source. As above, so below. As below, so above. Once you lose your fear of death, you have so much at your disposal to navigate the world—it truly is very freeing.

"I bring this up because when we were traveling, we came across people with illnesses, including infectious ones like the pandemic you experienced in this lifetime. We spoke earlier of our connection to the Essenes. Even though we didn't agree with everything the Essenes taught us, purification and cleanliness were aspects we integrated into our work, especially when we worked amongst those with a disease."

"Was healing a bigger part of your work in Gaul, or was it teaching Yeshua's message?" Rochelle asked.

"We did both, of course; however, when you teach, are you not also healing people and vice versa?" she replied. "To return to my point, we combined faith with knowledge, but we also subscribed to common sense to keep our bodies protected as well. Times were more challenging for us, so focusing on survival was part of our lives, especially in the small villages where we had less access to things available in the wealthier towns and cities.

"All of the experiences with and teachings from the Essenes, the Isis movement, and Yeshua went with us as we walked from village to village. We weren't traveling far, but we took our time, building relationships and connections along the way since these communities would become followers of our teachings. While we kept practical hygienic practices along with faith, it was our trust in Yeshua who guided us to rely on the people we would meet. As a result, we didn't take many belongings with us and learned to restrict our physical possessions when we traveled. We would live by this motto: Take only what you need and let everything else be provided to you. Of course, that was easier said than done and we often went without dinner, but we didn't starve. People were kind and often provided for us."

Rochelle sat quietly sipping her tea, wondering what it was like to be a healer when there were no modern medicines, clinics or hospitals, and limited knowledge about severe illnesses and infections. During Miriam's time, many had leprosy, but later people had to deal with the bubonic plague, the Spanish flu, and others far worse than what she and Angelo had lived through.

"We made our way through these small villages that led further up into the mountains," Miriam resumed. "It was a slow journey because we wanted to establish rapport with others, but other factors included the weather and traveling with a baby. By then, we were moving into late fall and early winter, so the weather was getting even colder, something we weren't accustomed to in our homeland.

"Locals took us in when we stopped for more extended periods; however, lodging was quite basic compared to today's standards. People didn't have guest rooms or beds, so we slept on the floor in their homes. Where did we go to the bathroom? Outside. We would bathe in rivers or with buckets of water from wells, not as you do now. We couldn't maintain the same purification as we did with Yeshua either; given our circumstances, we could only bathe every few days, which was much more customary. We also didn't have towels as you're accustomed to, but we used a cloth to dry ourselves.

"Everyone lived this way because it was what we had available. Word passed from village to village about seven women traveling with Miriam's and Yeshua's baby and people asked those who lived there to give us food and shelter. Many felt they would be blessed by taking us in, providing provisions, and caring for us. This is not written down in your Bible, the Gospels, or the Coptic writings."

Rochelle asked, "Since you were educated, why didn't you write?"

"I did," Miriam said. "I wrote on thin pieces of papyrus—it's like paper but thinner; unfortunately, it disintegrates easily."

"If that's true, how did what we now refer to as the Gnostic Gospels last so long?" Rochelle asked.

"They were placed underground in jars and caves so they would endure," she replied.

"Were any of your writings saved in a similar way?" Rochelle asked. "What about the *Gospel of Mary*?"

The energy through Angelo changed, and a sense of sadness came through when she responded.

"My gospel? My words? Most of it was destroyed."

"But what about the little that has been found?" Rochelle prodded.

"Very little of my story survived, and what did survive was dictated by me," said Miriam. "During our travels, our greatest need was not to write but to survive. Reading and writing were privileges for those who had leisure time, something we didn't have, especially when we were on the move. For us, our priority was survival. Before we left for Gaul, some of the female apostles would scribe what I learned from Yeshua since all of the women in our group could read and write. The men wouldn't scribe what women said because it was of no significance to them.

"It's important to remember most of the male apostles didn't support or believe much of what I said, although Thomas was an exception. Thomas, a gentle and kind man with a great deal of faith, was more of a brother to me, and we shared a kinship I didn't have with the others. You might call him an empath today as he had a sensitive side and expressed his emotions. He was a great support to me."

Even though Rochelle was curious to hear more about Thomas, Miriam seemed eager to continue her account of their nomadic life in those early days.

"As we made our way northeast, we spent enough time in each village to get to know people and establish ourselves," she went on. "Building community and trust in others where we planned to live for the rest of our lives was essential. We needed to understand the language, the food, and the customs as well as prepare for the changing of the seasons, all of which were new for us. We also needed to learn how to gather food, which roads were safe, and which ones were dangerous. The multiple forests were filled with animals, so we had to be careful when traveling, especially by foot.

"The people in this part of the world were primarily Pagans, not Jewish, and most believed in multiple deities. Many didn't adhere to the Greek and Roman deities as they had their own gods and goddesses that supported their strong connection to nature.

"With much more rain than we were accustomed to in Judea, we weren't exposed to as much sun as we once had either, and as a result, our skin became lighter over time. The people we met in the villages were caring, considerate, and thoughtful. Although they were superstitious in many ways, they didn't try to force their beliefs and customs upon us; instead, many would integrate the teachings we brought to them from Yeshua. They simply saw Yeshua as a great shaman, one they had heard could perform healings, as was typical for shamans then.

"Modern-day India has many of the same healing practices. Remember even in Judea, not everyone was Jewish. Each culture, including those from Sumeria and Egypt—the most prominent during our time—had its own unique way of healing. In many cases, they combined natural forces with supernatural forces.

"You and Angelo don't even realize how much you heal others through our energy. You might say you are combining the supernatural with what you call natural—your science and alternative medicine—to heal others. During our time, we used herbs, flowers, roots, and bark. We would grind antler cartilage and plants from the forest to create herbal concoctions. Your natural, alternative medicine, and conventional Western medicine have both come a long way, so you should embrace them both, not choose one over the other. In other words, learn how to combine both disciplines and practices in an integrated and healthy way. We were not purists or narrow in our teachings. Back then, I combined my knowledge from the Isis teachings with Yeshua's teachings; some would accept this combination, and some wouldn't. We didn't force our message on the Pagans in the area, most of whom were Druids, and they didn't force their way of life upon us."

They simply saw Yeshua
as a great shaman,
one they had heard
could perform healings.

Rochelle asked her, "What did you do in the villages during all those months? What was your daily life like?"

She appeared to go into the Akashic Records for five minutes or more. Was she diving into that timeline to access the visuals and other memories more vividly? A long pause followed as if she was trying to determine how she could communicate a narrative through Angelo in a way that made sense to their modern ears. Eventually, Miriam picked up her story again.

"I mentioned earlier people saw us as nuns even though this wasn't the terminology then. It was mainly because people saw us as bringing messages of and from God to them, but we were more like nurses and spiritual teachers. We offered our services in exchange for free lodging, and occasionally people gave us a little money for our teaching and healing as well. Funds were essential for us to continue our journey; however, we often didn't get paid at all. Nevertheless, we always had shelter and comfort as we made our way through the region.

"When we stopped to live in a village for a while, we became part of their society, so they began to trust us. We might stay in a southern Gaul village for three to four months or so and then move on to another one. It was a great way to connect to each community, as we knew this would be important later in our work after the teachings grew and spread.

"Sa'rah became multilingual and multicultural because of our nomadic way of life. She spoke the Gaulish languages and Latin, and she understood the language I spoke best: Aramaic. Remember the more languages you spoke, the better it was for commerce and making connections, so I wanted Sa'rah to grow up with that kind of knowledge and, I might add, privilege. I wanted her to live a life without hardship.

"Whenever we arrived in a new village, we split up as a group because the houses were relatively small. Typically, two of the sisters went to one home. Naturally, I was always with Sa'rah, but all of us spent much time together and became a closeknit family. The nine of us (counting Sa'rah) gathered once a week to break bread and drink wine together. Yeshua came to us in his Merkabah during those special gatherings."

Rochelle asked, "How long did his Merkabah last? Or perhaps I should ask, how long was it able to appear to you in a form you could see in this realm?"

Miriam stopped speaking while she searched for what to say and how to say it.

"It wouldn't be accurate to say his Merkabah didn't last because time had passed since it could stay for an infinite amount of time; however, the necessity for his apparition in energy form grew less and less for all of us over time," she explained. "He wasn't the same Yeshua, the same Isha I knew. He appeared to me only in spirit form, so the emotional attachment wasn't the same way as it had been, and we all knew we had work to do. We needed to move forward and be as strong as he had been, teaching what he taught us but in our own unique ways.

"Yeshua could experience human emotions when he came through Chaei'el, very similar to what we can both do now through you and Angelo. It is hard to explain how this works in a way that makes sense to your linear ways of understanding the world, but I will try my best. As I bring these messages through your auric fields now, I am Miriam of Magdala, and I'm not. I am the energy of who that being once was in human form; however, I am not precisely the same as I was through the body of Miriam of Magdala.

"You see, I can't have the same human essence as I did two thousand years ago because I am coming through a different host with a different DNA than what I once had in my human form, so it's never going to be exact. This is why there are variances of styles and messages through what some call channelers today. However, since you allow us to take hold of your auric field in a more integrated way, we can see, hear, taste, touch, and feel through you both, a unique phenomenon. For me to return precisely as I once was, the host must let go of everything."

"Everything?" asked Rochelle, unsure what she meant.

"A complete surrendering, very similar to what you refer to as avatars today, although it's quite unique in your case since I come through you sometimes as an individualized energy and sometimes as the All."

Rochelle tried to grasp what Miriam was saying. She knew what Miriam meant by the avatar state. In Sanskrit, the word means descent; however, Rochelle remembered reading about avatars in Yogananda's autobiography and then later in texts related to him: "Paramhansa Yogananda explained that the term *avatar* refers to a soul who has been freed from maya (delusion) and is sent by the will of God back into manifested existence to help others."[3]

"Over time, the more you connect to Yeshua and me, the closer you become to the true essences and energies of who we once were when we were physical beings as Miriam and Yeshua," Miriam said. "This explanation is perhaps the best way for you to understand it in your modern human form."

The energy shifted and Yeshua came through to speak.

"There is no separation between Miriam and me, and there is no separation between Miriam, myself, Angelo, and you," said Yeshua. "As I have told you countless times and in various ways, there is no separation between both of you and both of us. I repeat it often because I want you to comprehend its importance. Do you understand?" he asked. "You are as much a part of us as we are a part of you. You are also Jewish."

She was baffled by the last comment. "Not in this lifetime," she piped in since neither she nor Angelo had been raised Jewish, but Yeshua moved on without skipping a beat.

"Why do you think you connect to the Kabbalah, have lived on a kibbutz, and relate to so many Jewish traditions?" he asked Rochelle. "You are both Jewish in this lifetime, but you just don't know it."

Silence followed as if he wanted her to reflect on what he had just said. It didn't take long to see the connections. The truth is that Rochelle always felt familiar with Judaic traditions and living on a kibbutz in Israel had to count for something. She resonated with Jewish culture and often found herself at social and business gatherings where she was the only gentile in the room, and yet she never felt like an outlier.

She knew Angelo felt a similar connection because he had worked in several Jewish synagogues and community centers and always felt at home. Yet, they had many childhood roots in Catholicism and various Christian religious beliefs. What didn't they know or understand about their upbringing and the pull toward other beliefs? she wondered to herself.

Yeshua began to speak again, this time with questions.

"Are you prepared for the inquiries that will come your way?" Yeshua asked her. "Are you prepared for how people will react to you? How many people will doubt your words?"

What's with the questions? Rochelle thought. Was she being tested? Were they being tested? Although she always felt this incredible warmth and connection to Yeshua's energy, she also felt she was being asked to step into something greater, even if it didn't always make sense to her or Angelo. Then again, his indirect guidance resembled his parables of two thousand years ago, hard to decipher even by his closest apostles.

"When we come through and work on your energetic bodies, you could say we're igniting a spark in your auric fields to help you slowly remember who you are at a soul level. When this happens, your physical body moves into a healthier, more unified alignment, and you become more of who you truly are, or what Miriam often calls, the Authentic Self, the Authentic You. Some teachers refer to it as your True Self. Essentially, your field becomes enlivened, and there's more congruency and coherence, giving you broader and deeper access to all the knowledge and experience in your Akashic Records within the etheric template, where the Akashic data is accessible."

"Etheric template?" asked Rochelle.

"The etheric template is the template for the etheric body," he replied. "For example, when a modern-day medical intuitive receives information through one of their clairs, it is often through the etheric template, although few can actually see it. Within this template, one can often detect disease and illness, even before it manifests itself in the physical body."

Then Yeshua posed several more questions to Rochelle.

"Do you believe you can heal?

Do you believe you can turn water into wine?

Do you believe you can teach my words?

Do you believe you can teach the Gospel?"

At this point, Rochelle interrupted Yeshua and asked, "Why would I want to teach the Gospel or turn water into wine?"

Of course, she knew Angelo was curious about the alchemy of the latter, and he was also curious about levitation, but for her, his first question was the most compelling.

Within the etheric template,
one can often detect disease
and illness, even before it
manifests itself in
the physical body.

"You don't feel the energy shifts in your body as deeply as Angelo does, but it's for a reason," Yeshua responded. "How would you be able to stay grounded? You embody creatrix energy."

"Creatrix energy?" asked Rochelle. "Do you mean an energy connected to the feminine source of creative power?"

"You have manifested so much in your business and home because creatrix energy runs through you as it did for Miriam two thousand years ago and for so many women today," he replied. "This is why another sister brought my energy through her auric field, so Miriam could stay grounded, build the necessary community, and extend my teachings' reach.

"Angelo will lift and move things, but he doesn't create things—you do. The work you do together is a blend of masculine and feminine energy coming together in unison, which is the balance needed to heal. When I say heal, I don't mean it in the way modern people think of the word."

Yeshua went on to clarify.

"Healing comes in many forms. Yes, it can occur in your auric field which affects the physical body, but emotional trauma is directly connected to physical disease as well because everything is interconnected. The same applies to the earth, so what is out of equilibrium now will be restored by balancing feminine and masculine energy again to heal the planet. This is how the natural laws of the universe work. You understand this, don't you? This is Yeshua, and these are my words."

Rochelle began to feel a little dizzy as he spoke. What exactly was he saying? Were they now healers? She would sometimes feel woozy as if she was going through a dimensional shift when he was there for long periods. As the months progressed, she grew more accustomed to his energy, and rather than feeling knocked out, she began to feel energized, warmed, and filled with love. As Yeshua stepped back, Miriam came forward to speak again.

"In our villages, we didn't perform miracles per se since our main focus was on teaching what you might call the Gospel or the *Good News,* as we have mentioned many times; however, this message was nothing more than 'we are one with God.' Many continued to believe in Polytheism which was fine for us. If you realized you were part of one Source, you felt that divine presence within you. You'd understand that we are all interconnected and live your life that way.

"This story is about all of us; it's not just about me, and my story back then wasn't about me either—we were all family and supported each other. I know how hard this is for you and Angelo because we see how much sacrifice you're making in trying to comprehend all our visitations and messages from the moment you wake up until the time you go to bed. Being one with Spirit and entering multidimensional realities requires taking care of your temple. We are with you when you meditate and exercise, and when Angelo does his martial arts forms. You two represent the hard and the soft coming together again as one."

Why does she always toss us into the mix? Rochelle wondered. Were they trying to get them to teach and heal as they had? For what purpose? And if so, why the story of her journey? Did they both need to feel what she and Yeshua felt to understand who they were so many years ago?

"Since there was safety in numbers, we'd squat in small groups when we went to the bathroom outside," she continued. "Although it was a personal act, it also left you incredibly vulnerable, so it wasn't uncommon for us to squat together as women. You probably won't be surprised to hear we often menstruated around the same time as well. The cycles of our physical body became unified within our auric fields, and because we had each other, we didn't need to hide anywhere. We used rags, but physically our cycles were not as heavy, and they didn't last as long as they do today.

"We didn't have time to exercise in the way you do since we were constantly moving—every day included some form of physical labor. Everything had to be done manually, such as walking, carrying, cutting, and washing. Remember also these villages were tiny. In the center of the village, you could buy your materials and food, but people lived on the outskirts in the forests and on farms, so we always had to walk. Obviously, the closer you lived to the water, the larger the village, which is the case today as well."

"What did you do during your days?" Rochelle asked.

"We woke up naturally as there were no clocks," Miriam responded. "The sun woke us up at times, which changed with the seasons. Sa'rah always slept by my side as it was important to me. When we were in private, Yeshua would visit us. The rooms we were given were extremely small because they were all they could offer us, but it was enough space for bedding on the floor and perhaps a small low table for a candle.

"Of course, we didn't have modern beds, but we made a mattress of hay and straw raised off the floor to keep our bodies away from the vermin. The rooms were rather simple but so were our needs. I would sing to Sa'rah every morning; then each day's schedule would depend on what we wanted to accomplish in a given day. I wanted my daughter to learn about her father and what he stood for, so we didn't hide anything.

"There were plenty of cows, so we always had milk. Berries, grains, and fish were bountiful as well. We boiled grains to make what you might call porridge. Even though we were in the mountains, it wasn't far from the coast, so we could get spices from the merchants at the port. We ate eggs as there were chickens on every farm, and the climate in Gaul produced more meat and game than in Judea. More rain made the land much more fertile, so we also had access to a greater amount and diversity of fruits and vegetables. People dug holes in the ground to create cellars which we used to keep things cool, and we salted the food to preserve it.

"Animals were an integral part of our life. While I never killed the animals I ate, we taught Sa'rah that whenever you take the life of an animal, you must give it a prayer and thank it before you take its life. And, of course, there was always a way to make it kosher from our Jewish roots. We used more humane methods to kill animals, so they didn't suffer so much. I didn't always maintain my kosher practices; however, I kept my oneness with and respect for the food I ate, and so did the sisters. If the meat wasn't freshly killed the same day, we added spices and salt to keep it fresh. When we didn't have meat, we ate eggs, grains, nuts, berries, and bread. Bread and cakes were plentiful here which were less common in Judea. The foods changed the further north we ventured, dictated mainly by the climate and soil.

"During the days, we'd often go and teach children in the villages; other times, we would visit a community to cook, assist others, or heal. The sisters took turns, but some preferred spending time with the children in the villages. We'd always regroup for meals together."

"What was your favorite thing to do?" Rochelle asked her.

"Being with Sa'rah and sharing my knowledge, mostly about how to be of compassion and love," she replied with a tenderness in the voice. "Extremely smart, Sa'rah was a fast learner and easily absorbed knowledge everywhere we went. Like Yeshua, she was full of love and like me, she was a sponge for learning. I slowly integrated her into the Egyptian Isis teachings so she could understand our esoteric and mysterious ways."

Suddenly, Angelo's right hand lifted, and his fingers began to scribe in the air, somehow bringing them both to another timeline in the process. It appeared to be a pyramid followed by spirals, his hands mysteriously etching shapes and codes from an ancient land. They appeared incomprehensible and yet also seemed to spark a memory from long, long ago.

Mesmerized by the fluidity of his drawings, Rochelle felt transported, as if the unspoken shapes and codes he continued to draw carried them both beyond space and time. She lost all sense of her earthly surroundings as an etheric realm appeared. Images of temples, ancient baths, adorning robes, clay pots, gold shawls, and plates of fruit all floated past her. Isis and Thoth, the ancient god of wisdom, writing, the moon, science, art, and magic both appeared and acknowledged Rochelle. Had she and Angelo just traveled back in time through a portal, or were they somehow the portal just as much as Miriam and Yeshua were?

"You know us and we know you," Thoth said to her. That flare of recognition made Rochelle feel a sense of harmony and oneness with the present moment until logic interfered. As her rational mind appeared, she found it hard to accept the experience. She shook her head and shouted, "This can't be happening," and shortly, Rochelle became aware once again of familiar surroundings in their cottage. It was as if something as simple as an intention was the magic key to shift her from one world to another. She didn't understand how it happened, but she was well aware it was beyond the boundaries of rational thought and imagination.

Rochelle blinked several times before she became aware of Angelo's deep breathing and his body writhing on the floor as if he was carrying more energy than he could handle. After a few minutes, his body began to rest, and the tips of his fingers clutched the floor as if he were merging with it.

"Life was callous and simple at the same time, always fixated on what we needed to do in each emerging moment," Miriam continued, interrupting Rochelle's observation and experience. "Sometimes, an entire day would be spent washing our clothes. We didn't have to go to a river because we had wells, but it was still time-consuming as we had to do them all by hand. At other times, our days were filled with walking into town and buying provisions, but each trip always turned into an adventure and an opportunity to meet with others.

"In your contemporary world, you can wash your clothes, clean your car, go to the supermarket, exercise, and work at a job all in one day. Even when you're on your exercise machines, you can watch a movie or listen to an audiobook on your phone. Think of all the things you did today: You prepared food and worked while machines washed your dishes and clothes. These efficiencies were not available to us. When we washed our clothes, we would talk and laugh as we scrubbed the materials by hand. We were much more present than you are today, which is why it was easier to go somewhere and just sit. Sitting was one of the best luxuries because we could simply be present with nature around us while we meditated or prayed.

Life was callous
and simple at
the same time.

"Everyone in modern times wants to reach the summit, yet they don't want to put in the time and effort to reach it or be present on that journey. Back then, it was always about the journey because we understood its importance. We were also aware life was short, so we valued each and every moment and activity.

"Our days were basic, filled with one or two activities because it took so much longer to do an activity than it would today. Humanity is now trying to remember how to return to the simplicity of how we lived, away from the wheel you're spinning on every day—that's why people run off to retreats, go on vacations, join a gym, and try to slow down. Your pandemic forced humanity to slow down and become more present with each other. People don't give themselves time to be present, to be one with their breath and to be one with Spirit."

Miriam then drew a parallel to Rochelle's and Angelo's own lives as a way to clarify a spiritual path for her.

"Think back to when you and Angelo spent a month in Japan," she said to Rochelle. "What was a day like for a Shinto monk or priest? It was quite modest, wasn't it? They didn't do much, did they? You saw them sweep, clean, read, and write. In China, monks do the same. How do you choose to reach enlightenment? It all depends on you. Even warrior monks with all their emphasis on clearing the body so they can clear the mind, live a simple life. Connecting your spiritual and physical bodies together is vital as is genuinely understanding the balance between the two. Many people in Gaul lived with nature and integrated that oneness into their daily lives, so it was common to have altars for the Pagan gods and goddesses, and animals were everywhere. Cultures find different ways to create balance and connection, but all aim for unity at the deepest level.

"What you're doing now is learning new knowledge across cultures, traditions, religions, and belief systems. You've done the hardest part earlier in your lives, and unlike previous incarnations, you no longer need to get up at four in the morning to do laborious tasks simply to survive. It's important to be present so you can be one with Spirit and your auric field, not just your physical body. Meditation is nothing more than being present, and being present can come in many forms—you both already know this. You decide on your meditation and what works best for you and teach that flexibility to others. It's essential to slow down and sit with your breath each day, but you don't need to be a slave to it. And many paths are possible. What works for one person may not work for another. Embrace diversity and *feel into* the things that nurture and feed your soul.

"What do your memories tell you? What do you think? Are you not your own book of memories? The question is this: How do you want to reach the mountain's summit? What journey will you take? Will you head straight up the mountain or take a slower and more connected path? What foods will you eat, and what clothes will you wear along the way? Are you going to explore by yourself or with others?

It is different for everyone, and as we teach through you now, it's important to honor the unique way that best serves each person."

What do your memories tell you? What do you think? Are you not your own book of memories?

Then she pivoted back to life in the villages.

"Our lives were unsophisticated and unassuming. They wouldn't have made for a great movie since your modern movies love to include fighting, death, and turmoil, and our small villages didn't see much death except by natural causes. Our elders were not treated like pariahs but with love and respect, and we took care of one another. Staying close lent a feeling of kinship, and even with our disparities, we bonded together as a community."

"How large were the populations of the villages back then?" Rochelle asked.

"Maybe three or four hundred; however, that was quite large compared to some of the other smaller villages further north," Miriam replied. "In the bigger towns closer to the port, you would see some crime, primarily petty theft, although occasionally we had murder. It was in the larger towns where you'd find more Roman military and authorities since they were focused on accumulating a lot of money, a bit like many Americans have become today.

"Village life was nothing extraordinary, but what was precious was having time to sit and be present with one another. There were no soldiers following us. You see, with Yeshua's physical death, things became easier for us. Even though many had heard of us and what happened to Yeshua, they didn't know us like they did back in Judea. This anonymity allowed me to spend quality time raising Sa'rah without fear or looking over my shoulder. So, you could say we were more at peace in Gaul than in Judea."

"Why not stay in those villages rather than go further north into the forests if you were comfortable and at peace?" Rochelle asked.

"Why do you both continue to exist in a multidimensional realm to learn about our lives?" she said. "To learn from us as we learn from you. What was pulling us to the caves and forest? We went the distance because of our faith and trust in something bigger."

"It would seem to me you would reach more people with your message in the villages further south, closer to the coast," Rochelle said.

Miriam stepped back, and Yeshua came forth to speak and it was a smooth and quick transition.

"I knew if they went to the smaller villages in the north, they would find pure tranquility," said Yeshua. "I needed them all to become warriors of love, and it was in the caves where I would visit them. These caves were not unoccupied previously, but unlike what some of your books say, Miriam did not live in a cave. Instead, she went there to meet others in private, and this is where I came, showed my Merkabah and taught. There were too many people in the larger villages, and many were stuck in their ways, so they were not as open to the message of being one with God. You see, further north, there was more inquiry and curiosity about who I once was, so they were more open to my energy and our teachings. You might say it was like an Egyptian community or cult, especially at the start, because it was primarily women who led the groups. They had been trained in the ancient Egyptian esoteric ways and over time, men joined the gatherings as well. It didn't take long to gather many in my name."

Rochelle asked, "Could everyone see your Merkabah?"

"It didn't take long for people to gather in my name," he said again.

Angelo's head tilted down, and there was another energy shift before Miriam returned.

"Why did he repeat what he just said?" Miriam asked Rochelle. "Because he wants you both to have faith. He wants you to call forth and convey a message of love and communion, one of connectedness and oneness. Do you understand? There's no separation between all of us. What makes you think we are separate? The energy is what matters."

Miriam's energy was getting stronger, and as she had experienced before, Rochelle felt like she was listening to Martin Luther King speak.

"We didn't come to this planet to make peace—I came here to make waves just as we did two thousand years ago," Miriam continued, but with power in the voice coming through Angelo. "Yeshua did not die on the cross for anyone's sins, as your religions have you believe, but he did it for what he believed in and because he had faith in something bigger than himself—in what we called the Father back then and you all now call God or Source. Would any of you do that? I think not."

She spoke with elevated inspiration, so Rochelle let her continue as her fingers flew across the keyboard to capture her teachings in real time.

"For us to become strong again as we were in our physical bodies, *you must become us,"* she said. "To do this, you must be humble, but you also need some ego to propel you forward. You will need to combine the strength and drive of the ego with love and peace from the heart. Feel with your hearts, don't think with your heads. You are both human beings, and that's why we are here: To feel everything again through you and your emotions as we share our messages. Put another way, it is through your heart chakra we can connect, speak and heal, and the combination of your emotions makes you both strong.

"Some speak to you about drama when they hear my name and don't like or understand it since they don't have an image of me that matches an intense and rebellious personality. Was there no drama when we lived? Unlike the slow quiet countryside of Gaul, Judea was filled with drama, which is why the sisters and I escaped so we could find peace and freedom for ourselves, and of course Sa'rah. I didn't want to raise my child in a society with nothing but murder, chaos, and Roman military around us, all of whom were corrupt beyond corrupt. It would have been an extremely stressful life for us and potentially dangerous as well.

"What you see with your governments is nothing compared to what we experienced. I was a strong woman back then, a strength I am attempting to project through Angelo now. I have a story to tell. I was much less a saint than what you have depicted me as and more like the women you now see in your government. In other words, I was a powerful woman who wasn't afraid to speak the truth about male dominance at a time when almost no one else was.

"I can enjoy this human experience in the present moment through both of you in this lifetime. Through you, my beacon of light is the brightest, and my light shines as Miriam of Magdala who walked the earth plane over two thousand years ago. You both have a hard time with some of these messages, but I will not hold back my truth, nor will Yeshua."

Then Angelo's head fell, and his breathing became labored. Soon, Angelo's soul stepped forward and reconnected with the here-and-now dimensional reality. They both looked at each other and smiled. It looked like they were done for the evening. Angelo got up and opened a 2016 Bordeaux.

Rochelle asked why he was opening such a special bottle, and he responded, "To celebrate the fact we have such incredible wine to drink when they didn't even have clean water. I think we should toast to their lives because as we understand them better, we begin to understand ourselves better and every living thing in this universe."

Rochelle knew he was right.

• • • • • •

CHAPTER 16

GAUL'S ALPS: TWO WORLDS AS ONE

Hope is the thing with feathers that
perches in the soul—and sings the
tunes without the words—
and never stops at all.
—Emily Dickinson

Eager to spend more time in the West, Rochelle and Angelo flew to northern California where they rented a lake house. From there, they'd rent a Yosemite cabin and then camp before heading back to Boston. When they arrived, fires were scorching much of the forests in the Northwest, covering everything outside in soot and ashes. The charred remains darkened the skies and left imprints everywhere. They hosed things down only to have to repeat the task two hours later. Their rental car, porch chairs, and benches all received a layer of ash, as did the herbs and flowers in the garden.

After a week, they began to feel a bit depressed from the poor air quality and lack of sunshine. One evening, when the sky was particularly gray, Rochelle made her usual pot of tea, lit a candle and some frankincense, and thought it would be a good time to rekindle a dialogue with Miriam and Yeshua. Rochelle and Angelo were both keen to learn more about Miriam's life in Gaul. It wasn't until around nine pm that Miriam came into their dimension, and it was one of her abrupt entrances.

"I am ready to tell you about my life in the *Alpes Cottiae* region which you now call Saint-Maximin-la-Sainte-Baume," she announced. "Of course it didn't have the same name during our time."

"The place with the caves?" asked Rochelle.

"We will get to them in time, but first, I want to tell you about our arrival. After living a nomadic lifestyle for nearly two years, we left the last village to head to our final destination."

Rochelle began to type everything she said as Miriam's determination to tell her story unfolded.

"We had started to obtain a name for ourselves as we ventured from village to village," she continued. "Through word-of-mouth, we became known as the *Feminae Christi,* for we taught about the practice of love. It wasn't our mission to change people's minds from one God to another but rather to speak about love and oneness, all of us as part of God, and there is no separation. The so-called *Good News* at the time was really about the unity of All That Is. Each village was unique, largely because they worshipped Pagan gods and goddesses in their unique distinctive ways. Still, many were open to our teachings since Pagan rituals emphasized a strong connection with nature, which made it easier for them to understand their personal version of oneness.

"At this time, Latin was starting to take hold amongst the Gaul languages, so we began to learn and speak Latin with a Gaulish accent. Every village had specific linguistic characteristics despite being close, and each prided itself on those differences. We started to become a part of Gaul, and Gaul became a part of us. So, who was in charge? Well, let me ask you this: Who is in charge of bringing forth our messages in your timeline?"

Rochelle replied, "Both of us."

"Yes," Miriam said. "For beings like us to work with you, permission must be granted. The soul permits the soul to work with energies from other dimensions such as ascended masters, gods, goddesses, angelic realms, elementals, and others. No one else does. To teach in the human realm, an agreement must be granted. Both of your souls are working in conjunction with other dimensions and realms to communicate this message.

"Some modern teachers call energies they communicate with by names, such as a federation, a council, a team, a group, or a collective whereas others simply call them angels. You can connect to these energies whenever you choose, but fundamentally they all come from God, and you are Godde. Do you see the circle I've just taken you into and around? It's *your own choice*, not an *approved choice* from some Galactic federation, council, or collective."

Rochelle and Angelo had read articles and listened to podcasts from those who reported they were working on an "approved project" or in collaboration with a council or federation. They felt this implied that other spiritual teachers were not legitimate if they didn't confirm the same thing. Not only did the language seem dual in nature and counter to Yeshua's and Miriam's teachings of oneness and love, but exclusive in the same way institutions have pushed on society for millennia.

"Although we didn't have the level of understanding and awareness over two thousand years ago we now have in our spirit form, we were aware people didn't need to live by the rules of an organization, monk, rabbi, or priest," Miriam explained. "We didn't say you had to become like us or even think like us. On the contrary, we found affinities with others. For example, we understood shamans and Pagans well because, in many ways, we also lived our lives being one with nature. Yeshua was a great shaman who understood Paganism better than anyone in those parts. His diverse and deep knowledge stemmed from the Essenes and other Judaic sects to ancient Egypt and the sages in India with countless stops along the way."

Since they had been talking about Paganism, Rochelle was curious to learn more about how they connected to nature. She wanted to hear Miriam's perspective on the moon and the stars and their impact on human beings.

"Living amongst Pagans, you must have learned a lot from them about our connection to nature as well," Rochelle said and then launched her questions. "Did you look to the moon, stars, and sun for answers? Did you notice changes during a full moon? Is there any truth to the claim that the veil to the other side was thinner during that time?"

"The full moon often makes it easier for a connection and messages to come through," Miriam responded.

"How?" Rochelle asked.

"Now, Angelo has to get out of the way," she said, sensing his discomfort with the topic. "How does this happen? You have a magnetic field around you and your Akashic Records are made up of magnetic resonance, both of which are impacted when the moon is full. This is also true of our energies, so we can communicate with you more easily during a full moon.

"It's not just the moon you are connected to, but the subatomic particles of your universe. The universe is in you as much as you are in it. People have such a hard time understanding they are made of energy. If you were to rewind the clock by billions of years, you'd be awestruck by the connection between your human bodies and Gaia. You have more in common with a meteorite than you think. Organic life as you have come to know it has had quite a journey."

Rochelle recently read something about the connection between our human anatomy and the universe. In Jude Currivan's *The Story of Gaia*, she said, "The nucleic acids of RNA and DNA, the amino acids which make up proteins and more, form the basis of Gaia's biosphere."[1] Later, she wrote, "Discoveries are revealing ever-more evidence of prebiotic convergence and collaboration, gestating as organic molecules in interstellar molecular clouds, delivered by asteroids and leading to the sibling relationships of RNA and DNA, amino acids, sugars, and lipids in the early waters of Gaia's gaiasphere."[2]

Miriam's and Jude's words took Rochelle far, deep, and wide. As the visions exploded in her mind's eye, Miriam stopped speaking for a while before she returned to her days in the mountains. It was as if she wanted Rochelle to digest and absorb and process what she had just said, not just hear it.

It's not just the moon you
are connected to, but the
subatomic particles of
your universe. The
universe is in you as
much as you are in it.

We settled permanently in the fifth or sixth village within Gaul's Alps," Miriam went on. "The villages were quite close, perhaps only ten kilometers apart, but as I said, we spent time living in each one. Remember my Isha was leading us to our final destination where we could begin our teaching in earnest. The villages to the north were similar to others we had lived in along the way; however, the village where we finally set up home was at a higher elevation physically, so it was much cooler, especially at night. This meant we had to acquire more suitable clothing such as animal furs and hides for warmth. Plenty of goats, cows, and foxes roamed the area where we landed, so we used feathers from ducks and geese as well—no part of an animal went to waste. The Druids of Gaul were highly attuned to their environment and deeply respected animals and the land.

"Every meal was sacred, and consuming various types of food was acceptable there. We would sometimes eat wild boar, a new experience for us. In the Judaic religion, scavenging pigs were considered dirty, so we were prohibited from eating pork. Yeshua said it was okay to now partake although we kept other learned kosher ways. Our meat was always blessed, and we were grateful for all we received, something we said aloud before each meal. The indigenous of your country long ago also blessed their meat and the hides they used and still do today. Each time an animal was sacrificed for the betterment of humanity, it was thanked for what it gave to us. We frequently had ceremonies to honor animals and their contribution to our lives. This is why we always tell you and Angelo to thank and bless your food too, so you understand how connected you are to everything. When you bless your food, make your intentions authentic."

The indigenous of your country long ago also blessed their meat and the hides they used and still do today.

Rochelle asked, "Where did you live when you first arrived at your final destination?"

"A number of families offered us a place to sleep while we had a home built for us," she said. "The construction of our home was made of wood, straw, stones, bricks, and mud. Locals in the village were willing to assist us with our endeavors, including building a special house where all nine of us could live together. During the six months it took to build the house, we established our footing by developing relationships with shamans and healers. First and foremost, we sought spiritual people out because they would best understand us and be most likely to assist us.

"Consider when a spiritual teacher comes to America and needs a place to stay for a week. Even if they might stay in a hotel during your current times, they might also opt to stay with people from their extended community. For example, people might offer to put them up and likely a few of their friends as well, so it was similar for us. As I mentioned earlier, word spread of our teachings from men on the boats who were selling their commerce from as far away as Judea, the Roman coast, up along Gaul's coast, the villages nearby, and further north. It felt good to have a new life although we missed our language, food, culture, and the warmer weather. Naturally, we missed our homeland, but we no longer worried about persecution from the Romans. We gave up everything to go on this journey, to trust in Yeshua's teachings, and to bring his messages to a new culture, a new country, and a new way of life."

Rochelle asked, "Who paid to build the house?"

"We gave our time in return for labor, as we did with all of our work," she responded.

"We were a bit like priestesses who always served, helping the poor and the sick amongst other things. As sisters, people saw us as the Mother Teresas of the time, so provisions were provided for us by the community. We taught, healed, and cared for local people, and they welcomed the priestesses of Yeshua with open arms.

"Life in the *Alpes Cottiae* was tough for us as women; however, by nature, we were great multi-taskers back then and still are today. Although not everyone will admit this, women are often considered more apt at survival than men, not because we're stronger, but because we're smarter. We didn't use our brute force but our intellect and intuition to survive and prevail. In reality, women don't need men except for the seed they give. While I don't want to denigrate men or downplay their usefulness, I only say this because there must be a shift in energy. The harmony and balance of feminine and masculine power have been disrupted for far too long. It is from this vantage point I speak now since balance must be restored. You're starting to see things change. It will happen in your lifetime, and men who understand will also assist in this transition.

"We had more liberty to speak our minds in Gaul's mountains than in Judea. They honor me in southern France today but more as a saint. I did not want to become a saint or to be seen as a saint, and neither Yeshua nor I wanted to be elevated in any way. The Catholic Church will do whatever it takes to promote itself to prolong its life. How many pilgrimages have been made to a place where I didn't live but only prayed and meditated? Nevertheless, we spent a lot of time in these caves, and they continue to have powerful energy in them today."

Miriam's cynicism took Rochelle aback, but she understood her frustration and dismay.

"While our house was being built, we were split up, two of us living in each home," Miriam continued without skipping a beat. "Because we were far away from the larger towns, and ports, it was an ideal place to become one with nature and focus on spiritual life. During those six or so months, we went to the caves to meditate, pray, and discuss how we would spread Yeshua's teachings. The Druids lived amongst us. Tree lovers and forest dwellers, they embraced us because, like your modern-day indigenous people, they truly understood Spirit.

"It wasn't unusual to meet shamans and medicine healers since communing with Spirit, gods, and goddesses was a regular part of their everyday life. They just did it in other ways than we did, but we were as open to learning from them as they were from us. While we were becoming accustomed to our new environment, we became warriors of love. You could say we were the caretakers of children, the elderly, and the sick, but we were also the teachers for those who had no teachers."

"What about healing?" Rochelle asked.

Miriam responded with a question: "Healing is like love, isn't it? It comes in many forms, shapes, and sizes. Healing can be a word or a sentence, but it can also be a thought, phrase, or even how you look at someone. It can mean binding a wound of an old man. Healing can be kissing a scratch on an arm when the person is crying out in pain, and healing can be hugging a loved one who is in need of solace. Healing can be emotions of love toward others and healing can include your intentions. Healing can be cooking for someone, as you have experienced many times in your own lives. Here I speak through you and Angelo, and I heal you as you heal me. Healing is always reciprocal: it's never a one-way street, nor is it a dead end. Healing occurs when the recipient is willing to receive it, and the giver provides it freely. I give myself unto you freely, and you receive me freely. The words I speak now are healing. Another aspect of our healing was the intimacy we had with each other as women, much of what we learned and continued to practice through the Way of Isis."

Healing is always
reciprocal: it's never
a one-way street,
nor is it a dead end.

"So, the Way of Isis was an ancient version of what we call a cult or a counter-cultural organization today?" Rochelle asked.

"It was an underground movement, if you like, for women, which I'll explain in more detail a bit later. Teachings and rituals were part of it, so you can think of it as a Way or Tao if you wish," Miriam responded.

"After the house was built, it became easier to do our work because we were all together every day and night," she went on. "For the time, it was considered a big house as it had two levels, a large room downstairs where we would eat and spend time together and an upper loft for sleeping. Most of us slept upstairs in the loft area because the heat would rise to the top and straw was used to help insulate the house. They placed wooden planks on the floors, which most others didn't do. On top of the wooden planks, we used animal skins and thick wool from sheep to help us stay warm during the colder months.

"It was quite uncommon to have a house with a second floor. We didn't have furniture as you have today. Sometimes we sat on little stools, but more often we'd sit cross-legged in a circle on the floor. We had a few low tables we would sit around to eat together. Life wasn't always easy, but it was all we knew. I wish I could say there was a bathroom, but there wasn't. No one had bathrooms. All of the water had to be brought inside from wells which weren't even wells as you know them but rather big holes in the ground. We used to dig holes for excrement, and it wasn't particularly clean or hygienic, but remember you can use it for fertilizer as well and we did.

"We didn't have to worry about pesticides or chemicals because they didn't exist. What you put into your body came out clean—more or less—for the body expelled what it didn't need. We used water and vinegar on a cloth to clean ourselves when we excreted and cleaned it every time. We didn't disdain the act as you do today since we saw it as a natural process for all human beings and animals.

"The house we moved into was large enough for all nine of us even though you wouldn't think so by your modern standards. As I may have mentioned, it was necessary to live in groups for a better chance at survival, so the house was full of seven female sisters, Sa'rah and me. Another one came to join us, but I'll get to that later.

"My Sa'rah and I had our own nook downstairs, and Chaei'el and Sa'rah shared space near us. Meyra, Ruthu'ah, Tirah, and Bassat slept in the big loft on the upper level. Because Shallu'ah was such an independent, strong spirit, she would sometimes sleep upstairs and other times, downstairs. More like a man of those times, she was a guardian for all of us. She always knew who was coming into the home and who was leaving. Playing the role of protector, Shallu'ah slept on a mat and blankets. Each morning, we woke up when the sun rose, meditated, and performed some of our Isis rituals."

"What did these rituals consist of?" Rochelle wanted to know.

"I will get to them in time," she responded.

"After our morning purification, we had breakfast, which often consisted of eggs from chickens or some other fowl, and we'd often grind up millet, oat, or barley. Milk from goats and cows was also available although there was no refrigeration. Worms and insects were always an issue since we had limited storage capabilities. They were everywhere, so we had to be careful when grinding up grains; however, they were so plentiful that we sometimes ate them, not by necessity but by accident. Occasionally, we made unleavened pita bread—an integral part of our tradition—as we had plenty of flour from local grains. Unlike today, it was thick and grainy.

"We boiled water and then strained it. Most of the time, we drank fermented grains sweetened with honey. Our stomachs became accustomed to things your bodies couldn't handle today, but our immune systems adapted and learned how to manage them. There were rivers we trusted over time since we didn't get sick from them, but we had to be careful. We also discovered that wine had healing properties even though we didn't quite understand it. We observed that we wouldn't get sick from wine, especially when it fermented longer. If we mixed boiling water with grapes and cooled it, we could drink it without becoming ill.

"Even though we did not have such things as toothbrushes, we used mint leaves to keep our mouths smelling good and little splinters from trees to pick food out of our teeth. When we had what you now call a painful cavity, we'd have to pull the tooth. Since we didn't have drugs, we used alcohol to numb the pain. After the tooth was pulled, we ground up medicinal leaves to cleanse the area and assist with healing. When Sa'rah was a baby and she was what you call teething in today's times, we dipped the top parts of our fingers in honey and let her suck on them to ease the pain. Sometimes we put our fingers in cold water and then into her mouth to numb her gums. Of course, having the baby nurse from your breast also helped as this was a natural process for us. We'd also grind up leaves for infections when we cut ourselves, so we were always turning to nature for healing.

"For diapers, we used cloth materials bound together with pieces of string, or if the cloth was large enough, we'd simply tie the fabric together. A type of string we made from goat leather and other things was available to us. During our menstruation, some of us used leather holders over the cotton cloth for better protection, and others might only use cotton wrappings. We didn't have underwear as you know it—we had what you might call bloomers, which didn't properly secure the cloth in place."

Miriam was in a groove, so Rochelle let her continue as she took it all down . . . and in.

"We spent much of our time cleansing ourselves, as odd as this sounds, because it was important to stay clean as part of our tradition. This wasn't so easy to do without flowing water in the house. You see, water came from holes in the ground, so it wasn't as readily available as you are used to today. For us, water to drink, bathe, and clean our clothes was limited too. We walked to nearby rivers and lakes to wash and collect water to boil. Sometimes we'd heat water in caldrons and wash our bodies off with rags. We didn't have soap as you know it, but we would create a concoction made from animal fats and perfumes to help cleanse our bodies. We'd also grind up dried leaves such as sage to purify our home.

"After breakfast, we did our chores, which included washing clothes, cleaning the house, and tending to Sa'rah and her education. Of course, there was no school to send her to, so we were the school. Then, we might break up into teams of two or three and head into the town to assist people. Sometimes, we would teach children, and Sa'rah was often part of those teachings; other times, we would attend to the sick and elderly. If we had an evening ritual, it would be similar to your dinner time. It wasn't an Isis ritual but one given to us by Yeshua. He taught us that everything is sacred, including all food, and nothing was truly forbidden. Everything was organic and healthy back then, meaning it came from nature itself, not processed food out of a box. Today, processed foods are everywhere because convenience has become more important than your health.

"Yeshua told us all food on the planet is also a part of God—it's all the same. Gaia—the energy of the earth—and God are all connected; this connectedness is why wine was considered so sacred. Our evening meal consisted of wine, water, bread, some meat if available, vegetables, and eggs, which we usually hard-boiled. The meat often came from the forest. We ate rabbit, fowl, and deer, but also duck and goat as well as things you would not find very appealing like possums and squirrels. We often had nocturnal animals since fish wasn't as available as it was in Judea. The evening ritual always began with a prayer, a blessing of the food we were about to eat, and a blessing for all we had been given. On a plate, we placed bread. I would tear it apart, eat a piece with my hands, and then say, 'Let this bread be the body and the soul of Yeshua. Eat from it so you may be the body and the soul of Yeshua.'"

"That sounds very religious," Rochelle interjected.

"Religious, no. Consider it as symbolic of becoming one with Source, one with God," Miriam said. "Christianity or Catholicism didn't exist during our times; these were merely rituals we did, including our Isis rituals each morning. What you see as religious, in the sense of repeating some dogma, we only saw as rituals of oneness. Each sister would hold the plate, take a piece of bread, eat it in the name of Yeshua, and then say something like, 'May I be of love, light, and service to others.' However, each woman said something different, spontaneously from her heart rather than from a memorized script."

Rochelle recognized she had been so conditioned by teachings from the church as a child that her interpretation of what was religious and not religious was deeply ingrained. There was so much unwiring to do, she thought. For both of them.

Then she asked, "Was it always in the name of Yeshua?"

"Yes," Miriam replied. "Remember this was nothing more than an offering, similar to what you do with your altars as we didn't have a formal religion. We would also pour wine since it was plentiful back then. Wine has been around for thousands of years, but it was obviously not produced using your modern methods."

"Where would merchants get wine from?" Rochelle asked.

"People made wine in a rudimentary way and stored it in jugs or vases, which were used to hold other liquids as well," she said. "We consumed it quickly because there were so many of us. The wine would taste off to your modern taste buds, but we were accustomed to smells and flavors you might find bitter or even foul today. The wine represented the blood of Yeshua, so we would say at dinner, 'Let us partake in the blood of Yeshua, and in this blood, there is life, and there is love.' Again, each saying differed depending on who was speaking.

"The Catholic Church created sayings that never changed. They said his blood was shed for all of humanity, which isn't true. His blood was not shed for humanity. His blood was shed because the Romans put him on a cross and nailed him to it. Again, Yeshua didn't die for the sins of humanity, but he died for the work he was here to do . . . to teach and heal. He believed in his teachings wholeheartedly, just as you both believe in what you are doing in your own lives.

"So, our evening ritual was a blessing of bread and wine, and then we blessed each other as sisters. We gave Sa'rah water sweetened with berries while we drank wine. Every meal, whether breakfast, a daytime snack, or dinner, was always blessed in some way."

"Were there ever any men at the table?" Rochelle asked.

"No, not in the beginning, but in time there were which I will speak of later," Miriam responded.

The energy then shifted, and Yeshua came through to speak about their daily rituals.

"After dinner, I would come through Chaei'el and deliver messages to the sisters," Yeshua began. "She would go into a light, trance-like state, and I helped her improve the connection over time since I was working directly through her auric field."

"Did this happen every night?" Rochelle had to ask.

"No, not every night," he replied, "but it was frequent as a way to teach and prepare them for their path as we teach you and Angelo for your journey as well. It was similar to what you experience through us today. I was with Miriam often, speaking to her in some form."

"How was this done? In what form?" Rochelle asked, eager to know.

"Mostly, Miriam received messages mentally and intuitively," Yeshua responded. "When she went to the caves, she sat and meditated alone, but more often, she brought some of the village folks with her, primarily women at first. During the days, the sisters taught, healed, and cared for children. Miriam shared the same lessons we taught when we walked and healed together in Judea. You would consider it quite rustic for today's time. Sometimes a few of the sisters would join her, and other times the sisters would congregate to hold sacred ceremonies and induct new initiates into their circles.

"Their activities changed according to their needs. If the sisters had to take care of things in the village, such as looking after kids, caring for the elderly and sick, or watching Sa'rah, then they wouldn't hold a circle. The sisters were always assisting each other and the community, and as Miriam mentioned, people saw them as your modern-day priestesses or nuns. They were seen as having a great deal of faith because they did, and people could feel this and see it in their daily actions."

Then he was gone. Angelo had a shawl around him as he sat on the floor during that late evening encounter. He was drawn to this particular shawl since it was filled with earth-bound greens, soft browns, and blues, colors Rochelle also loved. Perhaps it reminded them of the forests and lakes in New England where they grew up.

Miriam's energy flowed back into their auric fields and using Angelo's body and larynx again as a vessel, she began to speak.

"Why do some gurus only wear white, and why are there people who show up at spiritual gatherings wearing all white?" Miriam asked Rochelle. "Some might see these groups as cults, but truthfully, people like belonging to a group, don't they? Every group doesn't automatically regiment behavior and demand total obedience to a leader. Remember this: To belong, we don't need to all wear shawls or all dress in white. You both must focus on independence so each person can show up revealing their own identity and flavor."

Show up where? Rochelle thought to herself. What was she alluding to?

"I told you when we blessed the wine and bread, each sister expressed herself in her own unique way," she continued. "They also wore their own shawls which represented who each sister was in her essence. Creativity comes in many colors and forms, so find clothes and shawls you like to wear and have fun with them. We all wore shawls upon our heads as it was a sign of humility. When Angelo wears a shawl, it represents me and takes on my feminine energy, but it also represents Yeshua for his humble ways."

To belong, we don't
need to all wear
shawls or all
dress in white.

Then she left, and Yeshua soon returned to share more textures and layers. Wow, thought Rochelle. It's as if their energies were dancing back and forth, flowing like those of a Qigong master as she balances the flow of energy and becomes one with both of them. She felt they were teaching them as much by what they didn't say as what they did say and also by the fluidity of their messages, as if they were truly united as one.

"It was important the women were supported during this transition from Judea to their new life in Gaul, and they were in multiple ways; however, not all of their teachings could be absorbed or understood," Yeshua said. "For this reason, they progressed slowly, building support and trust along the way. Soon, people had more confidence in the sisters because of their giving, loving, and nurturing ways, so things were constantly being given to them. Old sitting stools and table hand-me-downs came their way, and they would repair them, similar to what you and Angelo do with used furniture you find online or at yard sales. The sisters furnished their home this way, just as you have both done with cast-offs and antiques."

Rochelle considered the parallels that Miriam and Yeshua brought up about their personal lives. Over time, she began to see how the threads of their lives connected. Miriam and Yeshua seemed to be forever pointing to down-to-earth examples of how similar they were to Rochelle and Angelo regardless of the timeframe, belief system, culture, or language.

They indeed had similar situations and experiences in their travels, especially Rochelle during her younger nomadic days as a wandering backpacker. She often slept in a stranger's home who didn't speak English. She saw how everyone was drawn to other energy forms to learn, grow, and heal. This beautiful exchange happens all the time, but most are unaware of it.

Even though they had modern conveniences they couldn't conceive of two thousand years ago, Rochelle and Angelo knew many who lived very simple lives in villages and rural areas, some because they lacked the resources to move elsewhere but others because they chose to live a more spartan existence. There is serenity and peace in that simplicity, and it appeared Miriam and Yeshua were trying to echo those sentiments about the value of basic living. Even in our modern world, we can choose simplicity over complexity.

Yeshua returned to his earlier thread.

"You know I was a carpenter of sorts, and the tables we made back then were relatively short," he said. "With high tables, you'd have to build chairs, and in our times, we never ate alone—we would break bread with family and friends; therefore, there was always a spread. We always shared what we had with others, so sitting on the floor and using long, low tables made it easier for more people to share the space, food, and drink.

"As I observed the house being built from my energy form, I grew impatient because I wanted them all to be together as a family again. Most of all, I wanted to be able to visit them in secrecy. After the house was completed, the sisters created a jovial celebration and since game was plentiful, it was quite a feast.

"Would you believe I was there for their housewarming, to bless them and their new abode? During dinner time, I would often come to them, and we would break bread, drink wine, and eat a hearty meal. I would either appear in my Merkabah or allow Chaei'el to bring me forth so I could speak to the sisters. Of course, you must be receptive to see the energy, but it was no longer seen as a miracle after a while."

"What do you mean?" Rochelle asked.

"It became normal for them. You sit with Yeshua right now but is it a miracle anymore?" he said. "You've become accustomed to the two of us being in your life regularly. Angelo put this on for a reason," he added, pointing to the shawl around his shoulders as they sat on the front porch facing the lake. "As Miriam noted, Angelo sometimes puts a shawl or blanket over his head or around his shoulders because of Miriam's energy, but also because of mine. Angelo has always liked wearing things over his head, a bit like monks do, for it represents humility as well.

"For practical reasons, I covered my head with a blanket or shawl to protect myself from the sand and wind and to keep my hair from flying in my eyes. It was also the custom as we all wore hoods in our culture. Besides my longish hair, I was lanky, tall, and blue-eyed. I wasn't particularly muscular, but all of us got exercise through our work and physical labor."

Rochelle tried to imagine Yeshua walking from village to village teaching with a blanket or shawl over his head to keep the heat and wind at bay.

"You live in big houses in your modern times compared to our simple lives, but your problems are relatively the same," he continued. "Many of you are still as lost and divided as people were back then. You still believe God is separate from you; when I say you, I mean humanity. So many will not believe you as you write these words, but what's most important is capturing my message, which is still the same as it has always been: it's about love and unity, and that's what the sisters taught in the villages."

As if he wanted Rochelle to fully absorb his words, there was a delay before he went on to accentuate the higher truths of their journey.

"My purpose during this transitional time for Miriam, Sa'rah, and the other women was crucial in nature. You see, what they saw as the Holy Spirit through Yeshua directed them to Gaul's mountains where they would be safe and out of harm's way, and there, they could lead a life of spirituality and service. It was also a place where I could present myself to all of them without fear of persecution. As they gained more followers, I came through to others within the village to convey my messages. When Chaei'el was in a protected and safe environment, she felt more comfortable bringing me through to speak. I could even present myself in my Merkabah to the villagers who would accept me.

"There was no conversion to a new religion. We shared new ideas with the community—not a set of shoulds but a set of new understandings of what life could be. We empowered them to lead lives in a way they had never seen or experienced before. We understood the power of our message, but Miriam has told you she never wanted an effigy so people could pray to her, and this wasn't my intention either.

"People from your structured and static religions tend to see me as something to be worshipped, but I came to this planet to show humanity that I, as a human being, am the same as you. I not only shine in your auric field, but you shine within my auric field as well, so you might say we are shining within each other. Remember you are not one but many, and I am not one but many. This will not be an easy message to give others.

"I have shown you that the soul comes in many colors, shapes, and pieces. Here I, Yeshua of Nazareth, sit in front of you, Rochelle, and speak to you now in this present moment and in your dimension. When I say to you the soul is made up of a colossal range of frequencies, is that so hard to believe when Yeshua is now dictating this to you in your dimension and reality? Many energies speak to you as one."

Although Miriam and Yeshua had spoken about the multidimensional soul, Rochelle and Angelo still had not fully grasped the message. The collective many. The quantum nature of who they are as energy beings. She was still ruminating on these ideas when Yeshua began to speak again.

"You have your own unique light frequency, but over time, you have acquired an immeasurable spectrum of frequencies that make up your soul. Through your structured religions, you grew up having an aversion to who I once was in that context. Even though Angelo has always found me intriguing, he often disbelieved the validity of these messages, and some others will say the same. In the beginning of our direct connection, he often felt: Can this be real? Why are these energies coming through Rochelle and me to speak?"

Rochelle, of course, had felt the same.

"Because I am Yeshua, Jeshua, Isha, Isa, and to the religious amongst you, Jesus," he said. "*I Am who I Am*, aren't I? This is another difficult message to give people. *I Am that I Am*, Rochelle. You will, in time, come to know me intimately, and then you will see who I truly am. When you fully understand who I am, you will understand the same power in you, and you will grasp the interconnectedness of all things. These are the words of Yeshua. Peace be with you. Peace be in you and give your peace to others."

You have your own unique
light frequency, but over
time, you have acquired an
immeasurable spectrum
of frequencies that
make up your soul.

Then Yeshua left, and Miriam returned to finish a thread, which one Rochelle wasn't sure about, for they had darted all over the place, from the soul and light frequencies to village life in Gaul's Alps. The tone changed, and Rochelle felt the energy soften through Angelo as Miriam shared a summative insight about the value of moving to Gaul.

"My life in Gaul was placid, serene, and tranquil for the most part, all the things everyone ultimately seeks in life even if they won't admit it," Miriam said. "I had a much more peaceful life in Gaul than in my home country, for I was recognized and even revered. Do you know how wonderful it is to be recognized and revered? To be fully received by those who don't even know you brings a deep joy in your heart only God sends in a divine way."

Rochelle took it in and reflected on how Miriam must have felt in her new home—a foreign one—yet one where so many accepted their teachings and even embraced them.

• • • • • •

CHAPTER 17

THE CAVES: RITUAL MEETS THE SOUL

What you want to ignite
in others must first
burn inside yourself.
—Charlotte Brontë

Rochelle was becoming more and more enchanted with Miriam, or perhaps it was her story, the fragility and vulnerability of it at times, and yet the power and strength of it at others. Miriam's rawness propelled Rochelle to be more honest about her feelings, regardless of the situation or consequence. Miriam encouraged her to become bolder as a human being and speak her truth as a woman. She felt this authenticity, fortitude, and resilience every time Miriam came through. Sometimes, both Rochelle and Angelo grappled with the new perspectives or, you could say, new realities Miriam presented. At the same time, they both felt Miriam and Yeshua in their hearts—an inner knowing—even though they couldn't rationally explain the feeling.

One evening, as Rochelle settled into a wooden chair outside on the grass, Miriam came for a visit to speak about the caves where they gathered people to teach Yeshua's wisdom and the Tao of Isis in more depth. Rochelle poured herself a glass of Sonoma Valley Cabernet Sauvignon and prepared herself for a long evening with Miriam and possibly Yeshua.

"I wish to speak to you tonight about the caves you asked about earlier," Miriam began. "The townspeople led me to the caves because they held their Pagan rituals there and found them sacred. They had been used for hundreds of thousands of years, so everyone could sense and feel their history and energy. Where do you think your cave-dwelling ancestors lived? Let's take an example. Ancient temples built by human beings for their gods and goddesses were destroyed, and mosques, churches, and synagogues were built upon their foundation. The energy within the foundation is still there, so it remains sacred and holy. The energy doesn't disappear over time, and the same holds true with the caves—the sacred energy from your ancestors remains forever present, but you merely changed the names and meanings as time wore on.

"Initially, I went to the caves to sit and meditate, and during those visits, Yeshua came. At times, his Merkabah appeared to me; other times, messages came intuitively to me like your modern-day mental mediums receive today. I'd go alone while one of the sisters looked after Sa'rah, so I could receive new information about what we would do next. Although I didn't walk to the caves every day, I'd visit often. A spiritual journey takes a lifetime; many people don't understand this or choose to forget.

"As time passed, the caves became more significant because the sisters joined me and we began to hold our circles. The sisters and I communed there and Isha spoke to us in solitude; however, I also went there on my own to pray since it was quiet and free from village distractions."

Then there was a pause, and Rochelle noticed Angelo's arms were moving as if a substantial amount of energy was running through them and his entire body.

"People have said I lived out my life in a cave which is absurd," Miriam finally said. "They had sacred energy, but they were not places to live. We came from a civilization with homesteads, and I shudder to think why people believed I spent the rest of my life in a cave when it wasn't necessary, nor a place I would choose to raise a child. I didn't go to a cave to repent or live out thirty or more years of my life. Would I really live in a cave when I had to raise my daughter, and would I really repent for my sins which I never had in the first place? This fabricated story has lived for far too long."

Rochelle let out a soft laugh at her feisty attitude. "Go on," Rochelle said encouragingly.

"You asked me earlier about our early morning Isis rituals," Miriam said. "I will explain them to you now as we also performed some of these rituals in the caves where we taught. We focused on the Goddess Isis and meditated upon the two serpents rising through each chakra as we visualized our bodies being purified and cleansed. If you want an analogy, then you could say the serpents represent energy—both female and male energy—rising up through you as a form of purification.

"After each meditation, we drank warm water with honey, which was seen as another form of cleansing. We were taught to purify ourselves spiritually and physically—both had to be clean to be part of the Isis teachings. This drink was typical of our morning Isis purification ritual. Sometimes, we added mint leaves to hot water. As we drank, we imagined and visualized the warm water cleansing and purifying us. No morning passed without holding the rituals of both prayer and meditation with purification. By holding ceremonies together, we strengthened all of our Merkabah bodies.

"As we began to teach more, we invited others who filled the caves to hear the wisdom. The messages included oneness with all beings and living things, equality between both sexes or . . . you could also say amongst all sexes, the divinity of the soul, and the body of light orders. *Light orders* was the phrase we used for the chakras and through each order, you could extend yourself to become one with God. We also taught about the sanctity of marriage and the connection between sexuality and divinity. And we gave grace during each meal repeating, 'We are one with God and the All.'"

"I imagine many of the Pagans already practiced some of those rituals?" Rochelle said.

"Yes, of course," she replied, "but many believed that the gods and goddesses were separate from them, so they were blind to their own divinity. They simply followed the rules, didn't they? Like many today, they were afraid to break the rules to discover who they truly were and let go of the fears forever binding them to a diminished understanding of themselves. If you bring light to your fears, you can truly step into your power and divinity. Back then, I broke the rules often, just as you have always done in your life as a woman, Rochelle."

Rochelle smiled and asked, "What was the main focus of Yeshua's wisdom you taught in the caves?"

"You both have a great foundation in spiritual knowledge, which makes it easier for you to understand our messages and accept this transition, but we had to use simple language and go slowly," she responded.

"Transition to what?" asked Rochelle.

"Transition from how you once were taught to understand Source or God to knowing who you truly are, a divine soul with no separation from God," Miriam replied.

If you bring light to your fears, you can truly step into your power and divinity.

"We still don't understand it completely," said Rochelle. "You often tell us we are you, you are us, and no difference exists between us. I assume this is so we don't place gurus and prophets on pedestals and can embrace the notion that the power lies within?"

"Yes," Miriam responded. "It is part of what we say to you, so you can understand our unity as a species and with everything else in the multiverse. We also say we are you and you are us since we speak through both of you, even though it appears only Angelo is bringing forth our messages. Why is that important? Because of the blending of the divine masculine and divine feminine energies running through the two of you, a balance that was also a part of our message back then. This balance is essential to being at peace with who you truly are as energy beings.

"You have a lot of earth and Pagan energy working through you, but you also have Yeshua, Miriam of Magdala, and many of the ascended masters from a Judaic line coming through you as well," Miriam went on. "In this lifetime, you and Angelo are tapping into and bringing forth primarily a Judaic line of masters, and we are two of them. You most identify with them; however, you also connect to ascended masters from non-Judaic lines, such as Mohammed, Buddha, and others who come from other worlds you don't even know."

"Why would we most identify with the Judaic line of masters when neither of us is Jewish in this lifetime?" Rochelle asked since she still couldn't fully comprehend the Jewish connection.

"Your history runs deep through Judaic lines, but you simply don't know it in this human form," she responded.

"Both of us?" Rochelle asked.

"Yes, both of you," she said. "Is it an accident or coincidence you are bringing our truth to the world? I think not. We are here to tell you our story and to remind you who you truly are. When I say we are here to remind you who you truly are, we also want you to remember that I am more than one energy speaking to you as Miriam, just as Yeshua is more than one energy—I am not just one soul, as we explained earlier, and neither are you. Similarly, who is Yosef or Joseph? He's many just like each soul is, and parts of his soul have lived many other lives. But was the energy of Yosef also the energy and soul of St. Germaine, as some believe?"

Rochelle didn't know some people believed that Yosef reincarnated as St. Germaine. Truth be told, she knew precious little about saints, nor did she have much interest in them. Then Miriam tried another tack to help Rochelle understand.

"How many people do you have in your database?" she asked Rochelle. "What I'm trying to tell you is this: You are an incredible connector of energies, Rochelle, and so are we. I connect as a soul to all energies, as does Yeshua. His message is still the same as it was over two thousand years ago; nothing has changed except your science and culture. Because people's beliefs and understanding of the world have expanded, you will not be crucified or run out of town for telling our story in this lifetime. The worst that will happen is people will not believe you and may even mock you, but those who are open-minded and have ears will listen. Today, people are much more open-minded than they were back then."

True, thought Rochelle, but having others believing she and Angelo were shifting dimensions outside time and space as they had come to understand it was another kettle of fish. She thought of friends keen to experience altered states of consciousness who had gone on Ayahuasca journeys in the Amazon jungle and others who had tried psychedelics. Some embarked upon such a journey with hopes of healing past traumas.

Miriam seemed to think she had made her point because she returned to the caves.

"We would meet in two caves. When we held more intimate gatherings, we used the smaller cave, where Yeshua would come to us in his Merkabah body. It was also the small cave where we brought certain initiates and adepts—the more advanced in our community—to connect with them in a much more private and secretive way. You might say it was a more exclusive space where others didn't go. In the smaller cave, our ceremonies introduced initiates to all the sisters and others who would be teaching them, a bit like guides. You have them everywhere today but under other names, and you even have many communal houses where spiritual people live. More and more spiritual gatherings, rituals and ceremonies are happening around the world than a generation ago."

She went back to their meetings.

"Over time, when the gatherings grew, we held our ceremonies in the larger cave. Occasionally, we met in people's homes or out in nature. We were able to expand our community largely due to our fairly remote location.

"The Druids and Romans had their own gods. The Romans left us alone, for their power didn't become substantial until they established a papacy and churches hundreds of years later. While the Romans didn't bother us, we still faced traditional beliefs and values that impeded the understanding of our message, particularly gender equality and balance. For example, Yeshua and I performed miracles together, yet none of them are recorded.

"Why is that? Let's just say it was a man's world that shaped perceptions. Many times, when individuals were going through a healing of grand proportion, they would fall asleep or lose consciousness for a few seconds, a minute, or even longer and then be revived again. These experiences were quite common with Yeshua. When they regained awareness, they would usually see his face first and not mine although I was always with him and assisted. Because of their patriarchal bias, they ignored me by his side and assumed that he alone had healed them. They never understood my value."

Yeshua and I
performed miracles
together, yet none
of them are recorded.

Rochelle sensed frustration in Miriam's tone. It must have been extremely difficult to be such a strong female force when women were never acknowledged for any of their contributions or merits.

"Despite this patriarchal bias, southern Gaul was ripe for spiritual knowledge, especially the power of the feminine because of their close connection to the land," Miriam continued. "During our meetings, we sat in a circle around a fire as you and Angelo do with your friends today. It was very rural in those forest-covered mountains and since people lived in nature, they were connected in a spiritually expansive way. You have lost your connection to nature as a species, just as you are out of balance and out of touch with feminine power, but you have many examples still alive with your indigenous elders, environmentalists, and others."

"Ritual and ceremonies help," Rochelle cut in.

"Yes, and honoring and respecting the land as well," Miriam said. "Being connected to nature means that you should always celebrate. Do you know why? Connecting to the seasons connects you to all of your ancestors, and your ancestors are directly connected to you. You are made up of your planet's rhythms through her resonance field. It's not as important to celebrate religious holidays as it is to celebrate the seasons. We lived amongst Druids, so we learned their unique ways of celebrating each season and embraced them."

Rochelle thought of the seasonal rituals she and Angelo held together with friends. They looked forward to their drum circles around the lambent light of a fire. She loved the smell of pine trees, the sound of crickets at night, and the connection they both felt to water.

"I enjoyed the Druid ways as they were highly spiritual people and their ways were not something we were exposed to in Judea," Miriam went on. "For them, Spirit was everywhere, a knowing which continues to exist today in many parts of the world, such as South America, Australia, and Hawaii. Your indigenous people communicate with Spirit all the time as did the Druids at the time, so the idea of apparitions or energy bodies was nothing new to them. Going on spiritual journeys through herbal medicine wasn't new for them either. But learning how to balance the masculine and feminine energies to become one with Source was unique for them.

"Even as they stumbled at times, they were open to many of the Yeshua's teachings and simply incorporated them into their spiritual beliefs and rituals. A perfect example in your current time is how many are now combining quantum physics with spirituality. The same was true for the seven sisters and me in Gaul; when we felt their resonance, we combined the Druid practices of honoring the land with our personal practices."

Miriam paused before she dove deeper into feminine power.

"Rochelle, do you remember when you and Angelo saw an Italian documentary where someone asked an Italian woman, 'Are you a *strega?*' and the woman replied, 'All women are *streghe.*'"

She remembered it well, for they both loved the film, and Angelo had strong Italian roots.

"The word *strega* in Italian translates to witch, and the plural form is *streghe*," she went on. "When she said in the film that all women were *streghe*, she meant all women were healers because they all learned how to heal using natural means. I would say to women back then, 'You need to learn how to heal yourselves and others, not just your children.' I needed women to find their voice again and feel confident since their strength vanished due to the patriarchal society that dominated them for many, many years. It wasn't always that way, but things changed long before our time."

Rochelle had read about the prominence of matriarchal societies in the region as many worshipped the Goddess, the Queen of Heaven so to speak. It was as if each culture created their own unique names for her, but she was merely an adaptation of the divine feminine which was endeared by societies for a long time. Whether it was the long-worshipped Isis, Ishtar, Artemis, Demeter, or Hathor, the parallels have long been documented.

As Rochelle noted in R.E. Witt's *Isis in the Ancient World*: "For thousands of years, as the evidence in Asia Minor indicates, men's religious needs were best answered by their adoration of a Mother Figure. Even in the strictly patriarchal religion of Jewry her presence can be glimpsed as an influence at work in the background of the Diaspora."[1]

Although the Goddess was often identified as nothing more than a fertility figure, people—both men and women—prayed to her, made offerings and even made cakes. Rochelle recalled just how powerful Isis had become across borders over time. Isis who has been called the "Mother of Gods" and the "Life Force Indwelling Nature," ultimately grew in popularity and became known well beyond Egypt . . . throughout the Mediterranean and beyond.[2]

"Counter to how you may have been programmed to understand history, women were once respected and life was different," Miriam went on. "You see, women used to be the dominant force in the household. Women were child bearers, healers, and cooks; they took care of everything while men hunted. It isn't so unlike today except now women make a living as well and often take care of the home on top of their careers. Why did society become patriarchal? What changed?

"When food production could support a larger population, the older division of labor between men and women lost its function in maintaining life. Specialization developed as the human species evolved. As the population grew, towns could support diversification and new types of jobs. Some animals, such as horses, became domesticated and assisted human beings, which helped expand food production. Not everyone had to hunt and gather anymore. It's not to say that you didn't raise your livestock or live on a farm, but people began turning to other things like woodworking, metalwork, painting, and even writing.

"Opportunities started to arise in these more cultivated societies, though not as plentifully as what you have today in your modern world. Physical strength and size didn't matter as much in many of these new jobs, but men were accustomed to an active role when hunting and fishing and trained to overcome prey. They may have felt a noble need to protect too, but these habits led them to take charge, and unfortunately, they took charge by demeaning women. I hate to say this, but they blamed problems on women whenever they arose, and a pattern developed. Through conditioning, it became acceptable to blame, chastise, abuse, and denigrate women. Making women subordinate became an integral part of society as other things evolved. Not all communities developed patriarchally; some of the indigenous groups maintained a maternal structure, perhaps because of their close connection to and respect for nature. But the predominant pattern was patriarchal."

Rochelle was temporarily distracted by her own historical and academic references, but Miriam appeared to be on a roll and continued her story.

"During our circles, I helped women regain their voice, which was vital for our time. This need still holds true even though you've come a long way since then. My teachings back then resemble my teachings of today in many ways; however, now I focus much more on the core messages of Yeshua because the messages of Isis and Horus are not as relevant as they were during my life as Miriam of Magdala. Connection to particular roots and cultures has shifted. Put another way, what once resonated has changed. In ancient Judea, some of the Egyptian wisdom, including the connection to their gods and goddesses, was an integral part of our life, and after I moved to Gaul, we incorporated some of the Pagan and indigenous ways. As we learned from each other, a synergetic relationship and dance between cultures arose which led to a healthy balance for all of us.

"We naturally related information to people in a way that could be understood and accepted, so you might say that we combined heaven and earth-based teachings. When religions developed and diversified, teachings and understandings changed yet again. Think of how many strands or sects developed from your Christian roots all over the world. When people broke away from the Catholic Church, new leaders surfaced and began to extend far and wide."

"Like the sixteenth-century German monk Martin Luther," Rochelle interjected. "His teaching and efforts launched what we have come to know as the Protestant Reformation."

"Yes, and so many more," Miriam said. "Rochelle, your great-grandmother, with her English roots, grew up in the Episcopal Church. Consider how many other offshoots emerged in your history, each with its own belief system and way of defining or seeing God.

"As a species, you are becoming more enlightened and you have been introduced to new scientific advancements and the quantum world. Today, I can relay information to you in multiple realities since you can understand the existence and meanings of quantum dimensions. Even as little as fifty years ago when people were still holding séances, Yeshua and I could not speak to you about the quantum implications on your lives. For so many years, humanity has held onto restrictive superstitions and fears which have held you back from expanding into your true Authentic Selves. We are part of the universe, and it is part of us.

"Quantum realities can help you open up to novel ideas from beyond your 3D world. For instance, you might assume all your technology is earth-based, but it's not. Let's say this: Much of your technology is channeled in some form or another. Other forms of knowledge also come through channeling. For instance, it's no coincidence that your science and spirituality are gradually becoming one again."

"By channeling, do you mean people are accessing information from non-local dimensions?" Rochelle asked.

"Channeling comes in numerous forms as you are learning when you connect to us outside the dimension you live in and perceive as a physical world," Miriam replied. "But everyone accesses information in their own unique way; some are seamless, and others are far more complex."

"Explain," said Rochelle, curious where Miriam was going to take her.

"When indigenous elders or your Pagan cultures perform ceremonies and rituals, what do you think is happening? It's a way to create a sacred space where you can focus your intention on a situation or person energetically—remember we are all made up of energy. These intentions allow you to expand your consciousness so more information can come in, for that too is energy. Connection. Clarity. It's why brilliant ideas—or you could say more expansive ideas—tend to show up when your mind is silent."

"Yes," Rochelle jumped in. "This is when I have those *aha moments* that seem brilliant when they first come, but often, they're the most natural and seamless solutions that simply didn't occur to me when I was stressed about something. I get the most clarity when I am present with what is transpiring right in front of me rather than focusing on a future worry or a painful memory."

Intentions allow you to expand your consciousness so more information can come in, for that too is energy.

"It's much easier to feel clear about a situation when you stay in the present moment, isn't it?" Miriam asked her, not waiting for a response.

Rochelle simply nodded, knowing she meant situations also applied to daily encounters and conversations with people. Often things can go awry when one person is assuming something that isn't true while the other person is assuming an erroneous idea as well. She considered the times when things didn't go well in their lives, and it was often amidst a major life transition when things were more chaotic than normal. Stress levels were high, and she didn't feel relaxed or stable. Rochelle grasped this feeling was also a perception, not reality.

"Others tap into this expansive consciousness using what they most resonate with as a way to quiet the mind," Miriam went on. "Rituals can come in a variety of forms. For example, taking a walk in the woods, sitting on a mountain top, fishing in the middle of a pond at dawn, planting flowers, herbs, and vegetables, or becoming one with a wave when surfing. Einstein took naps in the middle of the day. Some people escape to a remote island to draw and paint whereas others write computer codes in the middle of the night. Everyone is connecting to or channeling knowledge beyond this dimensional reality because you are all part of so much more than what you physically see and touch in this reality. When musicians tap into something that may at first sound otherworldly, it's because it is. In your modern world, some people refer to this process as channeling while others who are uncomfortable with that terminology might call it divine inspiration, or simply inspiration. All creators know of this inner source and express their unique experience of spiritual wisdom, innate yet beyond themselves. Creation is an expansive process, isn't it, Rochelle? When you close doors to what is possible, you have less available to you. Why would anyone want that?"

"Fear and uncertainty often get in the way," Rochelle said. "Rituals and ceremonies in organized religions may have started out as a way to connect to your divinity, but for many, it became something they did out of habit, following a set of rules they no longer resonated with or understood." She thought of some of the people she met at Catholic school who confessed their so-called sins to a priest, often feeling uncomfortable doing so, but fearing if they didn't, their souls would go to hell.

"Remember Rochelle, not all new ideas are advancements," Miriam said. "Don't think when many societies became monotheistic you advanced in your spirituality. People largely became monotheistic because it was forced upon them."

Rochelle recalled reading Murat Iyigun who wrote about the development of powerful institutions to control people. There were financial and political advantages for leaders and institutions to support a monotheist God religious view. Within this framework, people would be judged for their deeds in life (the infamous Judgment Day), which helped to maintain societal order, stability, and respect for property.[3]

It made sense to her, for if people wanted social, economic, and political security, it was an indirect way to impose change rather than people choosing it because it's what they truly wanted.

"By forcing one religion upon another, you take away the true essence of what spirituality is in its best and purest form," Miriam continued. "And that form often comes from divine inspiration within, intuition or channeling. It's all the same—you are simply accessing the expansiveness of who you are as a soul, so you're tapping into the wealth and depth of knowledge from within and without."

"As above, so below," Rochelle quickly added. She wondered: When we receive divine inspiration from within, intuitive downloads or channeled messages—whatever language we want to use to describe the experience—are we entering another dimensional reality, creating a new one or *both*? If this connection is possible, what else is available to us once we embrace it as an option?

You're simply accessing
the expansiveness of who you
are as a soul, so you're tapping
into the wealth and
depth of knowledge
from within and without.

"Things change over time as belief systems change," Miriam said. "As your traditions and spiritual practices change, old language you once used to describe divine connection will die off and a new language will emerge. Even after the death of Yeshua, the language we used to teach changed. In other words, we weren't there to impose a doctrine but to empower and inspire people. It wasn't my message to teach people they needed to believe in Yeshua to reach salvation, but instead that they too could become a great spiritual master. When we prayed, we connected to a resonance field with Yeshua and his energy of love. My message with the sisters was that we all have the same ability to be like Yeshua—we only need to intend it, practice it, and *become it*. We also taught there are many paths to get there, not just one, and Yeshua's wisdom was just one example. Your world has known many examples before Yeshua, as many ascended masters and prophets have also performed miracles. You have them today as well.

"As we have said many times, a central part of our teachings focused on the dance between masculine and feminine energies—the power of both of them working together in harmony. In the region of Gaul where we lived, while they did not fully understand this balance, they were much more open than people were in ancient Judea, what you know as Palestine and Israel today. They weren't confined to religious laws that blocked them from being their Authentic Selves. Nothing held them back. In essence, no laws jailed or incarcerated them from stepping into and living their true nature. There was no Judaism, Christianity, Islam, Hinduism, or Buddhism they were forced to follow. We were free to worship as we wanted, and not even the Romans could impose a religion upon us. We were part of a powerful, enriching community and flourished for years while teaching many, many people. The message from Yeshua was always the same; however, it would change according to each culture and language.

"Balancing your divine feminine and divine masculine energy can be incorporated into all societies willing to receive the message although it could challenge the social structure, for instance, a society built on patriarchal power. Unity with God or Source in masculine and feminine balance is ubiquitous in its true nature and is whole and complete. This unity can transform all societies built on division."

Miriam moved on as Rochelle reached for her tea cup and changed positions.

"As we chanted and sang with the Druids, we poured our combined energies into those caves. As we held our ceremonies, we became one with them as they became one with us. Over time, we began to lead sex rituals and activations in the caves, and as we grew larger, it became necessary to hide our teachings to protect ourselves. And so, clandestine we all were.

Our work combined Yeshua's spiritual wisdom with the ancient Egyptian Isis rituals, which included sacred sex. We did this quietly as the community needed to trust our teachings of love and unity, which included aspects of both—sacred relationship and sex.

Unity with God or Source in masculine and feminine balance is ubiquitous in its true nature and is whole and complete. This unity can transform all societies built on division.

"Remember we were women during a time when women had no respect or voice. Sacred sex was a way for us to connect to God or Source through foreplay, intercourse, masturbation, and ejaculation, all of which were frowned upon as much in Gaul as in our homeland of Judea. Knowledge of the sacred sex practices was taught by women for women, and as time wore on, there were those who took these practices home and taught their husbands as well. Some men enjoy having a woman lead them, and for others, it's a fantasy they hold. Many rituals and practices were taught to men in ways they didn't fully understand, as a way of helping the communion of both masculine and feminine energies. As women, we pleasured one another, which will be hard for many to read. Most of us were not what you would call lesbians, but we practiced with each other in private.

"The teachings were based on the Isis/Horus connection, the coming together of feminine and masculine energies as one. You see, it was about merging *all* of these energies—Osiris, Anubis, Isis, Horus, and beyond. Some teachers have referred to deities as archetypes which have always been part of our history across cultures."

"Myths are powerful ways for us to understand the mystical world and even connect to it. They always have been," Rochelle added. She thought of something she had read from Joseph Campbell in *The Power of Myth* about "identifying with the Christ in you. The Christ in you doesn't die. The Christ in you survives death and resurrects. Or you can identify that with Shiva."[4] He also said:

> Heaven and hell are within us, and all the gods are within us. This is the great realization of the Upanishads of India in the ninth-century B.C. All the gods, all the heavens, all the worlds, are within us. They are magnified dreams, and dreams are manifestations in image form of the energies of the body in conflict with each other. That is what myth is.[5]

"We incorporated a lot of Egyptian gods and goddesses into our rituals where we focused on the caduceus and the two snakes coming together to balance the energies," Miriam continued. "Even though we didn't refer to the path traveling through the chakra system then, we were aware of energy rising through the body—you might call this practice a kind of Kundalini awakening today."

"So, how would you practice?" Rochelle wanted to know, wondering how far she should prod.

"Women practiced masturbating so they could feel the energy flowing through all of their chakras," said Miriam, as if the answer was the only one. "When someone orgasmed, they connected with Source, God, or Universal Consciousness, whatever name you relate to most. The intention was the most crucial part. They activated a connection during this shift throughout the body and the auric field surrounding it. We masturbated with each other because men were never taught how to give a woman an orgasm. Although rare, a few men were open to understanding it, and eventually, they became part of our circles and rituals, but this took trust and time. When they realized it wasn't a game but a genuine practice of connecting to Source or God, we allowed them to be part of our group. Couples wouldn't share this practice with others but only between themselves as it was considered a sacred act. Partnerships were quite conservative during our time.

"Sa'rah was not privy to this information until she was much older, and by older, it is not the same as you might think today. Remember women had babies at sixteen or seventeen, so she learned about some of these teachings at fourteen or so. It is suffice to say that women during our time grew up extremely fast. When we imparted the Isis teachings to those interested in learning them, they became initiates. We asked them if they were willing to use the teachings of sacred relationship and sex to become one with Source, or we'd say to become one with the Father, as this was familiar language during our time. We asked them whether they were willing to connect to Isis and Horus and if they were ready to walk a path of spirituality."

Dare I ask about Horus? Rochelle wondered.

She and Angelo had attended a workshop on Egypt, which included historical teachings on Osiris, Isis, Horus, Thoth, and *The Book of the Dead*. But how much did they really know about ancient Egypt and its culture? They were both intimately aware of how little they knew, which kept them forever questioning and peeling back the layers of the proverbial onion.

She thought to herself, what was true and not true? When you realize you don't know what you don't know, yet you're armed with knowledge that changes as your learning expands, then perhaps you can also realize there really isn't one truth but innumerable perceptions that make up countless truths. This reality naturally leads us as human beings to surrender and have faith in the process of living and learning time and time again.

Overcoming her reticence, Rochelle decided to open a new can of worms when she asked, "What were the teachings of Horus?"

"Masculinity was part of the sexual initiation," Miriam replied, "which means Horus represented masculine energy and the balancing of masculinity and femininity, especially for men who would become part of the Isis teachings. The process for men through the Isis teachings was what we called the Horus initiation."

"What was the Horus initiation?" Rochelle asked under her breath, becoming aware of her conservative roots.

"The male initiate worked with his female partner, and they'd arouse each other. This was not a theater act or a performance, so please do not take it as such—it was simply the rite of the ritual."

Rochelle didn't expect that level of detail and Miriam felt her uneasiness.

"I can sense you do not appear to be amenable to my words," Miriam said to her, and the formality of her response almost made Rochelle laugh out loud.

"You and Angelo both have a wall that prevents you from understanding these teachings fully. What do you think Yeshua and I did together? We performed the Horus rituals together. It was part of a sacred relationship, and it wasn't done randomly, but from a place of deep love."

"Were they done openly, publicly?" Rochelle wanted to know. She thought of how traditional America's Northeast has always been, even in modern times, and these rituals took place over two thousand years ago. The old prudish ways of structured conditioning from past generations didn't let go easily. Perhaps, the Druids were simply more open because of their oneness with the earth and all it represents.

Rochelle recalled the open-minded attitudes of many of the European women she encountered on her travels. Women she met from Sweden, Australia,

Germany, and France certainly weren't shy about sharing their summer vacation stories with men, all of which were quite different from what Rochelle had been accustomed to hearing. Their stories certainly made for a much better romance novel or movie than those from her hometown.

Miriam's response to Rochelle's question came quickly.

"No," she replied. "Through humanity's religions, many have been raised to think of the sexual act as sinful."

Rochelle and Angelo were well aware of their upbringing, but that morality wasn't just programmed into the minds of New Englanders. Those who have been conditioned under any of the Abrahamic patriarchal religions will uncover ideologies and rules that came about as a way to condemn and eventually forbid the customs of the Goddess, which included sexuality and sensuality. Rochelle had read about this shift from historian L.R. Farnell as far back as 1896: Even though sex for reproduction was considered divine by many, early "Christian propagandists" exaggerated separateness from God, which led to dissonance between a "biological view" and the doctrine or dogma.[6]

Under the Goddess religions, Rochelle had come to realize that sex was sacred, a far cry from sinful and shameful.

"Although the Horus and Isis teachings shared sacred sex as a way to oneness with Source, the Horus rituals differed from the Isis practices," Miriam continued. "During a Horus ritual, the initiate required the partner to be with him to execute copulation. This became a kind of religion, so many viewed it as a cult. Both males and females reached a certain level and then maintained or held it so they could orgasm together. In this way, they became one with Source and its all-encompassing energy, the result of the sexual portion of the Horus initiation or cult as some saw it. The woman and man who chose each other must be life partners, and they could only demonstrate sexual love for each other. You see, this ritual needed to be done with life partners through love, not casual sex, but it was misunderstood in countless ways.

"Within the Isis teachings, sex was part of what we did to connect to Source. Sex is only one way to get there, but it's an incredibly potent way, and it's the most organic act for all human beings. Didn't your Pope say sex and food are divine pleasures from God? How long has it taken for this attitude to change its tune? This will have lasting repercussions within the Catholic community. If sex and food are pleasures to be enjoyed, then perhaps people can understand Yeshua and I had both a sexual and spiritual connection together that was divine. We enjoyed one another when we came together as one, something many of the religious amongst you will have a hard time hearing as well. We practiced controlling our experience so we could orgasm together."

Sensing Rochelle's surprise, Miriam then said in a softened voice, "All energies are here to serve you in any manner they come in, so don't overthink it or put a label on it because of how you think the information I am sharing with you now will be received. Remember sacred sex is just one way to connect to Source, but it also strengthens your Merkabah, immune system, and physical body. Why is this so hard for humanity to hear?"

Magdalene's energy left, and Yeshua came forward but only to relay a brief message.

"I wish to speak to you about Miriam and the everlasting and eternal love we had for each other," Yeshua said. "We shared an enormous amount of passion; however, a flame that burns at both ends of the candle can burn quickly. You have Miriam on one side and me on the other. Passion is a beautiful thing, but it can burn itself out in the blink of an eye. Be careful you don't burn out too fast."

Rochelle assumed his message meant to stay in balance. Yeshua left, and Miriam didn't return for a few hours. When she did, she first posed a question for Rochelle to reflect upon.

"Do you know how amazing it was to feel safe finally and embraced by a community like family, especially after having to flee our homeland?" Miriam asked her.

"We truly had merged with the energies of the nature dwellers," she continued. "The community we built was not only connected in so many ways but growing as well. I felt at peace. This joy you feel in your heart comes from your Higher Self, and this is when you know you are finally home. Together we held sacred ceremonies, and I became one with the Druids over time. We were all part of a more profound and greater love that grew into a beautiful community. I couldn't have asked for anything more since they became a family far greater than my own.

Do you know how amazing it was to feel safe finally and embraced by a community like family, especially after having to flee our homeland?

"Every night, we broke bread together and drank wine. Back then, we were always in a hurry to ferment the wine since it was better than the water; however, our wine was quite bitter. Life could be bitter in those days, and so was the wine. Wine is giving, it is life itself, and bitterness is part of it. The bitterness of wine also represented the blood of Yeshua—you might say bitter wine represented the cruelty he had to experience in his lifetime. This is why we tell you and Angelo only to drink good wine now. Taste a little bitter wine every now and then to remind you what you had experienced in past lives when times were tougher, but mostly consume good wine to represent who you are today. Yeshua would say to all of you now: 'You don't need to drink bitter wine. Drink good wine because it's unnecessary to carry a cross or be on the cross.' In other words, leave your bitter, tougher times and memories behind you and move on.

"Why would Yeshua or I, Miriam of Magdala, want any of you to suffer? Why would we desire any of you to carry a cross and suffer something that would burden you for your entire life? It makes no sense. Say your truth and speak up for what you believe in, which Yeshua and I did. I will tell you again: Yeshua did not die for the sins of humanity; he simply died for what he believed in, the truth of our own divinity and his love for all of humanity. He didn't say you had to die on the cross or bear that cross. Rather, he was simply saying you should speak from your heart for what you believe in and truly embrace it. This is the way to the deepest love and greatest joy."

And then, it appeared they were done for the evening.

"Wow," said Rochelle after Angelo regained consciousness in their present timeline. "She covered sex, magic, rituals, suffering, and guilt all in one evening. It's a lot to absorb."

"It's as if there are lessons upon lessons thrown into the layers of her life and therefore into ours," Angelo responded.

"Maybe, the less we try to figure it out, the more it will make sense. We may be integrating her messages even if we can't comprehend them all," Rochelle said, but she noticed that Angelo was lost in his thoughts, staring out of their screen doors into the dark night. An owl's soothing call broke the silence..

"It's about an innate truth. Hers. His," Angelo finally said. "Perhaps Miriam is right not to overthink things and be overly serious; letting her words be, we are integrating them in ways we don't fully understand. It's about speaking your truth as you see it, just as Yeshua did over two thousand years ago. He taught from his heart and fully embraced it, regardless of what those who opposed his teachings said or did. Yeshua believed in his message of oneness so much that he surrendered to it."

"It's also about moving beyond fear," Rochelle added, after reflecting for a few minutes on Angelo's insights. "Not that we won't ever be afraid because it's a natural part of being human. But how much suffering will we bring into our lives from choosing fear over and over again? What choices will we make? Ones which create unnecessary drama or ones which inspire, connect, and unite people?"

Rochelle smiled as the owl's call grew louder outside their cottage.

"I think Yeshua had fear, but his faith, commitment, and resolve were far stronger than fear," Angelo concluded. "His compassion was stronger than fear, and his love for God and humanity was stronger than fear."

Angelo took Rochelle's hand, and they listened to the owl call out to them once again before they fell into a deep sleep.

• • • • • •

CHAPTER 18

LETTING SA'RAH GO

The best protection any
woman can have
. . . is courage.
—Elizabeth Cady Stanton

Rochelle and Angelo wondered if the Isis teachings and rituals rolled over into other cults or groups over the years, but at least for the time being, Miriam appeared to be done with sacred sex. On her next visit, she took them from sex to the blessings and trials of motherhood. It was on a foggy, cool Saturday afternoon that Miriam shared her memories of Sa'rah and her life.

"In this lifetime, Sa'rah was my only daughter, and she was a precocious child," she said in a more serious tone than Rochelle had heard her use in a while. "She began to speak and walk early, and although she didn't have many playmates early on, the sisters imparted their knowledge and life experiences. Ruthu'ah was the first sister to assist, and because of her whimsical personality, she taught her fun language games for speech, basic math, numbers, and colors. You might say Ruthu'ah oversaw Sa'rah's elementary academics.

"Sa'rah remained with us from her infancy to her teens until she married at eighteen, not an uncommon age back then, and many married even earlier. She was more interested in a secular lifestyle than a spiritual one. Yeshua and I represented spiritual and secular worlds coming together as one, but without the religious dogma. You and Angelo have both in your life now, too. Sa'rah decided she also wanted both; however, she chose a more secular path of that integrated life."

"What was she like in childhood?" Rochelle asked.

"Sa'rah grew up much more quickly than children do now," Miriam replied. "In your modern world, you allow them to be children for much longer. I couldn't judge or predict how her life would unfold because I respected her free will—I would not be my father and dictate what she had to become, nor would Yeshua.

"She had completed all of her formal education by the age of fourteen. As hard as this may be to imagine for those times, she was schooled in mathematics, astronomy, alchemy, languages, and philosophy through the combined knowledge of the sisters and locals.

"By the time she turned sixteen, she was initiated in the Isis teachings but never truly advanced, not because she couldn't but because her life was with her husband John in what you know today as England. We took her on a spiritual journey but gave her the freedom to ultimately choose her own path—without judgment. I refused to be like my parents.

"Sa'rah ended up marrying John who wasn't much older than she was when they met. A man of wealth, he didn't speak English as you know it today but more of an ancient Anglo-Saxon variant and combination. Over time, Sa'rah learned to speak it as well. A merchant who passed through the ports along the southern Gaul coast, he was more of an emissary and promoter of items rather than a seller of them. I believe his parents were originally from elsewhere in Europe since they referred to him as Jean, but they changed it to John when they moved north as was standard at the time. His family was well-off; however, he was unique because he had a spiritual side people couldn't resist. He had also done spiritual work in India and was familiar with the stories of Yeshua. John would become an important man in time as he was a great connector and always making business introductions. His family were wealthy landowners, which made it easier to produce in quantity. Consider your current-day Amazon where you can get almost anything you want. John's family business was similar in that they offered nearly everything you or a business might need."

Rochelle had to know the answer to her most pressing question, so she asked, "How did Sa'rah fall in love with him?"

"The same way I looked into Yeshua's eyes and just knew," said Miriam tenderly. "The same way you and Angelo looked at each other when you met and just knew. You both knew, and they did too."

Miriam stepped back, and soon Yeshua came forward with the following message: "I too wanted to have a family when I walked the planet but didn't since I had a higher calling, didn't I? You both feel a higher calling in this life as well. The man they called John could provide Sa'rah with protection and comfort. I gave my blessing to them both, and although I didn't come to her as I once had now that she was a married woman, she knew I was always there because she could feel me. From time to time, I showed up in my Merkabah to her and John."

"He was open to it?" Rochelle asked.

"Yes, of course," Yeshua responded. "John was a profoundly spiritual man and knew what he was getting into when he married Sa'rah."

After his brief appearance, Yeshua took leave. Rochelle read the words she had just captured; she felt he wanted to acknowledge the relationship and show his support of the union by giving his blessing to them both. That evening, Miriam reemerged and picked up the story.

"When they decided to marry, I went with Sa'rah and John to Britannia for the ceremony and celebration," said Miriam which surprised Rochelle. "The sisters stayed behind in Gaul to teach, heal and reach more people with Yeshua's wisdom. We traveled by horse and carriage, and it took about a month or so to get there. Horses were our main transportation, and even though it was never an easy voyage, it was always an adventure. We had to travel with caution since you never knew what or who you'd encounter on the roads. Wild animals lived in the woods, so you had to know which routes were the safest ones; however, John was well aware of the roads and ensured we were well protected throughout our journey.

"John and Sa'rah's wedding was a wedding of weddings, the wedding I never had. Although I did wed Yeshua, it wasn't anything like the feast we had in Britannia. We were incredibly fortunate to have abundance flowing in our lives, so the wedding celebration lasted for a few days."

"Did Yeshua's Merkabah visit while you were up there?" Rochelle asked her.

"Yes," Miriam responded, "but only briefly. He showed up to let us know he was very proud of what we were doing. That said, he also told me my path was in Gaul and I would return there in time. He said it was safe to leave Sa'rah behind since she would be treated well, not like property. John was a gentle soul who offered her something other than what she had grown up with—a spiritual life with the seven sisters and me. Despite being spiritual, his more secular way of life appealed to her, so marrying him offered her a unique and alternate path to staying with us in Gaul for the rest of her life. They lived in the northeastern part of what is now England, north of what you call Hadrian's Wall."

Rochelle pulled up a few maps on her laptop and zoomed in on the region Miriam mentioned. Alnwick, Alnmouth, Amble, and Rothbury popped out.

"The names are not the same as they would have been during my time, but this area is roughly where they lived," she said curtly, as if the regional details were not what really mattered about her story.

"After the wedding feast, I lived with them for a few years," Miriam continued. "She had a daughter within the first year whom we named Mary Sa'rah, so I stayed to help her with the birth and Mary's early years.

"Although John wasn't a member of the Knights Templar as this organization didn't start until much later, he dabbled in a similar one that preceded it. To be part of it, you had to be single and devoted to its needs. Marriage and children were thought to compromise this devotion. Since he was both a business and family man as well as a baron, he never became fully involved, but his influence gave him access to prominent people and activities. He was a bit like a Mason without the Illuminati status of what the Knights Templars ultimately became. It was a male group that kept secrets hidden from the common man."

"How did Sa'rah and John meet?" Rochelle asked her, moving positions to get more comfortable as the story flowed.

"Months after they met at the port in southern Gaul, they started to have a relationship. First, they became friends, admired each other, and then became lovers. Their courtship lasted no more than a year before they agreed to marry. The only thing I knew about John after we met him was that he and his family had enormous amounts of land and he was mostly focused on business; however, there was one thing he yearned for—a deeper connection to spirituality. Sa'rah provided that connection for him. Behind a great man, there's always a greater woman, but you both already know this."

Rochelle's eyes got bigger as she was drawn into their love affair and, of course, the journey. She was eager to learn more about a married woman's life in those days.

"Did he travel a lot?" she asked Miriam.

"After he met Sa'rah and they had a baby, he didn't need to travel as much since his business was fairly established," Miriam replied. "Because his family had means, he could afford to hire others to travel for him. I never wanted Sa'rah to move from town to town and sleep in people's homes as I had done. As her mother, I wanted her to have a stable life, which is exactly what John provided. Having so much stability was wonderful for me too, but as time wore on, I knew my return to Gaul was fast approaching."

Rochelle asked, "Did Sa'rah's husband organize your trip back?"

"Of course," she responded. "John was instrumental in arranging the transportation and managing where we would stop and stay along the way. He had many connections, and we never lacked or needed anything although you would likely consider us poor by your modern standards. When my granddaughter Mary turned around two years and six months old, I made my preparations to return to Gaul. When I left Sa'rah, John, and Mary, I knew I wouldn't return for a long time but rejoiced in the knowledge my daughter was safe, happy, and loved and that she had a child with the name Mary, Yeshua's mother. I cried, leaving them behind, so the trip returning to Gaul wasn't as joyful as going there. Accompanying me on my journey were five others I met in Britannia through my Isis teachings."

Surprised by her last comment, Rochelle asked, "Because they wanted to help?"

"Yes," she said. "Of those five, three were single women and two were men, one of whom was a contact of John's, and one was an initiate in our circles. They were all coming back to Gaul to assist with our teachings, and they also had means. Money talked back then as well although we didn't call it money. Abundance will help you, so don't resist it when it comes, Rochelle."

She tried to take it all in while watching Angelo fidget and move around significantly before her tale flowed once again. He was likely in the Akashic Records with Miriam again, she thought.

"Our journey back down through Britannia took longer than the voyage north," Miriam related after a while. "We hugged the coast and went through small towns where we'd stay for a few days and then continue. We went by horse and carriage in a manner of speaking, but the carriage was much more basic than one you might be imagining from the 1800s."

Rochelle found it hard to fathom how difficult it must have been to travel during those times, especially as a woman.

"Truly, it was more of a basic cart, and others traveled only on horseback," Miriam added. "It wasn't an easy journey, so we took our time to ease the stress. There was no need to hurry since no one was chasing us, nor were we running from anything or anyone. We also knew the route we would take in advance because of John and his connections, so we were always protected during our voyage. After we reached Gaul's northern border, it took another four weeks to travel to our home. Transportation was limited back then as most of our options were Roman-created trading routes and roads, so we had very few choices for travel. For obvious reasons, we didn't want to use the roads built by the Romans, so we followed the safer trading routes. We were fortunate our adventure through

Britannia and Gaul went without any issues because unexpected excitement such as bandits could occur at any time.

"When I returned to Gaul about three and a half years later, I had to readjust. I missed Sa'rah and her family but receiving updates about them provided solace for me. People traveled between Britannia and Gaul, so even if it took months to get messages, we would still get them.

"While I was gone, the sisters had not only grown older and wiser but had also become well-established in their practice. Their circles and the people attracted to Yeshua's teachings had grown exponentially. When I left, only around thirty or forty people came to our circles, and when I returned, the number had grown to three hundred or more. People would travel fifty or so miles to hear the teachings; even back then, they were thirsty for spiritual knowledge."

"Who was in charge when you were gone?" Rochelle asked Miriam.

"Truly, the burden was put upon all of their shoulders as they all played a part in continuing our work," she responded. "The sisters went to as many towns as possible, so the numbers grew. They always knew where they would stay for safety reasons, so they never went to a place blindly. Sometimes they'd visit a town for a month or so, establish themselves, teach, and then return to our home base.

People would travel fifty or so miles to hear the teachings.

"As the administrator of our organization, the sister Sa'rah allocated certain tasks and maintained the records of where the students lived as well as their deeds. Sa'rah noted when people provided services or gave back to their families and community as this was required to be part of our organization. You might call it charity work in your modern-day tongue; it helped you grow on your spiritual path, so it was an essential part of the journey. Yeshua worked directly with both Sa'rah and Ruthu'ah, giving them information intuitively on who was ready to move forward in their studies. Everyone has direct access to this intuition, which is one of humanity's strongest gifts.

"As we expanded, needs for food, shelter, additional clothing, writing materials, and more also increased. To address monetary requirements, we eventually started charging for our teachings. Most students could pay the fee, and for those who couldn't, we still accepted them if they showed interest and a commitment. During my absence, Meyra came into her own as she grew in both confidence and resolve. Beyond industriously taking care of the other sisters, she had begun actively gathering young people to teach them about the *Good News* or *Word of God*. The *Supreme Being* was also used as they were words people could resonate with and comprehend. Meyra worked with the youth so she could understand their thinking.

"Remember we were teaching the Gnostic ways which was our form of Christianity at the time. We showed the local people how to incorporate our teachings into their spiritual beliefs with ease. Their religion was Earth, Sky, Water, Wind, Fire, Sun, and the Moon. Adding the *Word of Yeshua* was simple and natural for the people of the earth. Many of them were able to see Yeshua's apparition which made it easier for them to believe in his wisdom. They were all intimately connected to the Spirit, including the youth Meyra managed and taught.

"Of all the sisters, Basmat, a healer versed in natural remedies, was best able to connect to the nature-loving Druids. She gave alms to their gods and goddesses and simply saw Yeshua as one of them. She told people to continue their daily rituals but also to understand they were not separate from the deities they prayed to. You see, until then, the people of Gaul saw themselves as separate from those they invoked and worshipped even though they saw and knew their connection to the land. Basmat's natural medicine and ways made her a true shaman in their eyes.

"Women healers like Basmat would later be called witches and be put to death by the Catholic Church and other influential male political leaders. How many tens of thousands of European women were put to death, all in the name of a truncated and patriarchal Christianity? This was a tragedy because of false belief systems.

"While I was gone, people went to Tirah when they were confused about the message. She instructed others that the *Word of Yeshua* was the right message but also suggested other people's beliefs and ours could work together harmoniously. She informed the community Yeshua's teachings supported many ways to become one with God since there was no one path. She also encouraged the Druids to follow their rituals while integrating the energies of divine love Yeshua imparted. Tirah explained to others, including the sisters, how to be more proficient healers while bringing in the love of Christ energy."

How many tens of thousands of European women were put to death, all in the name of a truncated and patriarchal Christianity?

Rochelle interjected, "You mean Christ Consciousness?"

"We didn't call it Christ Consciousness," Miriam responded. "The language we used during our time was more the *Word of Christ* or the *Word of Yeshua*. We told them this Word meant all people have God and the Christ energy of love within them. Tirah also made it known that all people are healers, and no one is separate from the Christ energy. This message of inner knowing and healing was part of our teachings, but she had a knack for crossing barriers and conveying these teachings to them in a way they could understand more easily."

Angelo shifted positions and his face began twitching. Rochelle grabbed his hand and asked him, "Are you okay?" He squeezed her hand to acknowledge he was, but Rochelle wasn't sure by the look on his face.

"It's been a long day for him," said Miriam. "It's hard for him to hold our energy for this long, even with your help," she added.

"I don't quite understand," said Rochelle.

"We have a lot of energy, so I won't stay for much longer. I will finish after a few final thoughts about the volume of work the sisters carried out while I was in Britannia. Significant progress was made, but much more had to be done, and I knew I would live out my days teaching and healing with the sisters. I didn't know then I would not see Sa'rah, Mary, and John again until roughly eight years later when they returned to Gaul to see me."

Miriam's tone was sober and solemn as if she *needed* to convey this chapter of her life with Sa'rah. Being a mother was certainly an integral part of her life. Although she deeply loved her daughter, she also was committed to the sisters and their teachings. She understood her mission meant that she had to stay in Gaul and continue her work. It was indeed where she belonged.

• • • • • •

PART IV:

THROUGH THE HEART WE TRANSFORM

CHAPTER 19

QUANTUM MIRACLES

Alice laughed. "There's no use trying," she said. "One can't believe impossible things." "I daresay you haven't had much practice," said the Queen.
—Lewis Carroll

Rochelle and Angelo left their lakeside house and drove to Yosemite National Park, where a rustic cabin was waiting for them. On their first evening, there was a chill in the air, so they sat by a hot stove, commenting on how the décor was so like the cottage they had rented in Maine. Bear and squirrel statues sat on the floor, and landscape paintings adorned the walls. Rochelle made a large pot of turmeric almond tea, and as she poured some for both of them, she watched Angelo put a shawl around his head, the one laced with sacred geometry. She often wondered if the shawl didn't somehow bring Miriam's energy forth, not unlike an ancient symbol, artifact, or amulet might unlock a portal to another dimension.

It seemed as if Rochelle and Angelo were forever pulling threads from one dimension into another, similar to the stories from their shaman friends over the years. She wished more people could realize they live in a multidimensional universe where another realm of reality is a mere thread away from the perception of the reality they're currently having.

After a half an hour of relaxing in a meditative state, Angelo's breathing slowed down significantly, and his head tilted back. As Rochelle put another piece of wood into the stove, she felt the energy in the room amplify. She and Angelo never knew what each encounter would bring, but this time the topic took them by surprise.

"Did Yeshua really raise my brother Lazarus from the dead?" Miriam asked Rochelle when she arrived.

"Lazarus?!" Rochelle blurted, but then took a deep breath and considered the direction Miriam was about to take them.

Neither Rochelle nor Angelo knew much about Lazarus, Miriam's brother. It was recorded that he was raised from the dead, only one of many miracles Yeshua performed. They assumed it was more myth and legend than the gospel it had become, for hadn't Miriam herself said that recorded history got so many details of their lives wrong? Which was it: Myth, legend, a contingent perception, or a universal truth? If they understood their teachings correctly, we only access perceptions that, in turn, become someone's truth which then might spread and become a collective truth.

Miriam touched Rochelle up and down her arm and said, "You feel real—it's all very real, isn't it? Where is Angelo right now?"

Rochelle quickly answered, "He's right next to me, or at least this is my perception."

But her own response made Rochelle wonder: If Angelo was just a perception, then certainly she was too. It raised the question: Were they in some kind of matrix they couldn't fathom? If they were mere projections, were Miriam and Yeshua also projections, and was the world they inhabited a fabrication as well? Was anything *real?*

Seemingly aware of Rochelle's thoughts, Miriam added, "The question is this: Is your physical body real? This rug and pillow, are these real? What about your beautiful rings? Are they real? The stove feels real as well, doesn't it? We certainly need it this evening with the colder temperatures, but none of it is real. This human body you see before you and think is attractive is not real. Do you understand? All of these material things around you are not real but merely perceptions of reality, made up of energy."

"I love the physical perception of what I see," Rochelle jested, nodding toward her Italian partner.

If they were mere projections,
were Miriam and Yeshua also
projections? Was the world
they inhabited a fabrication
as well? Was anything real?

"Then, it's a great reality you have created, isn't it?" said Miriam. "If you're going to create a perception, then why not make it a beautiful one? The greater your perception, the more you will manifest in life. Yeshua's astute comprehension of perception also allowed him to bring Lazarus back into our realm; however, other spiritual masters have also performed such a task as well."

"So, how did he do it?" Rochelle asked her, eager to learn more.

"Yeshua knew Lazarus was nothing more than a perception in a magnetic state of existence and reality; therefore, Lazarus only appeared to be dead," she replied. "Put another way, he was dead for everyone else but for Yeshua; Lazarus was an illusion, so he communicated with the consciousness of Lazarus and said, 'Lazarus, you're not dead; now, wake up.' You see, this is how strong Yeshua's connection to God or Source was."

Miriam paused before adding, "You both keep your bodies in great physical shape, which is an important part of spiritual life as well."

"If we are merely perceptions, then why does it matter?" asked Rochelle.

"Because you're having a physical experience in this realm, so why not have a healthy one?" Miriam responded. "In this dimension, certain laws apply. You can't simply jump off a cliff or drive into another car and not reap the consequences. If you don't take care of your physical body, illness may follow in this realm. Some people only practice spiritual wellness and forget the physical piece of the puzzle, so despite their faith, they get sick. What you do in your energy body, you do in your physical body and vice versa as they are really one and the same. They are interconnected and woven into the fabric of one."

There was a break in her flow while Angelo moved around as if energy was running up through his body and into Rochelle's, or was it the other way around? She was trying to digest what Miriam had just shared while also sensing the strength of the energy growing around them.

"I am deep into Angelo now, so much so there's no distinction between him and me," Miriam noted. "This little nugget of information is extremely important for your spiritual journeys and those you will teach. Do you comprehend my message?"

Teach? Did Miriam really think she and Angelo were going to teach others? Sure, she was transcribing and recording what they said, but she still didn't know if she had the courage to share any of it with the world. What would academics and historians think? The religious would likely shout blasphemy at them as they had done with Miriam and Yeshua over two thousand years ago. They were correct in that Rochelle and Angelo wouldn't be hung, quartered, shot, or sent to prison for teaching something not aligned with a church, institution, or political authority. Still, they could be ridiculed or labeled as unhinged, cracked, and irrational. Rather than go down that path with her, however, she decided to probe deeper. She wanted to know more about the physical body and perceptions.

"Speak to me more about how this happened between Yeshua and Lazarus," Rochelle said.

"I wish I could say it was symbolic because it was hard to believe back then, and even today most will not believe this is possible," said Miriam. "You see, Yeshua simply called back his soul to reunite with his physical body. When you think in quantum terms about who you are as individuals, it is easier to fathom new possibilities beyond your current realm of thinking."

Rochelle shifted positions. She tried to imagine how anyone would believe this story.

Miriam asked, "How do you wish to see yourselves? As three-dimensional beings living in a three-dimensional world? Yeshua understood we were multidimensional beings living in sundry realities, so nothing was impossible for him. Of course, he didn't use language in those times, but he was aware of our power as human beings. It was quite difficult to explain this to people, so he chose his words carefully.

When you think in quantum terms about who you are as individuals, it is easier to fathom new possibilities beyond your current realm of thinking.

"You're sitting here typing and listening to a multidimensional being dictating a story to you from over two thousand years ago. You have a vision and memory of it; however, a sense of what is real is a *perception of consciousness*. The whole idea of a universe is nothing more than consciousness in action creating and recreating itself endlessly."

Rochelle tried to process the explanations coming her way, but it was still dizzying.

"So, you ask me whether Yeshua brought Lazarus back to life?" Miriam asked Rochelle. "The real answer is that he wasn't really dead in the first place. Put another way, Yeshua didn't believe he was dead. It's just as difficult to believe now as it was back then. You must see yourself as a multidimensional being where death itself doesn't exist. Don't you see the miracle in what's occurring even at this time? Let's translate what is happening now into quantum language and thinking."

Quantum again, observed Rochelle. Didn't they know she and Angelo were creative types? What did either of them know about science, never mind quantum physics and multidimensional cosmology? Couldn't Miriam talk to them about the things they were most passionate about, like art and music? Miriam was dead set on going down the quantum rabbit hole again. Rochelle moved closer to the stove and added another pillow beneath her as she adjusted her laptop and waited for Miriam to continue.

"*I Am who I Am* and have come through many," Miriam finally said. "I am Sophia, or rather, some might call me the Sophia, which is the feminine portion or face of God. Some refer to it as wisdom. I just manifest myself in multiple forms through different people, but I show up in those who act in the name of love to teach in unique ways. For some, it is through art, others through music, and for others, through books or simply healing."

The whole idea of a universe
is nothing more than
consciousness in action creating
and recreating itself endlessly.

"Why don't you come to us through art or music?" asked Rochelle. "This quantum stuff is way over our heads."

"Isn't writing a form of art?" Miriam replied with another question. "Some people who connect to me are not bringing through pure versions because some of the messages are getting muddled with other aspects of who they are and their own interpretations. It's much easier to come through you both since you two are a check and balance of energies. You also keep yourselves pure, and I can work through both of your auric fields, not just one. This is the quantum portion of who I am, and Lazarus is the same."

Rochelle was about to correct her and say, "You mean, Lazarus *was* the same," but Miriam would likely remind her there's no past, there's no future, there is only *right now.* Rochelle also wondered what she meant by the purity and cross-check part, but she allowed Miriam to move on.

"If you look at it from a quantum perspective, Lazarus wasn't dead; his soul had simply separated, and Yeshua called it back," she explained. And that was the last thing Miriam said before Yeshua arrived to clarify more of what happened.

Yeshua Speaks

"It is true when I resurrected my friend Lazarus that his physical body, as you see it, was dead and being prepared for burial by his family," Yeshua began. "I never intended to show people I was greater than them through my miracles. It truly wasn't my intention. My hope was to show them they all have the same potential and capacity I had through their words, thoughts, and belief systems.

"I never really healed anyone; I simply made them believe they were healed. How was this done? You might say I created a perfect *match* with their frequencies and then *invited them to believe* they were healed. I had the gift of speaking to a person's soul and creating a perfect frequency match. Even though healing transpired as a result, remember all healing is a two-way street. All human beings have the ability to speak to other souls, so I'll remind you again: I am not any different from you. You see, we are all the same energy, meaning we are all healers, but most people don't believe it today and certainly didn't believe it back then."

"You were able to create a perfect match with a person's frequency?" Rochelle asked, a bit dazed by this revelation.

"It appeared I brought Lazarus back to life, and it was a miracle of miracles for the time; however, here's what actually occurred: I was able to match my frequencies with his, but this only happened because his soul was willing to not only listen but respond. Healing cannot happen if the soul isn't willing to listen, but *if it agrees* and *heeds the call*, then what you call a miracle occurs. Our souls knew each other well before our incarnation into this life, or you could say, into this reality. As a human being, I had a deep connection with Lazarus and sensed it would lead to something, but neither of us knew exactly what might transpire until I heard Lazarus was dying. At that point, I knew I needed to go back and heal him. When I arrived, I was surprised to find him deceased, so was suddenly aware that I was about to meet my greatest challenge head on as you say in your modern tongue.

"How do you heal a dead man? You can't, or can you? So, you see, this was when God spoke to and through me. This was the moment to become what was foretold I would become, and then I knew. In so many ways, I said, 'I am the Way to God, and only through me, you will reach God.' But I only used those words since this was the language people could understand. It didn't mean you could only get to God through me. What I meant was that you must be who you truly are and step into your own power as I had. My work with Lazarus made this message clear to me and solidified my purpose: to teach everyone they can be as I was and do as I did."

Healing cannot happen if the soul isn't willing to listen, but if it agrees and heeds the call, then what you call a miracle occurs.

Rochelle nodded, trying to process his explanation as she savored the words he chose to use, noting what he omitted. Clearly, there is profound wisdom buried under the phrases "frequency match" and "when God spoke to and through me," she thought.

"Apostles with me bore witness to the resurrection of Lazarus as well and could see the deep implications of the experience for me," Yeshua went on. "You might say everything I had learned on my spiritual path came down to this one occasion. The belief in who I was as an energy form was critical at this time. If I say to the mountain move, then the mountain must move. If I say unto Lazarus, rise, then Lazarus must rise, and he did. From that moment on, I never doubted my path again. As time progressed and the series of events unfolded, I suspected my most probable outcome, but I didn't resist my purpose anymore. So, my dear friend Lazarus assisted me on my journey more than he could ever have imagined. During this time, I also felt driven to move forward with Miriam on our path. We both knew our purpose.

"I understand," said Rochelle softly, touched by the unfolding events . . . the rawness of it all.

"Do you understand your purpose in this lifetime?" he asked her. "Don't have any more doubts, especially when I sit here with both of you and speak my truth."

Still bewildered or perhaps dumbfounded was more accurate, Rochelle asked him, "How do you match your frequencies to another to heal or bring someone's physical body back to life?"

"My time in India was spent with numerous gurus," Yeshua responded. "Do you know how I was able to levitate? It was by matching the frequencies of the earth realm and then allowing myself to become one with it. I could control and give the illusion, if you will, that I was floating on air. I wasn't really levitating as much as I was giving the perception I was floating since I was nothing more than energy—then and now—just as you are. Everything is about energy and the perception you create with that energy.

"How did I turn water into wine? I simply connected to and matched the frequencies of the wine. What about the stigmata in the hands? The great saints and sages didn't receive the stigmata because they were so holy and sacred but because they believed they could, and so it happened. You don't need to be a sage or a saint to turn water into wine or to heal others. Rather, you simply need to have the right belief system to heal or, as you say, to create miracles. In other words, you must have immeasurable faith that it's possible. This is what we taught two thousand years ago, but most didn't understand or believe it. How many will believe it today?"

Next, Yeshua turned next to macro shifts in society which excited Rochelle.

"Once your governments and healthcare providers accept, integrate, and promote holistic healing, you will see humanity's consciousness shift significantly," he went on. "Finally, you will see humanity in its true energy form which will stun you, in the same way the explosion of your technology and AI have astonished you. Science and spirituality are advancing at the same speed and frequency."

Although they had seen increased adoption of integrative medicine and holistic practices in the West, Rochelle wondered how much of it was truly being integrated into established institutions and organizations. What would it take for society to change its thinking? And when would all insurance companies cover these emerging alternative methods? She remembered hearing an interview with a renowned doctor who spoke about the importance of having insurance companies on board for programs he was integrating into his practice, including diet and lifestyle changes. Integrated and whole-body healthcare approaches would transform healing, she thought. Before she could turn to the challenges Big Pharma has created for the entire industry, Yeshua changed course.

Science and spirituality
are advancing at the
same speed and frequency.

"I will admit when Lazarus did arise, I was stunned," Yeshua noted. His comment startled Rochelle, but she too found it hard to fathom.

"Yes, I was shocked when it happened, but I didn't convey this to others. You see, your churches and Christian organizations want to believe I was some type of all-knowing God. For them to read that even I was skeptical at the time would be considered blasphemy. But in truth, I was surprised everything I had learned and practiced came to fruition at that precise moment. I had performed what you call miracles before, but I had never been able to bring a body back from death. Afterward, we laughed and cried, and then we celebrated with food and wine."

"It was only the beginning of what I would do after my Crucifixion," Yeshua continued. "I would rise or resurrect myself into a Merkabah body. The event with Lazarus gave me an understanding of what was yet to come and what was possible. Raising someone else is one thing but to raise your own self is a bird of another feather."

"So, you didn't bring your physical body back as some believe?" Rochelle cut in.

"My physical body was a mess—it had been beaten and torn into pieces, and resurrecting the physical body was not the aim," he replied. "The aim or goal of my Resurrection was to show humanity what you are in your true essence, an energy form. And I demonstrated this to others by showing up in my energy form people could see. Unfortunately, humanity corrupted the true message because people had so much doubt and fear back then, and so many still do. Hopefully, with a lot of tender loving care and advancements in science, people will start to understand. Finally . . . "

Yeshua broke off as if contemplating what to say next in a way that would expand Rochelle's knowledge and understanding.

"Sometimes Angelo is confused about the boundary between him and me," Yeshua resumed. "There is no difference between you, Angelo, and me—we are all one, and there is no separation as I have said before. This is precisely why and how human beings can create their own miracles. I am not one, but many, and so are you, and I keep repeating it since it is such a hard message to grasp.

"Rochelle, you and Angelo have the ability to heal anyone you choose to heal instantly; however, you both lack faith right now, and it takes a great deal of practice on this path to realize this faith, as you already know. You just need to reprogram your energy field, not unlike what some of your more courageous scientists and biologists are speaking about now with bioenergy healing. Remember, you don't know what you don't know. Take nothing for granted, know when to be humble, give back and heal others, and you will heal yourselves."

Yeshua left, but she sensed they weren't done for the evening.

Whoa, what a message, thought Rochelle. It seems that we are all individual souls and also one with all souls and one with Source. Just as we are all drops in the ocean and the entire ocean, we are individual extensions of Source and also Source itself.

Soon, Miriam reappeared as she wanted to talk about the preparation for and arrival of Lazarus.

Preparing for Lazarus

"Lazarus had a fairly clear idea of where I went, and we had always thought we would meet up again," Miriam remarked as Rochelle gazed out their cabin window.

Moonlight shone through the window and off in the distance crickets chirped. The mist had begun to settle in, and the stove needed another log, so she grabbed one to keep the room warm as Miriam continued her story.

"There were emissaries who brought information from Lazarus to me in Gaul," she said. "Money was also sent from my family and some of the families of the seven sisters. My father still refused to help, behaving as if I had gone off to join a cult; however, my mother was even stronger than I was in many ways for she always found ways to get money to us despite my father's resistance and other obstacles at home. My parents were still alive, but their health was failing. I knew I would not see them again, another aspect of life not so uncommon back then. It was more difficult since we didn't have fast transportation between countries as you do today, but it was also much more normal during our time because people's circumstances and situations didn't make it easy for them to leave.

"It had been around twenty or so years since I had left Judea, so we were both in our forties when Lazarus came to Gaul. He came alone but bearing gifts.

"What drew him to come?" Rochelle asked her.

"The stories of Yeshua grew," Miriam responded. "Sometimes, when you put a man to death who claims to be the *Son of God*, that man and the image of who he once was becomes even greater, and that's what happened in certain communities in Judea. The apostles continued to teach his Word; however, the messages of the apostles had altered from the original teachings of Yeshua, so much so they began to take on the apostles' points of view. A message can change quickly as it gets passed along.

"The teachings took on more of a Jewish and patriarchal vision, but I wasn't part of that vision, nor would I ever be. So, it wasn't just the Catholic Church that excluded me from the initial teachings; it was my own friends and community, the apostles with whom I had lived, taught, and walked with as well. Most of them didn't care much for me anyway, so I suppose it was to be expected.

"Lazarus became part of the apostles after I left and he taught their story or a version of it anyway, but even he could no longer bear witness to the injustices created in the name of Yeshua which only increased over time. The apostles asked Lazarus to head up a group to bring the message to other parts of the world, but he wasn't willing to do it. Just as the Jewish Orthodoxy had created their own rules and laws you had to follow, so too did the apostles start to make up their own rules and laws you had to follow in the name of Yeshua. It's important to remember no rules or laws were part of Yeshua's true teachings."

Despite the fog, Rochelle and Angelo left the porch of their cabin open so they could hear the calming sounds of crickets and croaking frogs. They knew dawn would bring new sounds, such as the ducks and hummingbirds sure to greet them over morning coffee.

"Cornucopia of nature you have here," Miriam said after a while. Rochelle laughed as she observed the trees swaying back and forth in the wind and heard a bird's call off in the distance. She was always aware of their rhythms and the diverse birdsong they shared. Soon, Miriam went back to Lazarus' story.

"After my brother's profound experience of returning to life so to speak, his views of life dramatically changed, which led to a yearning to see us again and observe how we were teaching Yeshua's wisdom. For nearly two decades, he taught with the male apostles, but he also made quite a lot of money in his profession. Today, you would call him a lawyer as he interpreted Jewish law."

"Tell me more about his arrival," Rochelle interjected.

"When we heard he was coming, I knew then I would spend the rest of my days with my brother teaching the true words of Yeshua," she said. "Many of his fellow Jews no longer accepted him since they felt he was tainted by his coming back to life, which seemed like an unnatural experience to them. Other people also found what happened to him hard to believe. So, he became a man with no country and few friends.

"I had sent letters to him over the years about my life in Gaul, and he was fascinated with the idea of people accepting Yeshua's true message. How could this be when he had to fight tooth and nail against his own people and the Roman government, all while hiding in secrecy most of the time? How could these Druids who knew nothing of Yeshua accept the message so willingly? He was intrigued by the life I had created in Gaul. You might say he was curious to see this unfolding community for himself. When he arrived, we created a feast to welcome him. Joining us were the seven sisters but others as well."

Rochelle never saw this episode coming since she never thought Lazarus would be part of Miriam's story, at least not in such a significant way. As she was reflecting, she noticed that Angelo's energy changed, his eyes closed, and his head went down. Rochelle felt a quieting and softening of his body, and the room felt very tranquil. After several minutes, Yeshua began to speak.

"By that time, I was rarely appearing to the sisters anymore because many years had passed; however, for this occasion, I appeared in my energy form," Yeshua said. "These things have never been written about either. People won't believe these words now, especially your religious scholars, but then again, many people didn't believe me back then either.

"I appeared once again in my Merkabah during this feast to honor Lazarus' coming. The celebration happened in the sisters' house, and just as a society or group expands over time, the house became bigger too. They added what you might refer to as a hall in today's vernacular. It was a room officially made for bigger gatherings, and although it wouldn't be considered large by today's standards, back then, it was a significant size and could hold around forty or so people. Food and wine were created for the occasion, and Miriam was aware I would return on the day of his arrival for this feast. It was as if Lazarus was resurrected again—symbolically this time, of course—but truly a new beginning for all of us. It was like I was resurrected again in a way as well, in the love of a dear friend I had known when I once walked the land in my physical body.

"Some of your religious people ask: Is there a second coming? People in Miriam's community in Gaul never asked this question. I taught them paradise was here already, but it was hard for them to grasp such a message, especially due to their life circumstances. Many people suffered, and times were hard, so it was difficult for people to feel they lived in paradise on the earth since it wasn't how they perceived their lives. Remember, how you live and see your life is a perception of how and where you live. Your perception becomes your reality and truth as it had for them at the time."

Rochelle nodded, for she tried to be aware of how their perceptions could create chaos or joy in their lives.

"This story of ours you are writing will be my and Miriam's message to the world," Yeshua continued. "Our hope is that it will go far and wide and be translated into multiple languages so many will read it. I want them to know that I, Yeshua, am here sitting with you, giving you these messages through you and Angelo. You didn't believe in me for many years, yet here you are, scribing my words. Angelo had forgotten all about me for a long time as well, but here he is in an alternate realm bringing my soul through his auric field. We will write books together, and we will heal through you. You will use our energy to heal and scribe our messages in this lifetime. If you're stepping into your purpose or Authentic Self, does it really matter who believes you and who doesn't?"

Remember, how you live and
see your life is a perception
of how and where you live.
Your perception becomes
your reality and truth.

Rochelle was less worried about people buying into their surreal visitations and more about people thinking they simply imagined all of it, even though they had never touched psychedelics or had an Ayahuasca journey. But then again, how could she and Angelo make up someone's life story they knew nothing about? And more important, why would they want to? They were not religious, nor did they care about religion, so they had no agenda. And they didn't have a scientific background to fully comprehend or convey the quantum realities Miriam and Yeshua had shared.

True, they saw themselves as spiritual, but nature was more of their guide than any belief system, including the ones taught by Yeshua and Miriam. Nonetheless, they began to see they really didn't have a belief system or dogma either. Above all else, their teachings were founded on love and oneness. From this vantage point, it felt very grounded, a far cry from crazy. And yet, she knew there would be many who wouldn't—couldn't—understand their journey, never mind accept it. After all, how long did it take her and Angelo to process their ongoing interactions with Yeshua and Miriam?

Yeshua seemed to respond to her thoughts as if reading her mind. Again.

"Yeshua isn't the only name I went by as Miriam has said. I go by quite a few names, and wherever there is love, you will find me. Heal in my name, teach in my name, but do not create any laws and rules in my name and say they are the laws of God or the laws of Jesus, for it wouldn't be true. Simply love one another in all the aspects of where you have manifested yourselves.

"There is no death. There is no birth. There is no sin. You must start seeing yourselves as Spirit, the energy you are in this lifetime. Then, you will start seeing who you truly are throughout the universe as multidimensional beings. You are not just a part of God but Godde herself/itself/himself. There is no separation. That is all for now. My name is Yeshua, and these are my words. Peace be in you, peace be with you, and give your peace to others."

Yeshua's energy suddenly left, and for about twenty minutes or so, Rochelle and Angelo sat in silence. Then Miriam returned to continue the thread of where they left off. In the meantime, Rochelle's head was spinning.

Miriam appeared to be excited about expanding upon Lazarus, whom Rochelle would soon learn had made quite an impact on Miriam's and the sisters' lives during the later chapter of their lives.

You are not just a
part of God but Godde
herself/itself/himself.

"He knew of our work in southern Gaul and throughout the nearby provinces," Miriam said. "When Lazarus left Judea, he had accumulated a reasonable sum of money, enough to be set for the rest of his life. By then, we were both in our forties which is much older than people in their forties today. If you weren't killed by outsiders, an animal, your own family, or a disease, then you were lucky to live past sixty. He didn't come with all his money because it was stored in several locations. Even so, he came bearing some of it along with gifts, including artifacts from the Egyptian Isis teachings. Lazarus showed up with ritual tools and stones, many of which we used when I was living in Judea, and he also brought writings scribed by or for some of the apostles. Remember the apostles had gone on their own path, but he was in contact with all of them, so he brought some of their writings. The apostles didn't really write themselves but had scribes capture their words, some of which ended up in parts of the New Testament.

"Over time, the Romans and the Catholic Church significantly changed these writings. They altered the original versions dramatically to fit the politicians of Rome and their motives and later to bolster the Catholic Church's power. Lazarus had many papyrus rolls with him, but they were copies of the original, scribed teachings. They truly were gems for us. Variations amongst them reflected how each apostle construed Yeshua's wisdom."

"Were some more aligned with the true teachings of Yeshua?" Rochelle asked, eager to know.

"Yeshua often spoke in parables which had to be interpreted," Miriam said. "I would never say one disciple was wrong and another was right because it wouldn't be true at all. Each disciple deciphered the meanings in the ways he felt were accurate from his understanding and experience of them. Although distortion arose from the patriarchal and traditional views I mentioned before, remember that there was no hierarchy of authority in Yeshua's original teachings. Even the Gospels state there is no need for a church, there is no need for a synagogue, and there is no need for an official house or temple of God to be connected to God. There is only you, and that is the true gospel."

Rochelle took a deep breath as she let Miriam's words wash over her.

"Amongst the treasures arriving with Lazarus were exotic spices from India and other parts of the Middle East we didn't have in Gaul," Miriam went on. "He also brought a variety of materials made of cotton and silk, which we often used on tables. Seamstresses and garment makers nearby helped us create new clothes. It was a lucrative profession back then since everyone needed clothes. Later on, they called them tailors, as you know. He brought sandals with him as well. Lazarus hadn't realized how much cooler it would be, but we wore the sandals during the warmer summer months. The leather was beautifully decorated with stained inks and colors, some of which had stones on top of them. Bear in mind we lived rustically in a remote, woodsy area, so these gifts made us feel like queens and goddesses, and we deemed them sacred."

Rochelle tried to imagine what it must have been like for the sisters to receive such gifts, especially after twenty or so years away from Judea . . . and for Miriam to see her brother again.

"Lazarus also arrived with blankets made of lamb's and sheep's wool which were extremely useful for the fall and winter months. The quantity of things he brought with him was the result of his accumulated wealth from working for so many years, and his additional funds allowed our organization to expand and flourish even more. You see, money doesn't bring happiness, but it brings opportunities to do positive things for people. We used the money to serve humanity, so in this way, abundance is a beautiful thing and should be relished."

After a long silence, she resumed with a personal message for Rochelle and Angelo.

"Don't forget this message on your own journeys. All too often, people who do humanitarian work or spiritual teachers and healers feel they should charge modestly for their gifts and always be serving others. It is important to fill your temple with what you need so you can continue to do the work. Exercise, sleep, and healthy food are an integral part of it, as is meditation and having faith, but abundance comes in many forms, and financial wealth can extend healing messages to a larger group of people. The contributions from Lazarus helped us grow by traveling to more provinces with our teachings. What do you say in your modern time? Don't look a gift horse in the mouth, and we didn't."

After Miriam left, Rochelle and Angelo were stunned by her parting message as it brought them back to Yeshua's discussion of the work Rochelle and Angelo would do in the world. Nevertheless, they assumed the next topic would focus on the expansion of their community and teachings in Gaul. The last thing they expected was for Lazarus to show up and actually speak. But four days after leaving the cabin and pitching a tent at a nearby camping site, that is precisely what happened.

• • • • • •

CHAPTER 20

THE GOSPEL ACCORDING TO LAZARUS

One may have a blazing hearth in one's soul
and yet no one ever came to sit by it.
Passers-by see only a wisp of smoke from
the chimney and continue on their way.
—Vincent Van Gogh

They had just finished cooking dinner around the campfire, both huddled under blankets and the glistening stars. Unexpectedly, Angelo started shaking, so Rochelle was especially vigilant. For several minutes, it was clear he was being pulled elsewhere. The effort to match frequencies was labored at first, and Rochelle sensed the energy belonged neither to the soul of Yeshua nor Miriam's, both of whom they had grown accustomed to for many months. This energy felt new, and it felt like a strained connection. Was this what Yeshua meant by a difficult frequency match? she wondered.

"Angelo, can you hear me?" she asked. His left thumb went up, so she knew he was aware of her presence even though he didn't appear to be *fully* in her realm or reality. She had begun to feel he was in both dimensions simultaneously or perhaps it wasn't really *both*, but more like *many*. Rochelle was fatigued that evening after their hike earlier in the day, so she knew she needed to revive herself to prepare for an ethereal visit.

She grabbed a pillow from inside the tent and threw another log on the fire when suddenly a voice began to speak, one with a different tone and energy than the two ascended masters who had started to feel like family to both of them.

Lazarus Speaks

"This is the one you know as Lazarus, the brother of Miriam from her time in the earth realm," the voice began, although it came out slow and choppy at first.

Even though Rochelle and Angelo had been talking about Lazarus with Miriam and Yeshua, they didn't expect to hear from him directly. Were they really going to learn about Magdalene's life through his eyes?

"The connection will get clearer," Lazarus said next. "Give me a few minutes to adjust the frequency so we can align with each other's fields."

After what felt like an eternity, he spoke again.

"I want to shed some light from my perspective, or you could say, the perspective of the soul who once inhabited the auric field of Lazarus when he/I once walked on this planet," Lazarus explained. "During our time, Yeshua's father Yosef and my father Joachim were friends."

"Joachim?" Rochelle asked.

"Yes, but for your modern-day English, a similar name might be James," said Lazarus. "However, the names back then were a mix of what you might call old Hebrew, Aramaic, and even Latin, so even James is not an accurate translation since James might be more likened to Jacob. The closest rendition of our mother's name might be Rayna; however, even this is not precise. I am trying to give Angelo names he can most easily pronounce in your language and dialect."

Hmmm, thought Rochelle. How could they communicate ancient names to either of them when they didn't have exposure to the language or culture of the time? Receiving the sisters' names took weeks, and Miriam had also said they too were not completely accurate, but as close as she could manage with Rochelle's and Angelo's linguistic skills.

"Our families knew each other fairly well," Lazarus continued, "and Mary, Yeshua's mother, and Rayna practiced the Isis teachings together, so they saw each other often."

More reference to the Isis teachings, Rochelle noted to herself. Evidently, it loomed large in women's lives, especially those who were perhaps more privileged and had the courage to join this underground movement for support from and connection to other women.

"Our fathers were a bit like Renaissance men since they studied a variety of ancient ideas and practices, but this didn't mean they weren't stuck in their patriarchal ways," he said. "It was quite common for families of means to practice ancient ways to bring them abundance and enlightenment. My mother was part of the Isis group or cult, which she passed on to my sister. For your contemporary ears, the Tao of Isis may make more sense."

She recalled Miriam had used the same term . . . probably for the same reason. Rochelle also noted how easy his communication was to process. I bet Lazarus was witty and smart, she thought. After a strenuous energy match initially, there was an ease and flow to the dialogue. It felt smoother than their connection to Miriam and Yeshua although she didn't understand why until later. He moved on.

"Yeshua was aware of my sister Miriam when they were younger, but not until he returned from the East did I notice their spark. You might say it was predestined my friend Yeshua would be betrothed to Miriam of Magdala.

"I loved my sister Miriam a great deal, but I did not understand her so well in those days. Both sets of parents were well aware their children were strong-headed and had a mission. Like Mary, my mother had a vision about Miriam before she was born. Both mothers had intuitive and psychic abilities; however, we didn't use these terms. It was common for some people to receive messages and visions from what we referred to as angels. Are they truly angels? Let's just say they are light beings without lives as you, Angelo, and others experience in various planes.

"Yeshua and I broke bread together when we were quite young," Lazarus reflected. "We became friends through acquaintances of our parents since we were educated in the same schools. I knew Yeshua as a child before he left for India to study at around twelve or thirteen years of age, and he didn't return until he was in his twenties. Truthfully, he was always odd, even as a child. We had heard rumors of him as a boy about possibly being a deliverer or a Messiah, but those stories of a coming Messiah had been told for thousands of years. How could Yeshua be the one, he who was a woodworker and lived amongst us? And so we didn't pay much attention to the rumors; however, he had a presence and unique gifts, so many were aware of him.

"When he returned home to Judea, we got back together, but our paths diverged substantially during our time apart. I embraced earthly and secular things, and he focused on spiritual things, but we still enjoyed our friendship. He was on a much deeper spiritual path than I was, and when he returned from his years of study, he was a new man."

"A new man?" Rochelle asked. "In what way?"

"He was deeply reflective and inward as if something transformed him when he was abroad," Lazarus replied. "The change felt drastic. As strange as this may sound, it seemed like he had experienced death. What do I mean? Although all people change as they grow up, he had changed so much I didn't recognize him at all. No one did. Yeshua had become an authentic spiritual leader and healer during his time away, but only when I saw him teach and speak to the masses did I understand his gifts and who he was as a person. When I witnessed him healing individuals with a touch or words, I truly grasped his impact and power.

"Remember, I was not much of a religious man at the time, even though I knew the Judaic laws extremely well in my role as what you would call a lawyer today. To help Jews who supposedly broke the law, I negotiated with the Pharisees who enforced strict rules, regulations, and statutes. The Romans left these matters to the predominant Jewish religious order of the time; however, if they couldn't take care of a matter, they stepped in to handle it as they did with Yeshua."

Lazarus stopped speaking as if to let Rochelle understand he was validating the history of what the Romans did with Yeshua once he became a threat to those in power.

"Miriam saw him as both a rebel and hero, which appealed to her because she was a rebel herself," he finally said. "At this time, Yeshua wasn't in trouble yet since it was still in the early days of his teachings. He had just started gathering people around him to teach all he knew, including what he had learned in India. His ways were foreign to me, so although I cherished my time with him, I resisted the wisdom at first. How could I teach about breaking God's law when I was there to promote it or, at a minimum, represent those laws? But it didn't take long to trust him.

"After he returned home, he gradually started gathering followers. And then . . . his disciples. Miriam joined his caravan of followers and teachers. How do you think my father felt about her decision? Our mother supported her mystical ways, but my father and sisters weren't as accommodating. I understood only because I saw her attraction to Yeshua and felt the intensity of their connection, but I had no idea what was coming—none of us did.

"Miriam and Yeshua grew closer in the first couple of years, and then they started to live in communities with others. For a while, they lived with the Essenes, an outcast group that other sects saw as breaking God's law. They were there to learn their unique ways and to perfect their teachings and healing techniques. Shortly after they left the Essenes, I became sick.

"My heart was enlarged and had a defect, so you might call it a congenital abnormality, but we didn't have language for it back then. My parents knew something was wrong since I was often short of breath, so they didn't allow me to partake in physical activities. They forced education upon me instead of physical labor, primarily because of my situation. During my studies, a viral infection spread throughout my entire body and turned systemic. My heart became inflamed and couldn't bear the brunt of the infection, which resulted in what you refer to as a heart attack. Put another way, my body stopped functioning and expired."

Rochelle nodded and murmured "expired" under her breath. Then, after a few seconds, she repeated it louder. "Expired?"

"Yes," Lazarus responded. "Do you want to know what it was like to pass? It was like coming back to who you *truly* are again, so it was a reunion of sorts. Although I didn't see God, as many would understand this term during this passing process, I recognized the sensation and feeling of being one with everything. In other words, I recognized something I already knew."

Lazarus halted briefly and then said in a resonant voice that seemed to shake the ground they were sitting on, "It was like going home."

Rochelle nodded attentively for she felt the significance of his message.

"A sister reported my condition to Yeshua, and he came immediately; however, he was several hours if not a day away," he went on. "I had been dead for well over a day by the time Yeshua arrived. You must understand my family was preparing me for burial, and my burial gown had been cleansed with oils and sweet-smelling perfumes. Please make it known I wouldn't come to you if I didn't think it was so important to tell you these things, but I also know what you are recording now will cause problems for you as well."

Silence followed. Problems? Rochelle thought to herself. More like a stir, the kind of stir that would either turn doubters into bigger skeptics or wannabe believers into obsessed fanatics. Maybe both. She began to fidget but then he picked up the thread.

"The custom of the time involved preparing bodies in a sacred place. Mine was laid in a small cave the family considered sacred. Later, human beings used catacombs or little houses made of stones. Those small caves often functioned as catacombs during our times. When Yeshua arrived, he came to the cave where my body lay."

Ten or so minutes passed before his story marched on. Rochelle began to wonder if he was pausing more for himself than for her. Perhaps the connection wasn't as strong as it had become with Miriam and Yeshua. It turned out it had to do with semantics.

"I am looking for the words to give to Angelo," he explained. "In your language, Yeshua said to me, 'Lazarus, get up.' To make it more poetic, let's say: 'Lazarus, Rise.' That was it. It was as if your mother would come into a room and say, 'Get up; it's time for school.' It was a bit like that, as strange as this might sound. At that time, my energy body connected again with my soul."

Rochelle interjected, "You mean your physical body reconnected to your soul?"

"The soul reconnected to my physical body, but truthfully it is *really* my energy body, for that is what we are . . . energy," Lazarus responded. "This chocolate wafer in front of you is nothing more than a field of energy," he continued, pointing to the small plate of cookies on the coffee table. "When I put it into Angelo's mouth, I can taste it. I can sense it. I move it around in Angelo's mouth, but it's pure energy, and this cup of tea before you is also nothing more than energy. What seems to be solid material form is nothing more than particles of energy you believe exist in a solid form, but I'm showing Angelo a picture right now of what merely appears to be real.

"What I am telling you now will be incredibly controversial. Yeshua didn't really save my life, nor did he resurrect my body—it only appeared that way. Many of your Christians and Catholics will not like this message. You see, Yeshua gave the *appearance* of resurrecting me."

Now wide awake, Rochelle blurted out, "So, he did or didn't?"

"My physical body did become *alive* again, at least as you perceive the word alive, but I say it was the appearance because it truly is a perception," he replied.

"Okay, so in our understanding, you were resurrected," she retorted, growing frustrated by how his explanation didn't make sense to her conditioned mind. Her rational mind. Her logical reasoning. Her *rooted in science* thinking. After reflecting for a minute or two, she added, "How is it actually possible?"

"Let me respond with a quantum understanding," Lazarus said. "Both energy fields must be equal to each other, and the frequencies must match identically for it to be successful in the way it occurred during my lifetime as Lazarus. It is a frequency and vibrational match between two energy fields, and they must be aligned. The energy field of a human being is like that of a tuning fork. Rochelle, when you play your crystal bowls, you create vibrational frequencies that match ours. When this connection takes place, Angelo is able to bring these frequencies and vibrations into your dimension, including our energies, but it must be an exact match."

"It wouldn't be an identical match every time I strum the same crystal bowl, right? Or would it?" Rochelle asked.

"Frequencies will come through that will match what you play and how you play it," Lazarus replied. "Crystal bowls give off the same frequencies as many energies in the angelic realm. Humanity in your reality gave this realm and the energies within it the name of angels although it's not really what you think of as angels within your linear frame of mind. Think of it in this way: Imagine a tuning fork is struck, and a glass is nearby. When the frequency of the glass and the tuning fork are in perfect resonance, the glass will vibrate, but when there's too much, it creates an extreme amount of energy—what you call interference—and the glass breaks. Interference is nothing more than resistance. If my soul had resisted Yeshua's energy when he called it forth, I would not have returned to this three-dimensional human realm, but there was no resistance nor interference. At a soul and energetic level, I knew exactly what I had to do; however, it's easier to explain what happened in terms of energy."

The energy field of a human being is like that of a tuning fork.

Rochelle took a deep breath, trying to absorb and process the wisdom. It made her think of the *Star Trek* transporter that could dematerialize a crew member and then rematerialize them somewhere else.

"I simply reenergized the conscious portion of my body, and it appeared my physical body came back to life in a three-dimensional world," Lazarus continued. "It wasn't really Yeshua bringing me back to life as it was a communication between our two energy fields outside this dimension. You cannot heal someone unless the other soul is in alignment with your frequency. Yeshua had the ability to tap into the frequencies of the individuals he healed at a microscopic level, so if they were healed, it was because their frequencies and energetic selves *recognized it* and agreed."

Recalling a similar although not as detailed explanation from Yeshua, Rochelle felt only awe and wonder. Staring up at the stars, she heard crickets in the distance, a reminder of her childhood—no matter where she was or who she was with—not unlike morning birdsong. The sound of crickets seemed to connect the stars with the earth, grounding her as she contemplated these mind-blowing revelations. Aside from nature's melodious orchestra, it was relatively quiet, and the night was serene, dulcet, and magical. She marveled at how comfortable she was with Lazarus' energy in a relatively short period of time.

"Yeshua was aware he was an energy being, a spirit being—not a physical form," Lazarus went on. "All he needed to do was match his vibration with the other spirit being in front of him, and he would heal. This was immeasurably profound, especially two thousand years ago. This is even profound by today's standards, isn't it?"

Her pupils got bigger as she considered the words pouring out of Angelo's mouth, still astonished she was speaking to Lazarus, Miriam's brother from another time. He was on a roll.

"Now, let me try again to explain to you how this happened. One energy being was speaking to another energy being, but *soul-to-soul.* Both energies of pure light assisted each other, but not on a three-dimensional plane as you call it, but more in an energy-verse—like a multiverse—so it occurred outside the construct of space and time as you know it in the realm in which you live."

Rochelle blinked, trying to comprehend it all. "You mean in other realms our human eyes can't see, and our ears can't hear, at least for most of us?" Rochelle asked.

"This is what I mean," he clarified. "Yeshua was able to place himself into the same energy-verse as mine, and as such, he created miracles, which is how people saw his healings. I will also tell you this: No other man on this planet has ever been able to connect to multiple realities in the same way he was able to do again and again. He was able to match his energy directly with mine and to enliven and restore my physical body again. As a result, it called forth what you refer to as the soul.

"You see yourselves as physical beings, just as I saw myself when I manifested myself as Lazarus on the human plane over two thousand years ago. However, when Yeshua called my soul and matched his energy to mine, I was aware I was no longer a physical form but merely taking the shape of a physical form in an alternate dimension or reality. I brought light to the energy body again, which then manifested back into physical, material form. As peculiar as this is going to sound to you, it was not as difficult for me to come back into this energy form as you think."

No other man on this planet has ever been able to connect to multiple realities in the same way he was able to do again and again.

Rochelle processed what he said for a few moments and then asked, "So, it was possible because your physical body was still somewhat intact and hadn't been dead for too long? Yeshua was able to reconnect your so-called physical body to the soul itself again?"

Contemplating for a moment, she added, "But I assume it would be much more complex to do for himself?"

"Correct," he replied, "as he only appeared in what you would call an energetic imprint of sorts, but it was much more profound than that. Let's see if we can get this straight. Yeshua reappeared as his soul with a projected image of his physical body. In other words, a body without the physicality of DNA. How will you explain this to people, especially your scientists and doctors? We know the physical body also has a conscious aspect; however, if the soul separates itself from the physical body, the physical shell dies, but the larger consciousness of the soul lives on."

Rochelle was wired at this point, but she wasn't sure if it was because she had drunk five cups of tea or because she was talking to a multidimensional being in her realm. Perhaps she was in his realm instead and unaware of it, or maybe they met in between.

I brought light to the
energy body again,
which then manifested
back into physical,
material form.

She knew she could never truly understand what was happening, but she also knew the visitations and experiences with Miriam, Yeshua, and Lazarus were as real as the perceived material life she dealt with every day. Rochelle was more convinced than ever that multidimensional realms existed, even if she couldn't get her linear mind around how and where they existed. Angelo knew this too. They weren't on a mushroom journey, nor were they in the blue-pill illusory world of *The Matrix* (or were they?), but these subtle and not-so-subtle realms—depending on your lens—existed. Then again, why can some spiritual masters perform miracles, and others can't? Why do some people have instantaneous healing from stage four cancer while others pass away and return to what you might call Universal Consciousness or All That Is?

They certainly didn't have all the answers, but they were beginning not just to understand the concept of maya or illusion all the spiritual greats have spoken of for thousands of years but also to experience it all. They knew indigenous elders and shamans who tapped into other realms to perform ceremonies and heal. Each spiritual master and healer may use their own language—depending on their culture and perception—for these unseen realms and dimensions we can all tap into. They understand and have always understood that these subtle realms and dimensions are as real as the flames in the firepit flickering before them. It's not magic, she thought, even if some of it appears to be so to their human ears, eyes, and minds.

Lazarus must have sensed Rochelle's mind was spinning. He went on to give another example.

"The physical body is presented here in this three-dimensional realm as an image of who you are in this lifetime or reality. Let's just say that it is an image projected or given by the soul. As Miriam may have told you, the Egyptians and many who studied the Isis teachings called it the Ka Body.

"In Yeshua's case, the soul did not reconnect to the physical body, but his soul was able to project an imprint people could see, and he was able to do this for long periods of time. Yeshua was able to manifest his Merkabah into the earth realm again and again. This ability was another thing that made Yeshua so unique and not just for our time. In contrast, the essences you refer to as ghosts are nothing more than shadows of what they once were. A ghost is more of a low vibrational energy, a remnant of the conscious portion of your body appearing as a projection, but without a soul because the soul had already separated."

Rochelle asked, "So, what's projected without physicality is almost like an imprint?"

In response, Lazarus decided to add yet another example to clarify his explanation even further.

"The soul doesn't need to go back to the so-called light since it's already there," he replied. "But it is also connected to all its lifetimes. Imagine pine needles on a tree as the countless lifetimes you've had, the branches on a tree as the essences and personas that made up all those lifetimes, and the tree as the soul itself. The tree, needles, and branches are not separate but one, just as you are one with many essences or energies. Now think of what you see as ghost energy in this way: A few pine needles are still experiencing a three-dimensional realm—meaning a realm vibrating in a slower and denser way—projecting energy that is further away from light and love."

Rochelle acknowledged the explanation, for it was a similar analogy Miriam and Yeshua had shared with them before. Denser and slower seemed to be one way they used to explain those with a consciousness of separateness. But was this only because they were simple analogies Miriam, Yeshua, and Lazarus thought she and Angelo could understand? And why was Lazarus using a similar example? Did they all share a collective mind in the other realms? Or were they able to meld with Rochelle's and Angelo's minds somehow to use language they could relate to?

"This lesson was one of the most important," he continued. "I truly understood it when I returned to my physical body two thousand years ago. I knew this would be one of the most challenging teachings to give others so they could connect to Source or God again. There was no way people could understand such a message back then, but it also wasn't my role to share it with others.

We all have a mission and purpose in life, don't we? Well, supporting them was mine, so I did everything I could to assist Miriam, Yeshua, and the apostles on their journey. I would have loved to have been a powerful spiritual teacher and healer, but it simply wasn't my purpose in that lifetime.

"Yeshua taught that everyone could heal; however, his gifts were extraordinary. Therein lay his uniqueness. Like no other healer, Yeshua was able to match frequencies and vibrational patterns simply through his ability to think it. Yeshua was able to be in multiple realms simultaneously, similar to what Angelo is doing at this time. He is not completely here in this realm, but he's not completely in the other realm either—he's in both."

She wondered what being in both realms really meant. If we are all multidimensional beings, are parts of our souls not existing in *multiple* realms or realities?

Like no other healer,
Yeshua was able to
match frequencies and
vibrational patterns simply
through his ability to think it.

It was late, but it didn't appear Lazarus was finished. She put a blanket around Angelo, who was leaning up against a large log not far from their tent. Rochelle knew she and Angelo would never forget this camping trip. She got up to add more wood to the fire and looked up into the sky, teeming with stars. In between the barrage of crickets attempting to harmonize, she could hear the occasional frog croak, as if it too wanted to be part of the orchestra.

Just like Lazarus, Miriam, Yeshua, Angelo, and her, each living thing plays its role in this beautiful and mind-bending universe, all contributing in mysterious and magical ways. We may not understand the grand plan, but sometimes we don't need to, because when we surrender to our purpose in an aligned and authentic way, everything seems to fall into place. She considered: If we are truly interconnected with All That Is, then we are interconnected not only to other human beings but to the trees, animals, oceans, bird life, and everything beyond the planet as well. She wondered if the stars had consciousness. Could they sense her somehow? Weren't we all stardust after all?

She mused, Lazarus wasn't one for small talk, was he? And neither was she. As she thought of her life with Angelo, she realized they had both begun to see these multidimensional beings as family. Even though they were energy forms they couldn't physically see in their reality, Angelo often saw visions of them through his third eye. She suddenly laughed out loud at the wonder of their lives, and as her laughter echoed into the night sky, Lazarus' soul activated once again to resume the dialogue.

"So, at the time, my resurrection was indeed a miracle, wasn't it?" he then said. "It wasn't so much that Yeshua resurrected me, but it appeared Yeshua resurrected me. This really was the purpose—to show others that a physical body could reignite. I was aware of his soul there with me telling me to get up and rise, and then I understood our mission together. As you likely know, no soul can command another. Each soul has free will to do as it chooses, and although Yeshua's soul could not command mine, by matching my frequencies it could *deliver a message*. It was up to me to receive that message and respond or not, and so I did.

"Similarly, Yeshua couldn't heal unless those in need of healing both received and accepted it. It's not so much about the message but how you receive it, as I suspect Miriam and Yeshua have said and taught you both. How does the soul receive what's coming its way? Do you choose it, or do you not choose it? Whether the message is healing in the form of words, energy, or a touch, do you embrace the wisdom or reject it?

"I should add that Yeshua brought more awareness to the situation as well. Put another way, he squeezed some of my physical body's skin, and as he pinched it, he said, 'This is not who you are.' People think they are physical forms only with flesh, bones, and muscles, and I used to believe that too when I was Lazarus. After my experience, I realized this wasn't the case at all."

Rochelle countered, "But we are in this dimension, so whether it's really more a projection or not, it's still a reality *to us.*"

"If you could only see what I see right now," he responded without skipping a beat. "I see the two of you sitting next to each other, and you're telling my story through your auric field even though you don't quite see it that way. I am showing Angelo a picture of you both in this reality in your energy forms.

"You see, Yeshua called me, or you could say he was able to match his vibrational energy directly with mine, which allowed me to understand who I truly was in that lifetime. Many have had near-death experiences, known as NDEs. I had a near-death experience, but I also had a real-death experience. In actuality, that's what near-death experiences are—when your physical body dies and separates from the soul. Often, the soul chooses to return to become enlightened as a means to assist others on their spiritual paths. An NDE is one way to contribute to people's lives since people can return to tell their stories. This is what I chose to do as well. You could also say I came back to assist Yeshua on his spiritual path."

After a long silence, Lazarus spoke again.

"The period you refer to as death is actually life," he said with a reverberating tone. "It's where I was after the body died. But where is that? Where did I go? Let me try to explain it to you using an example."

He pointed to the small, green-painted table with a lit candle on it near the tent.

"Imagine your table has one hundred candles lit on it, and let's say those one hundred candles represent your soul, but only fifty of them are lit. Each time you have an experience, more candles become lit, representing a life or an experience, however you want to say or see it. The more candles that are aflame, the more experiences you are having, so ultimately, your soul becomes wiser as a direct result of having more experiences. When a candle goes out or is snuffed out, that experience ends.

"So, when Yeshua said to me, 'Lazarus, Rise,' his soul was telling my soul to relight the candle and make the physical body breathe again. Put another way, bring life to that candle or bring light to that body *once again* so you may shine your light to others, and so I did."

The period you
refer to as death
is actually life.

It was much easier to comprehend what he was saying in the context of brightly lit candles, so she loved the analogy.

"Where was I in between all of this?" he went on. "Everywhere. Understand, even when all the candles are out and there is no light, I am still everywhere as a soul. What do I mean exactly? You actually don't need to have any experiences to be alive because you are *always* one with Source and living vicariously through others as we do through you. Put another way, my candles are always lit since this is what I and others you might call ascended masters do. We're always teaching and healing others and giving experiences to those who need or want more experiences."

Even though it must have been four am, Rochelle was still wide awake and eager to hear more.

"So, where does the soul go?" she asked him, aching for more clarity.

"The soul goes everywhere and can experience everything if it chooses," Lazarus replied. "When Yeshua called me and said, 'Lazarus, Rise,' he allowed me to relight one candle and continue my experience as Lazarus on the earth plane. You see it as a miracle, but it was merely a way I could assist Yeshua on his journey—one soul assisting another soul, but in a human dimension. I allowed my candle to be lit again so others could see what Yeshua could do and perhaps better understand his message. You might say I had to die to be reborn. I sacrificed myself so Yeshua could be the true authentic healer he was in that lifetime. In a way, I put myself on the proverbial cross or became the sacrificial lamb."

Wow, thought Rochelle, there was so much to process. Considering some of the indigenous traditions she had experienced on her travels, she asked him, "So if people choose to expand spiritually and assist others in this realm, do they have to go through a kind of death, but perhaps not always a physical one?" She wondered whether Lazarus would correct her to say, "a perceived physical one."

"You both already died, but not in the way I did," he responded. "Often, people on a spiritual path die to step into their soul's journey, whether through an NDE or, as both of you have experienced, through an emotional death. Now, you're igniting your candles again so Yeshua and Miriam can come to heal and teach through both of you. And tell their story, of course. Others want to hear I was welcomed through the heavenly gates with open arms, but it's not really what happens unless you choose to have that perception. Remember, we create our own realities in our spirit form as much as we do in our perceived physical form. Do you understand?"

Although Rochelle was riveted by the teaching, she also felt slightly groggy, and it wasn't just because she had been up nearly all night talking to Miriam's brother's soul. She noticed she felt overwhelmed with energy whenever a new soul came through Angelo's auric field. Miriam had told her several times their energies filtered through her first. Truth be told, she had problems staying alert for the first few months of their visits. Over time, she had grown accustomed to them, but it was hard to describe. For Rochelle, it felt a bit like smoking a joint; it was relaxing but also transcendental in that it brought a deep sense of peace and serenity. In this case, Lazarus' powerful energy seemed to both exhaust and captivate her simultaneously.

We create our own realities
in our spirit form as
much as we do in our
perceived physical form.

Rochelle asked, "Why do I feel so knocked out when new energies like you or the Essenes come through? I can somehow stay grounded while Miriam is here, but when others visit, it feels like I'm being drugged or drawn into another realm, perhaps both concurrently. It's as if I'm not quite here even though I can physically see material objects such as the furniture and paintings in a room or the tent and fire before me now."

Lazarus addressed her question, echoing pieces of what Miriam had also shared with her.

"It's because you are acting as a filter, which allows Angelo to bring forth a multitude of energies, including novel ones like mine. You might say this: We come through you, Rochelle, as particles but flow into Angelo as waves. I am the same energy, but I change my molecular structure into and through Angelo. Imagine stronger energy cables and chords placed through you and Angelo so you can handle all of our energies."

Rochelle's head got dizzy again. *Is this for real?* Was she really talking to Lazarus about quantum particles? Her brain froze while she tried to process what he just shared.

She felt one more explanation might just transpose words into bubbles that would inexorably pop and blow her mind.

"These stronger energy chords and connections we place through both of you allow your meridians to connect to stronger and bigger energies, like all of ours," he clarified. "It allows you to have freedom of choice whether you want to speak to individual frequencies or collective ones although truly all of it is one."

It was overwhelming despite her sense of calm and interconnectedness with the stars earlier. She knew they were planning a canoe ride and a hike in the woods later and wondered how they would stay awake for it after staying up all night. Frankly, she was eager to connect to nature and the birds despite fatigue because she knew they'd make her feel grounded after such a surreal rollercoaster ride with Lazarus. Animals reminded her of what it was to be human, whereas Lazarus took her to far-reaching spiritual heights that wore her out. Rather than go deeper into things her brain was too tired to grasp, she simply asked him, "Did you always know or feel you would see Miriam again?"

"Returning to life, as you call it, shook me up in a momentous way, and I began to look at life in a fresh new way," Lazarus replied. "After such an extreme soul encounter, my resistance gave way to an all-embracing belief in his teachings, so I assisted the apostles where I could. But I always felt something bigger had to be done, so I continued to practice law and save money so I could travel or make a significant impact.

"Remember, Miriam and I were able to send messages through merchants and sailors although they were slow. As news came from Miriam about the growing community and their acceptance of Yeshua's true teachings, my curiosity grew. I felt the need to see what was happening in this land of Gaul, but first, I wanted to save up enough money to leave Judea. I knew there was a strong possibility I wouldn't return."

And then his energy was gone. It took longer for Angelo to come back fully to her reality, but once he did, he greeted her confusion with his own. They were both dumbfounded at first since they never imagined Lazarus would actually visit them. The fire was out, and they could feel the dew from the early morning fog. Before crawling into their tent, they briefly looked at the green forest around them growing brighter in the light of the rising sun. Despite the mind-boggling story from Lazarus, they were exhausted and ready for some sleep. Outside, birdsong echoed into the dawn's light, and they both nested in their tent until the sun's heat drove them outside. They spoke of the previous night as they prepared eggs over a late morning fire and heated grains, water, and milk in Rochelle's grandfather's old coffee pot.

"Did last night's adventure really happen?" Rochelle asked Angelo.

"We know so little about Lazarus," Angelo replied.

"You mean, we knew so little about Lazarus," she responded. "I now feel like he's a long-lost cousin." She broke off for a few seconds before adding, "I'm at least relieved we were together in the same dimension last night."

Rochelle poured some fresh coffee into her favorite camping mug and looked out at the fluffy clouds beginning to fill the same sky shrouded with pink mist as they retired several hours earlier.

"The mystery of what is unveiling before our eyes," Angelo said. "I still don't understand it all."

She pinched his arm. "You sure feel real to me," she said.

"At least we still have that," he added and laughed.

"As a reality?" she asked.

"Well, at least one of them," he replied. "If we truly are multidimensional in nature, shouldn't we be able to experience perceived physical and expanded realities from the subtle realms simultaneously?"

"It appears we do," she said. "Perhaps others don't because they don't believe it's possible."

Angelo wasn't sure if it was a question or a statement, but in the silence that followed, they stared into the dense thicket of trees, sipping their coffee as the geese flew above them.

• • • • • •

When they returned to Cambridge a week later, Rochelle engaged in grounding activities to remind her they were also here to have a quotidian human experience, even if it was a perception or projection. It was a Saturday evening when Lazarus reappeared in their sitting room. She decided to light candles and incense to prepare for another journey with Lazarus since the last one was rather intense. As if he had known her for years (or lifetimes), he began observing their home.

"*Domus* is a Latin word for home," he said. "Peasant folks used the term to refer to the home of aristocrats, and this is the kind of home I see when I look around your place, but not because of the structure of the building itself. I am using this analogy for several reasons. You have created a frequency of wealth from the music you play, the books you read and display on your shelves, the plants you surround yourselves with, and even the food in your cupboards.

"To experience abundance in your life, you must believe you are *of* abundance and *worth* abundance in all aspects. As you look around, see and feel the wealth and abundance in its myriad forms. View your statues of gods and goddesses as wealth. You have symbols here of Pagans, indigenous relics, and books upon books of knowledge from Hinduism, Buddhism, Christianity, Judaism, Islam, Sufism, Zoroastrianism, Shamanism, and Shintoism. I see your books on neuroscience, psychology, the biofield, quantum physics, and philosophy too. I feel wealth in every corner of your home in so many textures and layers.

"When I was Lazarus in a human body, this perception of diverse wealth is what I tried to instill in the common people although most couldn't grasp it. I would tell them the real wealth was within each of them and it would materialize in ways beyond their imagination. I truly began to discover what my life purpose was after I was resurrected. To expand upon this, let's go back to my life from two thousand years ago and recount the time I spent in ancient Judea before I joined Miriam again in southern Gaul."

There was a dynamic presence and charisma about his energy, and Rochelle expected he was larger-than-life in his day. As Lazarus related his story, she wished she could see what his human form once looked like.

"After this so-called miracle of resurrection, I knew what my mission was and what it was not," Lazarus continued. "It wasn't to join the apostles and teach the *Word of Yeshua* to others, especially since the Word was being changed as time marched on. Not only with the apostles but also with others scribing what he said, Yeshua's true teachings had morphed into something else fairly quickly."

It made sense to Rochelle. Consider how many people copied, translated, and updated the text over a millennium, all with their own agendas and biases even if some were not aware of them consciously.

"Even with Yeshua's original teachings, not everyone understood or received them. 'Pay no mind to those who do not have ears to listen but give your all to those who are willing to hear you,' was Yeshua's message. Those with ears listened, and those with eyes saw the truth. It is the same now; not everyone has ears to listen and eyes to see, so they cannot accept the wisdom he once taught.

"Given my status and connections in life, I knew my purpose was to provide financial support for those who were teaching his actual truth. I had no idea exactly how I would do this; however, after my life-changing experience, I transitioned from practicing law casually into a more committed role, an easy move for me since my father was in the same profession, and I could join him. I knew it would give me financial stability and elevate me to what you'd call a favorable place, an echelon of esteemed individuals. Influential people introduced me to others with political clout, a necessary game, if you like, to make things happen. I studied religious law with none other than the Pharisees. I also studied Latin and Greek Philosophy, Sumerian Philosophy, and Egyptian culture, all of which became useful when debating with the Roman magistrates about the laws governing the people of Judea."

Mysteriously, as Lazarus began to speak more and more about Egyptian culture and Jewish law, the music on their playlist began to change. Sometimes when other energies entered their dimension, a new song would randomly start to play, or the volume might change. Often when Miriam and Yeshua came for a visit, the audio suddenly turned off, or a tune they had never heard of began. Song switching happened twice during that evening's visit with Lazarus, and oddly, Gregorian Chants came on, taking Rochelle by surprise.

"Naturally, it was also crucial that I study the Roman laws imposed upon us," he said, not taking notice of the music shifts around them. "To best assist my clients, I had to argue and debate the laws most relative to whatever issue or crime they were facing at the time. You see, there were two bodies of law a Judean had to abide by—those imposed by Judea and those inflicted by the Romans. Bargaining always took place between them, and I was well positioned to be an instrumental and effective negotiator."

Rochelle noticed a sense of pride in the words bellowing from Angelo's mouth as he spoke of his career so many years ago. "What were you doing before practicing law?" she asked.

"I was involved with several spiritual organizations," he replied. "My work didn't include serious spiritual studies as Yeshua had done, but it brought me into contact with various cultures, languages, and ways of life. I enjoyed learning from others and had the liberty to do so until I got sick. I never wanted anyone to enforce their religious beliefs upon me, so you could say I was more of a free spirit like Miriam—we were similar that way. She was much more into mystical and spiritual studies than I was; however, when you had means, as we did, you were given opportunities to travel. You see, wealth allowed me to explore unfamiliar lands. The cultures, languages, and laws I learned along the way were instrumental in my becoming a successful lawyer. There's a lot to be said about that path, for it shaped who I became."

Rochelle now understood why his language was more fluid and sophisticated than she expected or was used to with Miriam and Yeshua. If he was tapping into the frequencies of who he once was as Lazarus, those cultured ways, including language, would come along with it. She lit another stick of incense as Lazarus continued.

"After you die and come back to life, so to speak, you have an awakening. Most people do—just look around your planet, and you will see this to be true across cultures and countries. With my awakening came clarity, so after that fateful day I became serious about my life. What I mean is this: I had a greater understanding of what life was truly about and a sense of purpose and direction of where I wanted to go. You and Angelo can both relate to this in your own lives, can't you?"

"In countless ways," she responded, "including this experience with you now."

"It's funny that I sit here in front of you and can savor all of the sensory experiences and sensibilities you and Angelo are having at this moment—the incense, the candles, the tea," he marveled. "You know, when I woke up and rose again, I knew there was no turning back to the desultory life I had been leading. I started having visions, ringing in my ears, and hearing voices talking to me about the importance of my position in life. I guess you could say the angels conveyed what I needed to do to assist Yeshua and Miriam on their journeys. Remember angels were what people believed in and all we knew; therefore, it was the language we used. So, you see, I spent twenty or so years establishing a law business and helping my father, which led to my ability to financially support Yeshua's teachings.

"During that stage of my life, I assisted some of Yeshua's apostles. Many of them were pigheaded as you would say and not always kind to my sister Miriam, a woman who was also married to Yeshua, a dear friend of mine for so many years. That said, I don't want to downplay their importance in history because what they had to endure as disciples of Yeshua was unimaginable. The psychological and physical abuse of simply being associated with him and his teachings was no easy task for any of us. Everyone knew if they had been found in the early days following Yeshua's death that they too would have been executed. Many decided to move into neighboring towns to teach after he had been crucified since they feared for their lives. I admired them for taking the stance they took, for it truly was courageous.

"Being reborn through Yeshua gave me a free pass to whomever I wished to see, so I had access to his apostles at any time. They had many of their memories, experiences, and teachings scribed through pamphlets and papyrus scrolls, some of which I collected. But it's important to understand why they differ.

The psychological and physical abuse of simply being associated with him and his teachings was no easy task for any of us.

“Let me try an analogy: Latin developed into various dialects which in turn grew into other languages. Creating multiple translations is one reason why the writings diverged over time. Although they started relatively the same, many of the words changed before they were published in what you now call the Gospels. You see, the writings were copied and recopied from one language to another, obviously influenced by the individuals who transcribed them. Political and spiritual beliefs and their cultural influences demonstrably impacted their translations. All of them had changed—not only in language which shapes meaning—but also in some content from their original texts even before Rome turned Christian.

“What you now refer to as the Gnostic Gospels are in essence much closer to the true identity of Yeshua's teachings than what you have in your Bible. More will also be discovered, some of which will happen in your lifetimes. I would love to say my gospel will be discovered one day, but I never wrote one,” he admitted wryly, “so I suppose you could say this is it.”

Rochelle let out a short laugh as he went on.

“I did my fair share of traveling with the apostles, but it wasn't my purpose to teach or try to heal others with them. Even though many knew who I was, my job was primarily to help my parents, my sister Miriam, and the female apostles. I felt I was advancing Yeshua's teachings by sending money to Miriam and the seven sisters and financially supporting the male apostles in Judea as much as I could. I became fairly well off through my legal profession, even wealthier than my father who strictly followed all the religious ways and laws of the time. My father was stricter about following the codes than I was, and his rigidity kept him from expanding and becoming more successful.”

“Which laws did your father follow?” Rochelle asked.

“"All of the strict laws, rules and orders of the traditional Jewish faith,” he said. “We had little say in shaping our government, and remember the Roman

Empire controlled our government despite the fact we were not considered Roman citizens. Primarily, we obeyed the laws of our own faith, but we also had to navigate between them and the Roman laws. It was a complex time in history, and I was frequently the one negotiating and helping others. You are fortunate to be able to participate in your government's decisions, for we couldn't do so.

"And a greater inclusiveness is coming your way. Today, things are shifting toward an awakening of consciousness amongst humanity. You can witness this shift occurring not just in your United States but throughout the world, and no government or group can stop it, try as they might. Your government has crushed and decimated your American natives and also enslaved your African community, overtly and covertly. Marginalized individuals are still mistreated in both poor and wealthy nations. May you never forget the death of my people simply because of their religious beliefs either; however, there's a reason for everything, and the true ascended soul or master can see the good and love in all of it. The soul who has done the work can recognize and acknowledge the beauty in all things even when they appear evil. While working as a lawyer, I had to see good where there was evil and protect those who couldn't defend themselves.

"Our father accepted my life choices, but he was not as supportive as my mother was about Miriam's decisions. He would have preferred her to marry a man of means who lived by the conventional rule books. Then again, he had other daughters who followed his instructions more traditionally, which gave him more status in our community. Thankfully, my mother made sure money was sent Miriam's way.

"After my miracle, my life was relatively routine, mostly because I worked and earned money, but I never married. Truthfully, I never had a desire to marry, have children, and live a family life. When someone is reborn the way I was, having children doesn't become as important as it once was since I felt a strong desire and need to support others and take care of the world. You both feel and understand a larger calling and know the people you care for are like your children in a way. The thing is, after my awakening, I had a mission and purpose, and it was to serve others, not to raise a family."

Rochelle understood, acknowledging his profound message by crossing her arms and hands over her heart. An overwhelming feeling of compassion arose in her as the words of Lazarus poured through.

"When I moved to Gaul to reconnect to Miriam, I felt free for the first time. I was liberated from the Jewish laws that bound us in unnecessary ways, and from the Roman laws that oppressed us. Some Roman laws controlled southern Gaul at the time, but enforcement was much softer. I spent the rest of my life pursuing truth, knowledge, and happiness after Yeshua changed my life forever. He was one of the greatest spiritual teachers and healers your planet has ever known."

And then the charismatic energy Rochelle and Angelo had started to become fond of left as quickly as he had appeared.

"I wish I knew Lazarus in his human form," Rochelle said after Angelo had come out of his multidimensional state.

"What an energy," Angelo responded. "What a powerful energy."

They both wished they could go back in time to break bread with him, but in a way they just had.

• • • • • •

CHAPTER 21

YESHUA: THESE ARE MY WORDS

Educating the mind without
educating the heart
is no education at all.
—Aristotle

Rochelle and Angelo wondered how much more would be shared about Miriam's life in Gaul and whether they would ever hear from Lazarus again. They were also curious how deep Miriam would go into Yeshua's teachings, especially after she had returned from Britannia and continued their gatherings. A week after Lazarus' last appearance, it was neither Lazarus nor Miriam who came for a visit but Yeshua.

Yeshua Speaks

"My Merkabah had been appearing to Miriam and the sisters for nearly twenty years, but my time was coming to a close," Yeshua began with a soft but serious tone. "Although I made visitations for a significant portion of Miriam's life, it was no longer necessary in time. As they began to expand their community in Gaul, the eight of them became spiritual teachers and healers in their own right. People often wanted to see an apparition of me, but I showed up in their dreams, meditations, and prayers instead, just as I do with people today. It is the same. You and Angelo are fortunate since I speak directly through a human host even though you can't see an image. In this particular realm, I am the energy of who

Yeshua once was, but I also incorporate Christ Consciousness which is an energy of pure divine love.

"Miriam knew one day I would no longer come to visit unless she requested me to, but even then that desire grew less and less over time. Showing up in my Merkabah wasn't needed as much anymore, for she could communicate with me telepathically in a psychic manner. Over time, Miriam's character, resolve and ability to heal had become formidable. She needed to go out on her own.

"Although she could have easily remarried, she chose not to; none of the seven sisters married, for they were all fully focused on their mission to teach, heal and help people. They had established a committed group of disciples and some of them became apostles who began teaching others. Miriam and I both agreed on when I would stop showing my apparition, so she knew it would happen and moved on as all great spiritual teachers do."

"Were the messages similar to the wisdom from the Gospels?" Rochelle asked.

"Yes, somewhat," Yeshua said. "Many of the teachings in the Bible were not necessarily written by Luke, John, Matthew, or Mark but written a few hundred years later. The Catholic Church decided what would be included in the Bible and what would be left out, based on what would benefit their agendas at the time."

"Were Matthew, Mark, Luke, and John *real?*" Rochelle asked. She had to know. Didn't so many wonder the same thing?

"They were amongst my apostles, but their writings were rewritten again and again, and the Catholic Church edited them again and again," he replied. "Things that didn't fulfill the Church's needs or desires were removed and changed. Some of my apostles were fishermen, and others were more learned, but most had a basic education, so they knew how to write. They took notes about what I taught and some of the things I said, and others you don't know of did the same. Some had scribes write for them, and others took down their own words. Writing took a great deal of effort since you needed a point for the ink. Managing the process took time, so most people found it easier to get others to scribe for them. Miriam used a scribe as well, not because she couldn't write but since it was easier to dictate and have someone more versed in writing take it all down.

"Today, you can just speak, and it converts to text on your computer automatically. The laptop you're using right now, Rochelle, has quantum characteristics. One day, you'll be able to interface with your laptops and tablets in even more quantum ways, meaning your thoughts will automatically connect to your devices. Although this may not happen in your lifetime, it is coming. Computers will be able to speak with and interact with you in deeper ways, as you've seen in some of your movies, and robots are already part of some people's lives. All the quantum material and books you're reading now don't seem as strange to you as they once did. It's up to you and Angelo to combine the quantum data and realities with the religions and faiths of the world."

"We aren't scientists and don't understand the world of quantum, nor are we qualified to speak of it," Rochelle said quickly, not wanting to take on the task of making sense of quantum realities amidst the esoteric messages coming from Miriam, Yeshua, and Lazarus. She knew that not only did they not have the education or experience to convey the quantum science scattered throughout their messages, but even those who were well-versed on the topic had a tough time explaining the implications, at least in a meaningful way. But Yeshua carried on, ignoring Rochelle's comment.

"When I say quantum realities, this is what I'm trying to say: Often, you ask about various strata within dimensions, and they are dimensions in that they do exist in distinct ways. You see, each dimension is relative to the frequencies it holds, and these are the quantum realities, or quanta, as you call them. To put it another way, these quantum realities are nothing more than different dimensional realities holding unique frequency patterns or vibrational states of being. Right now, you and Angelo exist in a vibrational pattern and state of being that makes you appear whole, and by whole, I mean thick."

"Thick?" Rochelle echoed, finding the word choice odd and wondering what he meant.

"Physical. Material. Energy taking on physicality," he said. "It's fun to experience this reality where consciousness integrates with physical form, as it's markedly different than being in a reality where you're just an energy form. You can view yourself in whatever form you choose. It truly all depends on the energy vibration pattern. In this dimension, by the way, you take on more forms than just human. Millions of species exist in this dimensional reality, and you're just one of them. Many are similar to you, but others are much more technologically advanced."

Rochelle thought of people like Nikola Tesla. Where was Yeshua going to take her next?

"I'm speaking about quantum realities and how they relate to spirituality," he continued. "When you see pictures of me depicted in this dimension, you may see a halo above or around my head, which is really nothing but my aura some people saw around me. When your auric field shines so bright, you appear to look like an angel in the earth realm, so many saw me that way. Those who shine their light brightly through their words and actions have the same thing; some can see auras, and others cannot. It was the same during my time as Yeshua in this realm and dimension. The truth is that everyone always has access to my energy, a bit like the Tree of Life that also makes up the sequence of your DNA."

It's fun to experience this reality in which consciousness integrates with physical form, as it's markedly different from being in a reality where you're just an energy form.

"What do you mean?" Rochelle asked, confused about why she needed to know this.

Yeshua explained, "I am the sequence of your DNA and the quantum of all of your realities. I am the beginning, and I am the end. I am the Alpha, and I am the Omega. I am every holy book ever written. I am not one, but I am All, and All are me. We are divinely interconnected and always have been. Recall what our message was back then and still is today: There isn't one path but many paths to obtaining love or enlightenment. These are my words, and I am Yeshua."

And then his energy was gone, and Rochelle and Angelo decided to grab a bite to eat and ruminate on his message. Three hours later, they were sitting under their oak tree with the lights off so they could see the stars. It was a chilly night, but they had plenty of blankets, and their heads weren't quite ready to hit the pillow. Rochelle loved watching the glistening twinkles of the stars off in the distance and listening to the enchanting sounds of the night. They held hands and gazed in all directions, appreciating the majestic solitude of the cosmos all around them.

Unexpectedly, Yeshua quietly returned. As Rochelle squeezed Angelo's hand, she could see his eyes were closed. Since she didn't have a notebook or her laptop, she turned her cell phone on so she could record his words in real time. Other times when Miriam or Yeshua spoke to them, she didn't capture their words at all, either in written or audio form. Often, one or both of them might check in about their day and occasionally, they'd say, "We are here just to strengthen the connection between us and both of you," and in those cases, Miriam and Yeshua wouldn't stay long. Rochelle could usually sense what was going to be important to capture and sometimes Miriam would blatantly tell her to write down what she was saying. That evening was special, and they could both feel it. She had hoped the visitation would be from Miriam since she had questions for her, but it was Yeshua once again who spoke as they lay there under the mesmerizing night sky.

"If there is something I must conclude in this part of the story, I will say this: Miriam, Lazarus, and many of the apostles followed what I guided them to do. Remember, I was considered the *Word of God*, the *Right Hand of God*, and through me, God spoke. But my actual mission was to let people know they were also the *Right Hand of God*, meaning all of us are beings of God and one with God. Most people at that time and even today don't understand this message. If you truly know who you are as a light being, then you will have no need or reason to try to interpret my words."

With such profound commentary, Rochelle wondered if he might dive into parables.

"So often, humanity takes things out of context, and amongst other things, my Crucifixion was taken out of context," he continued. "Well before the Church, my death was misunderstood, for you see, even my own apostles thought I was dying because it was my mission. My mission wasn't to die on the cross but to teach and to heal. I had no intention of dying; as Yeshua, I was just as human as you are now. My abilities were the same as yours since we all have these gifts; however, I just had faith and most people don't.

"You and Angelo could have more faith than you do. As children, you had a lot of faith, but you didn't understand who I really was then. You thought I was a man, the *Son of God*, but I am energy, a sequence, a spectrum of frequencies, just as you are. I came to your world to deliver a message, and I did. Humanity created a religion from my message and slaughtered many in my name, especially women. Far too many have justified malice in my name, yet all you need to do is love in my name, or your own name, for all of us."

Yeshua seemed to be on a roll, and it was powerful. She loved it when he combined love with mind-boggling quantum connections. Rochelle remained quiet and let him continue.

"We know you wonder how you can share Miriam's journey and life with others. We also know you both worry about this story and the validity of it. I am the Christ whom humanity has fought over for millennia, and I will say these words: You must all wake up now and realize I am in all of you. You must all understand that your time of discord and fighting needs to end. You must understand God is you and that no separation exists between you and God. God never judges you; it is only you who judges you.

"Creation comes directly from humanity, and humanity is part of the consciousness of this universe. You are all a part of a great cosmic consciousness, yet so many of you don't realize it, or perhaps don't want to believe it. You are not alone in this galaxy and certainly are not alone in this universe. You must stop thinking of yourselves as singular; instead, you must think of yourselves as being connected to everything, not just your planet but the entire universe as well. You must see yourself as pure light and love and begin treating each other as such.

"Human consciousness is constantly creating and evolving; however, you need to move beyond your current humanness to see who you indeed are as energy beings, which is so much more than the flesh and bones you perceive as your only existence and reality. Step out of your bags of skin and see the actual light beings you are rather than physical forms with excuses that only create boxes to limit you. You are so caught up in your daily lives, thinking about where the next meal and paycheck will come from, you have forgotten who you really are as energy beings.

"One vital way human beings can tap into this higher consciousness is to slow down. Everything must slow down. When you decide to walk, when you decide to sit, when you decide to turn off all of your digital media, you can begin to connect to something deeper. Your society has given you the freedom to simply do nothing, but you don't take advantage of it. Rather than using your technology to free yourself from more busyness, you remain glued to it. You often feel every moment must be filled with some kind of stimulus, digital screen, or entertainment, or you're missing out on something.

"I will tell you this: Blessed is she who can sit and do nothing. Blessed is he who walks with nothing in his ears and can just BE. Blessed are they who come in my name and show love and the energy I carried in my lifetime, the energy many of you call Christ Consciousness today. Blessed is humanity who knows itself as God."

"Wow," said Rochelle. "I can feel you." She could literally feel his serene and loving energy, and it was expanding. "I've never been good at doing nothing, yet I feel so at peace when I do," she added softly.

Rather than using your
technology to free yourself
from more busyness,
you remain glued to it.

"Humanity has created technology capable of going faster than the speed of light. Simply push a button, and you can connect yourself to the other side of the world instantly," Yeshua continued. "Yes, your technology has advanced quickly, but your spirituality is severely lagging. Your spirituality must reach the same level as your technology, for they are one and the same. Humanity has tried to divide them for years and seems dead set on keeping it that way. This separation is how technology becomes an end in itself, a distraction from connection and a higher purpose. Your materialists, psychologists, scientists, philosophers, spiritualists, and scholars have been arguing over human existence and the metaphysical world for millennia and beyond without this awareness.

"How do you connect now, Rochelle? Your modern pandemic showed you how to communicate with more people around the world than ever before. The viral infection demonstrated you're all the same and have the same desire to be healthy and connected. The virus showed the world you are all susceptible to becoming sick and dying. For those awake during that period, it also revealed that humanity must evolve and become one consciousness and, I will add, become *one consciousness in love.* You must stop seeing yourself as separate. You must begin to help each other and stop hurting each other as you have been doing for so long. Your governments are always playing games about how to one up each other, which doesn't serve any of you long term, does it? In a few hundred years, you will have one earth government and one people, so a sense of oneness will come in time. Europe will start to come together as one government, and then South America and North America will come together as one. Soon, you'll begin to have contact with other beings in your galaxy, driving you to come together as one species. You will understand you are *homo sapiens sapiens* as you call yourselves, and this new understanding will impel you to come together in harmony."

Rochelle wanted to hear more about the contact with other beings Yeshua spoke of, but he seemed to be on fire with a mission to speak of love and interconnectedness. The tone was focused and almost urgent.

"This expanded knowledge is inevitable since you will not destroy yourselves; you will come together peacefully as time progresses," he continued. "Once you all put aside your petty disparities and find love and humanity in all people, positive ramifications for everyone will abound. Your spirituality will start to develop as fast as your technology because you will finally comprehend they are one and the same, and you can no longer divide them.

"Human beings are born now with greater abilities to access other dimensions. Whatever you wish to call these new children, they can connect—much more easily and seamlessly than their ancestors ever could—to a higher consciousness. You and Angelo are seen as bridges to a higher consciousness, but you will all be able to do this by simply *willing it* within a few hundred years."

Seen as? Rochelle thought to herself. Willing it? She sat there pondering Yeshua's message.

They had told a few of their friends about their otherworldly experiences, some of whom had believed them; however, others found it too far-reaching to be true. Some asked them for proof which was also difficult. Did people ask others who have had psychedelic experiences for proof of their unique recollections, whether it be visions or something else? After all, psychedelics are often equated to an altered state of consciousness or even a transcendental super-experience, altering the mind in the process. Some psychologists have reported positive results using micro-dosing of psychedelics with patients. If such an experience could lead to someone being more open to hearing an expanded view and different meanings about their state and place in life, then it could potentially allow a new way forward to ease trauma and pain. Rochelle also read about a writer who used psychedelics to "help him emerge from a pandemic brain fog that had snatched away his ability to write."[1]

She and Angelo had never ingested a thing, yet they were taken to multidimensional shifts in consciousness and in multidimensional realities. She mused: Who's to say what's *real* and *true* for anyone? Isn't that what Yeshua and Miriam were trying to say about belief systems in the context of limited versus expanded awareness and consciousness? We make choices and manifest in every single moment of our day, and if we truly are the universe, why not tap into its expansive knowledge, power, and creative juice? Rochelle came back to the present moment as soon as Yeshua picked up his thread.

"You, Angelo, and others like you are the impetus to initiate the beginning of Universal Consciousness. As I said, I work through you two but also through others, not just as Christ Consciousness but also as a love that is known, experienced, and felt in different ways, as you both felt on your last trip to Japan. How efficient would it be if I only worked through one or two? It wouldn't be a very efficient computer, would it? I also work through humanity's technology to connect people to each other in more sophisticated ways. Japan has forgotten its roots like most of the world, but you're all gaining it back little by little again.

We tell you to go slowly for a very good reason, and this is because there will be no end. You now realize there is *no end*."

"Work through us?" repeated Rochelle, as she contemplated his words. "No end," she added under her breath, but Yeshua didn't elaborate.

Perhaps that's what they were doing, she thought, for she felt their energy uniting as one. Now she began to understand Miriam's message so many months ago, that it wasn't just her story or journey but the experience of all four of them. Magdalene's life was told in their collective voice, not Miriam's or Angelo's. Maybe they were all merging, and that experience was part of the lesson. That we are interconnected and all one. Yes, all of humanity is connected if we can only realize it—wasn't this what they had been telling them all along?

"In your lifetime, you now understand your purpose, and in all your lifetimes to come, you will comprehend the same," Yeshua went on. "You'll continue on this journey, for it is the magic that will make you as powerful, mystical, and needed as I was during my time. You will slow down as you age in this lifetime, but you'll never stop because we will give you continuous energy. Stay on your path and help others on their own. You must believe in your power.

Maybe they were all merging, and that experience was part of the lesson.

"As the great Buddha focused on: Do the right things, speak the right words, think the right thoughts. Miriam and I will add to these wise teachings: Take care of your physical shell by eating the right food, exercising, and meditating. Find time for sitting and doing nothing every day. Create a daily practice—whatever that ritual is for you—but do it.

"As you quiet your mind, you will rest into your heart and connect to your Higher Self. As you rest into your heart, you will connect to us and to Source or God. Here in this silence, you will realize the interconnectedness of all things and know the oneness in the All That Is. Great peace can be found here, and when you experience this peace, you will truly know God, and you will know *you*. And you will also experience the serenity and inner knowing of the *I Am*

Consciousness in its profound nothingness and everythingness all at the same time. This is the end of my transmission."

And with that, Yeshua was gone. Rochelle and Angelo knew it was their time to make sense of all he had shared. Or perhaps it was time to simply breathe it all in and *become one* with it.

They looked at each other with tears of profound love in their eyes, marveling at his words, all of which amplified Yeshua's and Miriam's earlier teachings about oneness and love. As they smiled in recognition of the transformative connection they had just experienced, a great horned owl began to hoot into the night sky. She had apparently heard the message too.

• • • • • •

CHAPTER 22

I AM WHO I AM

Life is the flower
for which love
is the honey.
—Victor Hugo

As the weeks flowed by, Rochelle and Angelo became increasingly aware of the powerful interconnectedness of *all of us*. It was as if the expanded consciousness they were sharing with Miriam and Yeshua had caused a big ripple in the multiverse.

They realized the world needed to hear Magdalene's story because, within it, others would find their spiritual journey just as they had. They also knew the messages came from a collective consciousness begging to be heard even if some of them were beyond their comprehension. When the soul acknowledges that cosmic knowing and embraces it, there's nothing left to do but surrender to the *beyond,* for in that mysterious void is an omnipresence that needs no explanation or proof.

Although there was still a cold breeze in the air, spring was in blossom and all of their favorite flowers were springing up; the birdbaths were active again, and the evenings were growing warmer.

Rochelle said to Angelo one Saturday evening as she cut some tulips from their garden, "Perhaps the life force of the universe will assist us, the same one Miriam and Yeshua have spoken to us about time and time again. It's a unified field full of synchronicity once we realize our connection to it. I believe we understand that beautiful dance of energy now."

"It's hard to imagine this expanded reality with outdated thinking," he responded, "but it seems that when we surrender and become one with the unified field, everything begins to flow. Dance. Harmonize."

"Matching our frequencies to the All," she added, laughing joyfully. "We are forever evolving and recreating ourselves through the universe, and the universe is forever evolving and recreating itself through us."

Angelo fired up the grill, and Rochelle set up a wooden folding table for dinner under their old oak tree. He opened a special bottle of Barolo they had brought back with them from northern Italy several years ago. After dinner, they grabbed their still half-full wine glasses and sat on a blanket in an open patch of grass nearby.

We are forever evolving and recreating ourselves through the universe, and the universe is forever evolving and recreating itself through us.

Above them lay Venus and the shimmering stars; the largest one felt as if you could reach up and touch it. Behind them, lights hung from their oak tree, reminding them of summer parties and celebrations even though they hadn't had one in a long time. After discussing non-local consciousness for an hour or so, Angelo's body began to shake, surprising both of them.

"Who's coming?" she said out loud, but before Angelo could respond, his head went back, and he grabbed her right arm as her left arm reached for the wine glass in his other hand.

"Is it you, Miriam?" Rochelle asked. "We were talking about non-local consciousness and merging with the universe," she added with a soft laugh. "Did you hear us?"

Angelo's breathing became labored, so much so that Rochelle wasn't sure if he was going into a deep theta brain wave state or actually falling asleep this time. She felt a shift in her body too, and her head began to shake back and forth, and suddenly she felt tingles in the palms of her hands.

"I Am who I Am. I Am that I Am. I make up all essences and all frequencies," a voice suddenly boomed. The energy and tone differed significantly from those of Miriam, Yeshua, or Lazarus.

"Who is here?" asked Rochelle anxiously.

"Some call me Elohim, but you can also call me *I Am who I Am*," said the voice.

It felt somewhat familiar to Rochelle and carried a similar energy to the Angelo she slept beside every night. The voice had his same strange wit, sarcasm, and charm. Feeling a bit uncertain, she asked Elohim, "Why does it feel like Angelo? Why do I feel a sense of ego? Who are you?"

"The ego is you," came the response. "I am you, and you are me, so if the ego shows up, then it is just your human self, making itself known."

She was curious whether the Elohim energy replicated or mirrored the ego personality when it came through a human form or host. Or perhaps it's a perfect match to a human, where the ego and personality are the most dominant aspects.

Reflecting, Rochelle asked, "Why don't you remove the ego or shine a light on it when you come through to speak? Surely you can do that if you are Elohim and make up all essences, all frequencies, and all energies?"

"Remember I am working through a human being, and while you are both open-hearted, it doesn't mean the ego doesn't get in the way," Elohim replied. "I cannot remove the ego because human beings always have a choice to either make their ego dominant or just another aspect of themselves. You've released ego in your own lives when you felt uncertainty and fear. For instance, you both came to realize you don't have to be financially poor to be spiritually rich although you were both raised with this conditioning. To be spiritual, you can be rich in your bank account and your heart, for remember abundance comes in myriad forms. In this case, you removed your egos to rise above the limiting perception you once had."

"Hmmm," said Rochelle, not sure what to say. "But in our human forms, the ego will always be part of our so-called blueprint, right?"

"Source is your original blueprint," Elohim responded. "You truly are connected to everything."

"Okay, I understand that connection," said Rochelle. "But right now, your energy feels so human-like, something I don't feel with Miriam, Yeshua, or even Lazarus."

"Yes," Elohim quickly said. "Because I represent the All That Is, the I/we/it/they/us is a perfect match to Angelo's frequency. So, unlike other energies you connect to, the persona or voice of the *I Am Frequency*, if you like, will feel and sound like the human being including the ego-self.

Fortunately, you are both free of negative energies since you don't allow them to get in the way of your purpose. They're there, but you tend to ignore them when you step into helping and serving others, which is when you're doing your best work."

Source is your
original blueprint.
You truly are
connected to everything.

"Wow," Rochelle said softly. Watching Angelo's head sway side to side as if he were in an intensely deep trance, she added, "Where was he just then?" She had sometimes gone on these quantum journeys with him in what appeared to be outside space and time, but that evening wasn't one of them. And quite frankly, traveling throughout the multiverse with Elohim was another kettle of fish.

"Don't you understand that doing God's work is doing your work?" Elohim asked Rochelle. "You're just living from your true light being, and there's no ego when you live from this place. At the same time, it's also true ego isn't always a bad thing when it does show up. For some things you need to do in your human form, it helps propel you forward, gives you drive, and even saves your life. Ego can be used to push you beyond what you think is humanly possible. The key is to use the ego when you need it and then shove it off to the side when it doesn't serve you or humanity."

Rather than responding to the last message, Rochelle asked, "Can you shed some light on why your energy came through tonight? Why now? Are you part of Miriam's and Yeshua's story?"

In hindsight, asking the question seemed ridiculous. Had she really asked Elohim/Source/God whether it/he/she/they was/were part of their story?

"Because Miriam and Yeshua taught and still teach about unity and love," Elohim replied. "Some feel they know my energy because they've read holy books or prayed to me, but is that truly *knowing God*? Is that truly understanding and experiencing Source and the oneness with themselves and everything as Yeshua and Miriam teach?

"I am your God, and I am not. I want you to know you are also Godde. God is simply creation and love for the betterment of humanity. You're creating for Godde or Source, just as you're creating for you and the universe. This is simply what Magdalene and Yeshua did two thousand years ago. Your ancient sages and mages from the East did as well. Shamans and your indigenous elders contribute to Universal Consciousness in their own unique way by creating harmony and oneness with the earth. You separate your belief systems and religions with distinctions to divide you as a species rather than seeing the commonalities to unite you. Humanity fights the very thing that can bring them peace and serenity. Why not focus on love and oneness as all of your spiritual masters across cultures and time have taught?"

Angelo's head went forward abruptly, and as the Elohim energy dimmed its collective light, Miriam arrived with a bang.

"Did you understand the message, *I Am who I Am*?" asked Miriam. "These words carry a powerful frequency, as do the words *I Am that I Am.* Do you understand, Rochelle? *I Am who I Am?"*

Rochelle sat there trying to absorb the intensity of it all. Miriam didn't wait for an answer.

You separate your belief systems and religions with distinctions to divide you as a species rather than seeing the commonalities to unite you.

"Do you know why you are receiving this message? It's because God is here in all of us. This was the message we delivered eons ago, and it's still the same message now. We are all God, for Godde is in all of us. God is within us. Godde is part of us. God is us. And being Godde, we are always in a state of peace which includes all things and all creatures. Our energies represent the void or the emptiness of all things, for, within that void, all frequencies and all energies exist."

"So, where do our souls go, and what do they experience when we're not in this realm?" Rochelle asked.

She speculated: If Miriam's soul was indeed made up of unending frequencies, whether her spectrum of frequencies responded or the *collective* spectra of frequencies did, they were still connecting to God and the All That Is, were they not?

"You keep thinking in linear terms, which is singular in essence. But even in a singular sense, you can become aware of countless forms of abundance," Miriam responded. "The singularity[1] is all about knowing you and all beings are one with the All That Is. And this oneness is not fixed, but fluid. As human beings, you have created far too many limitations because of your linear thinking. When you think in multidimensional terms, everything changes. Once you shift away from this old pattern of thinking, then you will open yourself up to unlimited possibilities, probabilities, and realities. It's hard to fathom this, but once you do, you will finally realize your power as energy beings."

Rochelle blinked. It was precisely what she and Angelo had discussed at dinner earlier that evening. They could both articulate it, so the teaching had been absorbed; however, Miriam was right. If they continued to think in linear terms, they wouldn't truly understand their profound wisdom, the expansiveness of the consciousness they were part of but also one with at the same time.

"You mean that we are one with God, one with Source, one with the universe, one with the All That Is, whatever language you wish to use and most resonate with," Rochelle said. "We aren't separate from Source. We are not only part of Source, but we are also Source—the drop of water in the ocean, but also the wave and the ocean itself."

"Yes, it is true you are one with Source and you are Source; however, I also want to tell you something else which may complicate things for you and Angelo when you share this knowledge with others," Miriam said.

When you think
in multidimensional
terms, everything
changes.

Rochelle braced herself for what was about to come. She hoped Miriam wasn't going to impart a lesson on string theory because she wasn't sure she could handle it at that moment.

"You have asked me about the nuances of messages, some of which differ slightly from the ones I am sharing now," Miriam continued. "In our timeline, Sa'rah didn't have a baby at sixteen, and she met with Yeshua's Merkabah many times when she was a child. But you may have heard about my life from others with discrepancies from the story you are receiving from Yeshua and me. There are even stories of my living in Turkey, but this also didn't happen in our timeline, the one in which you and Angelo are currently living. Now, you understand the problem you'll have when my journey becomes public."

Rochelle asked, "You mean, there are multiple timelines in which you existed, outside the one humanity has learned about and come to know? Why don't all human beings who can connect to you and your dimension only bring information through from this timeline since we all exist in the same timeline together now?"

Miriam said something that took Rochelle by surprise.

"Some people are new to this timeline, so they might have a stronger connection or frequency match to another one. You weren't part of some of these other timelines, but you both were part of the timeline I am giving you now, namely this earth realm and dimension. Remember that you and Angelo are also having a similar experience in other realms with only slight variances. In addition to this timeline, you exist on another earth, in an alternate timeline, and in a different dimensional field and so do others. Like the multiverse some of your scientists speculate about today. Raising your vibration in this timeline affects the many expressions of you—what you see as other lives—in the other dimensions. And your earths can merge into each other as well; you can think of it as one reality going into another or one earth plane jumping into another dimensional plane."

"How does this happen?" Rochelle asked, feeling overwhelmed by Miriam's initial response. It was as if quantum theory, the esoteric, philosophy, and astronomy were all folding in on themselves. Her brain was aching to return to something simple like breaking bread around a table, but Miriam was done with village life in Gaul. She went on to explain how dimensions merge.

"Because they become so similar in their dimension and their ability to vibrate at the same pattern, the frequencies and amplitudes merge as one," she said. "In a sense, two or more earths can merge as one. Beyond earth timelines merging, many hope your planet will merge with higher dimensional frequency planets."

"Why?" asked Rochelle. It was the only thing she could think to say. Why did they need to know about multiple earths jumping into other planetary realities and timelines? Was it because she and Angelo were experiencing the early stages of how these shifts would occur for humanity? As strange as it was for both of them, perhaps their experiences in other realities and realms with Miriam and Yeshua would become normal for human beings over time. Rochelle's mind was racing, and suddenly she had a dozen questions to ask.

Before Miriam could answer, Rochelle asked her, "What does merging with higher dimensional frequency planets mean? What will that look and feel like?"

"It will put you closer to God or Source. Closer to love. Closer to unity consciousness," Miriam replied.

This response was also something Rochelle didn't expect to hear, and it immediately raised another question. She thought of their earlier teachings on frequencies and their reference to lower vibrational energies.

"On these other earth planes, are we vibrating at higher or faster frequencies?" she asked. "I suppose vibrating faster as a species means we become lighter in a way—closer to our true energy forms. Yeshua used the word thick to describe humanity at this time, referring to our dense physical bodies."

"In some planes, you are vibrating faster and are lighter in your forms, and in others, you are not," Miriam said. "The journey I am sharing with you now is based on quantum realities—your and Angelo's reality—which is narrating my story from this timeline in this earth realm and dimension."

At this point, Rochelle had to ask her most pressing question to ensure she wasn't losing her mind or sense of reality, at least in her dimension with its linear framework and constructs.

"Do you mean the same dimension of the Bible, Quran, Vedas, Torah, Kabbalah, Hermes, and Plato that we have all read and studied in this lifetime on this earth realm? Please tell me you are referring to the timeline we have grown up learning in our history and holy books and not a timeline some science fiction writers tap into."

Rochelle knew Angelo wanted to know the answer to the same question. Although they both had a deep curiosity for better understanding the unknown beyond their dimension, she had to know whether *Magdalene's Journey* was a reality in the earth dimension and timeline where they existed. In other words: Was it true in the history of their *here and now?*

"Yes, this dimension and timeline, the one you are in now," she said abruptly.

"So, others might be tuning into another timeline when they connect to you, Yeshua, or others, and this is why their information varies?" Rochelle probed, somewhat relieved by Miriam's answer, not that she fully understood it. "I suppose it would be the same for indigenous elders when they take shamanic journeys," she surmised.

"Remember the merging and overlapping of earths we spoke of earlier?" Miriam asked Rochelle. "The slight variances in information can happen when these timelines overlap, but they are so minuscule people may not even realize they've made a dimensional shift. Names, faces, and other factors could remain the same, so the interpretation and narrative might change somewhat because the perception changes, but often, things feel incredibly similar.

"People will ask you, 'How do you know if Miriam's story is real? How do you know Miriam and Yeshua are real?' They may think my story . . . your story . . . only exists in the realm of imagination or lucid dreaming. Even though some understand that imagination and lucid dreaming can be a means of accessing higher dimensions, others may simply choose to see it as fantasy."

"People can't deny your story . . . our story . . . *now,"* Rochelle said, knowing that plenty would. For months, they thought long and hard about skeptics, but at this point, she felt differently and knew Angelo did too.

"What if someone has another idea or story of who I am? Is one correct and one incorrect?" Miriam asked Rochelle. "No, not really, a response your religious skeptics, researchers, and scientists will not accept. We can say yours is accurate for this timeline, but it doesn't mean that other information isn't valid, for others may be tapping into another timeline and reality, *not this one.*

"Of course, the scientific community wants to see things appear exactly the same. 'Where are the repeatable observations?' they will ask. That said, quantum physicists know perception affects how a subatomic particle behaves when viewing it. Is it a wave or particle, energy or matter? Energy matters, and you are all energy. Perception matters. Timelines matter. Dimensions matter. The quantum aspect of your multiverse creates multiple probabilities and realities."

And then Miriam was gone, and it was sudden, much sooner than Rochelle expected. Her eyes were bulging when Angelo came back into their dimension. "I know, I know," he said gently when he saw the look on her face. "Where do we go from here?"

Perception affects how a subatomic particle behaves when viewing it. Is it a wave or particle, energy or matter?

Although disorienting more often than not, they loved some of the tangents Miriam and Yeshua were forever taking them on; it was as if they were leaving breadcrumbs on a path toward and ultimately into a quantum rabbit hole filled with one mind-blowing revelation after another.

"Maybe that's the point," Rochelle said under her breath, as she began to write down what she felt in that expansive moment.

Perhaps the idea is to dumbfound humanity so much that we simply surrender, let go of everything, and become part of the emptiness of the void spiritual masters so often speak of and inherently know. Maybe—just maybe—it's to turn our beliefs upside down and inside out so we can become open to broader and deeper ways of thinking and seeing the world.

To say Miriam's and Yeshua's teachings were not in their wheelhouse was an understatement, Rochelle thought. This part of their teaching is so beyond their background and formal study they couldn't help but feel like kids who accidentally went through a wormhole and landed in a version of *Alice in Wonderland* that seemed as real as their summer conversations around a campfire. As real as the flowers blooming in their garden and the tomatoes exploding every August. Indeed, these tangents seemed to raise questions far beyond the double-slit experiment, Schrödinger's cat, and Einstein's spooky action at a distance.

But at the end of the day, if we are all truly energy beings existing beyond time and space, then perhaps connecting to souls from a particular timeline, including this dimension and earth realm, was possible after all. Even more, as Miriam, Yeshua, and Lazarus shared, there is no past or future; there *just is*.

What a beautiful segue into the wisdom of every great sage, mage, master, and guru: It is much easier to live from your heart and to be of love when you stay in the present moment. In the here and now, it's easier to embrace gratitude. To encompass serenity. To become grace.

Rochelle felt the words as they flowed through her fingers and onto the screen.

When love is in the driver's seat, does it even matter whether we understand the unfolding of multiple realities and the merging of countless earths? Is anything true or real in an energy-verse outside time and space besides love?

Miriam would likely say "yes and no" because what we perceive becomes our projected reality. Put another way, our intention of something creates a ripple in the multiverse that ignites an idea and results in countless probabilities. How we perceive what emerges leads to another choice and intention, opening up yet more probabilities and realities. No wonder Einstein didn't want to go there.

From this lens, regardless of whether we work within science or the mystical arts, we begin to understand how much our voice and daily actions matter. How we think and treat people matters. Whether we throw vibrations of love and unity or anger and divisiveness into our day matters. These vibrations not only create ripple effects in our own lives but also affect other living things on this planet and beyond.

She stopped writing and looked around their sitting room at all the antiquities and books she and Angelo had collected over the years, all contributing to the belief systems they held and the reality they were having, at least in this dimension and timeline. Their perceptions had changed countless times over the years as their consciousness continued to expand. As their understanding of the universe evolved, so too did the ripples they created through their thoughts, words, and actions. It was as if the universe was mirroring them, matching their energy in each and every moment. Maybe we all mirrored each other in an exquisite cosmic dance that was forever unfolding.

Rochelle and Angelo now understood Yeshua didn't die for the sins of humanity as is commonly believed and taught. He died for what he believed in—faith and love—both of which he demonstrated every day. When Miriam and Yeshua saw people wake up and understand their own power and divinity, rather than follow dogmatic rules of how to behave and live, they saw this awakening as the true miracle, far greater than the physical healings they performed.

The *real miracle* is when love within us shines so brightly to the world our light heals ourselves and others. That light is our intuitive compass telling us who we are, far beyond the perceived physical shell we wear. We are God, Godde, and the Goddess. We are the grains of sand and stardust, and we are also the All That Is. Most important, we are love. And the *real magic* happens when love is both the leader and driver of our lives.

One late night under the stars as Rochelle and Angelo looked out to eternity, they talked about their bond with Miriam and Yeshua and understood that connection extended beyond what their minds could imagine. They realized if there was a key takeaway of Miriam's and Yeshua's journey with them, it was not which religion had it right or what path or spiritual master was the best way to enlightenment, but it was to be of love. Love really is the glue that binds all energies together, starting with your family and community. Only fear keeps us resistant to this powerful force that truly connects and binds us.

That light is our intuitive
compass telling us who
we are, far beyond the
perceived physical
shell we wear.

In a participatory universe, when we realize we are interconnected, then the "no" part of the answer to "Are we real?" takes on a new meaning, a multidimensional one outside our current comprehension. Can we be okay with that . . . just for now? Perhaps we can come to understand that regardless of how much of our existence is a perception, the real miracles lie within. The ripple effect in the multiverse—when we magnificent mortals lead with love—may be just the thing to save the human species.

It's so simple, it's hard. *But is it?* Maybe it's as simple as making a different choice. As our collective consciousness expands, we will be able to feel, sense, hear, taste, and touch a new profound beauty in the interconnectedness of All That Is. Then we will realize we are not separate from God, Godde, Source, or Universal Consciousness. Even more, in this marvelous cosmic soup of awareness, we will innately feel and know the oneness of Source.

In each moment of our existence, we are becoming that which we are becoming and experiencing becoming God again. When we feel this truth, we will no longer need to search *out there,* for the *in here* will be acknowledged, recognized, and known again. In that celebration, our souls can breathe life into our human shells, and our breath will be the daily reminder we are always in an intimate collaboration and co-creation with Godde and every living thing.

Indeed, we create the dance, and we are the dance at the same time. Breathe into that delicious and unifying dance. Do you feel the marvelous and universal truth? Your soul is calling. Can you hear it? What will you do when you answer its call?

THE END ???

• • • • • •

AFTERWORD

The book points to the work of both early visionaries and contemporary thinkers, while also weaving in popular culture references and authors who have moved our understanding of dimensions, probabilities, energy, and matter forward.

We have come to see *Magdalene's Journey* as an interesting blend of historical fiction and visionary literature. Historical fiction mixes fact and imagination whereas visionary literature focuses on spiritual wisdom or inner knowing. These two genres most capture the unique mix of characteristics this book represents, but not entirely. Notably, they do not account for the science that backs up the fantasy and realism in this narrative, nor do they reveal the non-local consciousness of Miriam's story.

Historical Fiction

Like history, *Magdalene's Journey* includes people who once lived and walked the planet, actual incidents, and real settings in terms of time and place. Like fiction, however, the book invites the reader to understand emotions and motives inside the historical reality. This fusion of historical externals and inner experiences characterizes historical fiction. As historical novelist Linda Kass writes:

> Reading history allows us to understand what happened. Reading historical fiction allows us to be moved by what happened. Even after we know the facts, we continue to search for sense and meaning. That is at the essence of our humanity. The historical novelist exposes the reader to the inner lives of people across time and place, and in doing so illuminates history's untold stories, allowing the reader to experience a more complex truth.[1]

Most would agree that historical fiction blends imagination and facts about the past to make the past come alive. But beyond such a broad generalization, historical fiction is a "genre of controversy and contradiction."[2] For example, what constitutes a past setting? A common minimum for the event or story seems to be at least fifty years, but whatever the minimum, it has to do with knowing a period not through personal experience but through research.[3]

In a twist on research, the book often cites or illustrates parts of her story through modern examples or a parallel situation in current times as a way to further illuminate what Miriam is saying. Does such a reference lend historical veracity or make her words more palpable and compelling?

Magdalene's Journey incorporates both historical fiction and alternative history. It is biographical as the riveting story of Mary Magdalene's and Yeshua's lives, and alternative since her narrative challenges religious and scientific orthodoxy and their mainstream paradigms of reality.

Enter Visionary Literature

You'll find New Age, Mind and Body, and Mysticism labels under the visionary literature umbrella. Depending on whom you ask or where you unearth your definition of this lesser-known genre, you'll discover a whole host of descriptions and informally related categories, which include consciousness and spirituality but also those further afield like parapsychology. A key feature of the story or content is that it expands one's mind[4] or a "growth in consciousness."[5]

> Visionary Fiction embraces spiritual and esoteric wisdom, often from ancient sources, and makes it relevant to our modern life. Gems of this spiritual wisdom are brought forth in story form so that readers can experience the wisdom from within themselves.[6]

Two other key features are a plot that is "universal in worldview and scope" and a story that may use "reincarnation, dreams, visions, paranormal events, psychic abilities, and other metaphysical plot devices."[7]

While this understanding of the genre is fairly recent, visionary art is far from a new term. In his essay, "Psychology and Literature," Carl Jung divided art into the psychological and the visionary; the former connects to realism and conscious, individual experiences while the latter emerges from what we might deem the imagination or collective unconscious and something that feels unfamiliar.[8] For example, Dante's early fourteenth-century epic poem *The Divine Comedy* features a spiritual journey, using Virgil as a guide for Dante to pilgrim through hell and purgatory.

Blake has often been called visionary because of the visions and prophecies he expressed in poetry, including prose and images.[9] Going further back, we can look to Virgil (70 BCE), the ancient Roman poet from the Augustan Period, known for *The Aeneid*, a visionary epic depicting relations with the gods.

If we rewind the clock even further, the legendary poet Homer comes to mind. Regarded as the author of two great classical works foundational to Greek and by extension to all Western literature: *The Odyssey* and *The Iliad*. Both are seen as epic poetry, some of whose features overlap with the visionary. Both portray journeys—Achilles' metaphorical journey of the hero in *The Iliad* and Odysseus' journey as the core plot; contain dreams and divine intervention; and illustrate growth in wisdom applicable to all humans, such as persistence and trusting in one's instincts. At the same time, they overlap with historical fiction since they include the Trojan War.[10] We could see *The Alchemist* as a defining contemporary example;[11] Paulo Coelho's allegorical fable weaves together a journey with spiritual growth and enlightenment.

Together, these examples—old and new—demonstrate that although visionary literature is often equated with content that is religious in nature, this is not always the case; it can be quite broad, just as the loosely related genre of metaphysical literature is broad in nature. Today, metaphysical literature has taken on additional meanings, for it includes not only poetry[12] but also content that is supernatural, Gnostic, and transcendent in nature.

Fantasy Meets Reality

Consider how James Redfield's *The Celestine Prophecy* and Tolkien's *The Hobbit* mix elements of reality or history to draw the reader into a world of magic and mystery with their surreal underpinnings. The series *Outlander* also blends fantasy and historical reality although it remains grounded in actual locations.

Similarly, *Magdalene's Journey* is designed to entice you into a world of historical enchantment from yesteryear that feels familiar and comfortable at times and far-reaching, ethereal, and otherworldly at others. Love and resilience stand out in the parallels between two sets of couples, one from the past visiting another in the present. In the reactions and growing understandings of Rochelle and her partner Angelo who live in the recognizable reality of modern-day New England, readers are invited to accept an alternative reality of Miriam of Magdala and Yeshua of Nazareth from two thousand years ago.

How many works of art, music, literature, and film play with our minds in equally dizzying ways? Jostein Gaarder's *Sophie's World* is a novel about the history of philosophy, and yet the mesmerizing story takes you on a wild roller-coaster ride involving two worlds that challenge the nature of reality itself, just as many great philosophers across time have done. Where did he get his ideas from?

Consider where all creators get their ideas from. Was it a vision, a dream, or a daytime imaginary stroke of brilliance? Does one life possibility exist instead of the other, or do the two proposed lives exist in parallel dimensions happening simultaneously? Can our consciousness access both in ways that cannot be dismissed as mere imagination or make-believe? Perhaps most important of all, can imagination be a pathway to higher realities?

These questions are at the heart of the book, upending categories of fact and imagined realities. Miriam certainly claims a higher truth to her journey. This work postulates more than one truth exists, and that reality depends on perception rather than a purely external, provable claim. And while some may decide such a message makes this book a work of the imagination, sections of it resonate with the implications of quantum physics.

History & Visionary Meet Science

Buttressing the plausibility of the alternating ancient and modern storylines in the book are scientific explanations of the surreal exchanges. The jumps in timelines and other seemingly fantastic phenomena sometimes reference quantum science although we—the authors—do not have an accurate understanding of the field nor would we assert such a claim.

Yet, more and more scientists and physicians are finally professing we need to explore things beyond where traditional research has taken us to date—beyond Newtonian laws as we have come to understand them. Moving past Newtonian laws does not mean abandoning them. With such practical use, rather than replacing Newtonian laws as an explanation for how our universe is governed, perhaps we look to Newtonian laws and quantum physics plus something else yet to be understood or even still to be discovered.

Over the past twenty years, countless books have probed even deeper to attempt to explain new scientific discoveries and their relationship to God, spirituality, and consciousness. While some scientists and philosophers debate the validity of new findings, or at least their practical applications in our daily lives, we have come to realize things may be happening we can't comprehend, including within the void and dark matter our human eyes can't see.

As science makes more discoveries and unravels more quantum mysteries, it seems likely humanity will better understand the complex, mind-bending ways the universe works, particularly how the energies within it exist in a non-linear, non-local dimension. New studies keep emerging about this connection we have to a data bank *out there*. Here's how Amit Goswami describes it:

> If the different brain areas oscillate in place as in musical instruments, they are quantum, and they become correlated by neuronal signals transmitted via the glial cells. Then, consciousness binds them together via its non-locality forming a trap called the tangled hierarchy. And in the process of quantum measurement, consciousness, trying to look through the brain, gets caught in the trap and splits itself into two: a subject looking at an object. We call it co-arising.[13]

In essence, reality is a beautiful dance between the local and non-local world, between local consciousness and non-local consciousness and everything contained within the omnipresent All That Is.

We've come a long way in the last century. Although relativity and string theory are not yet everyday twenty-first-century dinner conversations, they have indeed entered our awareness. Within this expanded awareness exist unlimited possibilities and probabilities or paths we can take.

We now realize every action has an impact elsewhere, which some refer to as cause-and-effect. We know now the universe is more connected than we realize, an idea that has advanced substantially since Schrödinger first coined entanglement.[14] While this idea is far from new, understanding various complex interactions, effects, and entanglements in many spheres, from everyday reality to subatomic dynamics, is continuing to grow. It truly is an interconnected and participatory universe, even if we've yet to fully process it.

The *butterfly effect*—which was mentioned in Chapter 11—suggests one small change in one state can change a state somewhere else in the world. And the multiple worlds theory implies an infinite number of universes and even the folding of ours into other universes we simply can't see. In other words, this ripple effect is much more profound than we can grasp with our linear minds.

If we can truly tap into another field outside of our current awareness, *The Matrix* and Lewis Carroll's *Alice in Wonderland* will look like puppy play. In other words, perhaps such notions of consciousness and perception in these creative works are not science fiction or fantasy after all, at least not as we currently define them. We invite readers to cross the compelling but controversial bridge between these two worlds.

Stephen Hawking once said, "The universe, according to quantum physics, has no single past or history. The fact that the past takes no definite form means observations you make on a system in the present affect its past."[15] And author William Faulkner was known to have said, "The past is never dead. It's not even past."[16] That said, it still isn't easy to grasp that multidimensional awareness exists outside time and space, even if brilliant minds have attempted to explain things beyond the observable with mathematical equations to back it up.

Perhaps we're only seeing the tip of the iceberg of what David Bohm, Einstein, Schrödinger, and other forward-looking and cutting-edge thinkers have uncovered. To their dismay, some of the newfound truths looked more like metaphysics than traditional science. Courageous and bold visionaries have been shot down for suggesting an interrelationship between the metaphysical and the physical worlds. Materialists have tried to cement a separation between the two, but more and more have been brave enough to step forward and speak their challenging and controversial truth.

These emerging answers to profound questions remain tentative because they have been beyond what we can prove with physical evidence, whether by direct observation or by consistent scientific measurement. More recently, Western science has made progress in understanding quantum dynamics. Moving from theory to evidence, three scientists from three different countries received the 2022 Nobel Prize in physics for developing tools to identify entanglement in particles normally considered too far apart to affect each other.[17]

Miriam's narrative offers a glimpse into the world of interconnected multidimensionality, a concept that closes a gap long dividing mystics, spiritualists, and philosophers on one side and materialists, scientists, and physicists on the other. It also brings you into the world of non-local consciousness beyond the observable physical world where Newtonian laws apply.

Understanding Non-Locality

The notion of non-local consciousness is central to understanding the source of stories from Miriam, Yeshua, Lazarus, the Essenes, and Elohim. Also critical is the means to accessing this non-local consciousness.

If we accept the assertion that consciousness is ubiquitous and forever emerging, it would seem that we can access it at all times. Knowing we are connected to the Universal Consciousness of All That Is which includes non-locality, it doesn't seem like such a far stretch to claim knowledge beyond our individual, ego consciousness. Cosmologist Jude Currivan explains it this way:

> By understanding that *all* that we call reality, not only on the physical plane but also beyond, *is* consciousness exploring and experiencing itself on myriad levels, the cosmic hologram offers an all-encompassing model of the Cosmos. . . . [E]xperiences of non-local awareness that are capable of transcending space-time, while nonetheless extraordinary, should come to be seen as innate abilities.[18]

In the book, Miriam speaks of a female apostle who channeled Yeshua—bringing his energy and words into her auric field—although she notes they didn't have such terminology during their time. She uses modern vernacular as a way to explain and connect what was happening *then* with what is happening *now* through Angelo and Rochelle.

Other practices gaining acceptance today also explain how human beings can access expanded awareness and consciousness, including non-local information. These include shamanic journeying, psychedelic experiences, meditation, Kundalini yoga, and soft martial arts, amongst a host of other examples. Many have ancient roots. As Miriam reminds Rochelle, age-old sages, indigenous elders, and spiritual masters have been able to bilocate and access subtle realms and dimensions for eons.

In Helané Wahbeh's *The Science of Channeling*, her premise is that "all humans can channel. That everyone can reveal information and energy from beyond time and space."[19] Yet for some, the word still invites ridicule or conjures a certain unseemliness, giving rise to skewed labels and biases; some even stigmatize it as energies or outside "forces" taking over the human body. Perhaps these negative connotations, especially the idea of possession, reveal perceptions based on superstition and fear, drilled into us through traditional religion for so long that most people avoid the term—at least publicly—so as to avoid dismissive judgment by the masses and the media.

Channeling could be thought of as the ability to access a creative databank in the non-local "cloud" as well as trustworthy inner guidance anyone can access whenever they choose. Naturally, people may choose different words to describe the experience. For example, a dialogue with a friend who had given a talk in an auditorium full of 2,000 people went something like this:

Us: "There were times when you were on fire up there. You were in the zone, and your talk just flowed like a river, as if you were tapping into something beyond this world."

Friend: "You know, no one has ever said that to me, but I've always felt it. When I paint and write, I get out of my own way and it's as if a creative force comes through me. The same is true when I'm on stage. You could say I *allow* the words to come through me rather than forcing words to come out in a rehearsed way. And yeah, it sometimes feels like I'm accessing ideas beyond my mind and even beyond this world."

Our friend's comment was even more remarkable because he is more mathematically minded than spiritually minded, at least in the way he describes or sees himself. Even so, like other creators and visionaries, he acknowledged that he allows inspiration from *the beyond* to assist. When our ego mind doesn't resist and gives way instead, nothing short of what we refer to as "genius" can make its way through.

Best-selling author Neale Donald Walsch of the *Conversations with God* series of books says the wisdom (as conversations) come *through him* which he then relays as a—in his words—"modern spiritual messenger." His books have given solace and inspiration to many who were once glued to an old paradigm they couldn't relate to or understand.

Consider fantasy authors like J.R.R. Tolkien (notably *The Hobbit* and *The Lord of the Rings*) and science fiction producers like George Lucas (*Star Wars* and *Indiana Jones,* amongst others). Conceivably their award-winning masterpieces are a combination of their vivid imaginations, dreams, and intuitive minds. As co-creators, however, our perception of what we each experience through those masterpieces may well place the stories in a realm beyond our everyday world. Put another way, what we give energy to ultimately breeds life; it becomes a living entity in its own right, part of and yet also beyond creator and reader or audience. And the language or label of any creation process dictates where it lives in humanity's collective consciousness.

Throughout the story, the characters Rochelle and Angelo question how their consciousness can expand to such a degree that information outside their "known" understanding can be relayed to them. They ask themselves: "Are we traveling through a portal to access knowledge from two thousand years ago? Are Miriam and Yeshua traveling through a portal to speak to us?" They eventually conclude that we are *all* portals of knowledge or consciousness, always connected to each other.

Yeshua Meets the Science of Consciousness

While they may not have used scientific language to explain their knowledge, shamans and ancient spiritual masters have been receiving messages from other dimensions to assist with healing over thousands of years, as did Yeshua of Nazareth. Could it not be possible that Yeshua healed using these subtle unseen fields and learned how to reappear long after his physical death? Was this not the same dimension or realm other ancient sages and mages in the East have used to bilocate, levitate, and reverse life-threatening diseases? These wise masters didn't have access to words like multiverses and quantum fields; however, they have always known and understood that dimensional shifts into other realms and vibrations exist beyond the human plane. In other words, they knew their everyday experiences and realities weren't the only ones. These ancient masters also knew that matter, which is ultimately energy—including our physical shells—was merely a perception or, as some refer to it maya, a Sanskrit word meaning illusion or even magic. Indigenous elders in the Americas knew the same thing, back then and today.

Miriam and Yeshua call attention to the congruences between humanity's modern science and their direct spiritual experiences from their time on the planet. Their story exemplifies the connections between science and spirituality that some scientists and philosophers have also embraced.

The German physicist Werner Heisenberg, most known for his *Uncertainty Principle*, said, "Quantum theory provides us with a striking illustration of the fact that we can fully understand a connection though we can only speak of it in images and parables."[20]

Ironically, Yeshua taught through parables. Yeshua beckoned his audiences to pay attention and open themselves to understanding the messages behind his parables. He knew, however, that people often ignored the messages back then. Some may have let daily worries or the love of money seduce them, but often people sensed the danger to the prevailing power structure. His rebellious nature of turning limiting beliefs upside down and inside out challenged the understanding of the common people, who strongly believed in multiple gods and the myriad superstitions connected to them. Yeshua's teachings threatened those like the Romans, who, wanting to control communities far and wide, promulgated their own belief systems that bolstered their power.

Today, many human beings still have a hard time understanding Yeshua's teachings, including the core idea that the *kingdom lies within.* We are the innate wisdom we so often seek outside. Our Higher Self knows a much richer way to live than the autopilot our protective ego-based selves default to time and time again.

Personal Choices

The narrative woven inside *Magdalene's Journey* brings old and new worlds together. Miriam's story is designed to lead you down a path of discovery, encouraging you to ask deeper questions about the nature of reality itself. To that end, we might now ask: Could this work be real *and* imagined, true *and* envisioned?

In your daily lives, perhaps you can begin to test out the notion we do not face an either/or choice of spirituality and science, but a both/and choice. Once open to it, we can experience spiritual reality infusing everyday material reality and transforming anxiety and uncertainty into a deep peace and inner knowing.

Regardless of your belief system, this book may, at a minimum, get you to think in a broader, more encompassing way about our very existence—for instance, to consider everything as energy, including us as human beings. In other words, we are energy beings having a human experience. Embracing this notion in your everyday life will change how you show up in the world and from that place, "miracles" may just start to become commonplace.

You have a choice to make in each and every moment: a perception of separation and divisiveness or a perception of connection and unity. That perception is everything, for it creates a life filled with fear and suffering or one filled with joy and love. You decide.

• • • • • •

FREE RESOURCES

We have a website dedicated to *Magdalene's Journey,* where you can read through a Q&A and learn more about the inspiration behind the book.

On our Resources page, you'll receive a glossary of terms, book group discussion questions, and a recommended reading list, which includes some of our favorites in both science and spirituality.

On our Offerings page, you'll find our latest free gifts for readers.

VISIT:

https://magdalenesjourney.com
https://magdalenesjourney.com/resources
and
https://www.magdalenesjourney.com/offerings

NOTES

PREFACE

1. Pruitt, Sarah. "How Early Church Leaders Downplayed Mary Magdalene's Influence." History, A&E Television Networks, 2 Apr. 2021, https://www.history.com/news/mary-magdalene-jesus-wife-prostitute-saint#. Accessed 12 Jul. 2023.
2. Bourgeault, Cynthia. "The Gospel of Mary Magdalene." *Parabola,* vol. 40, no. 1, "Sin," Spring 2015, https://parabola.org/2015/01/29/the-gospel-of-mary-magdalene/. Accessed 10 Aug. 2022.
3. King, Karen L. *The Gospel of Mary of Magdala: Jesus and the First Woman Apostle.* Polebridge Press, 2003.

Note about *The Gospel of Mary* mentioned in the Preface. It is sometimes referred to as a Gnostic text, but more so, a non-canonical text or gospel that was discovered in 1896 in a fifth century papyrus codex, said to have been written in Sahidic Coptic, but not translated fully until 1955. Referred to as the Berlin Codex, or the Akhmim Codex, after the name where it was found, the papyrus bound book was purchased by German diplomat Carl Reinhardt in Cairo and brought to Berlin. Parts of the gospel are missing. See *The Nag Hamadi Library,* edited by James M. Robinson, HarperOne, 1990.

CHAPTER 2

1. Pinkham, Mark. "The Truth About the Holy Grail: Magical Chalices Around the World." *Ancient Origins,* 9 Dec. 2021, https://www.ancient-origins.net/human-origins-religions/holy-grail-005124. Accessed 12 Jan. 2023.
2. Laszlo, Ervin. *The Upshift: The Path to Healing and Evolution of Planet Earth.* Waterside Productions, 2022.
3. McGowan, Michael. "'Remember to look up at the stars': the best Stephen Hawking quotes." *The Guardian,* 14 Mar. 2018, https://www.theguardian.com/science/2018/mar/14/best-stephen-hawking-quotes-quotations. Accessed 1 Feb. 2023.

4. Jung, Carl G. *Psychological Types. Collected Works of C.G. Jung.* Bollingen Series XX. Translated by Gerhard Adler and R.F.C. Hull, 3rd ed., Volume 6. Princeton UP, 1976, p.52.
5. Ibid.

CHAPTER 3

1. McKusick, Eileen Day: *Electric Body, Electric Health.* St. Martin's Essentials, an imprint of St. Marin's Publishing Group. Copyright© 2021, p.xxiii
2. Schwartz, Gary E. *The Afterlife Experiments: Breakthrough Scientific Evidence of Life After Death.* Atria; Reprint edition (March 18, 2003). p.267.
3. Alexander, Eben: Near Death Experiences: The Mind-Body Debate & The Nature of Reality' in The *Science of Near-Death Experiences*, ed. John C. Hagan III. p.108-109.
4. Lévi-Strauss, Claude: *The Elementary Structures of Kinship.* Published first in France under the title *Les Structures Elementaires de la Parente* in 1949. A revised edition was published under the same title in France in 1967. Translation copyright© 1969 by Beacon Press. Reprinted with permission from Beacon Press, Boston Massachusetts, p.115.
5. Lerner, Gerda. *The Creation of Patriarchy.* New York, Oxford: Oxford University Press, 1986.
6. Shlain, Leonard: *The Alphabet Versus The Goddess: The Conflict Between Word and Image.* Viking (Penguin Group). New York. 1998, p.3.
7. Ibid, pp.6-7.
8. Lerner, Gerda. *The Creation of Patriarchy.* New York, Oxford: Oxford University Press, 1986, p.200.
9. Osborn, Lil Abdo, "Mary Magdalene 'The Lioness of God' in the Baha'i Faith" *Alternative Spirituality and Religion Review*, Volume 3, Issue 2, 2012, pp.181-197. https://doi.org/10.5840/asrr2012323. Also see PDF download at Library of Congress: https://www.loc.gov/item/18012992.
10. AshtangaYoga.info: https://www.ashtangayoga.info/philosophy/source-texts-and-mantra/upanishads/chadogya-upanishad/. Accessed 1 April 2024.
11. Engels, Frederick. *The Origin of the Family, Private Property and the State*, ed. Eleanor Burke Leacock. New York, 1972. International Publishers Co; First Ed.

12. Lerner, Gerda. *The Creation of Patriarchy*. New York, Oxford: Oxford University Press, 1986, p.218.

13. Ibid, p.178.

14. Plutarch, De Iside et Osiride 27: FRA 232, 34. Refer to this reference for more on Plutarch' writing on the many trials and tribulations that Isis had endured and how people looked to her for encouragement.

CHAPTER 4

1. Stone, Merlin. *When God was a Woman.* New York. Mariner Books/Imprint of HarperCollins, 1976, p.234.

2. Crow, Duncan. *The Victorian Woman.* London. Allen & Unwin, 1971.

CHAPTER 5

1. Abegg Jr., Martin G., et al. *The Dead Sea Scrolls: A New Translation.* 1st ed., HarperCollins, 1996. The scrolls were found in 11 caves near the Qumrān Ruins, in the northern part of the Dead Sea. They are said to offer a wider spectrum of ancient Jewish beliefs and groups at the time than what we originally believed to be true. According to the official Israeli Antiquities Authority's The *Leon Levy Dead Sea Scrolls Digital Library*, "While some of the writings survived as nearly intact scrolls, most of the archive consists of thousands of parchment and papyrus fragments." This same source also points out that they consisted of two types: "'biblical' manuscripts—books found in today's Hebrew Bible—and 'non-biblical' manuscripts—other religious writings circulating during the Second Temple era, often related to the texts now in the Hebrew Bible." See "Introduction." *The Leon Levy Dead Sea Scrolls Digital Library,* Israeli Antiquities Authority, 2023, https://www.deadseascrolls.org.il/learn-about-the-scrolls/introduction. Accessed 12 Feb. 2023.

2. Than, Ker. "Dead Sea Scrolls Mystery Solved?" *National Geographic*, 27 July 2010, https://www.nationalgeographic.com/culture/article/100727-who-wrote-dead-sea-scrolls-bible-science-tv. Than states, ". . . because it was believed that the Essenes occupied the Qumr*ān region* during the first centuries B.C. and A.D., it is why ancient Jewish historians believed that they were the authors of *The Dead Sea Scrolls*." The article also speaks of research that "suggests that many of *The Dead Sea Scrolls* originated elsewhere and may have been written by multiple Jewish groups," a point echoed by archeologist Robert Cargill whose insights are included in the National Geographic 2010 documentary, *Writing The Dead Sea Scrolls.*

3. Modern scholars have suggested that, when the Qumrān sect was forced to abandon its community life because of the great Jewish revolt against Rome in AD 66–70, its members hid their library in nearby caves. The large number of preserved manuscripts indicates its importance. Also refer to notation 6 for additional reading.

4. "Ancient Jewish History: Pharisees, Sadducees, & Essenes." *Jewish Virtual Library*, https://www.jewishvirtuallibrary.org/pharisees-sadducees-and-essenes. Accessed 5 Feb. 2023.

5. Lawler, Andrew, "Who Wrote the Dead Sea Scrolls?" *Smithsonian Magazine*, Jan 2010, https://www.smithsonianmag.com/history/who-wrote-the-dead-sea-scrolls-11781900/. Accessed 12 Feb. 2023.

6. Denova, Rebecca. "Essenes." *World History Encyclopedia*, 4 Feb. 2022, https://www.worldhistory.org/Essenes/. Accessed 12 Feb. 2023; Singh, Shiveta. "Essene: Ancient Jewish Sect." *Encyclopedia Britannica*, 3 Apr. 2008, https://www.britannica.com/topic/Essene. Accessed 12 Feb. 2023; Lawler, Andrew.

7. Tabor, James. "Understanding the Essene/Dead Sea Scroll Calendar–and Alternatives, *TaborBlog*, 12 Mar. 2022, https://jamestabor.com/understanding-the-essene-dead-sea-scroll-calendar-and-alternatives/. Accessed 2 Feb. 2023.

8. Tigchelaar, Eibert J.C. "The White Dress of the Essenes and the Pythagoreans." Jerusalem, Alexandria, Rome: Studies in Ancient Cultural Interaction in Honour of A. Hilhorst, edited by Florentino García Martínez and Gerard P. Luttikhuizen, Leiden: Brill, 2003, pp.301-321, https://doi.org/10.1163/9789047402794_024.

9. Magness, Jodi. "The Impurity of Oil and Spit amongst the Qumran Sectarians." *With Letters of Light: Studies in the Dead Sea Scrolls, Early Jewish Apocalypticism, Magic, and Mysticism*, edited by Daphna V. Arbel and Andrei A. Orlov, De Gruyter, 2011, pp.223-231, https://doi.org/10.1515/9783110222029.2.223.

10. Yogananda, Paramahansa. *Autobiography of a Yogi.* 13th ed., Self-Realization Fellowship, 2019 printing, p.252. Los Angeles, CA. All rights reserved. This is a later reprint; however, the original book was published in 1946.

CHAPTER 7

1. Stone, Merlin. *When God Was a Woman*. Mariner Books, an imprint of HarperCollins Publishers, 1976. pp.154-155.

CHAPTER 10

1. Patten, Terry. "Our Wicked Predicament and the Consensus Trance." *A New Republic of the Heart: An Ethos for Revolutionaries.* North Atlantic Books, 2018, pp.15-44.

CHAPTER 11

1. "Chaos Theory: Mathematics and Mechanics." *Encyclopedia Britannica*, 14 Nov. 2022, https://www.britannica.com/science/chaos-theory. Accessed 16 Dec. 2022. From the website: "Chaos Theory, in mechanics and mathematics, the study of apparently random or unpredictable behaviour in systems governed by deterministic laws. A more accurate term, deterministic chaos, suggests a paradox because it connects two notions that are familiar and commonly regarded as incompatible. . . . . For example, the meteorologist Edward Lorenz discovered that a simple model of heat convection possesses intrinsic unpredictability, a circumstance he called the 'butterfly effect', suggesting that the mere flapping of a butterfly's wing can change the weather." See also Vernon, Jamie L. "Understanding the Butterfly Effect." *American Scientist*, vol.105, no. 3, May-June 2017, p.130, https://www.americanscientist.org/article/understanding-the-butterfly-effect. Accessed 30 Mar 2023.
2. *City of Angels.* The film was directed by Brad Silberling, Warner Bros, 1998.

CHAPTER 12

1. Nelson-Isaacs, Sky. *Living in Flow: The Science of Synchronicity and How Your Choices Shape Your World.* North Atlantic Books, Berkeley CA. 2019, p.245.
2. Houston, Jean. *The Passion of Isis and Osiris: The Union of Two Souls.* Ballantine Books, New York. 1995, p.141.
3. Blackburn, Simon. "Nous." *The Oxford Dictionary of Philosophy (Oxford Quick Reference).* 3rd ed., Oxford UP, 2016, https://www.oxfordreference.com/display/10.1093/oi/authority.20110803100240441;jsessionid=54D56A1E0A45919EBA8EEEF8C2886491. Accessed 30 Mar 2023.
4. LeLoup, Jean-Yves. *The Gospel of Mary Magdalene.* Translated by Joseph Rowe, Inner Traditions, 2002, p.131.
5. Barnstone, Willis and Marvin Meyer, Editors. *The Gnostic Bible.* Shambhala, 2009, Citation on the *nous* from *The Gospel of Mary*, p.499.

**Epigraph at the start of the chapter: Dōgen, Eihei. *The Zen Poetry of Dōgen: Verses from the Mountain of Eternal Peace.* Translated by Steven Heine, Tuttle Publishing, 1997, p.61. https://quotepark.com/quotes/1747580-dogen-but-do-not-ask-me-where-i-am-going-as-i-travel-i/

CHAPTER 13

1. "What is Heart Coherence." *HeartMath*, 13 Sept. 2022, https://www.heartmath.com/blog/health-and-wellness/what-is-heart-coherence/. Accessed 10 Feb. 2023. HeartMath defines it as a "synchronized and empowering state, physically, emotionally, mentally, spiritually."

CHAPTER 15

1. Thakkar, Chirayu. "Karma: Definition, Early Sources." *World History Encyclopedia*, 4 Dec. 2014, https://www.worldhistory.org/Karma/. Accessed 22 Sept. 2022.

2. For examples of a more complex history of the relationship of science and religion see the following: Swindal, James. "Faith: Historical Perspectives." *Internet Encyclopedia of Philosophy*, https://iep.utm.edu/faith-re/. Accessed 3 June 2023; Raymo, Chet. "In the church-science split, both sides have suffered." *Science Musings*, 6 Nov. 2020, https://www.sciencemusings.com/in-the-church-science-split-both-sides-have-suffered/. Accessed 3 June 2020; Baglow, Christopher. "A Catholic History of the Fake Conflict Between Science and Religion." *Church Life Journal: A Journal of the McGrath Institute for Church Life, University of Notre Dame*, 4 May 2020, https://churchlifejournal.nd.edu/articles/a-catholic-history-of-the-conflict-between-religion-and-science/. Accessed 3 June 2023.

3. "What is an Avatar?" *The Yogic Encyclopedia*, https://www.ananda.org/yogapedia/avatar/. Accessed 3 Oct. 2022. For further reading on Yogananda's teachings and life, see Yogananda, Paramahansa. *Autobiography of a Yogi.* 13th ed., Self-Realization Fellowship, 2000. Also see *Journey to Self-Realization: Collected Talks and Essays on Realizing God in Daily Life*, Volume III. Self-Realization Fellowship. Los Angeles, CA. All rights reserved. For his discussion of avatars, see Chapter 33, "Babaji, the Yogi-Christ of Modern India."

CHAPTER 16

1. Currivan, Jude. *The Story of Gaia: The Big Breath & the Evolutionary Journey of our Conscious Planet.* 1st ed., Inner Traditions, 2022, p.99.

2. Currivan, Jude. *The Story of Gaia: The Big Breath & the Evolutionary Journey of our Conscious Planet.* 1st ed., Inner Traditions, 2022, p.105.

CHAPTER 17

1. R.E. Witt, *Isis in the Ancient World.* Excerpt from book © 1997 Thames & Hudson Ltd, London. Note for serious academics: Originally published as *Isis in the Graeco-Roman World* by Cornell University Press, Ithaca NY, 1971.

2. Bergman, J. *Ich bin Isis (Acta Univ. Uppsal.: Historia Religionum 3).* Uppsala, 1968. p. 98, with his notes. Also noted in *Isis in the Ancient World* (see above)

3. Iyigun, Murat. "Monotheism (From a Sociopolitical and Economic Perspective)." *Center for International Development: CID Faculty Working Paper 151*, 2007, pp.1-62.

4. Campbell, Joseph. *The Power of Myth* with Bill Moyers, edited by Betty Sue Flowers. 1988. Anchor Books-Random House, 1991, p.46. ©Alvin H. Perlmutter, Inc. and Public Affairs Television. From Episode 3: *The First Storytellers.*

   The series: https://www.amazon.com/Power-Myth-25th-Anniversary/dp/B00A4E8E1O/. The book: https://www.amazon.com/Power-Myth-Joseph-Campbell/dp/0385418868. The audio: https://www.audible.com/pd/The-Power-of-Myth-Programs-1-6-Audiobook/B002V59WRE.

5. Ibid. From Episode 2: *The Message of the Myth.* See the above links for series, book and audio.

6. Farnell, L.R. *The Cults of the Greek States.* Oxford, Clarendon Press, 1896.

CHAPTER 21

1. Nayak, Sandeep, and Matthew W. Johnson. "Psychedelics and Psychotherapy." *Pharmacopsychiatry,* vol. 54, no. 4, 2021, p.169, https://doi.org/10.1055/a-1312-7297. Accessed 4 Apr. 2023.

2. Duncan, David Ewing. "Stolen Words: COVID, Ketamine, and Me." *Vanity Fair,* 30 May 2022, https://www.vanityfair.com/news/2022/05/stolen-words-covid-ketamine-and-me. Accessed 4 Apr. 2023.

CHAPTER 22

1. Sutter, Paul. "What is Singularity?" 27 Oct. 2021, https://www.livescience.com/what-is-singularity. Accessed 14 Nov. 2022. A more complex scientific

definition of singularity can be found on the website, *Live Science,* and other websites of its ilk. Sutter explains, "To understand what a singularity is, imagine the force of gravity compressing you down into an infinitely tiny point, so that you occupy literally no volume. That sounds impossible … and it is. These 'singularities' are found in the centers of black holes and at the beginning of the Big Bang. These singularities don't represent something physical." Also see the work of Ray Kurzweil, for instance, Kurzweil, Ray. *The Singularity is Near: When Humans Transcend Biology*. Viking, 2005. Kurzweil's book discusses "an era in which our intelligence will become increasingly nonbiological and trillions of times more powerful than it is today—the dawning of a new civilization that will enable us to transcend our biological limitations and amplify our creativity." See "About the Book." *The Singularity is Near*, http://www.singularity.com/aboutthebook.html?utm_content=bufferc4b75&utm_medium=social&utm_source=facebook.com&utm_campaign=buffer. In the context of *Magdalene's Journey*, it is explained in a conversation that the singularity is about knowing that you and all beings are one with the All That Is.

AFTERWORD

1. Kass, Linda. "Why We Read Historical Fiction." *Gramercy Books,* 2017, https://www.gramercybooksbexley.com/blog/why-we-read-historical-fiction. Accessed 8 Apr. 2023.
2. Johnson, Sarah. "Defining the Genre: What are the rules for historical fiction?" *Historical Novel Society*, 2002, https://historicalnovelsociety.org/defining-the-genre-what-are-the-rules-for-historical-fiction/. Accessed 9 Apr. 2023.
3. Lee, Richard. "Defining the Genre." *Historical Novel Society*, archived 11 July 2018, https://web.archive.org/web/20180711120201/https://historicalnovelsociety.org/guides/defining-the-genre. Accessed 9 Apr. 2023.
4. Smith, Victor E. "What is Visionary Literature?: Defining the Genre from Content." 2006, https://victoresmith.com/creative-ventures/visionary-literature/. Accessed 12 Dec. 2022.
5. "What is Visionary Fiction?: Characteristic Features of Visionary Fiction." 2023, https://visionaryfictionalliance.com/what-is-visionary-fiction/. Accessed 04 Apr. 2023.
6. "What is Visionary Fiction?: Characteristic Features of Visionary Fiction." 2023, https://visionaryfictionalliance.com/what-is-visionary-fiction/. Accessed 04 Apr. 2023.

7. "What is Visionary Fiction?: Characteristic Features of Visionary Fiction." 2023, https://visionaryfictionalliance.com/what-is-visionary-fiction/. Accessed 04 Apr. 2023.

8. Jung, Carl G. "Psychology and Literature." *Modern Man in Search of a Soul.* 1933. Martino Fine Books, 2017, pp.175-199. See also Jung, C. G. "On the Relation of Analytical Psychology to Poetry." *Collected Works of C.G. Jung, Volume 15: Spirit in Man, Art, And Literature*, edited by Gerhard Adler and R. F. C. HU, Princeton University Press, 1966, pp.65–83.

9. Greg, Andrew. "William Blake, the Romantic visionary." *Art UK*, 28 Nov. 2017, https://artuk.org/discover/stories/william-blake-the-romantic-visionary. Accessed 5 Apr. 2023.

10. The Center for Hellenic Studies: https://chs.harvard.edu/center-for-hellenic-studies-online-resources-for-homeric-studies/ and https://en.wikipedia.org/wiki/Iliad. For a discussion of the historical reality of the Trojan War, see Dunn, Daisy. "Did the Trojan War actually happen?" BBC, 20 Jan. 2020, https://www.bbc.com/culture/article/20200106-did-the-trojan-war-actually-happen#:~:text=For%20most%20ancient%20Greeks%2C%20indeed,have%20been%20a%20real%20event. Accessed 14 Apr. 2023. Dunn writes, "For most ancient Greeks, indeed, the Trojan War was much more than a myth. It was an epoch defining moment in their distant past. As the historical sources–Herodotus and Eratosthenes–show, it was generally assumed to have been a real event."

11. "The Alchemist by Paul Coelho." 2023, https://visionaryfictionalliance.com/product/the-alchemist-by-paulo-coelho/. Accessed 07 Apr. 2023.

12. "Metaphysical Poetry: Definition, Characteristics & Examples." Accessed 28 Aug 2021, https://study.com/academy/lesson/metaphysical-poetry-definition-characteristics-examples.html. Accessed 13 Feb. 2023. "Literary critic and poet Samuel Johnson first coined the term 'metaphysical poetry' in his book *Lives of the Most Eminent English Poets (1179-1781).* Samuel Johnson also used the term "metaphysical poets" in a chapter from his *Lives of the Poets* titled "Metaphysical Wit" (1779).

13. Goswami, Amit. *The Quantum Brain: Understand, Rewire and Optimize Your Brain*. Bluerose Publishers, 2021, p.112.

14. Schrödinger, Erwin. 1935. "Discussion of Probability Relations Between Separated Systems." *Proceedings of the Cambridge Philosophical Society*, vol. 31, 1935, pp.555–563. In a two-part article from 1935-36, Schrödinger (1887-1961) coined the term "entanglement" to describe this peculiar connection between quantum

systems. He writes, "When two systems, of which we know the states by their respective representatives, enter into temporary physical interaction due to known forces between them, and when after a time of mutual influence the systems separate again, then they can no longer be described in the same way as before, viz. by endowing each of them with a representative of its own. I would not call that *one* but rather *the* characteristic trait of quantum mechanics, the one that enforces its entire departure from classical lines of thought. By the interaction the two representatives [the quantum states] have become entangled."

15. Hawking, Stephen and Leonard Mlodinow. *The Grand Design*. Bantam, 2010, p.82.

16. Faulkner, William. *Requiem for a Nun*. 1951. Vintage, 2012, p.73.

17. "Nobel Prize in Physics 2022." *The Nobel Prize*. 4 Oct. 2022, https://www.nobelprize.org/prizes/physics/2022/press-release/. Accessed 11 Nov. 2022. The announcement read in part, "Alain Aspect, John Clauser and Anton Zeilinger have each conducted groundbreaking experiments using entangled quantum states, where two particles behave like a single unit even when they are separated. Their results have cleared the way for new technology based upon quantum information."

18. Currivan, Jude. *The Cosmic Hologram: In-formation at the Center of Creation*. Inner Traditions, 2017, p.197.

19. Wahbeh, Helané. *The Science of Channeling: Why You Should Trust Your Intuition and Embrace the Force That Connects Us All*. Reveal-New Harbinger, 2021, p.121.

20. Heisenberg, Werner. *The Physical Principles of the Quantum Theory*. Translated by Carl Eckhart, and F.C. Hoyt, Dover Publications, 1949. Werner writes, "Quantum theory provides us with a striking illustration of the fact that we can fully understand a connection though we can only speak of it in images and parables."

BIBLIOGRAPHY

Books

- Abegg Jr., Martin G., et al. *The Dead Sea Scrolls: A New Translation.* 1st ed., HarperCollins, 1996.
- Barnstone, Willis and Marvin Meyer, Editors & Translators. *Essential Gnostic Scriptures.* Shambhala, 2010.
- Barnstone, Willis and Marvin Meyer, Editors. *The Gnostic Bible.* Shambhala, 2009, Citation on the *nous* from *The Gospel of Mary.*
- Bourgeault, Cynthia. *The Meaning of Mary Magdalene.* Shambhala; 9.1.2010 edition (September 14, 2010).
- Brown, Dan. *The Da Vinci Code.* 1st ed. Doubleday, 2003.
- Campbell, Joseph. *The Power of Myth,* collaboration with Bill Moyers, edited by Betty Sue Flowers. 1988. Anchor Books-Random House, 1991.
- Coelho, Paul. *The Alchemist.* HarperOne; Anniversary edition. 15 Apr, 2014.
- Crow, Duncan. *The Victorian Woman.* London. Allen & Unwin, 1971.
- Currivan, Jude. *The Cosmic Hologram: In-formation at the Center of Creation.* Inner Traditions, 2017.
- Currivan, Jude. *The Story of Gaia: The Big Breath & the Evolutionary Journey of our Conscious Planet.* 1st ed., Inner Traditions, 2022.
- D'Adamo, Arthur J. *Science Without Bounds: A Synthesis of Science, Religion and Mysticism.* 2nd ed., CreateSpace Independent Publishing Platform, 2015.
- Diamant, Anita. *The Red Tent.* 1st ed., St. Martin's Press, 1997.
- Faulkner, William. *Requiem for a Nun.* 1951. Vintage, 2012.
- Feynman, Richard. *QED: The Strange Theory of Light and Matter.* Princeton UP, 2006.
- Gaarder, Jostein. *Sophie's World: A Novel about the History of Philosophy.* Translated by Paulette Moller. 1991. Farrar, Straus and Giroux, 2007.

- Goswami, Amit. *The Quantum Brain: Understand, Rewire and Optimize Your Brain*. Bluerose Publishers, 2021.
- Hawking, Stephen and Leonard Mlodinow. *The Grand Design*. Bantam, 2010.
- Heine, Steven (translator of) Dōgen, Eihei. *The Zen Poetry of Dōgen: Verses from the Mountain of Eternal Peace*. Translated by, Tuttle Publishing, 1997, https://quotepark.com/quotes/1747580-dogen-but-do-not-ask-me-where-i-am-going-as-i-travel-i/
- Heisenberg, Werner. *The Physical Principles of the Quantum Theory*. Translated by Carl Eckhart, and F.C. Hoyt, Dover Publications, 1949.
- Houston, Jean: *The Passion of Isis and Osiris: The Union of Two Souls*. Ballantine Books, New York. 1995.
- Jain, Shamini. *Healing Ourselves: Biofield Science and the Future of Health*. Sounds True Publishing. 2022.
- Jung, Carl G. *C.G. Jung Letters, Vol. 1: 1906-1950*. Bollingen Series Translated by R.F.C. Hull, Princeton UP, 1973.
- Jung, Carl G. "Psychology and Literature." *Modern Man in Search of a Soul*. 1933. Martino Fine Books, 2017.
- Jung, C. G. "On the Relation of Analytical Psychology to Poetry." *Collected Works of C.G. Jung, Volume 15: Spirit in Man, Art, And Literature*, edited by Gerhard Adler and R. F. C. HU, Princeton University Press, 1966.
- Jung, Carl G. *Psychological Types*. *Collected Works of C.G. Jung*. Bollingen Series XX. Translated by Gerhard Adler and R.F.C. Hull, 3rd ed., Volume 6. Princeton UP, 1971
- Kurzweil, Ray. *The Singularity is Near: When Humans Transcend Biology*. Viking, 2005.
- Laszlo, Ervin. *The Upshift: The Path to Healing and Evolution of Planet Earth*. Waterside Productions, 2022.
- LeLoup, Jean-Yves. *The Gospel of Mary Magdalene*. Translated by Joseph Rowe, Inner Traditions, 2002.
- Lerner, Gerda. *The Creation of Patriarchy*. Oxford University Press, New York. 1986.
- Lerner, Gerda. *The Creation of Feminine Consciousness*. Oxford University Press, New York. 1993.
- Lévi-Strauss, Claude: Lévi-Strauss, Claude: *The Elementary Structures of Kinship*, Boston: Macmillan, 1969.

- McKusick, Eileen Day: Electric Body, Electric Health. St. Martin's Essentials, an imprint of St. Marin's Publishing Group. Copyright© 2021.
- Nelson-Isaacs, Sky. *Living in Flow: The Science of Synchronicity and How Your Choices Shape Your World.* North Atlantic Books, Berkeley CA. 2019.
- Pagels, Elaine. *The Gnostic Gospels*. Vintage, 1989.
- Patten, Terry. "Our Wicked Predicament and the Consensus Trance." *A New Republic of the Heart: An Ethos for Revolutionaries*. North Atlantic Books, 2018.
- Robinson, James M. (edited by). *The Nag Hamadi Library*. HarperOne. 1990.
- Schrödinger, Erwin. 1935. "Discussion of Probability Relations Between Separated Systems." *Proceedings of the Cambridge Philosophical Society*, vol. 31, 1935.
- Schwartz, Gary E. *The Afterlife Experiments: Breakthrough Scientific Evidence of Life After Death*. Atria; Reprint edition (March 18, 2003).
- Selig, Paul. *I Am the Word.* TarcherPerigee; 40655th edition (June 24, 2010).
- Shlain, Leonard: *The Alphabet Versus The Goddess: The Conflict Between Word and Image*. Viking (Penguin Group). New York. 1998.
- Starr, Mirabai. *God of Love: A Guide to the Heart of Judaism, Christianity and Islam*. Monkfish Book Publishing Company, 2012.
- Stone, Merlin. *When God was a Woman*. Mariner Books/Imprint of HarperCollins. 1976.
- Wahbeh, Helané. *The Science of Channeling: Why You Should Trust Your Intuition and Embrace the Force That Connects Us All.* Reveal-New Harbinger, 2021.
- Walsch, Neale Donald. *Conversations with God: 4 Books Collection Set.* Hodder and Stoughton/Watkins Publishing, 2019.
- Yogananda, Paramahansa. *Autobiography of a Yogi.* 13th ed., Self-Realization Fellowship, 2019 printing.

Articles

- "Ancient Jewish History: Pharisees, Sadducees, & Essenes." *Jewish Virtual Library*, https://www.jewishvirtuallibrary.org/pharisees-sadducees-and-essenes.
- Baglow, Christopher. "A Catholic History of the Fake Conflict Between Science and Religion." *Church Life Journal: A Journal of the McGrath Institute for Church Life, University of Notre Dame,* 4 May 2020, https://churchlifejournal.nd.edu/articles/a-catholic-history-of-the-conflict-between-religion-and-science/

- Blackburn, Simon. "Nous." *The Oxford Dictionary of Philosophy (Oxford Quick Reference).* 3rd ed., Oxford UP, 2016, https://www.oxfordreference.com/display/10.1093/oi/authority.20110803100240441;jsessionid=54D56A1E0A45919EBA8EEEF8C2886491
- Bourgeault, Cynthia. "The Gospel of Mary Magdalene." *Parabola,* vol. 40, no. 1, "Sin," Spring 2015, https://parabola.org/2015/01/29/the-gospel-of-mary-magdalene/.
- "Chaos Theory: Mathematics and Mechanics." *Encyclopedia Britannica*, 14 Nov. 2022, https://www.britannica.com/science/chaos-theory.
- Denova, Rebecca. "Essenes." *World History Encyclopedia*, https://www.worldhistory.org/Essenes/.
- Duncan, David Ewing. "Stolen Words: COVID, Ketamine, and Me." *Vanity Fair*, 30 May 2022, https://www.vanityfair.com/news/2022/05/stolen-words-covid-ketamine-and-me.
- Dunn, Daisy. "Did the Trojan War actually happen?" *BBC*, 20 Jan. 2020, https://www.bbc.com/culture/article/20200106-did-the-trojan-war-actually-happen#:~:text=For%20most%20ancient%20Greeks%2C%20indeed,have%20been%20a%20real%20event
- García Martínez and Gerard P. Luttikhuizen, Leiden: Brill, 2003. https://doi.org/10.1163/9789047402794_024.
- Gilman, Larry, et al. "Physics: Newtonian Physics." *Scientific Thought: In Context.* 14 Feb. 2023, *https://www.encyclopedia.com/science/science-magazines/physics-newtonian-physics.*
- Greg, Andrew. "William Blake, the Romantic visionary." *Art UK*, 28 Nov. 2017, https://artuk.org/discover/stories/william-blake-the-romantic-visionary.
- "Guide: Defining the historical fiction genre." *Historical Novel Society*, n.d., https://historicalnovelsociety.org/defining-the-genre-2/.
- Johnson, Sarah. "Defining the Genre: What are the rules for historical fiction?" *Historical Novel Society*, 2002, https://historicalnovelsociety.org/defining-the-genre-what-are-the-rules-for-historical-fiction/.
- Kass, Linda. "Why We Read Historical Fiction." *Gramercy Books,* 2017, https://www.gramercybooksbexley.com/blog/why-we-read-historical-fiction.
- Lawler, Andrew. "Who Wrote the Dead Sea Scrolls?" *Smithsonian Magazine*, Jan 2010, https://www.smithsonianmag.com/history/who-wrote-the-dead-sea-scrolls-11781900/.

- Lee, Richard. "Defining the Genre." *Historical Novel Society*, archived 11 July 2018, https://web.archive.org/web/20180711120201/https://historicalnovelsociety.org/guides/defining-the-genre.
- Lee, Richard. "History is But a Fable Agreed Upon: The Problem of Truth in History and Fiction." *Historical Novel Society*, 2000, https://historicalnovelsociety.org/but-a-fable-agreed-upon-speech-by-richard-lee/.
- Maclaine, David. "*The Iliad* by Homer." *HistoricalNovels.info,* n.d., http://www.historicalnovels.info/Iliad.html.
- Magness, Jodi. "The Impurity of Oil and Spit amongst the Qumran Sectarians." *With Letters of Light: Studies in the Dead Sea Scrolls, Early Jewish Apocalypticism, Magic, and Mysticism*, edited by Daphna V. Arbel and Andrei A. Orlov, De Gruyter, 2011, https://doi.org/10.1515/9783110222029.2.223.
- McGowan, Michael. "'Remember to look up at the stars': the best Stephen Hawking quotes." *The Guardian*, 14 Mar. 2018, https://www.theguardian.com/science/2018/mar/14/best-stephen-hawking-quotes-quotations.
- "Metaphysical Poetry: Definition, Characteristics & Examples." 28 Aug 2021, https://study.com/academy/lesson/metaphysical-poetry-definition-characteristics-examples.html.
- Nayak, Sandeep, and Matthew W. Johnson. "Psychedelics and Psychotherapy." *Pharmacopsychiatry*, vol. 54, no. 4, 2021, p. 169, https://doi.org/10.1055/a-1312-7297.
- Osborn, Lil. "Mary Magdalene: 'The Lioness of God' in the Baha'i Faith." Baha'i Library Online, 2012, https://bahai-library.com/pdf/o/osborn_mary_magdalene.pdf
- "Physics in a Minute: The Double-Slit Experiment." *Plus: Bringing Mathematics to Life*, 2 May 2017, https://plus.maths.org/content/physics-minute-double-slit-experiment-0.
- Pinkham, Mark. "The Truth About the Holy Grail: Magical Chalices Around the World." *Ancient Origins*, 9 Dec. 2021, https://www.ancient-origins.net/human-origins-religions/holy-grail-005124.
- Pruitt, Sarah. "How Early Church Leaders Downplayed Mary Magdalene's Influence." History, A&E Television Networks, 2 Apr. 2021, https://www.history.com/news/mary-magdalene-jesus-wife-prostitute-saint#
- Singh, Shiveta. "Essene: Ancient Jewish Sect." *Encyclopedia Britannica*, 3 Apr. 2008, https://www.britannica.com/topic/Essene.
- Smith, Victor E. "What is Visionary Literature?: Defining the Genre from Content." 2006, https://victoresmith.com/creative-ventures/visionary-literature/.

- Sutter, Paul. "What is Singularity?" 27 Oct. 2021, https://www.livescience.com/what-is-singularity.
- Swindal, James. "Faith: Historical Perspectives." *Internet Encyclopedia of Philosophy,* Raymo, Chet. "In the church-science split, both sides have suffered." *Science Musings,* 6 Nov. 2020, https://www.sciencemusings.com/in-the-church-science-split-both-sides-have-suffered/.
- Tabor, James. "Understanding the Essene/Dead Sea Scroll Calendar–and Alternatives, *TaborBlog,* 12 Mar. 2022, https://jamestabor.com/understanding-the-essene-dead-sea-scroll-calendar-and-alternatives/.
- Thakkar, Chirayu. "Karma: Definition, Early Sources." *World History Encyclopedia,* 4 Dec. 2014, https://www.worldhistory.org/Karma/.
- Than, Ker. "Dead Sea Scrolls Mystery Solved?" *National Geographic,* 27 July 2010, https://www.nationalgeographic.com/culture/article/100727-who-wrote-dead-sea-scrolls-bible-science-tv.
- "Nobel Prize in Physics 2022." *The Nobel Prize.* 4 Oct. 2022, https://www.nobelprize.org/prizes/physics/2022/press-release/.
- Tigchelaar, Eibert J.C. "The White Dress of the Essenes and the Pythagoreans." Jerusalem, Alexandria, Rome: Studies in Ancient Cultural Interaction in Honour of A. Hilhorst, edited by Florentino.
- Vernon, Jamie L. "Understanding the Butterfly Effect." *American Scientist,* vol.105, no. 3, May-June 2017, p.130, https://www.americanscientist.org/article/understanding-the-butterfly-effect.
- "What is an Avatar?" *The Yogic Encyclopedia,* https://www.ananda.org/yogapedia/avatar/.
- "What is Heart Coherence." *HeartMath,* 13 Sept. 2022, https://www.heartmath.com/blog/health-and-wellness/what-is-heart-coherence/.
- "What is Visionary Fiction?: Characteristic Features of Visionary Fiction." 2023, https://visionaryfictionalliance.com/what-is-visionary-fiction/.

Documentaries, TV Series & Films

- Dunn, Daisy. "Did the Trojan War actually happen?" *BBC,* 20 Jan. 2020, https://www.bbc.com/culture/article/20200106-did-the-trojan-war-actually-happen#:~:text=For%20most%20ancient%20Greeks%2C%20indeed,have%20been%20a%20real%20event

- *Outlander*. Based on *Outlander* novels by Diana Gabaldon, developed by Ronald D. Moore, performances by Caitriona Balfe, Sam Heughan, Sony Pictures Television, 6 seasons to date, 2014-present.
- *Sliding Doors.* Directed by Peter Howitt, Performances by Gwyneth Paltrow, John. Hannah. John Lynch, Jeanne Triplehorn, Intermedia/Mirage Enterprises, 1998.
- *The Da Vinci Code* (film) Directed by Ron Howard, Screenplay by Akiva Goldsman, Performances by Tom Hanks, Audrey Tautou, and Jean Reno, Sony Pictures Releasing, 2006. Original book by Dan Brown. (see books)
- *What the Bleep Do We Know!?* Directed and Produced by William Arntz, Betsy Chasse, Mark Vicente, Written by William Arntz, Matthew Hoffman, Betsy Chasse, Mark Vicente, Roadside Attractions, Samuel Goldwyn Films, 2004. *What the Bleep Do We Know!?* was both a book and a film; the film was a documentary that served as a "radical departure from convention." See: https://amzn.to/3AvZ0fg

ACKNOWLEDGEMENTS

Any piece of art, music or written creation is indeed a process before its ultimate fruition. A book is sprung into the universe from a creative seat of inspiration. It truly is a birthing. Those who are familiar with the analogy that it takes a village to raise a child will also understand that it takes a community to launch a book. We are incredibly grateful for our online and live communities who have been with us from the early days of this riveting journey.

We would like to acknowledge the following people for their tremendous support, creative input and insights, editing, marketing, as well as their deeply heartfelt encouragement to get *Magdalene's Journey* out to the world.

Our deepest gratitude goes to Dr. Gabriele Hilberg for believing in us and our work from the very beginning and for her ongoing guidance, love, and support. As a soul who shines bright in the world, you've been a guiding light for many years, and we can't thank you enough.

A monumental thank you goes to Shirley Shultz Myers. Your edits, direction, suggestions, and insights significantly contributed to the book's fluidity, consistency, and accuracy. More than just an editor and advisor, you've become a dear friend and we are so glad we teamed up on this project—the persistence and resilience over many long hours have truly paid off. You kept Renée sane through many versions.

Appreciation, gratitude, and a deep heart-felt thanks go to our dear friend Dunja Kacic-Alesic for her artistic flare; you created the book cover and sketches for each section of *Magdalene's Journey* that we instantly loved. Thanks for *getting* us time and time again and more importantly, for *getting* Miriam. Gabriele, Shirley, and Dunja: You have been beacons for us along the way for which we are forever grateful.

Loretta Falcone, thank you for the gifts you have given us as a scientist, a loyal friend and a sister. A deep and big love to you for who you are and all that you do. Thank you Eileen Drevitson for your insights, contributions, and support that has gone above and beyond again and again. You're a natural giver, which has been instrumental for us on this book journey. We are deeply grateful for your persistence and reminders to stay the course despite the hiccups along the way.

Dr. Jean Houston has been a beacon of light for decades. Thanks for speaking your truth again and again. Your words of inspiration in the final throes of this book process were such a comfort.

We are grateful for the editorial input and advice from David Bolinsky, Diane Rezendes, Janet Rae-Dupree, Eric Gabster, Mark Gober, Bill Blodgett, and Mark Boslet—your support means more than you can possibly know.

We are moved by the ongoing support from our video editor Tommy Clifford, who worked with us side-by-side to ignite and elevate this ever-winding journey, including this book. Thanks for keeping Renée organized along the way.

And what can we say to our dear friend Celia Canfield who not only agreed to read early drafts but gave us ideas that helped reshape the structure of the original manuscript? We are in deep gratitude soul sister.

Hats off to the wonder and mystery of your abilities Stephen Ashworth. Without you, our technology would never work, connect or deliver. We don't know how you do it, but the gifts keep coming and we are eternally grateful.

A deep appreciation to Carmen Hughes—you have always gone the extra mile to assist with publicity, research, and advice, without asking for anything in return. And thank you Ceree Eberly for your fact-digging contributions, love and continued support along the way.

Thanks to Dr. Brian Swimme, Sky Nelson-Isaacs and Jerry Gin whose esteemed work in cosmology, physics, and biology gave us their unique and thoughtful input where scientific references are made. Your insights helped us better understand that important bridge between the worlds. May your work forever illuminate those on a traditional path.

We also appreciate the encouragement and ongoing nudging—both soft and hard—from our friends Christine Mason, Katie & Kyle Hunt, Jill Lublin, Steve Lillo, Commander Jeff Jones, and Dr. Natalie Petouhoff. Thanks also to Geoff Affleck for helping us finally get to print. We appreciate your guidance and most importantly, your patience.

We bow down to the members of our programs who have been part of our journey for many years. Thank you from the bottom of our hearts. You make it so easy to show up again and again.

Renée would also like to acknowledge her grandparents Irene and Theron Blodgett who bought her a typewriter when she was a child, encouraging her to get ideas onto paper and submit letters to newspaper and magazine editors to make the world more harmonious. Believing in a child and giving them unconditional love are two of the most important things you can gift in a lifetime and you both succeeded.

You have all become like family to us, and we are so grateful for how you show up in the world, and the light you have shown to this project and our lives. Without your love and support, this visionary masterpiece wouldn't be what it is today.

Before the seed was planted, there were pioneers who shaped our views and changed the trajectory of our lives. We've been inspired by far too many way showers to mention them all. We honor those who have had the bravery and strength to rise above their fears and speak their truth, paving the way for a more united world.

As we moved from science to spirituality and then back around again, we have been in awe of these remarkable women who continue to give us the courage to pursue our dreams—they make leadership in their fields look easy and do so with grace and dignity: Lynne Twist, Cynthia Bourgeault, Dr. Jude Currivan, Mirabai Starr, Dr. Shamini Jain, Rev Deborah Johnson, Kala Ambrose, and Skye Alexander. A big toast to your authenticity, intelligence, wisdom, and resilience. We learn from you every day.

Renée wishes to raise a toast to the profound teachings she has garnered over the years from those she considers mentors: Yogananda, Wayne Dyer, Herbie Hancock, Tony Robbins, and Ray Kurzweil—your profound words, insights and encouragement pushed me to go further and deeper.

We love you Dema Premal and Miten—your songs and chants have both ignited and soothed us often over the years. May your voices continue to heal many.

Without these visionaries' hunger for a different truth than the polarizing views of the world that have only served to separate us rather than unite us, we'd still be stagnating in outdated paradigms.

Lastly, our relationship with nature has shaped us in profound ways; to not acknowledge her as a living entity would be a significant omission. We revere those who have dedicated their lives to honoring the planet and her valuable resources, including our Pagan and Indigenous grandfathers and grandmothers as well as the Shinto Masters who taught us vital life lessons in Japan. Once we lose sight of the oneness we share with all living things, we lose our humanity altogether. As Leo Tolstoy once said, "One of the first conditions of happiness is that the link between Man and Nature shall not be broken." A'ho. And so it is.

ABOUT THE AUTHORS

Renée Blodgett and Anthony Compagnone are the founders of Blue Soul Earth® where they lead programs, workshops, and global retreats focused on expanding and deepening humanity's awareness and consciousness. With a foundation in heart-centered living, they ignite human potential, helping others transform by tapping into their innate wisdom so they can lead with purpose and connection. They are also the producers of the Blue Soul CHATS podcast and Blue Soul Summit® which is a video series with visionaries across disciplines that educate, inspire, and liberate.

As founder of Magic Sauce Media and Blue Soul Media, Renée spent three decades in media, marketing and technology, creating award-winning campaigns. She is also the founder of *We Blog the World,* an online magazine focused on transformative travel. She has been writing articles about business, technology, travel, mindfulness and consciousness for twenty years and as an avid photographer, she has published five destination photo books.

Anthony has served as a bilingual speech and language pathologist and therapist for thirty years and is the founder of Speech Synergy which serves the San

Francisco Bay area. He is also a martial arts master with several accreditations in Chinese Kempo and Kungfu, and is a Sifi in both Dan Black Belt Chinese Kempo and Shippalgi Korean Kungfu. Anthony is also a meditator, yogi and pranayama breath facilitator. He is passionate about linguistics and speaks five languages. This is their first book together.

Visit www.bluesoulearth.com, www.bluesoulmedia.com, and www.bluesoul-summit.com to learn more about their work. The website www.magdalenesjourney.com is dedicated to this book and includes free resources and insights.

Follow @magdalenesjourney on Instagram and @bluesoulearth on all social media platforms. You can subscribe to their podcast at anchor.fm/bluesoulchats.

INDEX